'TIL ALL THESE
THINGS BE DONE

'TIL ALL THESE THINGS BE DONE

A Novel

Suzanne Moyers

SHE WRITES PRESS

Published 2022
Printed in the United States of America
Print ISBN: 978-1-64742-235-6
E-ISBN: 978-1-64742-236-3
Library of Congress Control Number: 2022905536

For information, address:
She Writes Press
1569 Solano Ave #546
Berkeley, CA 94707

She Writes Press is a division of SparkPoint Studio, LLC.

For my children, SaraJane and Jassi.
Here's to second—and third and fourth—chances,
and never giving up on love.

CHAPTER 1

W*here am I?*
Leola looked around. Was this the house in Bronway where she'd lived as a girl? There was a fireplace, yes, but not the one of raw pine with Mama's treasured clock upon it. This mantel was glossy white, decorated with brass candlesticks, a painting of ships, bright-colored china birds. On the floor, not the rug Mama had woven from old clothes but one made of wool, with fringe and swirling designs. And the divan where she sat: Leola ran her hands along the smooth fabric, pressed the over-soft cushions. This was a fancy thing, not threadbare and rickety like the one in Mama's parlor.

Leola gazed at the small table nearby with its vase of delicate roses—peach, pink, yellow. Yellow roses of Texas! She smiled, snatches of song circling her brain:

You may talk about your Clementine
And sing of Rosalee
But the Yellow Rose of Texas
Is the only girl for me!

Rosalee! Someone had called her that once. Had it been Joe, her husband? She studied the roses again. Were these his flowers? Lord knew that man could turn a wretched patch of desert green! P'rhaps this was Tyler then, the small, pretty house she'd shared with him and their children.

From the next room came piping laughter, a high voice chattering away. Was that one of those children? Her son, what was his name? Paul? No, Peter! Was it Peter or the other one? The girl named . . . Leola squeezed her eyes shut. *Thinkthinkthink.* But the memory slid by like the underwater silhouette of a legendary fish when you'd left your rod at home.

She glanced out the window, wondering again where she was. No trumpet vines or hummingbirds like in Tyler. No wide sky arcing above the chinaberry trees; instead, low russet hills, branches that reached and reached, peeps of blue showing between. Probably wasn't that other place she'd lived either, noisy with the sounds of many children. Never much of a home but *the* Home in Wixa . . . Waxa . . . Whatever the town was called.

Suddenly something in the corner caught Leola's eye, a shadow shaped like—a man! She leaned forward, trying to make out who it was. Joe? Peter? Brother Giles with the camera and . . . and the pinching contraption? Leola shuddered, thinking she should hide. But the figure moved now, lifting a hand. *Beckoning.* And then she noticed his other side, the sagging, hollow sleeve, missing its arm.

"Papa? Is that. . ." her voice was choked, "is that you?"

The figure grew clearer, the face more familiar: small, well-formed nose like her own; square chin (with a deeper cleft than hers); full mouth (her lips were thin). And those eyes—wide-spaced, curved upward at the corners, the trait she shared with her father more than any other.

"Papa!" She struggled to go to him, but the sofa cushions sucked her back, a quicksand of fabric and foam.

"Don't leave!" Leola's voice cracked with panic. "Tell me first why you couldn't . . . why you didn't—"

"Mother?"

A woman stood in the doorway holding something in her hand—a food-scooper. A froon? To stir a pot with. A *spoon*, that was it!

"Who were you talking to?" the woman asked, glancing around.

Leola's heart quickened, wondering if she should tell. She was fairly certain this was the same person who took her money. Kept her here against her will. Would not let her go home. But before she could answer, the woman rushed over, setting the spoon on the table.

"Mom." She crouched, staring into Leola's eyes. "Are you okay?"

Leola leaned back. "Who are *you*?"

The woman flinched. "I'm your daughter, Rose. Don't you remember?"

Leola hesitated, not wanting to admit she hadn't, in fact, remembered.

"'Course I do." She peeked at the vase. "*Rose.*"

Her daughter sighed, lightly touching one of the flowers.

"Last crop of the year, cut from the garden yesterday. The peachy bud is one of Daddy's—*the Leola Rose*, he named it. They do well even this far north. Pretty but hardy." Her eyes sparkled. "Like their namesake."

Daddy? Did she mean *Papa*? Leola wagged her head, like settling a sack of cotton, trying to make more room.

Rose shifted her position, and Leola could see into the corner again—it was empty! She groaned aloud.

"What is it?" Rose asked.

Leola couldn't help herself. "My father—he was here. I mean there. *Over there!*"

Rose checked behind her. When she looked at Leola again, her face was filled with doubt.

"How about I make you a snack?" She stood, grabbing the spoon. "Got home late so supper won't be ready for a bit. You must be hungry."

Leola *had* been hungry a few times in her life but certainly wasn't at the moment, not with Papa near, trying to tell her something. All she wanted was the woman—her *daughter*—to leave so he'd come out of hiding.

"A snack would be nice," she murmured, and Rose seemed relieved.

"All righty then." She turned away. "Back in a jif."

Leola could tell her daughter didn't believe her about Papa's visitation. She'd noticed the way Rose regarded her, like a child or a crazy person. Leola wondered if she'd worn that same expression looking at her own sister—which one was it, Mae or Karla?—who'd also claimed to see their father's ghost, who'd never been quite right after all she'd been through. *Blessed are the poor in spirit.* Well there was nothing *blessed* about being touched in the head. Nothing at all.

Leola recalled someone explaining recently about her own wasting mind. *A disease that comes with aging,* they'd told her. Something called *Dimension? Dime-in-shaw?* A disease of dimming, whatever the name. Still, no matter how mauddled . . . auddled . . . *addled* her thoughts, she was sure Papa had been here, in this very room, trying to tell her something. And now he'd disappeared again.

Leola wiped her eyes with a sleeve, lifting her face to the sun, feeling warm—for once. She'd been cold night and day since coming North. *Yankeeland*, she and Joe had called it in private after their daughter had moved to . . . wherever this place was. Something *new*. Not New Mexico, not New York . . . New Jersey! That was it. Joe used to say how funny it was that Rose had grown up where people couldn't be bothered to pronounce their last name, yet nowadays lived around folks who didn't believe an Italian could speak with a Texas twang. *A person just can't win*, he'd say, shaking his head.

Leola sunk back into the divan, closing her eyes, letting the sun sink into her. Letting it sink in where she was, not Bronway or Tyler or the orphanage nor anywhere else but New Jersey, the home of her daughter. The Rose she'd made with Joe.

At least she remembered that—and other things, too, bits and pieces of her past. The buttery crumble of cornbread on her tongue. Joe's lips on hers, urgent and warm—the thrilling ache his kiss brought down deep. Brilliant woven cloth swaying in a hot breeze. The red of a hummingbird's throat and another shade of red, crimson blood trailing a floor, leading to, or from, *Papa.*

CHAPTER 2

It happened too fast for Leola to drop the half-peeled potato and knife. Too fast for Mama to move from the window where she'd gone to see what the racket was, cartwheels on packed earth, male voices shouting, boots clattering across the porch. Too fast even to open the door, as the men from the mill kicked it in themselves, Gus Lister and Ralph Newsom hefting Papa's body onto the kitchen table, scattering the beans Mama'd been picking over moments ago.

"Arm got caught up in the saw blade," Gus shouted. "Someone's ridin' to town to summon Doc."

Seeing Gus press Papa's shoulder, stanching the blood, Leola dropped her knife, finally, into the sink. Dropped the potato also, lunging toward her father . . . except Mama blocked the way.

"Go to your sisters." Her eyes were like burnt coals in her paper-pale face. "They'll be wakin' soon from their naps. Keep 'em from," she glanced at Papa, "this."

Leola warbled all over like Auntie did from the palsy sometimes. She wiped her hands on her apron, trying to answer, but nothing came out. Not that she would've been heard, as Doc Hickley blustered in then, shouting orders left and right.

"Boil water, Orlie! And I'll need all the clean cloths ya got!" He turned to Ralph. "Ride on down to the Gumbses' place, see if Nancy has some of her sugar-soot concoction for makin' a compress."

6

Leola wanted to add, *And bring Nancy back with you,* but stopped herself. Doc would never allow a root healer or any other Black person to work beside him, however much he respected their medicine.

Cutting away Papa's shirt, the doctor noticed Leola for the first time.

"This child's got no business here!" he snapped, and Leola bristled. At fifteen, she was hardly a child, had helped birth the piglets last spring and nursed her sisters through measles. She could pump water and cut up bandages and . . .

Mama's fingers pressed hard around her wrist.

"Do as I asked, Lee. Go to your sisters. *This instant.*"

Leola started to argue, but there was the corpse-like body of her father. The ashen skin. A foul smell rising in her nose: metallic, mixed with rot—flesh, already dying. She couldn't stand to see Papa this way. She was a coward after all. A child, not a woman. She *wanted* to be gone.

So she stumbled down the narrow hallway to the stifling bedroom she shared with her sisters, curtains shut against the afternoon glare. Wouldn'a done a lick of good to pull them back neither, for summer had been blistering and autumn promising more of the same.

In the corner bed, two-year-old Karla napped peacefully, finger in her mouth, but Mae sat up, dark hair mussed every which'a way.

"What is it, Lee-lee? We got visitors?"

"No." Leola coughed, hiding the quaver in her voice. "It's Papa, got hurt down at the mill."

Mae frowned.

"Hurt bad?"

Bad enough to die, Leola thought but did not say.

"Nothing Doc Hickley can't fix right up." She lowered onto the bed. "Meanwhile, Mama says we ought stay here, keep from getting underfoot."

Mae narrowed her indigo eyes. *Stubborn since the day she arrived,* Mama sometimes said of her middle child. Born too early during a January freeze, it hadn't seemed Mae would live out the night. Papa had set her in a shoebox lined with cotton batting and placed it by the stove, but Mae refused to stay put, squalling until someone picked her up. After a few days, the fretting stopped and she began to eat, turning plump and pink overnight. *Well, didn't* she *tell off ol' Death!* Papa had declared, though that same determination made Mae a trial at times. As now.

"I wanna see my papa!" Thrusting her spindly legs from beneath the quilt, she slid to the floor. "And I'm hungry 'sides!"

"No!" Leola jumped up, forcing the gentler tone Mama might use. "I told you, darlin', Papa needs tending. I'll get you something to eat, soon's I can."

Mae hardly faltered. As she made a beeline for the door, Leola grabbed the china doll off her bed.

"Reckon a girl of seven is ready to play with such a fine thing, don't you agree?"

Mae stopped, mouth open wide enough to catch a barnful of flies. For years, she'd begged to play with Bettie, but Leola always answered, *Not 'til you're bigger.* The doll—bisque head and limbs, sateen dress, blush-painted cheeks—was Leola's most precious possession, a present from Papa after he'd started teaching down in Mixon. Back then school ran eight months a year instead of five, so Papa hadn't needed that second job at the sawmill—a job she thought he'd never have again nor another like it. If he even lived.

As Mae moved closer, Leola held the doll out of reach.

"You may have Bettie for a time but only if you promise to stay put like Mama said."

The girl nodded, somber enough for baptismal vows, then settled herself on the bed again. Cradling Bettie, she hummed Papa's favorite ballad, while Leola took up the words: *If I roam away, I'll come back again/Though I roam ten thousand miles, my dear . . .*

Hearing the familiar song, Karla stirred, and Leola pulled her close.

"Hush, sweetness," she whispered, stroking the girl's butter-soft cheek.

The sea will never run dry, my dear/Nor the rocks never melt with the sun . . .

From down the hall came a sharp cry—Papa's voice!—and Leola felt ashamed for *not* defying orders, for *not* insisting she help—until she recalled his battered body, lifeless as the doll on Mae's lap, the oozing cloth where his arm had been.

Noticing her sister's wary expression, Leola feigned bravery, taking up her song again:

But never will I prove false, to the bonny lass I love;
'Til all these things be done, my lass,
'Til all these things be done.

Early June 1919

CHAPTER 3

The sun was licking the sky awake as Leola pulled on her new dress. Well, not *new* exactly, and hardly the fashionable one she'd seen in the mail-order catalog: lightweight silk, tiered skirt, batwing sleeves. No, this was a *work* dress, made by Mama from old picking sacks, the material soft from countless washings. Was shaped like a sack, too, with wide armholes to let the air circulate—whatever air there'd be on such a hot day. Leola sighed, thinking at least this was an improvement over the denim overalls she used to wear—so scratchy it took all her mettle not to rip them off before she'd even quit the field.

After braiding her hair, Leola hurried to the kitchen, where Mama stood over the stove, spooning batter into a skillet.

"Mornin'."

Leola shoved a steaming corn patty all of a piece into her mouth.

"Mercy, child!" Mama scolded. "It's a wonder you don't burn your mouth off or choke, the way you bolt your food."

Leola took a second cake, swirling it with sorghum syrup.

"Can't help myself," she replied, gulping it down. "One whiff of these things makes me hungry as a stray cat. Besides, I don't have time to let 'em cool. I'm late as it is."

She wiped her hands on a towel, then reached behind the door for her picking sack—also new, also made by Mama, with padded straps and a reinforced bottom so it wouldn't rip. At nine feet long, it was meant to hold as much cotton as possible. Both bag and dress, she often thought, had been designed to keep her at this hateful task forever.

"You sure you're up for pickin' today?" Mama asked, noticing her pained expression. "Seems you still got an ache from the last time."

'Course I'm not up for pickin', Leola wanted to answer. She was never up for the tormenting clouds of 'skeeters, the cricked neck muscles from stooping and reaching and reaching some more. But Mama knew this well enough and only asked because she was a mother and hated her child having to do what needed doing.

"Was just the strap pinching my skin," Leola lied, "but I set it right."

She gathered the bag's excess fabric to keep from stumbling as she walked.

"Besides, the drouth's over and the cotton coming up fast—better take advantage while I can."

Her mother pointed at the sweating jar on the table.

"Hope that lemonade'll keep you gettin' too thirsty. I'll stop at Farmer McGee's, later, to bring you more."

"No need." Leola slipped the jar into a smaller cloth bag that also contained a ham sandwich and apple for the noon meal. "Mr. McGee keeps plenty of water jugs 'neath the wagons to take when we need."

Her mother flashed a warning look.

"Then make sure to *take* when you *need*, hear? Last time you came home halfway dead with thirst."

A rustling sound caught their attention—Papa, standing in the doorway.

"Mornin'," he mumbled, buttoning one of the shirts Mama had altered so the empty sleeve wouldn't dangle.

"Morning, Papa!"

Leola hurried to embrace him, but he sat down too quick, leaving her teetering in mid-reach. She swallowed, gesturing out the window.

"Look at that sunrise! Pretty as a picture, wouldn't you say?"

Papa barely glanced from his coffee cup. "Reckon so."

Standing there, Leola recalled how her father used to be. *Before Papa*, she called him, who'd never fail to wax poetic over a wondrous dawn or hug his daughter first chance he got. But that man got lost in the saw blade sure as his left arm.

In the months following his accident, Leola had bargained with the Lord to let her father live. When her prayers were answered—when Papa passed through endless rounds of fever and they could dress the wound without him squirming and cussing—it seemed nothing less than a miracle . . . except that, as the days had passed, his spirit sunk deeper, a shiny coin tumbling down a dark well. He never read his prized books anymore nor played his French harp. Even Mrs. Gumbs's pokeroot tonic had failed to raise him from despair.

At first Leola figured it was the shock of the accident, the pain of losing his arm, that had changed her father. But it soon became clear he'd no memory of falling onto the blade nor the frightful struggle after and these days, his stump ached only when a storm approached. 'Course, a man losing an arm was no small matter 'round here, with muscle labor the main way to earn a living. Papa had attended a year of college, was smart as a whip and had a head for numbers, but those qualifications meant little when it came to driving horses or putting roofs on barns.

Brings a man down, Mama had told Leola, *to beg for work and find none.*

Still, Leola suspected more to the story of Papa's melancholy. Thought maybe it had to do with the longstanding spite between him and her cantankerous grandfather, Mr. Owen, who often accused Papa of getting maimed on purpose so he could "laze about, gatherin' wool."

Only yesterday, when he'd come to collect his rent, Mr. Owen had addressed Mama as if her husband weren't sitting nearby.

I been forgivin' of your circumstance, Orlena, seein' you're my daughter, but I can't always make exceptions 'cuz y'all are kin. Gotta meet my obligations, whatever fixes you get yourself into.

Which had riled Leola no end. Mr. Owen had suffered his own share of misfortune—like buying this sandy-land farm right before the corn market failed, taking on two mortgages he couldn't afford. Then his wife, Big Leola—for whom Leola was named—had died and, without her help, Mr. Owen was further doomed. The man considered himself *charitable* for allowing his daughter's family to rent his old sharecropper's cottage, but it hardly seemed an equal bargain. Mama was the only one of Mr. Owen's children who'd moved back after Big Leola died, doing all her father's cooking and cleaning with next to no thanks. And far's their living quarters were concerned, Mama said the place wasn't fit for mice until she and Papa put considerable elbow grease into fixing it up.

Leola had asked her mother, time to time, about the bad blood between Papa and Mr. Owen, but Mama claimed it was on account of the old man's *disposition,* which Leola figured was true. He kept mostly to himself—had no friends that Leola could see—and never smiled at his granddaughters, insisting they call him by his surname instead of PawPaw or Grandaddy or any other term of endearment.

Mama's voice intruded on Leola's thoughts.

"Best get on your way, girl, 'fore the best rows are claimed."

Taking her brimmed hat from its peg, Leola peeked at Papa, hoping he might tap his cheek, begging for a kiss. But no, this stranger—this *After Papa*—still stared listlessly into his plate. And so she slipped away.

CHAPTER 4

Even at such an early hour, the sun was wicked on Leola's back, the day's humidity adding extra weight to the sack she dragged behind. Judging by the size and shape of it, she'd picked some thirty pounds of cotton so far. Another seventy and she might earn enough wages for a bag of flour, real coffee instead of the usual chicory root they brewed, maybe some bacon to tide them over until hog killing. P'rhaps she'd even put some aside for that mail-order dress—or the pattern and fabric so Mama could make it, if she ever had time.

Leola looked across the field where the farmer's larger wagon sat beneath a sycamore tree, awaiting their cotton. From here she could make out the jugs beneath it, burlap tied tight around their tops. Seemed a miracle how, even on the hottest days, evaporation cooled that water. 'Course Leola had her own miracle to look forward to— the jar of Mama's lemonade she'd left in the shade—and she licked her thirst-scabbed lips. *Five more pounds,* she promised herself, *pick five more pounds and you can have your drink.*

She bent over, slipping a feathery tuft from its sharp boll without feeling a single sting. First few times Leola had picked, the plant's barbed leaves left her fingers so sore, she'd had to soak them in linseed oil for days on end. But she'd had plenty of practice since and now could remove the feathery tufts neater than a pickpocket filching wallets at a fair.

Cramming more cotton into her bag, Leola caught sight of the Colored pickers across the field—kept separate as always. The white workers were mostly children, with some women here and there, but the Black hands ranged from toddling babes to elders walking on their knees, spines bent from tending other folks' crops and kettles their whole lives. Colored men in their prime, too, doing the rare job that paid them a halfway-decent wage. Leola flicked a mosquito from her wrist, thinking at least she had some chance of escaping this life someday.

Laughter erupted from the next row: little Jimmy Suggs, poking an anthill with a rolled-up leaf. Poor thing was smudge-faced and scrawny, wearing oversized overalls with mud-crusted hems and a battered straw hat. Though he'd begun picking before Leola, he'd hardly made progress, stopping every few minutes to do a jig or study some interesting rock. Whenever his elder sister, Opal—far ahead on the same row—caught him slacking, she'd holler, *Stop that, Jimmy Ray! Hain't got time for monkey bidness, hear?*

Brought a pang to Leola's heart, imagining her own sisters at such a chore. Mae would find any excuse to dawdle, using cotton fibers to dress up sticks or gathering weeds into bouquets. But Karla— well, she was just a mite! Surely Papa would find a job before they'd have to send *her* out here.

"Jimmy!"

Opal's shout made Leola flinch yet again.

"That bag hain't hardly growed since last I checked. Git yourself to workin', this instant!"

Leola snorted, wondering why the girl couldn't let up on her brother. Opal had wide shoulders and tree-trunk legs, and could pick one-handed, steady as a locomotive's pistons—*reach-pluck-wad, reach-pluck-wad.* Already, she'd filled two whole bags; seemed she could more than make up for Jimmy's scant earnings.

Then again, Opal's kind tended to think with their appetites more than their brains—or so Mama said. *White trash*, some people called them, *low-downers*, scrabbling a living any way they could but always coming up short. Mama dubbed them *clay eaters*, saying they craved the loamy earth found near rivers and streams. When Leola asked why people would eat dirt, Mama had sniffed.

Their men believe it begets more children, and their women, that it gives them strength to deliver those children.

Overhearing this, Papa had frowned.

People only resort to such measures, Orlena—if they even do—to fill their empty bellies. Main difference between us and them is a long stretch of bad luck makes 'em forget who they once were.

Leola glanced at Jimmy, all bare feet and sickly complexion, and then at Opal, stained dress stretched tight across her back. *Bad luck*, she thought, as in having a drunken, no-account father who came home long enough to beat you and misuse your mother. Or *bad luck*, like your own papa getting his arm cut off, turning melancholy and never being right again. Either way, Leola reckoned, it'd be easy to forget who you might've been.

Swallowing her sadness, she settled into work, trying to match her picking rhythm to the names of the Animal Kingdoms.

Porifera

Cnidaria

Platy . . . platy . . . hel . . . minth . . . es

Anne . . . anne . . . annelinda? Annelita?

She cussed beneath her breath. If she'd any hopes of attending North Texas State with her best friend, Mary Shipley, she'd need straight As and a full scholarship. Ship went to boarding school, where she could take all the necessary courses, while Leola had gone on long as she could at puny ol' Bronway High, earning her remaining credits by mail, studying whenever she could—which, these days, wasn't often.

Reaching toward another plant, she pictured the animals along with their phylum:

Mollusca: snails clinging to the rocks in Caney Creek.

Arthropoda: insects, like the flies buzzing 'round her head.

Chor . . . chor . . . data: the four-pound catfish she'd caught one day at Lake Palestine.

"Jimmmmmy Suggs!"

Here came Opal, barreling toward her brother, slapping the ant-hill-poker from his hand. "Quit lollygaggin', kid!"

"I'm thirsty, Opes," the boy answered, rubbing his knuckles.

"You fill that bag." She waggled her finger in his face. "Then you can 'git water. Not a minute a'fore!"

Seeing Jimmy's quivering lip, Leola could no longer contain herself.

"You oughtta be ashamed," she shouted at the girl, "treating your own brother that way! And him so young!"

Opal spun around, face mottled with rage.

"Mind yer own bid'ness, missy! Just 'cuz your pappy's a school-teacher don't mean 'ya get to lord it over us." She let off a wheezy laugh. "Guess all that book-learnin' didn't keep him from falling on a sawblade, huh? And now he ain't no bett'r'n a gimp!"

Pressing an arm to her side, moving about in a fitful dance, Opal sang, "Step right up and see the deeeee-formed schoolteacher!"

Leola checked the insults wheeling through her brain. She'd spotted Mr. McGee at the edge of the field; if he caught her making trouble, she'd not be hired back. But then here was Opal, doing her loathsome dance, so Leola gave into her ire, stepping over the cotton plants, jamming her nose in the other girl's face.

"'Least my papa doesn't steal jug money from his own children but is a right and honorable man," she hissed, "not that a *clay eater* would understand the first thing about *honor!*"

Fast as lightning, Opal took Leola's arm, flipping her face down to the ground.

"Y'ain't no better'n me, nor anyone else." She yanked up Leola's dress, pulled down her drawers. "Got shit stuck to yer ass, same's the rest of us."

For an eternity after Opal climbed off her, Leola was aware only of the warm sun upon her private places, the taste of dirt in her mouth—like damp smoke and dried bone and *humiliation.* A few children tittered but the rest were silent—all except Jimmy, whose filthy feet appeared in Leola's line of sight.

"Mrs. La'ola? You awright?"

With some effort, Leola sat up, straightening her clothes, not daring to look from her lap, knowing there were boys here she'd see in town and school and church for the rest of her life. *Dear Lord,* she silently prayed, *please reach down, save me from my disgrace, and I will never do wrong, ever again.*

And then an arm *was* pulling her up, a familiar voice murmuring, "There, there, Rosalee."

Not God but Papa, calling her by the nickname he'd assigned at birth—which she hadn't heard him use since his accident.

"All is well." He pulled her close, stroking her hair. "I'm here now."

Relieved as she was, Leola couldn't help wondering if Papa had seen her exposed so rudely—a notion she couldn't dwell on long as Mr. McGee had shown up, waving his hands in the air.

"All my born days, ain't never heard such a ruckus! Y'all kids supposed to be pickin', remember?"

Papa removed his hat, slicking damp hair from his forehead.

"Seems like these young'uns could use a rest every so often, Tom, and more looking after, if you don't mind me saying."

The farmer hunched his shoulders.

"Matter of fact, Frank, I was about to make an announcement 'long those lines." He pointed at a surrey parking beneath the sycamore. "Mrs. McGee is just arrived with cookies and fresh-made lemonade. If y'all want any, y'all might head there straightaway."

The kids whooped, taking off across the field as if lit on fire—all except Opal, who glowered at the two men like she might very well shove *their* faces into the soil.

"Don't go dancin' in the pig trough, Opal," the farmer warned. "Best get some rest and somethin' to eat while you can."

When the girl still wouldn't move, Jimmy tugged her hand.

"Hurry up, Opes, a'fore all the cookies is gone."

She gave their group one last hard look, muttering, "Come on, then," pulling her brother across the field like yet another sack of cotton.

After they'd left, Farmer McGee studied Leola. "You hurt, child?"

"No sir," she mumbled, thinking the real pain was deep down where he couldn't see. Telling herself, too, that he couldn't have noted her part in the scuffle—nor the resulting disgrace. That the others wouldn't mention it either, out of fear of causing their own trouble.

"Leave your pickings in the wagon for weighing," the farmer said, pointing at her half-full bag. "Come by later to get your pay. But next time, make sure you choose a row far from that Suggs girl." He lowered his voice, addressing Papa. "If she weren't one'a my best workers, I'd have no truck with such cracker filth."

Papa frowned. "Good thing you do. Velma Suggs was bad off *before* her latest babe arrived and that consumption don't help. They'd hardly manage without Opal's wages."

Shaking his head, the farmer trudged off, and Leola turned to her father. "How did you know to come by just then?"

"I *didn't* know. Soon after you left this morning, I got to thinking 'bout you picking on such a hot day—a Saturday, no less. Felt the urge to fetch you back." He shook his head. "Was only by accident that I happened along when I did."

He whistled at their mule, Violet, who'd been patiently standing by.

"But it's time for us to go."

He retrieved her pickings from the ground.

"Mama borrowed some sugar and rock salt from Auntie." His eyes filled with their *Before Papa* gleam. "Reckon we can make it home in time to help turn the freezer crank?"

Leola's face warmed with love—and then worry. Even more than the idea of Papa seeing her in her natural-born state, she feared he'd heard what Opal had said about him and what she'd said in return.

"Opal . . . she . . . I called her a—"

He held up his hand.

"Any youngster doing a grown person's job is liable to go astray, child. You've worked yourself to a nub of late, which I do appreciate. But if you're to have a future free of such onerous toil—and I'm determined you will—you'll need to finish your education and also have some fun, such as folks your age are meant to do. As of today, we'll make sure that happens."

He helped her climb on Violet and they headed toward the sycamore. Though Leola struggled to keep her head high, the other children were too busy enjoying their snack to notice her presence—or kind enough to pretend as much.

Taking the lemonade jar from Papa, Leola spied the Suggs kids, removed apiece from the others. Jimmy sat on Opal's lap, a cookie in each hand, chattering away—although his sister wasn't paying attention, instead watching the Rideouts with a curious mixture of envy and longing.

Wrestling a torment of feeling over what she'd said to the girl, Leola gulped the drink, the tang of earth too raw on her tongue.

CHAPTER 5

A few days later, Leola found Papa on the back porch, examining a hunk of basswood.

"Isn't this a fine specimen, Rosalee? Found it by the river. Would be right nice for whittling, I reckon."

Leola took the branch, studying it close so he wouldn't see the pity in her eyes. Papa—or *Before Papa*—had been an expert whittler, able to carve wood and even walnut shells into anything you could imagine. Over the years, he'd made a menagerie of tiny wooden animals, both familiar (armadillos, deer, coyotes) and copied from books (zebras, elk, elephants), which Leola had played with for hours on end. Her sisters had too—until Mama hid them recently, saying such things only reminded Papa of his *incapacities*.

"I don't know about you," Papa was saying, pointing to a section of the branch, "but I keep seeing a particular creature right about here. What d'you think?"

Leola tipped the stick, imagining what it might become.

"Hmmm. This could be antlers—no, tusks. And here," she traced a bumpy spot, "could be a snout." She looked at him. "It's a wild pig like the one I kept as a pet when I was a kid—until it trampled Mama's garden and ate her chicks."

"I pictured the very same thing! Which only proves we are truly cut from the same cloth—er, *tree*." He peered at her. "Remember when you were little and loved to watch me carve? How I gave you a bar of Ivory soap and let you use a spoon handle to make a figure of your own?"

Leola smiled, recalling how satisfying it had been to press on the soap and watch it give way in clean-smelling curls of white.

"I think I made a bird once. Or that's what it was meant to be." She laughed, shaking her head. "Ended up looking more like a lop-sided snowman."

"Well, I thought you demonstrated a talent for whittling and wanted to teach you more."

"Except," Leola scoffed, "Mama said if I was going to spend extra time on handiwork, it ought be sewing, which, in her estimation, is a *far more practical life skill.*"

"Mama's not here to *estimate*, is she?" Papa gave her a wink. "And we can't let this fine wood go to waste, not when it so badly wants to be a fetching javelina." He stood. "Wait here."

After rustling around inside, Papa returned with the cigar box he used to store his whittling tools, handing her the pearl-handled penknife he'd had since childhood.

"Seein' I can't carve so well these days, it's up to you to help our porcine friend fulfill her destiny."

Leola cast him a doubtful look. "Mama won't be happy if supper isn't ready when she gets home and me sculpting sticks like a good-for-nothing boy."

"The beans only need heating, Lee, and you can whip up a batch of larrupin' good biscuits faster than anyone. Most likely, we'll have supper fixed long before your mother returns." Papa waggled his eyebrows. "Besides, I'll say I commanded you to help me. She can't protest that, can she?"

Before Leola could answer, he jiggled the hunk of wood like a saber.

"Daughter, I herewith order you to whittle or risk the wrath of your esteemed elder!"

Seeing how excited he was, Leola could hardly say *no*. So after they'd sharpened the knives on Mama's whetstone, he helped her peel the remaining bark and she began to carve. Though Leola could recall the gist of what he'd taught her before, Papa used his hand to guide her, at times, providing plenty of verbal encouragement too: *Don't use your wrist too much. Put the weight in your thumb . . . Turn it, work the other side . . .*

When the knife slipped, nicking her finger, Leola refused his ministrations, licking away the blood, not stopping until the thing resembled *something* besides a piece of wood.

"You're doing right nice work for a first effort!" Papa exclaimed, and Leola sniffed.

"You may be needing spectacles. This is more like one of those strange mixed-up creatures in your book of myths—half-cow and half-turtle, p'rhaps, but a cow-turtle with tusks and—what's this?" She ran a finger along the pig's jagged chin. "A beard?"

"It only needs finessing to bring the rest of the way out."

Papa removed another knife from the box, this one with a thinner blade.

"Here is what I always use—*used*—to make the shape more exact."

Glancing between his hand holding the knife and her hand with the carving, his face fell, as if he'd suddenly remembered the distance between what he *knew how* to do and what he *could*.

"No matter." He set the knife back in its box. "You can figure it out later, if you've a mind." Nodding at the shavings on the steps, he added, "Best we clean up. You're probably right—Mama will have our heads if supper isn't ready and the place a mess to boot. I'll go get the broom."

While he was gone, Leola closed the box, thinking if Papa had a proper workbench with a vise to act as a second hand, he might be able to whittle again. 'Course, they couldn't afford to buy one and even if Dell Meeker, their good neighbor, agreed to cobble something together, he'd be busy for a while yet harvesting crops.

But the next day, helping Mama can tomatoes, Leola spied their old apple peeler on a high shelf. Big Leola had bought the contraption in the eighties when it was considered the kitchen tool every farm wife *had to have*. She'd dubbed it The Apple Inquisitor as it did, indeed, resemble a torture device, with long spikes to hold the fruit and toothy gears for turning the shaft. Not that they ever used it much. In the time it took to set up, Leola and Mama could peel, core, *and* slice a dozen apples apiece. Yet there it was with its metal "arm" and sturdy "fingers," and a clamp to hold everything in place. Like a vise, only better.

Without a word, Leola climbed onto a chair, removing the heavy machine from its shelf—nearly losing her balance in the effort.

"What are you about, child?" Mama said, rushing to take it from her. "We've no apples for a pie!"

She nodded around the kitchen, every surface covered with jars and tins.

"And we're hardly done with this mess, besides."

Leola jumped to the floor, lifting the contraption from Mama's arms.

"Not making a pie. Think I've found a better use for this ol' thing—an invention of sorts. Won't take long to rig up, I promise."

Put out as she was, Mama watched her daughter closely as she clamped the device onto the small table Mae used for her lessons. Then Leola headed outside, where her sisters were leashing a captive cicada with thread.

"Come on, girls, let that poor creature take its rest. I got an important job for you!"

Mae and Karla abandoned their pet at once.

"What is it?" asked Mae, scratching the welt on her knee, a parting gift from some desperate late-summer mosquito.

"I'm testing out a special invention for Papa." Leola held up a sample branch. "We need to find sticks 'bout this size to see if it works."

It was as if she'd asked them to help find buried treasure, for the girls fell right to the task and did a good job of it too.

Back in the kitchen, even Mama got in on the scheme, hardly chiding Leola when her stroke of genius took longer to realize than planned. Finally, though, all was ready. As they'd been instructed, Mae and Karla met Papa on the porch, tying a cloth around his eyes before leading him inside.

"Am I to be walked from the plank then, mateys?" he asked, in a scalawag voice.

"One minute." Mae stopped him in front of the little table. "Go on, take off your blindfold!"

Papa did as he was told, studying the javelina Leola had started carving yesterday, its unfinished end impaled on the apple-peeler's spikes.

"It appears we're having a pig roast of sorts," he joked, though Leola could tell he knew more or less what he was looking at.

"This pig doesn't need cooking, Papa, only carving—which you can do yourself now with your new whittling arm."

She pointed to the butter knife wedged snugly beneath the crank shaft.

"This locks the arm in place so it won't move as you carve, but when you need to work another side," she pulled out the knife, turning the handle, "it's easy as, well, apple pie!"

Papa went quiet, inspecting the peeler-whittler from all sides.

Then he took up the mother-of-pearl penknife lying beside it. Locking the crank into place, he gingerly shaved a bit of the pig's hind leg, turned the sculpture, and added some curve to its belly.

Gazing at Leola, his face shone with pride.

"This is about the smartest invention I ever did see." He glanced at his wife. "I do believe, Orlie, a keen mind will serve our daughter—*all* our daughters—in life 'least as well as fancy stitching. Don't you think?"

Mama, holding Karla in her lap, kissed the child's head.

"And goodness in their hearts, too, Frank," she replied. "They've that in abundance too."

Papa pulled two chairs to the whittling machine.

"Let's see, Rosalee, if I can't teach you some of those special techniques I was talking about yesterday." He winked at the other girls. "Y'all watch too. Soon enough, it'll be your turn to try."

And the whittler set to work.

CHAPTER 6

A strange noise jostled Leola's sleep: not the midnight train shrieking across the plains nor Mae's nightly babblings—sounds she'd long grown accustomed to and barely noticed at all, anymore. No, this ruckus was peculiar enough to invade the sweetest dream she was having of her beau, Joe Belfigli.

I tell you, Orlena! It was Papa, shouting from the next room. *Houston is our last best hope!*

Leola, forced from the mirage of Joe's embrace, blinked the night-crust from her eyes. Mama spoke next, too soft to make out completely, so Leola pressed her ear to the wall, telling herself if eavesdropping were a sin, the Lord wouldn't have granted us curiosity in the first place.

"I could ask my father to forgive our rent again," Mama was saying, "just this month, until you—"

"No!" There was a sharp bang, like Papa pounding his hand on the furniture. "I will not ask that man for more of his so-called *charity!* Besides, Columbus Owen would welcome my leaving, the sooner the better, far's he's concerned."

Leola studied the breathing mounds in the other bed, praying her sisters wouldn't wake. Papa had seemed in better spirits lately—the whittling had helped—but there was a new strain between their parents the little girls hadn't seemed to notice—though, if this ruckus continued, surely they would.

It had begun the previous week, when Papa brought home the *Houston Chronicle* given him by Dell Meeker's nephew, in town for a visit.

That young Murl is making quite a success of himself in Houston, Papa had proclaimed. *Says there are plenty jobs available for a person can keep a ledger neat. Fellow don't need two arms to do that, I reckon!*

He'd read aloud the advertisements, clerks and bookkeepers offered top dollar by the oil and shipping companies, while Mama bent over her sewing, listening without a word—until it was done. Biting off the end of her thread with fearsome precision, she retorted, *I read that newspaper, too, Frank. Not only the job advertisements but the front-page article 'bout those three recent murders—one man shot while smoking a cigar, another while talking on the phone, and the third sitting at his desk, fountain pen in hand! Kil't all in the same day!*

This had ended their argument—but not, it seemed, for good.

"Murl's already had his boots stolen twice," Leola heard her mother say. "Told me if the flooding don't drown a person then the opportunities for sin will. Hardly seems the place for raisin' young ladies."

"If I don't find work soon, we will be sending our eldest *young lady* out to service soon, as once you were." Papa's laugh was sour. "And we know how *that* turned out!"

"Frank! You promised to let bygones be bygones!"

"I have tried to bygone that, Wife, but your father makes it hard, treating me all these years like I stole the mare he intended to trade for top dollar."

Mama's gasp was clear even through the layers of magazine pictures that papered their walls.

"What a lowly way to put it, Husband!"

"It's the truth, Orlena. The doctor's scheme was no better than . . ."

Here, his voice dropped so Leola caught only a snippet of his
reply: *kept woman.*

She pulled her ear away, unsure who this *kept woman* was, certain the physician in question wasn't Doc Hickley, but the one Mama
had worked for as a girl—a situation Leola had only discovered by
chance from her great-aunt Malvina, down the road.

One day, while helping Auntie clean her attic, they'd come
upon the old woman's trousseau, filled with blankets and tea towels
and other items put aside when she was young and still dreamt of
marrying.

At the bottom of the pile was a beautiful red-and-blue quilt in
a wedding ring pattern. *Plumb forgot I had this,* Malvina had said,
unfolding the delicate fabric. *Your mama made it when she was
hardly older than you.*

She'd traced the interlocking designs with a finger.

*Orlie could sew a quilt or fancy dress faster'n anyone I knew. Good
thing too. Kept her brothers and sisters from starving when she hired
out as a seamstress.* Auntie sat back, wrinkled brow creasing further.
*Most'a those families were nice enough, 'cept for the one—the doctor up
in Kilgore . . .* She looked away. *Nearly cost Orlie her salvation, that one.*

Leola's ears were pricked way up by then but too late, as Auntie
seemed suddenly reminded of her audience. Shoving the quilt away,
she mentioned some mayhaw bushes ripe with berries down by the
river, how she wanted to make one of her famous trifles and wouldn't
Leola like to help? Getting them right off the subject of Mama's past.

Then, not long afterward, Mama had been teaching Leola her

stitches—or trying, for the girl found sewing blame tedious and didn't have the knack besides. While her mother tore out another of her uneven hems, Leola had rummaged through the sewing basket, unearthing a tiny pair of silver scissors with flower engravings on their handle.

Where did you get these, Mama? she'd exclaimed. *Wouldn't they suit Bettie right well?*

Her mother flinched as if Leola had poked her with the scissors' sharp point.

The doctor's wife gave them to me. They're not for dolls but snipping loose threads. She'd held out a palm. *'Tain't for small children, neither.*

Then she'd pushed the scissors beneath a knitted doily and Leola hadn't seen them since.

Next door, Mama's voice rose so loud, Leola couldn't avoid eavesdropping if she'd tried.

"You are treadin' where it ain't wise to go, Frank! What happened with the doctor has nothin' to do with our present circumstance, which is about *you* not trying, hoping someone else will bear your load—that someone bein' *me!*"

Leola startled at the meanness of these words. Hadn't Mama herself pointed out Papa's shame at being unemployed, saying it wasn't his fault they had to sacrifice white sugar and new boots?

Then again, Mama's sentiments weren't entirely out of the blue, for sacrifice had always seemed her stock in trade. Even before his accident, Papa would come home from work to whittle or go fishing while Mama traded one job for a thousand others: cooking, cleaning, always on guard for snakes and uncapped wells, caring for her obstreperous father and when Papa got hurt, him too. P'rhaps she'd finally found the end of her rope and couldn't keep ahold of it anymore.

Hearing her father's boots thumping across the kitchen floor, the front door opening and shutting, Leola wanted to run after him. But she held back, remembering he often lit out these days, always returning in a better mood. And then she smelled his musky pipe smoke and knew Papa hadn't fled, after all, but was sitting on the front porch, *pondering* as he called it.

Though her father believed you could think yourself out of a problem, Leola wasn't so certain. The more she tried to untangle the confusions in her mind, the more snarled they became. Like why, when the Colored soldiers returned from the war, demanding better pay and more freedoms, Pastor Nickles said it was white folks' *Christian duty* to keep them in their places. Or why, last week, the father of her school chum, Birdie Wobel, shot his wife dead, all because she'd invited the starch salesman in for refreshment. And, of course, there was this business of Houston—why Papa wanted so badly to go, why Mama resisted, and what the *kept woman* had to do with any of it.

A breeze kicked up, blowing in another gust of tobacco smoke, its mellowy aroma finally settling Leola's unease. She reminded herself the mysterious lady they spoke of was likely a figure far in their pasts, that she'd heard her parents argue plenty over whether to seek their fortune elsewhere, though it never had happened. Mama and Papa would find a way around this trouble as they'd done a thousand others before.

From across the room, Mae sighed in her sleep while outside, a bachelor mockingbird trilled his nighttime serenade: *Love-er! Love-er!*

Leola thought of Joe's hands tender on her skin, the way he laughed—deep and throaty—like the world was pure delight. Like *she* was pure delight.

Love-er! The mockingbird teased. *Love-er!*

Easing onto her pillows again, she decided that whatever the future held, it was too far-off to predict, much less fret over. What mattered was the present, that she was loved and looked after, safe with her family—*home.*

CHAPTER 7

L eola and Mary Shipley climbed the verandah steps, wrangling
armfuls of pink and purple gladiolas from Mrs. Shipley's garden.
After dumping their harvest on the table, Leola motioned at the
clouds billowing on the horizon.

"Storm's coming. Reckon I should head out."

Ship rushed over, hugging her friend.

"I won't let you leave unless you promise to come back next weekend when I'm home again. Otherwise it'll be another two weeks 'til
we see each other and that is far too long!"

Leola returned the embrace, then stepped away.

"I'll do my best. Much as I love you, I'm mighty busy these days."
She gave Ship a long look. "Besides, it's you who stays at school so
often, attending your socials and such. Not that I blame you a whit. If
it weren't for Joe, I'd be outside my mind with boredom 'round here."

Mary picked up a flower.

"Thank goodness for what fun I *do* get. The teachers at MacComb's
take a peculiar pleasure in loading us with all manner of infernal
assignments." She tucked the bloom into one of the vases they'd collected earlier. "And how *is* your course on natural sciences? I can't for
the life of me get the animal kingdoms into my thick head."

Leola plucked a dead leaf from its stem, hesitant to answer. In
spite of Papa's promises, she'd had little time to study, not with

staying up late to help Mama sew, only to wake at dawn to work in the fields or a neighbor's kitchen. She didn't want to explain that such labor was no longer for pin money either, but so her family could *eat.* Some things were too embarrassing to share even with your fondest friend.

"I may not go to college," she replied slowly. "Might take up sewing for a profession. Seems I'm better at it than I ever imagined."

Mary chuckled, jabbing Leola with an elbow.

"You've the strangest sense of humor!"

"Isn't humor." Leola fussed with the bouquet, avoiding her friend's gaze. "Makes more sense if I take a vocation I already know. With me helping full-time, Mama can double her orders and—"

Ship stamped her foot.

"Hooey! You always said you'd rather clean chimney pipes for a livin' than spend your days jabbing needle into cloth." She narrowed her eyes. "You said you wanted to teach high school or at least learn stenography. Office girls in Dallas earn fifteen dollars per week—far more than your mama makes from needlework, I imagine."

Leola didn't answer, knowing her friend would never understand. Mary had been a sprite when her father lost his ginning business during the cotton bust of '05 and not much older during the uncertain early years of his rose-growing venture. She didn't remember attending their tiny one-room school—except that she'd met Leola there—for as soon as her family had money, they'd sent her to MacComb's Academy in Carthage. Mary would have to make an effort *not* to achieve her aspirations while it seemed impossible at times for Leola to remember she'd ever had them.

"Reckon all the work we did," Ship continued in a peevish voice, "ensuring ladies could vote and have their college educations and such . . ." She trimmed a stem too close, its flower thumping to the floor like the head of an executed queen. "S'pose it's all for naught."

Leola, reaching for the severed blossom, felt a flash of guilt. Mary and her mother were suffragettes, proud of their efforts to secure greater freedoms for their sex. Last year, after Governor Hobby ratified the female vote in local elections, Mary and Mrs. Shipley had helped sign qualified women—including Mama—to the rolls in Longview. Mary had worn a white dress that day and, when a businessman pelted her with a burning cigar, paraded the singed frock afterward as a badge of honor.

Leola always supported Ship's work—wished to be part of the movement—though she was too busy surviving to do more than applaud its efforts. An acid feeling roiled within her, suddenly, thinking it was easy for Mary to hold lofty ideals when she didn't need to worry about making ends meet. Only women of leisure could march in parades and write letters to the statehouse, while the rest pressed their noses to the grindstone day in and day out.

Then Leola remembered this was not some regular rich lady but dear Ship, who didn't have a superior-feeling bone in her body. If she wanted, the girl could cocoon herself inside her privilege, not caring fiddlesticks about the rest of the world. Except that wasn't her way.

"Oh, Ship, I'll go to college, you know that. Might not finish my courses same time as you but I *will* go."

Grinning, Mary took both Leola's hands.

"Promise? You're the smartest girl around. Shame if you let that mind go to waste."

"I'll finish my studies, I promise, and become a rich and famous science teacher. Someday you can say, *I knew her when* . . ."

Ship seemed too distracted by Leola's fingers to laugh.

"Nearly forgot. There's a present I been meaning to give you." She hurried inside, returning with a flower-decorated ceramic jar labeled, "*Crème de Roses du Texas.*"

"Father had a perfumer in Tyler concoct this from our own crops. Will make those hands of yours smooth as velvet." She laughed, showing small white teeth. "Will also make you smell like Shipley roses, which is why I won't wear it, for fear of being suffocated altogether."

Leola opened the jar, inhaling the potion's bloomy scent, wondering whether it was more than ragged hands marked her out these days, if she was beginning to stink, too—like Opal. Like a *clay eater.* Wondered whether Mary Shipley was only doing her charitable duty in staying friends.

"It's right nice," Leola murmured, but Ship was back to bouquet-making and didn't notice her strangled tone, chattering on about a teacher at MacComb's who was friends with Alice Paul, *fearless campaigner for women's rights!*

Right then, thunder rumbled from far away and the girls grabbed at each other like frightened children. As they broke into laughter, Leola told herself they'd loved each other through rich and poor and a thousand other things, and let go her ill feelings, certain the gift wasn't meant as insult.

"That storm'll be here in an hour's time," Leola said, slipping the jar into her pocket. "I better set out."

Ship squinted down the road.

"If you wait, Father can take you. He should be back any minute."

Leola was about to point out that an hour allowed plenty of time to make it home when Joe appeared in the driveway, driving the Shipley wagon.

"Aha!" Ship cried. "Look who it is! The answer to our prayers."

"Mary Lucille Shipley, you are slick as a boiled onion!"

Yet there was no real anger in Leola's tone. She and Joe were so busy lately, it was sometimes only through Ship's machinations that they saw each other at all.

As he walked toward them, Leola couldn't help thinking—yet again—that Joe was the handsomest man she'd ever seen, with jet black hair and sparkling brown eyes, skin burnished gold by the sun. There was an air about him, too—a cool confidence—that made her feel reassured in his presence. Joe didn't smile often but when he did, it seemed meant for the particular person it was directed upon— which right then was *her*.

"Fancy meeting you here, Rose o'Roses," he said, mounting the steps.

"I could say the same," she replied, and they both glanced at Ship, who imitated a blameless face made them all laugh.

"We should make hay while we can," Joe said, motioning into the distance. "Those are some mean clouds threatenin'."

Seeing the sky was still mostly blue, Leola grinned, knowing his haste was less about the weather and more about wanting time alone—an idea that sent shivers down her spine in spite of the beaming sun.

After Ship gave Leola a bouquet to take home, Joe helped her into the front seat of the wagon then climbed in himself, calling out to the horses, "*Arri*," which was *giddy up* in his father's language. He'd taught her other words, too, from Italian: *biscotto* for *biscuit*, though the ones his grandmother made were crunchy and full of almonds, not soft and yeasty like those Leola was accustomed to. He'd also taught her the words for sky (*cielo*), sweet (*dolce*), dear (*cara*)—and *mi amore*, for which he never did supply a meaning but didn't have to. The way his face shone when he said it was translation enough.

Joe had been raised in a veritable Tower of Babel. His mother,

Elodie Hebert—who died birthing him—came from an old New Orleans family. His father, Louis, had emigrated from Italy to build the railroad line out West, where he'd learned the hard way not to utter his native language in front of others, insisting his son speak only English at home. It was Joe's grandmother, Nonna Rae, who conversed with him in Italian as they cooked together or tended her garden—and what he'd learned in that garden got him the job with Mr. Shipley.

At first, Joe mainly drove supplies for Blanton's company though, when his boss noticed his knowledge of horticulture, was quickly put in charge of developing new breeds of flowers. He'd even invented one they'd christened the *Belfigli Blood Rose*, for it was the deepest red you could imagine.

Leola hardly recalled their introduction three years ago, while Joe claimed he was taken right away by her eyes, saying they changed from moss green to blue gray depending on her mood. He'd been beguiled, too, by the interest she took in the *whys* and *wherefores* of breeding flowers, as she did in so many things. Of course being five years her senior, he was hardly in a position at the time to act on his feelings. But six months ago, when Ship confided he was "near about mad" from thinking of her, Leola began to consider Joe as a serious suitor. And now he was her only one.

Driving through town, people greeted them—less from a friendly inclination, Leola believed, than a desire to report back to Mama. She imagined the look on her mother's face when meddlesome Mrs. Littlejohn or grouchy Mr. Slemmons mentioned seeing her with *that Eye-talian feller*. Imagined her mother lecturing again about the *dangers* of associating with *such kind*.

Like so many others, Mama believed that new arrivers, Catholics, and their ilk were ruining everything about America—and Texas in particular. *It's a strange religion,* she'd said upon learning of Joe's background. *Y'ain't seen the inside of a Papist chapel, Daughter, filled with bright-painted statues, which they worship like pagans in the temple of Ba'al.*

Joe's maternal ancestry didn't help matters, as Mama said it implied mixed blood—not only French but probably Spanish and Indian and *Lord knows what else.* Not to mention *that Orleans women have a reputation for, ahem, independent livin'.*

Though Papa was not so dead set against Joe, it was Leola who came to her sweetheart's defense.

Let me remind you, Mama, that Joe's Italian—she'd pronounced it properly, with a short *I*—*kin have built the biggest grocery in Jefferson and, as for his mother's people . . .* She'd tossed her head . . . *Joe's grandmother started a school for young prisoners and* her *mother built the first playgrounds in that city. So if by* independent living *you mean* willing to put themselves out for others, *then I reckon they fit that definition.*

She'd wanted to add more—how Mama claimed to be God-fearing yet often judged people based on outdated if not blame-fool ideas—but held her tongue. Mama would only tolerate a certain degree of disrespect and did seem somewhat humbled by Leola's rebuke.

Now Joe urged the horses faster, jolting her back to the present, and soon they'd arrived at the Dark Road, which ran through an ancient grove of cedars so thick hardly any sunlight got through—or rain, for that matter. Leola loved the idea it was only them around for miles. Most travelers chose another route, saying the Dark Road was *hainted,* relating stories of ghostly happenings—bobbing lights and otherworldly sounds to make your hair stand on end. Sometimes

Leola and Joe even spun their own spooky tales, mainly as an excuse to move closer on the buckboard.

Presently they turned into a little hidey-hole barely wide enough to fit the cart, where they'd stopped before. After lashing the horse to a sapling, Joe helped Leola into the back of the wagon then clambered in beside her. Rain pattered lightly on the trees overhead and, when a drop did land upon Leola's hand, Joe wiped it away gently.

"Can't have you getting wet," he said, reaching for the large oil-cloth in back, draping it over them. "This should protect you."

"Only from the rain, *mi caro*," Leola replied, placing a melting kiss upon his mouth. "Only the rain."

Giggling at her poor excuse for an accent, the two leaned close, forming their own shelter from the world's blustery judgments and whatever other bad weather might come—now and evermore.

CHAPTER 8

With the sun's heat blunted by clouds, Leola hit her picking-and-thinking stride quickly this day. Mostly she was figuring what to wear to the Old Maids' Convention in a couple weeks. Wouldn't be hard to rustle up a costume for the Parade of Spinsters, which only required a heavy skirt and high-necked blouse—the attire of most older women, single or otherwise. The riddle was what to don for the grand finale, when each of the girls would transform into so-called *eligible marriage material*, all for the benefit of the Smith County Free Kindergarten Association.

Leola considered the peach chiffon frock Mama had recently given her, saying she was too misshapen from child-birthing to fit in it any longer. 'Course having babies had done nothing to grow Mama taller than five-feet-one, so the dress barely reached past Leola's knees—all the fashion in other places, p'rhaps, but not here yet.

A verse of song rose from the Black pickers: *When I was a little boy, little boy, little boy* . . . snatched up by the white pickers, *When I was a little boy, twelve-year-old* . . .

Leola was too busy ruminating to join in, deciding whether the lace she'd seen at Laird's Dry Goods might add some length to the peach dress.

Papa went and left me, left me, left me, the Black pickers sang, and the white kids replied, *Papa went and left me so I'm told.*

Leola imagined reappearing onstage in the delicate gown, hair flowing, cheeks pinched bright. Imagined Joe in the audience, grinning at the sight of her.

Ha Ha this a'way. (Black folk)

Ha Ha that a'way. (white kids)

She hadn't yet asked permission to attend the Convention, well aware Mama condemned such to-dos as frivolous if not downright sinful. *Ain't what a girl wears on her outsides that attract a mate,* she'd said recently, studying a photo in *The Farm Semi-Weekly* of one such affair. *What matters are inward virtues. Cheerfulness. Humility.* She'd sighed. *Forbearance.*

Seemed ironical that Mama showed little such forbearance these days for her own husband, 'specially when the subject of Houston arose.

Ha Ha this a'way. (Black singers)

Ha Ha that a'way. (white)

Every time Papa so much as mentioned that city, Mama shot him a look that made him clam right up.

Then o' then. (All)

Leola stood, shaking her bag, settling the cotton to the bottom. Hard to admit, but she also believed Old Maids' Conventions were silly—not for the same reasons as Mama but because it seemed impossible to predict what made one person appealing to another. She was no beauty, her hair too straight for fashion, her complexion liable to spots. Where other girls seemed naturally graceful, Leola's angular build often made her feel gauche. Plenty of folks said she *thought too deep and hard for a girl,* and she found it impossible at times to be gentle, much less retiring. Yet Joe adored her in spite of— maybe *because of*—such attributes.

Likewise, she could never have predicted falling for a man who nurtured flowers as a vocation, spoke three languages (Spanish was easy to learn, he said, when you already knew Italian), and dressed in the high-crowned hats usually favored by rancheros, along with embroidered cowboy boots no decent farmer would be caught dead wearing. Didn't help that, whenever someone stared at his feet, Joe felt it necessary to explain that the boots, made by the Lucchese family of San Antonio, were prized around the world. Never mind he'd bought his pair third-hand, heels worn to nubs and original color masked by sunbaked grime.

Thinking of this, Leola laughed aloud. Eccentric as such habits might seem to others, they were what made Joe, *Joe*. Reaching for another cotton plant, she remembered their last meeting—how she'd unbuttoned the front of her dress, let him slip his hand inside. The way he'd groaned, with longing to the edge of pain.

Yowwwww!

A different cry interrupted Leola's reverie and she looked over to see Jimmy Suggs, two rows away, collapse. She hurried toward him, checking the ground as she went, sure a rattler or corn snake had made its strike. As she knelt beside the boy, a little girl pointed at a fat green worm with the telltale double triangle on its back, writhing about in echo of Jimmy's movements.

"Lookee, Leola! A pack saddle!"

Thwack!

One of the bigger boys squashed the bug with a rock, leaving a mess of guts behind, and Leola turned her attention to Jimmy again.

Though the worm's bite wouldn't kill, its poison could make a person—especially one small as Jimmy—*wish* they were dead. Luckily, as soon as she'd pried open the child's fist, Leola found the barb at the base of his thumb and eased it out.

"Where's Opal?" she asked Jimmy's brother, Earl, standing nearby.

"Mam took sick again so Opes had to stay with the baby. Might head down here later on."

Though Earl was no more than eleven or twelve years old, every other tooth in his mouth was black with rot, and Leola couldn't help feeling that same mixture of disgust and pity she always did where the Suggses were concerned.

She nodded at Jimmy. "He'll need the doctor, quick."

Earl edged nearer, speaking low. "Last time Doc came, Mam couldn'a pay him. Don't reckon it'd be any different today."

Leola looked for Wash Kane, sitting his horse across the field. Mr. McGee was in Tyler today so the hired man was full in charge. Not that Wash checked on the white kids much, choosing instead to supervise the Black workers, shouting at them to pick faster, saying McGee had plenty others to take their places and didn't they know time was money?

Finally, a Black fellow pointed out the kids' hullabaloo and Wash set his horse in their direction.

"What's the trouble?" he asked when he got there, like a small boy weren't thrashing about before him.

"Jimmy got bit by a pack saddle," Leola replied. "He needs help."

Wash checked the sky, which had suddenly filled with darkening clouds.

"Can't be traveling to town and back. If it rains, the cotton will come straight outta the boll. Picking's gotta get done 'fore then."

Leola showed him Jimmy's hand, twice its natural size and red as fresh-slaughtered beef.

"Well we got to do *something* or this boy will suffer worse than he is. Takes too long to get to town anyway." She paused. "We can bring him to Nancy Gumbs's down the road. She'll have a remedy."

With Earl listening, she didn't want to add that Nancy's fees were lower than Doc's and she might accept barter besides. Not that the boy would've appreciated it either way.

"Nancy Gumbs, the hoodoo?" Earl hissed, scuffing the ground. "She got magic blacker'n her skin. Mam wouldn'a like one bit for Jims to go there."

Leola frowned. "Mrs. Gumbs is not a hoodoo but a fine healer who tends my own family. Besides, your Mam's too sickly at the moment to care *what* color the person is helping Jimmy."

This quieted Earl, who could see his brother was suffering and nothing else to do.

Wash nodded at the little cart behind the cotton wagon.

"Only got the small gig to fit the little boy and Leola. She'll need to direct me to the healer's house." He nodded at Jimmy's brother. "Y'all can walk well enough."

Earl gave the ground another firm kick but the hired man was already turning his nag around, calling over his shoulder, "Won't be blamed if'n someone makes a fuss about a Nigra layin' hands upon a white child, y'hear?"

As Wash fetched the cart, Leola soothed Jimmy best she could.

"It's all right, little one. Mrs. Gumbs makes good medicine, good as Doc Hickley's, don't you worry about that."

She turned to Earl, mooning about like a dog that lost his bone.

"Go get some water for your brother and be quick about it."

Earl did what she'd asked and, by the time Wash returned, Leola had forced a few sips of liquid down Jimmy's throat. 'Course the way to Mrs. Gumbs's place was bumpy as all get-out so the child threw up twice, once in Leola's lap. He'd probably never smelt good a day in his life and by the time they got to Nancy's, both of them could've put a polecat to shame.

Leola was relieved to see Mrs. Gumbs in her side yard, turning tobacco leaves in a drying rack—though when the woman took notice of the unfamiliar driver, her eyes shone with fear. A white man driving up to a Black person's residence didn't often portend good.

"Mrs. Gumbs!" Leola waved her arms. "I've a boy here bit by a pack saddle!"

Realizing who she was, Nancy's face relaxed, for she'd a long acquaintance with the Owen-Rideout family. Her father, Elkin Bell, had been a sharecropper on Mr. Owen's farm and, through sheer hard work, eventually bought his own land nearby. Growing up, Orlena and Nancy played together often—not so unusual for Black and white children in those days. More unusual was the bond continuing after they'd grown.

When Leola was small, she and Mama visited the Gumbses often. While the two women sewed and talked, Nancy's much-older children, Neely and George, kept Leola company, teaching her clapping songs, telling her stories, helping her find moss and sticks for fairy forests. Sometimes the Rideouts stayed so late that Leola would curl up in the Gumbses' big bed and fall asleep. Not that the opposite ever happened, for a white family receiving Black visitors—much less allowing them to sleep in their beds—was a taboo written in the hardest stone, whatever bond they shared.

Approaching the cart, Mrs. Gumbs swabbed her forehead with a rag, as the clouds had cracked open and the day was heating fast again. Handing Jimmy over the side, Leola explained about the pack saddle bite, how she'd removed the stinger, but it hadn't helped much.

"Ain't this here a Suggs?" Nancy asked, frowning down at the child.

Leola, jumping to the ground, nodded. "Jimmy. The youngest."

For a moment, Leola thought Mrs. Gumbs might refuse to treat him and she wouldn't have blamed her for it. Opal and her family could be a splinter in the sides of certain white folk but were a three-foot spike of terror to anyone dark-complected. In the fields, Leola had witnessed the Suggs kids calling the Black pickers every kind of name, laughing as they kicked over their water jars, sometimes taking food right from their lunch buckets. 'Course they had a model of such behavior in their father, for Cyril Suggs, in his usual sozzled condition, was as likely to take his meanness out on Black folk as his family. Only last year, he and his drinking mates had set fire to the barns of several Colored farmers. Never got charged for it, either.

Now Mrs. Gumbs started toward the house.

"Reckon you came all this way," she mumbled, and Leola hurried to follow.

Nancy's cabin was lopsided and rough, with a primitive fireplace on one wall instead of a proper stove. The floors of the house were whitewashed and the walls covered with fresh newspaper, for Mrs. Gumbs believed like Mama that cleanliness was next to godliness, with healthfulness their natural heir.

In one corner stood the bed where Leola had fallen asleep so many times and, in another, the rocking chair where Elkin Bell sat, lacing a pair of deer-hide moccasins. It was a craft he'd learned years ago, living with the Choctaw, where he'd also found himself a bride—Nancy's mother, Jane, whose constant mourning for her people had sent her to an early grave. There was a *Mr.* Gumbs, a porter on the railroad and rarely home. Neely Gumbs had married and moved to North Carolina, while George rented a place closer to town—though, according to Mrs. Gumbs, possibly not for long.

Nancy had recently confided in Mama that her son had turned restless since serving in France, where he'd learned a great deal about gasoline engines and got his first real taste of equality too.

Seems those Frenchies let their Black folk enjoy their freedom, Mama told Leola afterwards. *And George got used to it. Wants to open his own mechanical shop but Nancy cannot fathom it, sayin' white folk own most'a the cars and would never frequent such a place.*

Now Mr. Bell looked up from his handiwork. The man was wrinkled as an apple left too long in the root bin yet had a brightness about his eyes could've belonged to a far younger man.

"What ya done brought us, Nance?"

"Only one of the Suggses, Dad. Got bit by a pack saddle." She wriggled a shoulder at Leola. "And you know Orlie's child."

"Sure do." Mr. Bell bobbed his head. "Y'all done growed since I seen ya last."

"Reckon so sir," Leola agreed. "Seems I might never stop neither."

Mr. Bell chuckled.

"I was a tall man once, could reach the sweetest pecans high on the trees. Old age will steal what height the good Lord grants you. Best have some extra inches to spare."

Nancy, about to lay Jimmy in the bed, studied his head with a stricken expression.

"This child is crawlin' with lice! Leola, bring my pallet from yonder. Will be easier to burn that when I'm done than a whole bed entire."

Leola dragged over the mattress of blankets and quilts and, as Mrs. Gumbs lay Jimmy upon it, tried not to think too hard on her own scalp, which suddenly itched like fire.

As soon as Nancy began washing Jimmy's wound, he set up such a caterwauling, anyone within a mile might believe murder was being committed. But then she smeared a rank-scented salve on his hand and the boy's groans ceased straightaway. Though she knew better,

Leola understood why some people thought the woman possessed magic powers.

"What was that remedy?" she asked as color rose in Jimmy's cheeks.

"Hog fat in turpentine." Nancy wrapped the boy's hand in a clean cloth. "Good for sore eyes, too, 'case you ever need it."

She spread a blanket over Jimmy, then perused her shelves, finding a glass bottle with a tiny piece of corncob in its top. After pouring some of the liquid into another vessel, she handed it to Leola.

"Add some of this here tincture to the hottest water you can stand and scrub your head in it. Should kill whatever nits you picked up. Will make you smell like sour fruit but that is better'n your current perfume."

Next she spooned a pale-gray powder into a newspaper envelope, handing that over too.

"Make a tea out this balmonia root, drink it three, four times a day. I'm guessing this child got a bad case of worms top of everythin' else and you most like to catch it. This'll clean you out before the worms hook your insides too deep."

Leola, feeling queasy already, nodded.

"'Preciate it, Mrs. Gumbs. I'll come by later to pay you what's owed."

The woman, fixated on Jimmy again, didn't reply.

"This child's dirty enough to light a fire with. Nothin' I'd like better than to give him a good scrubbing with some lye soap."

Elkin let out a cackle. "Imagine his kinfolk finding out, what a foofaraw that would cause!"

As if she'd overheard and without even a *Yoo-Hoo-Anyone-Home*, Opal Suggs bashed through the door, Earl trailing close behind.

"You got some nerve," Opal shouted at Leola like she was the only person in the room, "bringin' my baby brother to this here godforsaken place."

Leola trembled, recalling their encounter weeks ago—and this time the battle-axe had Earl on her side. Then again, here was Mrs. Gumbs with her square shoulders and sinewy arms, wearing a pair of oversized man's boots could kick Opal clear to the next county. Of course, there was the matter of Cyril Suggs, who might not care about his children yet would relish any excuse to torment those he despised. Nancy Gumbs's boots would be little match against him and his rummy thugs.

"Jimmy was in awful pain," Leola explained, calmly as she could, "and Nancy's was the closest to McGee's. Besides, Earl said the doctor wouldn't help, seeing you owed him already."

Soon as this last bit left her mouth, Leola regretted it—too late, as Opal heaved herself up like one of those female Viking warriors in Papa's folktale book.

"You sayin' Mam ain't good for her debts?"

Leola was scrabbling for a response when Elvin Bell made a noise, and everyone looked over to see him using his rifle to rock himself back and forth, back and forth. The gun was nearly as tall as Earle and although it looked old—p'rhaps was a relic from the Civil War— its gleaming metal parts meant it probably still got fired, time to time.

"Best take your brother home," Mrs. Gumbs said to Opal, breaking the silence, "and be done with it. He'll turn out fine if'n you apply this balm to the swelling."

She held out the bottle.

"Just enough left for what's needed. I got to make me a fresh batch anyhow."

Opal folded her arms. "Won't be obliged to any Nigra witch."

Leola flinched but Nancy only tipped her head, speaking in a sugary voice.

"All I done is what the good Lord commands, Miss Opal, treating the *least* of His children as we would treat Him." Her lips twitched. "Nothin' owed for that a'tall."

Opal seemed to be calculating whether this was a slight when Jimmy sat up, calling her name, and she knelt beside him.

"You like'ta scared me to death, Jims!"

Leola was shocked by the other girl's unexpected tenderness.

"Guess you was foolin' around again in the fields and look what done happened."

Jimmy sniffled. "The worm was so purty, Opes, painted up like he was. I din't know he'd bite me!" He glanced shyly at Nancy. "Don't hurt so much now anyways. The hoodoo made it better."

Opal snorted, hefting Jimmy as she stood.

Swiping the jar of salve from Nancy's hand, she called out to Earl, "Best get outta here, a'fore we are crawlin' with vermin or whatever else a person might find in a shithole such like this."

After their ragtag band was gone, Leola caught Mrs. Gumbs and her father shaking their heads at each other as folks do when they've heard a jest too often and are long past laughing at it.

CHAPTER 9

Leola knew their financial situation was dire when she caught her fastidious mother cutting skipper eggs from a cheap cut of pork. Couldn't bring herself to comment about it, forcing the meat down at supper, trying not to picture flies hatching in her intestines. Wondering if Mrs. Gumbs's hookworm tincture might help.

Though her parents had stopped arguing outright about Houston, the topic was a half-smothered fire licking the pauses of every conversation, to the point where Leola almost wished they'd quarrel. At least, that way, she'd know where everything stood.

But then Mr. McGee hired Papa to deliver his cotton to the gin each week and also do the final accounting, which offered a sorely needed ray of hope. Though the job didn't pay much, the prospect of work soothed Papa's mood, lightening Mama's disquiet too.

The arrangement suited Leola, as well, guaranteeing a ride to town on Saturdays. Usually two wagons were needed, so Vaughan Peeples drove one and Papa the other, with Leola sitting on the buckboard beside him. However, this week there was only one load for the gin, meaning she'd have to sit on the cotton in back.

"Don't be such a prissy miss," Papa said when she protested about mussing her good dress. "It's high time you found out what it's like to ride on the softest featherbed you can imagine before you're too old."

Leola shot him a look.

"I'm already too old for such a thing, thank you just the same."

"You're harder to refuse than your mama's custard pie, child." Papa's mouth crooked sideways. "But if it's more amenable, you can ride with Vaughn and I shall sit on the cotton stack. I could use some rest anyhow."

Mama glanced up from her sewing machine.

"I hardly believe you'd have your old father riding on the crops like a schoolboy, Lee. An apron over your clothes and a scarf upon your head will protect you just fine." She let out a puff of air. "Vanity's a sin and respecting your elders a virtue, last I looked."

Leola nearly laughed, thinking how she'd recently caught Mama studying herself in the mirror, tipping her head to find a flattering angle. Yet she didn't bother pointing this out. Truth was, she'd watched other kids riding their family's cotton loads over the years and it seemed like fun. And soon she *would* be too old to find out.

Next morning, when Vaughn pulled up with the loaded wagon, Mae and Karla insisted on jumping into the cotton like they did every week, and then it was Leola's turn to climb aboard. She'd begun to lower herself, proper, onto the pile when Papa grabbed her hand.

"It's not a cauldron of boiling water, Daughter. To do this right, you must jump like your sisters did."

Leola sighed yet couldn't help smiling. Papa seemed so happy this morning; least she could do was indulge him.

"Y'all are set on making a fool of me, it seems," she muttered, scrabbling onto the bench, waiting until Papa counted *one-two-three*, then falling headlong into the pile, shrieking louder than her sisters had.

As the team lurched into motion, Leola marveled this was the same rutted road she knew, as she barely felt a jolt. Rocked by the pitch-and-swell of the wagon, mesmerized by the pale dome of sky above, she nearly did fall asleep . . . until Vaughn brought the horses up so short, she almost tumbled over the side.

"Dag-blame it!" the driver shouted, as George Gumbs tore past in his automobile, while Papa only watched with an admiring expression.

"Guess that soldier really did learn 'bout engines over in France, like his mama said. Last I saw, that Hupmobile was broke down worse than a mule after summer harvest. And now look at it go!"

Vaughn, easing the cart onto the road, coughed dust from his lungs.

"I don't care what he learnt in the war, Frank. Boy's got no business runnin' us off the road. Could'a got us kilt!" More coughing. "Can't figure why Negroes get the right to drive. Y'see the menace they pose."

Papa shook his head. "I've seen more'n a few jalopies turned wheels-up in a ditch lately, Vaughn, and not a one of them driven by a Black person."

Vaughn didn't answer, flicking the reins harder, and Leola settled back into her cream-puff bed, rousing only when she heard the *hiss-clack* of the cotton gin. Being early yet, she stayed to watch Papa put the cotton through its paces, directing Vaughn as he backed the wagon into the barnlike building. After Papa shouted a signal to the gin operator, a long rubber tube dropped from the ceiling, sucking up the mass of cotton in a thunderous *whoooosh!* that made Leola clap in spite of herself.

As a crane delivered the finished bale into the yard for weighing, Papa waved his arm like a circus master.

"From fifteen hundred pounds of fluff to five hundred pounds of pure white gold! It's true, Rosalee; modern machines are humanity's greatest feat."

After he'd reconciled Mr. McGee's receipts, they left Vaughn to water the horses, heading for the dry goods store.

The place hummed as it always did on Saturday afternoons, customers perusing the cabinets of hosiery, bins of nails, and shelves of canned vegetables. Leola knew most everyone there but didn't stop to converse, heading straight for the candy counter. Since he'd started working for Mr. McGee, Papa insisted she keep some of her cotton-picking money to spend however she liked, and today she'd planned on buying a surprise for Ship. After debating between caramel creams, licorice pipes, and chewing gum, she finally settled on Chiclets, which Mary relished in defiance of her teachers at MacComb's.

The salesgirl was just handing over the gum when George Gumbs sauntered through the front door, and the place fell into a hush. Black folk tended to use the rear entrance of the store and, even then, mostly to pick up orders for their white employers. Yet Bronway was a tiny town where everyone knew everyone else and Laird's the only provisionary, so most folks turned a blind eye to the occasional lapse in custom and, soon enough, everyone went back to their business.

But not long afterwards, as Leola was inspecting the ribbon display, she spotted Mrs. Slemmons from church cutting George in the cashier's line.

"I declare, Rob," the woman trilled to the shopkeeper, "thought my appetite beat by this here heat, yet that orange cheddar of yours got me hankerin' already for supper."

Mr. Laird unlatched the cheese case.

"How about a sample then, Effie? I've some fresh soda crackers would go with it, real nice."

Mrs. Slemmons nodded. "That would be dandy."

As Mr. Laird carved the cheese, George took a small step forward.

"Beg pardon." He spoke low but firm. "I was next in line."

Mr. Laird and Mrs. Slemmons acted as if they hadn't heard him.

"Tell me, true, how you like this," Mr. Laird said, passing Effie Slemmons some cheese on a flaky cracker. "I've engaged a new dairy down in Rusk and have not yet decided whether it's worth the trouble."

Before she could answer, George spoke again—louder this time.

"I been waitin' awhile to pay."

Mrs. Slemmons didn't flinch nor did Mr. Laird react. Leola, on the other hand, could not tear her eyes away, watching as George's mouth flattened into a thin line, his face filling not with fear but indignation, maybe even *anger*—emotions Leola had never before seen in a Black person looking at a white one.

Papa had appeared by then, taking his place behind George, and Leola held her breath. At home, her father had been outspoken about the many recent savageries against Black folk: a well-respected businessman, jailed for complaining about his taxes; two young boys, whipped for "stealing" water from a white man's well. After Pastor Nickles preached about *pruning back the Coloreds, who will spread like Johnson grass otherwise*, Papa had skipped a few worship services in protest. But now all he did was study a rack of seed packets as if nothing were happening at all.

"Isn't proper," George said again, "to break the line like that."

Mrs. Slemmons still did not respond, but Mr. Laird leaned to one side, glaring.

"Have some patience, boy. When I'm done helping Mrs. Slemmons and Mr. Rideout, and if no one else is waiting to pay, then it will be your turn."

No one else white, Leola thought. *If no* white *person were waiting, then you'll be served.* That's what Mr. Laird meant.

A voice boomed in her mind: *Is not right!*

Leola started at this inner reproof, as unexpected as a tornado dipping from a clear blue summer sky. There were plenty other admonishments she knew by heart: *Is not right . . . to lick your fingers at the table, wear floppy shoes, dance, drink, kill.* But she'd never felt such a caution over this sort of circumstance—never mind she'd seen it played out thousands of times before.

She glanced at Papa, still studying those seeds. Saw the town banker staring at the cigar box in his hand. Heard Widow Harkness and her daughter debating the merits of plaid versus striped shirt-waists. *They must know,* she realized, *that it's wrong. Know but won't say.*

George turned his gaze in her direction and Leola had a sudden recollection of visiting the Gumbses' years earlier. Nancy had cut each child a sticky-sweet slice of ribbon cane and, when Leola dropped hers in the chicken yard, George had insisted—without any prodding—that she take his. And now he seemed to see the revelation in her face. Seemed to understand *she* knew what was happening was wrong. That *everything* she'd understood until this moment was wrong.

Leola could hardly stand the chafing, suffocating weight of her newfound awareness. Wanted to cast it aside like those cumbersome overalls she'd once worn in the fields—but the feeling only gripped her tighter. She perused the yellow Chiclet package, reading the fancy red script: *Candy-coated gum. Mint-flavored. Refreshing!* When she looked up again, George had turned his back on her.

"Thankee kindly, Rob," Mrs. Slemmons was saying, as the shop-keeper gave her change. "For the extra crackers too. I'm sure Mr. Slemmons will stop in shortly to say he enjoyed them."

Lifting her packages by their strings, she whirled around, letting them knock against George—and not lightly either.

"That didn'a take long, did it?" she murmured, the doorbells tinkling in her wake.

"C'mon, Frank." Mr. Laird beckoned at Papa. "You're next."

Except Papa wasn't next, and now George watched him as he had Leola—not with expectation but *daring*. She gulped, wondering if Papa was thinking of the white doctor in Tyler who'd been bull-whipped for treating a Black man. Or the milliner in Texarkana, driven from town for hiring a Black salesgirl.

Is not right Is not right Is not right . . . That deep-down voice was shouting now. Leola wanted Papa to let George step in front of him yet didn't want him to be beaten and harassed. Didn't want a cross burnt in their yard or to be singled out at school, shunned, whispered about.

"Papa!" She hurried to his side. "Let me check you got the proper needles, the crewelwork ones Mama wanted. She won't be happy if she can't finish Mr. Durnaydon's vest tonight."

Papa exhaled, flashing Mr. Laird a sheepish smile.

"Reckon I ought do as my daughter says. Don't want to risk the wrath of my wife." He stepped aside, gesturing at George. "Go on son, while we get this sorted."

George didn't move at first nor say a word in return to Papa, and Leola wondered if he might leave altogether. But finally he thumped his groceries, one by one, onto the counter.

Of course Leola already knew Papa had the right needles but pretended to check, just the same. Meanwhile, Mr. Laird toted George's bill and, instead of tying his goods in neat packages, made him fill his own sack, not thanking George for his business nor even saying goodbye. At least this got George off the hook for expressing gratitude to Mr. Laird which, it seemed, he had no intention of doing, walking toward the door with deliberate steps. Not looking around at all anymore.

After he was gone, the very floorboards of the building seemed to sigh with relief. People spoke again. The banker whistled a tune, Widow Harkness and her daughter took up a new argument—this time over lace versus cotton gloves. Leola was glad when Papa paid for their supplies and didn't make a fuss over the situation—though when the shopkeeper groused about *Negroes gettin' too big for their britches,* Papa replied, *He's a nice young man, Rob,* and left it at that.

Out in the warm sunshine, Papa appeared uneasy, like he wanted to say something—except Leola spoke first.

"If I don't hurry, Mary might think I got sucked up in the gin operation and eat my share of the strawberry shortcake."

Papa exhaled.

"Wouldn't want that to happen, would we?" He pecked her on the cheek. "Go on, Rosalee, and have a grand afternoon."

And so she went, the insistent refrain of *Is not right* muffled by the din of everyday life.

CHAPTER 10

When she arrived at the Shipleys, there was the promised cake on a silver-plated tray along with cheese-and-pimento sandwiches and, next to it, a pitcher of pink lemonade. Of course, Mrs. Shipley insisted on conversing with them a while—never mind all Leola wanted was to rip into the food and the topic of Ship's new beau, Henry Scales.

At long last, Mrs. Shipley glanced at her watch.

"Much as I'm enjoying this visit, girls, I ought head to Laird's, buy those mincemeat pies Mr. Shipley craves."

Hearing mention of the store, Leola reached into her bag for Mary's gift.

"I declare," Ship exclaimed, shaking the Chiclet package so the pieces clicked together, "you're the very best friend! These will come in handy when I am in close quarters with," she peeped at her mother, "my *chums* at MacComb's. *They* always complain I eat too many fried onions at suppertime and can hardly get close enough to," she cleared her throat, "*speak* to me."

Both girls sucked in their cheeks, trying not to laugh, while Mrs. Shipley acted like she hadn't understood the real meaning beneath her daughter's words. If Henry's family was as rich as Mary claimed, no doubt the Shipleys would see past certain indiscretions.

Mrs. Shipley picked up her gloves from the table.

"Was Laird's busy?" she asked Leola, who shrugged.

"Like a usual Saturday."

"Ach," Mrs. Shipley lamented. "Guess I'll be waiting in line then."

Leola recalled the scene at the store, George's questioning gaze, the newfound horror of *Is not right.*

"Mr. Laird was rude to George today," she ventured, and Ship looked confused.

"George?"

"George Gumbs, when he came in to buy something. Mrs. Slemmons barged in front of him in line and Mr. Laird didn't say one thing."

Nor did anyone.

"Oh, dear." Mrs. Shipley fiddled with a teardrop earring. "That Effie Slemmons is a she-bear in satin." She frowned at Leola. "But George should know better than to feel insulted. It's only some folk taking advantage of the laws. Nothing much for Rob Laird to do, is there?"

Leola licked her lips thinking, *What if the laws are wrong, too?*

"I don't understand Negroes resisting their separate place in our society," Mrs. Shipley continued. "Why would they *want* to mingle with low-down whites like Mrs. Slemmons, who will only cause them trouble?"

Ship, nibbling cake, nodded.

"I hear there's a fine new general store over in Mount Bristol run by another Black fellow. Keeps the same inventory as Laird's. George could shop there, save himself the aggravation *and* support a Negro merchant."

Leola shifted in her seat.

"Why should George have to travel an hour to get his groceries," she asked, "all because certain white folk can't abide the Golden Rule?"

Ship frowned at her mother, who also looked perplexed—not by what Leola had said, it seemed, but by the fact she'd said it at all.

"Laws are laws, dear," Mrs. Shipley replied. "Necessary for keeping things in order."

Leola peered at Mary, who shrugged as if to say, *What can we do?*

Is not right Is not right Is not right. The phrase hissed in Leola's mind.

Mrs. Shipley stood, smoothing her skirt.

"This is an argument for another time, girls. If Laird's is as crowded as you say, those mincemeat pies might already be gone. And so I bid you *adieu.*"

After she'd left, Ship and Leola sat in silence for a while. Leola didn't think the argument was for another time. She wanted her friend to agree, even if it had to be behind her mother's back, that the business at the store *was* not right. Wanted her to say she felt the horror too. Instead, Ship leaned over and picked up a sandwich triangle, shoving the whole thing in her mouth. Smacking loudly, she nodded at the platter of deviled eggs.

"Your turn, Miss Rideout."

Leola paused. It was their tradition to act uncivilized whenever they were alone, flaunting the normal decorum that might suffocate them otherwise—except it seemed some rules were not for flaunting. Regardless Ship was forever pointing out how poorly their sex got treated; never, ever could she say anything against *this.*

Leola reached for an egg, which she shoved without warning into Mary's face.

Ship went still, yellow and white dotting her face, and Leola was sure her friend might cry. Instead the other girl reached for a piece of shortcake, smashing it into Leola's mouth so forcefully, her teeth collided with her gums. Leola barely flinched, almost welcoming the violence of whipped cream and fruit, the acrid taste of blood amidst all that sugar, a punishment she somehow deserved.

Ship, eyes glittering with tears, brought a hand to her cheek.

"Lee! I'm so sorry!"

Leola stared at her knees. "I'm sorry too." *For a thousand things besides this.*

She longed to talk about the young man assaulted in Waco's town square for wearing his soldier uniform. Wanted to discuss the recent lynching in Karnack, how spectators munched popcorn as a man swung from a tree. Wanted to grab her friend by the front of her candy-stripe frock and scream, *Is not right!* But her lip was bleeding, so Leola reached for a napkin instead—upending the lemonade pitcher, showering Ship with sticky liquid.

For a long moment, the girls stared at each other, at the puddle in Mary's lap, the dripping furniture. And then they started to laugh, waves of shrieking, dark hilarity, the sound of madwomen kept too long in cramped dungeons.

The housemaid, Fiona, ran into the room, took one look at them, and burst into giggles too—apologizing to "my lady Mary," setting them to laughter again. Fiona was their age, more friend to Ship than servant. Except that when the laughter died down, she was the one to fetch the bucket and cloths, scrubbing the floor and settee. Leola tried to help, imagining herself in Fiona's place, cleaning up after reckless girls who squashed crumbs in the carpet and considered it fun. But Mary wouldn't have it, insisting Leola come upstairs while she changed her soaked dress, leaving Fiona to her labors.

After she'd donned a new outfit, Ship took a picture frame from her night table.

"Leola Rideout, meet Henry Scales."

Leola studied the photograph, thinking Henry was more or less as she'd imagined: handsome like the college men in tobacco advertisements, with pale eyes, light hair, and a smile suggesting mischiefs he'd never need to answer for.

"He's a dreamboat," she said, and Ship collapsed, face first, onto the bed, limbs flung every which a'way.

"Not only that, Lee! He's also a swell baseball player and prize debater too—can talk himself out of anything."

Leola set the photo aside, leaning down to whisper, "And talk certain girls *into* anything, I warrant."

Ship flipped over, cheeks bright.

"I hardly need persuading, Miss Rideout, as I believe is the case when you are alone with your own *dreamboat*."

Now it was Leola's turn to blush, but as she began describing her last meeting with Joe, they heard the front door opening and closing, a voice calling, "I'm home!"

"Father?" Ship sat up, confused. "He wasn't due from Longview until this evening."

Rushing to the window, they spied Joe outside, unhitching the horses from the hack.

"Dang," Ship said with a theatrical pout. "I guess you'll want to go to your love when I've barely confided half my revelations of Henry."

Leola was about to say Joe probably had other errands to attend and didn't plan to meet until later. But before she could, Mr. Shipley called up the stairs.

"Mary? Your father's home and expects a fonder greeting than what he's gotten so far."

Ship rolled her eyes but couldn't help grinning. Blanton Shipley worshiped the ground on which his only child walked. In a way, Leola felt sorry for poor Henry Scales, who would have to woo Mr. Shipley at least as hard as his daughter.

Downstairs, Blanton hugged Mary then gave Leola, whom he regarded as yet another member of their family, a quick kiss on the cheek.

"You're back early," Ship noted, and her father's smile vanished.

"There was bad business in Longview today." His glance at Leola made her throat tighten. "Nothing too terrible, don't worry. I'm just glad you're here. Might be good to know what happened before you see Joe."

"Joe? Is he all right?"

Leola tried to remember if he'd seemed hurt when she'd watched him from the bedroom window.

"Oh, he's fine. Not physically harmed, in any case." Mr. Shipley loosened his collar. "But he's taking the horses to the farrier now, so I'll have time to explain."

Leola wanted more than anything to run outside and see for herself how *fine* her beau was but didn't want to be rude.

"I'll get this dust off myself first," Blanton said, pointing toward the washroom, "and meet you in the parlor." He raised an eyebrow. "I prayed the whole way home you'd saved some of that strawberry shortcake Fiona made last night."

Ship and Leola exchanged guilty stares, having finished most of the dessert themselves. It was Fiona who rescued them again, poking her head from the kitchen.

"I made an extra cake, sir, though will have to stir up a new pitcher of lemonade." She struggled to keep a straight face. "Seems to go quickly on such a hot day."

Ship giggled, but Leola was feeling too uneasy to join in. As they waited for Mr. Shipley on the parlor couch and Fiona brought in the refreshments, Leola castigated herself for not seeing to Joe earlier.

Soon Blanton was back. As she poured his drink, Mary asked,

"What was this bad business, Father? We're on pins and needles—Leola especially."

Mr. Shipley took a swig of lemonade, patting his mouth with a napkin.

"The Klan was holding a carnival today right on the Longview town square, raising money to build a gymnasium at the high school."

Leola felt confused. The Klan she knew was notorious for making trouble for Negroes, and what did that have to do with Joe?

"There were hundreds in attendance." Blanton took the plate Mary handed him, balancing it on his lap. "Picnicking and playing games. They even had a marching band and a Better Baby contest." He snorted. "Those donation jars were crammed with dollar bills! Way they were going, they'll be able to build a gymnasium *and* a swimming pool."

He cut a bite of cake, chewing far too slowly for Leola's liking.

"Those klavern folk were somethin'," he said, swallowing, "parading about in their peaked hats—no robes however. Was too blame hot, even for them." Mr. Shipley let off a tart chuckle. "There was a man I knew among them, Sam Ormsby. Supplies me with fertilizer. I'd no idea he was a Klansman but there he was in that outlandish regalia."

Setting his plate down, he pressed the napkin to his sweat-dampened forehead.

"Ormsby shouted at Joe and me as we passed, asking why I hire *Papists*—*Dagos* was the other word he used—which Joe said proves how addle-brained such folk are, for the word comes from *Diego*, a name common among Spanish, not Italians. By then a couple other Klansmen had also taken notice and started chanting, *Dagos go home! Keep America great!* Their usual mealy-mouthed refrains."

"Poor Joe!" Mary murmured, though Leola was too mortified to comment.

"It was over quick enough." Blanton sighed. "But when Joe crossed town again later—by himself, this time—they were at their mischief again. Threw fruit and rocks, even shoes, if you can imagine! Joe didn't complain, though I could see he was shook up."

Leola no longer cared about being polite. She jumped from her seat, heading straight for the front door, but Ship caught up with her on the threshold, grabbing her arm.

"Wait until Joe comes back. Give him some time to collect himself."

"I'm going to him now," Leola insisted, "like you'd go to Henry, if he'd been treated likewise."

Flying down the street, she hardly felt the ground beneath her, didn't even see the passerby who called, cheery as anything, "Howdy there, Leola!"

When she got to the blacksmith's shop, Joe was just coming out, and it took all her resolve not to embrace him on the spot.

"Mr. Shipley told us about Longview," she panted, "that business with the Klan."

Joe looked like he might spit. "I asked him not to tell you!"

"He knew I'd want to know. And he was right."

"What did he say, exactly?" Joe glanced about. "And keep your voice down, please."

"He said the Klan called you bad names and—"

"They were only names, which cannot hurt me." He narrowed his eyes. "Hysterics don't help anyway. Not yours, not anyone's."

"I'm only offering my condolences. Telling you how sorry I am, and glad you're safe."

Joe's laugh scraped the air. "Safe as a fly in a glue pot, I'd say."

"Whatever happened in Longview would never happen to you here," Leola replied. "I can only imagine that—"

He grabbed her elbow, hustling her into a nearby alley.

"'Bout half the town is KKK, Lee," Joe hissed, nodding toward the street. "Mack Slemmons for one. Flake Honeycutt, the wheelwright, for another. And Morris Conway."

"Mr. Conway? The pharmacist? But he's a deacon in our church!"

Joe's face went rigid. "Go look in *Deacon* Conway's window, Leola, without bein' too plain about it. Read the blue sign. Come back, tell me what it says."

Leola stepped into the sunlight again, reading the placard behind the pharmacy's glass front: *100 percent.*

She returned and told Joe what she'd seen.

"That's right," he snorted, "as in *100 percent pure American.* There are signs in other stores, too, you probably hain't noticed. Some say *TWK* for *Trade with a Klansman.* Some only have the number *one hundred* on them. It's a signal—a code—telling folk those merchants will only hire and serve so-called *true white Americans.* Plenty of people—deacons and Freemasons, even teachers—not only appreciate but *approve of* such sentiment. Here in this town, where you were born."

Now Leola did recall seeing a few such signs, one at the gin and another at the shoe store. "That's shameful, Joe. Except I'm not a Kluxxer and don't care a whit what those folks think."

He paused, scowling at her.

"I been mulling it over and you ought care. You're one of *pure, unsullied* blood and I, a so-called *mongrel.*"

He scrunched the toe of his boot into the dirt like he was crushing into smithereens every 100 percent American he knew.

"How would you manage, knowin' there were folks who judged—even *hated*—you for being married to, as they call it, *Papish scum?*" His mouth puckered. "I 'spect it'd be too much for such a tender-hearted girl like you to handle."

Choking back tears, Leola tried to keep her tone light. Tried, even, to smile.

"My bloodline's hardly what those Kluxxers would call *pure*, Joe. There's Irish and Scottish and French in our family tree. It's thought my great-grandmother was Cherokee. Papa says we must have Eskimo inside us, too, for what little snow we ever get makes the girls happy as rabbits in the lettuce patch." She gave a little laugh. "We're far more mutt than you, I reckon, and nothin' wrong with that."

Joe didn't seem to appreciate her sentiment, regarding Leola as if she were some distant figure he couldn't quite make out.

"Tell me this then. If we married and I asked you to become a Catholic, would you?"

Leola went silent, for he'd never asked this before. She knew when he was home in Jefferson that Joe sometimes went to the Roman Catholic Church, but they rarely spoke of it. In fact, all she knew of Catholics was what her mother had told her, and now she tried to imagine worshipping among statues, murmuring strange incantations into strings of beads, genuflecting before a golden cross. Tried to imagine and couldn't.

"I—I don't know," she stammered, "about being Catholic. I been Baptist all my life and that's all I'm accustomed to."

"See?" There was the harsh laugh again. "Even you are prejudiced."

She flinched.

"That's not what I meant. It's something I've never considered before, is what I'm saying. Reckon you haven't considered being Baptist neither."

"You're right. I haven't." Joe's expression was steely. "Don't matter anyway. Whoever I marry, however *purely* American, will need to become Catholic. So I guess that is the end of that."

Leola wasn't sure what to say. Her faith had been a constant since

Day One, like Indian paintbrush in springtime, and Mama and Papa, and always *makin' do.* It'd never been her choice, what church she attended nor whether she went. That was what they did, what *everyone* did, not only for the sermons and redemption, but for the singing and socializing too.

As a child, she'd imagined what God looked like and how he found time for so many prayers, whether ascending to Heaven was like *bringing in the sheaves,* as in one hymn (which, to her mind, was not cause for *rejoicing* at all) or more like *Taking a trip/In an old gospel ship/And sailing through the air,* as in another.

Then, at age twelve, she'd received The Call and soon afterward got dipped in the creek wearing a white organdy dress. Her redemption assured, she was supposed to feel settled in such things. But over the years, Leola had learned there were more religions on Earth than countries, each claiming its own path to salvation. She began doubting that her faith held the only Keys to the Kingdom, despite Pastor Nickles's proclamations otherwise. Still, she'd clung to the surety of it, same way she took the well-worn path to town despite knowing faster routes.

Not that there was time for explaining all this, as Joe had started for the street and she ran to catch him.

"I love you." She clutched his arm. "Please—"

He shook her off. "There are things more important than love."

Leola felt struck by lightning. What—*what!*—was more important than love? As she watched him stalk away, she didn't care whether passersby noticed her sniveling like a baby.

"Leola?" It was Dora Meeker, hurrying over. "You all right, child?"

Leola didn't answer, turning in the direction of home, her vision so blurred by tears that it was good she knew the well-worn path after all. The day's events blurred in her mind too: the unfamiliar ache she'd felt when her neighbors had been vile to George, Mary seeming so unsympathetic about it, the Klan taunting Joe in Longview, the sign in Conway's Pharmacy. The signs *everywhere* she'd not seen.

Stumbling over a chipmunk hole, Leola couldn't forget, either, how Joe had rebuffed her own attempts at kindness, saying she'd have to convert. With sudden vehemence, she wondered if he was no better than those frothing, pointy-headed Klansmen, thinking one religion was better than another . . . namely, *his*.

By the time she got home, Leola's mind was as jumbled her heart. What the Klan—what Effie Slemmons, her own mother, just about every person she knew—believed seemed so clearly wrong and yet, for a brutal instant, she thought there might be some truth to their sentiments. Maybe she and Joe really *were* too different to understand each other, as foreign to each other as if they'd been born in separate countries, after all.

CHAPTER 11

L eola pushed away her breakfast, bracing for Mama's favorite aphorism: *Wasteful makes woeful wants*, which the woman probably uttered in her sleep, regretting the time squandered on dreaming when there was so much else to do.

But today Mama didn't upbraid Leola for leaving her food untouched, setting the plate on the sideboard and covering it with a cloth.

"In case you've a mind to eat later," she explained.

Leola pretended not to notice the worried expressions her folks exchanged, expressions she'd seen often since falling out with Joe two weeks earlier. She'd told no one—not even Ship—what had happened, even knowing her parents had a hunch. Joe had been absent their place all this time and she'd barely spoken his name aloud—except in the midst of night, crying into her pillows.

"You still attending that Old Maids' assembly this afternoon?" Mama asked, scraping a plate over the slop bucket.

Leola stood, distracted by a tiny emerald-and-ruby hummingbird darting about the trumpet vine outside. Was rare to see such birds so late in the season, and Leola felt a stirring of wonder inside her dampened soul.

"Lee?" Papa stared around his newspaper. "Your mother asked you a question."

"Yes?" Leola turned from the window. "Oh—the convention. No'm. Changed my mind." She slid her plate into the dishpan. "Think I'll stay home, finish the corn-shelling, study some. If I don't pass this latest science course, I'm sunk."

"The corn-shelling can wait 'til tomorrow," Mama replied. "As for the book-studyin' . . . You're not a hothouse flower, my girl. Fellowship with your friends will serve you better at the moment."

Picking up a cloth, Leola finally met Mama's gaze.

"Thought you considered Old Maids' Conventions foolish. You wouldn't let me go to the last one, remember?"

"True enough." Mama pushed hair from her face with the back of a sudsy hand. "But I been thinkin' on the matter. If it's to raise money for a good cause, can't be all foolishness." She raised an eyebrow. "Long's you understand—"

"I know, I know," Leola interrupted, swiping a damp plate with the cloth. "*Pretty is as pretty does* and so forth and so on."

She set the dried dish onto its brethren stack then picked up the heavy cast-iron skillet. Although the idea of parading herself on a stage didn't appeal all that much, Mama was probably right: Ship wouldn't be home again for a while, and seeing old friends could prove a diversion from her ceaseless thoughts of Joe.

Leola's mind had been a whirligig lately, trying to figure out who was most to blame for their quarrel—one minute certain it was him (he'd said she was prejudiced!), the next, thinking she was to blame (she'd been careless of his wounded pride). At this point, she wasn't even sure it mattered. They were through and nothing more to do about it.

"Guess I'll go then," she sighed, seasoning the clean skillet with some lard, "if'n I can hitch a ride with you."

Mama looked relieved.

"Certain you can but I must leave by eleven o'clock sharp. And I could use your help pinnin' Mrs. Durnaydon's gown 'long the way."

Leola hung the clean pan on its hook. "'Course."

"Oh, I nearly forgot . . ." Mama opened the door, flinging dishwater onto the tansy patch near the back steps. "I found a pair of old boots up at Auntie's the other day. Might go right well with your spinster attire."

Leola nodded, thinking of the peach frock she'd altered for this very occasion. She'd left it short after all, tucking the bodice to accentuate her meager bosom, adding lace to the square neckline. Done it all thinking of Joe, who wouldn't be there anyhow—might not be anywhere *near* Bronway today, might've upped and moved to Tyler to oversee construction of Mr. Shipley's new greenhouses. Leola swallowed, telling herself that would be for the best, give them a fresh start, a chance to go about their lives until some other sweetheart came along, a notion that made her insides twist like the towel she wrung over the sink.

"Reckon Joe will attend the Old Maid proceedings this afternoon?" Papa asked, as if reading her mind.

"I've no idea what *he* is about today." Leola bristled, sure her father was fishing—as he had often lately—for information about Joe. "Not my business nor anyone else's, far's I'm concerned."

The words came out rougher than intended and Mae, cutting paper dolls in the corner, was quick to call her on it.

"Y'ain't s'posed to sass. Ain't that right, Mama?"

"*Isn't*," Leola hissed, tossing the dishrag aside. "*Isn't* that right." She pivoted to face her sister. "You're big enough to speak proper and not like one of the Suggses, who hardly go to school at all."

The child's eyes sparked with equal anger. "'Least I don't cuss like you do!"

Leola glared a silent warning, to no avail.

"I heard you sayin' *dag blame* the other day," Mae went on, "and *Jesus Christmas* too." She pointed Mama's oversized scissors at the stove. "When you were gettin' ashes for soap-makin' and the pipe burnt'ed your fingers."

"Tattle-trap!" Leola shouted, tempted to grab the shears and cut every corkscrew tendril from her sister's head.

"Stop your bickering, girls," Mama ordered, "or I will take the broomweed switch to both your legs!"

"Ain't me." Mae stuck out her bottom lip. "Y'said yourself, Leola's been meaner than a stewed skunk of late and y'ain't—aren't—*haven't* done nothin' 'bout it!"

Papa stomped his heel on the floor.

"That's enough!" He narrowed his eyes at Leola. "No sassing and no cussing in this house." His gaze shifted to Mae. "And no tattling neither, 'specially when folks are carrying a heavy heart."

Leola rubbed away tears. She *had* acted like a stewed skunk lately, refusing to play with her sisters, getting irritated by the smallest things. And if she hadn't quite cussed up a storm, as Mae claimed, sure enough she'd wanted to.

Just then, Karla pattered over, waving a square of butcher paper.

"'Dis a pit-chure you, Wee," she said, unable to pronounce her Ls proper.

The sketch showed a lady with straight brown hair, wearing a puffy blue gown. Considering Karla's age, it was not a bad rendering of Leola or, in the background, their little house with its gnarled pecan tree and old Violet in her corral.

"What a fine job you've done, Karla," Leola murmured. "You've made me look like a queen!"

She pointed to the indistinct objects her illustrated self was holding.

"And what are these?"

"'Dat's a knife, Wee! For whit-win'!" Karla's gold-brown eyes danced as she pointed at another figure. "And 'dis is Papa wit' a new arm. You made it, outta wood!"

Leola's anger melted, and she lifted Karla up.

"It's the prettiest picture of me anyone ever did draw. And you're right: if I could, I *would* make a new arm for Papa."

She inhaled her sister's baby-sweet scent, which, if made into a tonic, would rival anything Mrs. Gumbs might produce.

"S'aw-right?" Karla patted her sister's chest. "Your heart fix't soon?"

"Oh, sweetness. I hope so."

As a sob escaped her throat, Mama moved close, wrapping both girls tight inside her grasp.

"Your father's right," she whispered. "Ain't nothin' worse in the world than falling out with those we love," and Leola started bawling once and for all.

Chapter 12

M rs. Durnaydon's fitting took longer than expected and, by the time Mama and Leola arrived at the fire station, there was a long line of folks waiting to get inside.

As she stepped from their buggy, peach chiffon on her forearm, Leola had second—or third or *fourth*—thoughts about playacting in public when she felt so low. But too late. She'd been spotted by Dot Furthold, who slipped from behind the ticket table, rushing toward her.

"Ain't it the bee's knees, Lee! We've already raised twenty dollars for the Free Kindergarten and brought plenty attention to the cause besides!" She nodded at two loose-limbed fellows in cheap suits, standing in line. "Reckon it'll bring *us* plenty attention, too, if you get my meaning."

"I'm sure you're right," Leola replied halfheartedly, not caring about attention from *other* boys, though Dot was too intent on getting back to certain dapper customers to notice her lack of enthusiasm.

"Go on up and find the other girls," she said, turning away. "They'll put you through your paces."

Leola climbed the stairs to the auxiliary hall, noticing most of the chairs were taken already, with children sitting on the floor in front and grown folk filling the sides and back of the room. Hurrying toward the curtained-off stage, Leola felt dizzied by the sea of faces yet couldn't keep from searching out one in particular: strong of jaw, with knife-blade cheekbones and piercing eyes, a face whose contours she'd memorized a thousand times over. When no such countenance came into view, she wanted to kick herself for even hoping.

Dipping behind the curtain—two sheets draped over a clothes-line—she found her friends practicing their dour expressions and spinsterish steps.

"Well, if it isn't Leola Rideout!" Exa Dove cried, nearly tripping over the train of her puce-green skirt on the way over. "Been a month of Sundays since we saw you last."

The other girls gathered 'round, admiring her spinster attire, claiming Leola did look "naturally frumpish" and "entirely without prospects," which might've been meant as praise but seemed ominous, given her present situation.

Exa pointed at the stage where a huge carton, painted white with red-and-black gauges and dials, stood.

"What d'ya think of our Makeover Machine? My brother, Wynn, lugged that box all the way from the gin. Spent hours decking it out."

"He's a real artist," Leola agreed, and Exa pushed open a door cut into the contraption's front.

"This is where you'll exit the stage after taking your turn as an Old Maid. I'll be inside, ready to help you transform."

Leola raised a doubtful eyebrow.

"It'll take some time, in such a tight space, to change outta these rags. Won't the audience be chompin' at the bit by then?"

Another girl, Berta Scher, laughed.

"I forgot this is your first convention, but don't worry. While you're changing, some of us will be down front entertaining the crowd, giving you plenty of time to be made over."

Leola, already sweating beneath her man-repelling garb, knew her eyes were swollen from the earlier crying jag and felt peevish from lack of food. Handing her frock to Exa, it seemed more likely she'd reenter the stage not as a budding beauty, but wilted and limp, like one of Joe's gardening experiments gone wrong.

Joe. She tamped down the familiar ache that came with every thought of him—right in time, too, for Dot had reappeared, brandishing a sturdy shoebox.

"Seems we've raised even more for our future kindergartners than we did for the destitute veterans last month." She gave the box a jangly shake. "Forty-two dollars to be exact! And this place packed to the rafters."

The Old Maids-in-Waiting barely got out their cheers before Dot shushed them.

"We'll have the chance to celebrate after our performance, girls. But it's near four o'clock, time for everyone to take their places."

Leola started for the hat room that would serve as their waiting area, but Dot held her up.

"Thought you'd want to know that ol' beau of yours, Joe *However-You-Say-His Name*, is here. Bought himself a ticket and gave an extra donation to boot." Her mouth puckered. "Proves he's like the rest of his slippery countrymen, always tryin' to get in good with folk like *us*." She squeezed Leola's arm. "We're so glad you've put that awful business behind you. Wait and see—soon enough, you'll have a slew of nice *American* suitors to choose among."

Leola winced, not only for knowing Joe was in the audience but because her friends looked down upon him as much as she'd imagined. However, the piano had sounded its warning chords, so she hurried away, and the show began.

As each performer appeared, Dot described the circumstances that might doom her to spinsterhood. Edith Sinnema would never sacrifice her picture-show habit for domestic responsibility; Bonita

Charpots found cooking a chore, burning every cake she made; Ima Atlas had fanciful notions of visiting the Great Pyramids, notions that excluded a husband and children tagging along.

"Yet there's hope," Dot would exclaim, as the sorry specimens disappeared inside the box, "in Dr. Makeover's Machine, the surefire remedy for the matrimonial-averse!"

The entertainment committee then sang, danced, or recited a poem until each girl reemerged, sporting fashionable clothes and equally fashionable smiles, sparkling yet demure, innocent, yet with the slightest suggestion of *savoir-faire*.

"Here's our Edith!" Dot announced. "Dr. Makeover has helped her realize—in the nick of time!—that picture shows are cold comfort when one needs a sturdy male shoulder to cry upon."

And: "After her treatment, Bonita understands the value of proper baking techniques, for there's nothing more rewarding than the satisfied sigh of a well-fed husband."

And: "Thanks to her makeover, Ima agrees: The Pyramids have stood five thousand years yet a good man will not wait!"

Then it was Leola's turn.

As she lurched onto the stage, feet pinched by Auntie's old boots, the audience hooted approval of her mincing gait and chagrined expression. Never mind it wasn't theatrics so much as knowing Joe was out there watching. Was he mocking her in his mind, glad they weren't associated any longer? Or yearning, as she was, to be more than friends again?

It seemed to take forever to arrive at the designated spot near the Makeover Machine, where Dot began her speech.

"Cast your eyes, dear friends, on poor Lulu Lost Love, a well-meaning country gal whose Christian compassion for mongrels and other downtrodden sorts she often mistakes for romance."

Leola froze, scanning the audience, hoping Joe was standing too far in back to hear. Dot, meanwhile, didn't seem to have the faintest idea of her offense, gesturing at Leola to exit into the Machine—which she did, numbly allowing Exa to help her into the peach chiffon, brush out her hair, and press a nosegay into her hand before shoving her onstage once more.

"Here is Lulu now!" Dot declared. "Under the tutelage of our esteemed professor, she finally understands the difference between charity and romance, and has sworn off *swarthy* types altogether. From here on out, it's only the fairest of marriage prospects—the *crème de la crème*—for our wholesome farm girl!"

As the spectators cheered, heat shot straight up Leola's spine and into her earlobes. She searched the crowd until she found Joe, peering from the side of the room, looking as he had after the Klan incident: befuddled. Hurt. Indignant. *Too much for a tender-hearted girl like you to handle,* he'd said. Yet he hadn't understood there was more to it, that those deep-down feelings were often the spark for whatever bravery she possessed.

She stepped to the front of the stage.

"*Crème de la crème?*" Her voice, however ragged, brought silence over the room. "Seems to me, there are plenty *crème de la crème* types 'round here whose so-called *pedigree* is in name only," she took a breath, "and who behave fairly to *certain* folk yet not to others. Who got no business callin' themselves *superior.*"

She peered at Dot.

"Y'all are wrong about your makeover machine. Seems the good doctor failed at his transformation, for I will take *swarthy* and righteous over creamy and mean any ol' day."

Dot frowned. Some of the other girls murmured. A chair leg scraped the floor. Joe leaned out from the wall, gaping, and Leola couldn't tell what he was thinking. Then, from the back of the room, a male voice rang out: "Guess your mama wouldn't approve of such a scene!"

Leola's mouth went dry. Gossip spread in this town faster than a prairie fire with a tail wind, meaning Mama would hear what had happened. Mama, who also disapproved of Joe for the circumstance of his birth, who did not like her daughters to sass or show disrespect to anyone. And yet . . . Mama had stood up to Papa about Houston. Had stood up to others, too, plenty of times—like the rich landowner who'd once prohibited Widow Breen and her brood from scrapping his fields after the regular pickers were done.

Leola had just finished work the day Mr. Hawley grabbed the wispy cotton fibers right from the hands of those starving children. *This ain't a charity operation,* he'd said, even though it was custom for prosperous growers to allow indigents to collect their leftover crops.

After Leola related the incident at home, Mama had ridden to the Hawley place, giving the man such a what-for, he'd shelled out an entire bag of coin, which she'd delivered to Mrs. Breen straightaway.

No, Mama had never *gone along with* things just because.

"Reckon my mother would say I got to listen to my heart," Leola replied, finally, "even if it causes a commotion."

The man—who she recognized as the miller's assistant—let out an ugly laugh. "Oh yes. Orlie Owen would understand right well 'bout causin' commotions, wouldn't she?"

The crowd tittered and Leola wondered if the man was refer- ring to that *near ruinous* episode from Mama's past. She spied Effie Slemmons in the front row, wagging her head as if to say, *for shame,* and Leola's courage faltered. People would believe what they would. She'd made a fool of herself for nothing.

Flinging aside the bouquet, she fled down the aisle, aware of Joe following, calling her name, not stopping until she was outside, sheltered by an overgrown lilac bush. When Joe caught up, he threw his arms around her and she did likewise, grateful for their shrubbery screen.

"Oh Joe! What've I done? Mama will tan my hide when she learns about this."

Joe stepped back, shaking his head.

"What I know of your mama—well, it's like you told that ol' buzzard's neck back there. She'd never want a simpering floor mat for a daughter, would be proud of you for expressing your beliefs, even if she didn't agree with 'em."

Lickety-split, Leola's anger toward Joe evaporated.

"I feel terrible," she said, burying her face in his chest, "about my part in our argument and for letting other folks' harebrained convictions get under my skin."

Joe kissed the top of her head.

"I've my own apologies to make, yet this ain't the best place to make 'em." He glanced about. "If you'd take a drive with me, somewhere we can—"

"Leola!"

They turned to see Dot and Exa heading toward them.

"Thought you might want these." Dot handed Leola her bag, along with the crumpled costume and boots.

"Thank you," she replied with little enthusiasm, and Dot cast her eyes to the ground.

"Reckon you're put out with us. I do regret if I—if *we*—caused you harm. Was mostly to distract you from your melancholy. Ain't that right, Exa?"

Exa nodded, addressing Joe.

"Wasn't meant against *you*. We always say you fit in right nice 'round here, to the point we've a hard time remembering this ain't your natural-born home."

Leola had a sudden wish to kick both girls hard in the shins and be done with it, but told herself they didn't understand the meaning of what they'd said—*were* saying—and how could Leola explain it when she'd only begun to understand such things herself? Even so, she knew she'd never again consider them good friends.

"Apologies accepted." She offered a tranquil smile. "I didn't mean to spoil your fundraiser. Y'all would never ridicule a person for where they were born or the tone of their skin or anything outlandish as that, I'm sure."

The two girls traded puzzled looks as if uncertain of her meaning—no matter, because Joe had stepped up, linking his arm through Leola's.

"If'n you'll excuse us, ladies. I promised Lulu here we'd find her lost heart." He motioned at the firehouse. "Y'all should get back to your beautificated customers 'fore they steal all the best suitors."

As they started for his cart, Leola added, loud enough for the other girls to hear, "*Second* best, Joe. Second best."

＋

When they arrived at their usual place on the Dark Road, Joe didn't bother tying up the horse, turning right away to speak to Leola.

"I'm sorry for what happened back there. Sorrier still for my part in our earlier row." His shoulders sagged. "And a large part it was, I reckon." His eyes went bright with pleading. "I meant what I said, Lee, about never wanting you troubled for my sake, except I didn't give you credit for having your own mind—and plenty of mettle—to make a choice in the matter. To shoulder the burden as you see fit."

Leola shook her head.

"Wasn't only you to blame. I been ignorant all my life, it seems, as if those terrible newspaper stories were things that happened elsewhere and nothing to do with me."

She watched the horse switch its tail.

"I never got to tell you . . . the day we argued? Mr. Laird and Effie Slemmons were so cruel to George Gumbs in the dry goods store. Yet how many times I seen that before and thought little of it, I cannot count. And then there was the to-do in Longview, our neighbors being in the Klan, those signs in the store windows . . . guess I'm greener than a willow sapling after all."

Joe exhaled.

"It's all a tangle, Lee. You'd think my own family being treated so badly would feel for others in the same boat." He pursed his lips. "Even so, my dad makes Negro customers use the back door of his store! I questioned him of it once and he acted like I was touched in the head."

Silence fell between them.

"P'rhaps we ought leave Texas, someday," Leola ventured. "Go to New York—or California!"

Joe's laugh was bitter.

"You think there aren't hateful folk in those places too? I read of Klansmen out in Cali raiding a union man's funeral, scalding his kids with hot coffee, saying it was Bolshie Catholics to blame for America's ills! And there were photos in the paper of a white mob up in Chicago hunting Blacks—with the police cheering them on!"

He gave her a searching look.

"Besides, how *could* we leave? You think your folks would move to Yankeeland with us? And my Nonna—whom you've never met and must soon—is on her last legs. She's going nowhere nor can I leave her, or this place. Texas is my home—*our* home, to improve however we can."

Another silence and then Leola asked, "Did you mean it when you said I'd have to convert to being Catholic, if we marry?"

He ducked his head.

"I said it out of pure-bald anger—not at *you*, but at the way things are. Truth be told, it was Nonna Rae made sure I got catechized. After that, my family hardly attended services at all. It'd be contrary to insist you convert to a religion I've little attachment to." He inched closer. "However, I *am* attached to you and hope you'll give me another chance to prove myself."

"Oh, Joe. You already have." She tipped her head. "But it's been the longest day and this hard seat's doing nothin' to make me feel rested. Wouldn't mind getting out of this buggy, stretching myself a bit." Another coy glance. "Don't imagine you brought that tarp from the Shipley wagon so we can have our rest?"

Joe's grin might have powered thousands of Thomas Edison's incandescent bulbs.

"I got something better than *that* ol' thing." He pulled a fine-stitched blanket from under the seat. "Nonna made this for me years ago. Not sure why I threw it into the cart last minute today." His mouth crooked sideways. "Guess I was hoping for a certain *final act*."

Leola, laughing, caressed the blanket's soft yellow yarn. "A thing made of love," she peeked at him, "*for* love."

After climbing from the carriage, they found a mossy spot beneath a tree, arranging the blanket on the ground and then themselves. Wasn't long before they went from a proper sitting position to lying down, nestled tight together.

"No wonder Dr. Makeover failed in his so-called magic," Joe whispered, "for there's not a thing about you needs changin'."

Leola hesitated, thinking she ought to set the man straight, confess her tendency to retell events with tiny threads of exaggeration; how impatient she felt sometimes with her sisters; that she envied prettier girls, snapped at her parents, held grudges.

But here he was, gazing at her with such trust. Such *hope*. At the very least his admiration gave her something to aspire to. And so she answered him with a kiss, encouraging yet firm, a pledge she intended to keep.

CHAPTER 13

Driving home, Leola asked Joe to leave her down the road apiece, knowing the sight of his buggy would raise further questions about where she'd been and why she was late. Then, reaching for the front door handle, she noticed a smear of dirt down the side of her dress that would make any such questions beside the point. Rubbing at the stain only made matters worse. Best she could do was drape her wrap strategically and sneak into her bedroom to change before anyone noticed.

She'd hardly got a foot through the door when Mae flew across the room, circling her like a whirling dervish.

"We're going to Houston, Lee! It's a big ol' city with lots of people and tall buildings, and—and a opera hall with chandeliers where I can sing," she paused to breathe, "and plenty jobs for Papa so Mama won't have to sew all night and," another breath, "and you can get learnt at a fine school and—"

"I'm aware what Houston is." Leola swerved from her sister's clutch. "And please stop massacring the English language, will you?"

She glanced between Mama, standing near the sink, and Papa, filling a lamp across the room. "Is it true?" Her voice quivered. "We're leaving our only home?"

Papa, blowing out the match, replaced the lamp's cover.

"In its essence, yes, though we hadn't meant to tell you in such a slapdash manner." He shot Mae a withering glance. "Your sister overheard me talkin' to the Meekers when they came calling earlier. Seems she couldn't keep the news to herself despite her promise otherwise."

He put the can of kerosene away.

"Get your supper, child, and we'll bring you up to speed. The news might be more agreeable when heard in its entirety."

Agreeable? she wanted to ask. *How could leaving Joe and Ship and everything I know be* agreeable *in any way, shape, or form?*

"I'm not hungry," she said—never mind that, minutes ago, she'd felt like bolting a horse.

She pitched her shawl over a chair, no longer caring whether anyone noticed the stained dress or her generally disheveled state. What punishment could her parents mete out worse than they already had? Still, as she dipped water from the barrel, Mama's up-and-down appraisal made her inwardly quake.

"We were worried about you, Lee," she said, removing two mugs from the shelf above the sink. "Good thing the Meekers *did* stop by or Papa might've gone searching for you."

Leola, braced for rebuke, was taken aback by Mama's gentle tone—until she added, "Dora was at the Old Maids' event today, Daughter. Saw you and Joe dashing away together."

Leola sat down, trying to compose herself.

"The convention got," she sipped her water, "tiresome. Joe and I, we . . . we prefered to be out in the fresh air like you said this morning, about it being good for my health."

Papa sat in the chair opposite Leola.

"We heard about that bad business at the fire station today. How you were singled out by some of the other girls and did your best to set things right."

"'Least they raised good money for their cause," Leola mumbled.

"I don't always understand what is happening to this country," Mama said, clicking her tongue, "with people flooding our shores, bringin' strange beliefs and foreign customs."

She took the coffee from the stove, filling Papa's cup.

"But to cast aspersions on such folks and those who befriend them . . . to make a public *shamin'* of their misfortune, all for the sake of entertainment? Well, I cannot make sense of that, either." Setting the pot down, she gazed at Leola. "Sure as the day is long, child, you showed those those bullies at the Convention for what they are."

Relieved as she was, Leola couldn't help wondering if Dora had related what the gin-worker said about Mama's own past *commotions.* Driving home with Joe, she'd almost made up her mind to finally ask about this long-ago incident, thinking if strangers knew of Orlena Rideout's secret past, shouldn't her own daughter?

But this revelation of Houston begged a thousand more urgent questions than some faded rumor . . . except those questions couldn't be asked because Mae chose that moment to burst into another makeshift song-and-dance number.

Houston! Houston!
Is where we're goin'
Houston! Houston!
And everyone's knowin'—

"Mae!"

Papa's sharp tone startled the girl into silence—made Leola jump also. She waited for Mae to burst into tears, but the child was too transfixed by the candies Papa fished from his pocket.

"You and Karla may each have a peppermint, Mae," he said, in a calmer voice, "only if you partake of them quietly in your room while we talk to Leola."

Mae's eyes bulged.

"I swan, we will be quiet and good as little mouses." Snatching the candy, she took Karla's hand. "Come along, darlin'. Be good for Sissy and we shall have a peppermint feast."

After they'd gone, Mama settled at the table with her own coffee.

"Hard enough, getting proper nutrients into either of those girls," she muttered. "Mae hardly touched her collards at supper."

Papa gave her a hangdog shrug.

"Peppermint is green in its natural form, is it not?"

No one, including him, laughed at the joke.

"So?" Leola asked, glancing between her parents. "When will we be leaving for Houston?"

Papa traced his thumb around the mug's handle.

"It's not y'all but I will be setting out first, to find a job and proper living arrangements before you join me."

"And how long will that take?"

"Hard to say." Papa shifted in his seat. "Not more than three months—four, tops."

She gawped at him. "Four months is an eternity!"

Leola couldn't fathom which was worse: the idea of leaving this place or staying behind without her father. But she could see the decision had been made.

"When will you go then?"

Papa hesitated. "A week from tomorrow, on the overnight train from Tyler."

"Why can't you wait until spring? If it's about the money . . . Mama's got plenty sewing commissions and I can help Mrs. McGee 'round the house, maybe take on other—"

Papa held up his hand.

"I appreciate your offer, Rosalee, except I need to make the best of an opportunity Murl Meeker told me about. Seems his employer will hire a quantity of clerks over the coming month. It's good-paying work with opportunity for advancement. If I apply in person instead of by mail, I'll have a leg up on the others. And if I don't get an offer, makes sense for me to stay, try for a position at another company."

Leola, wanting to find blame somewhere, glowered at Mama.

"And you're all right with this? With Papa leaving us so long? With us going in the first place? You said yourself Houston was full of vagabonds and oilmen who would steal our virtue along with our boots." She snorted. "Guess that was a made-up story from one of your dang ladies' magazines."

"Rosalee," Papa interrupted, "that's no way to speak to your mother!"

Mama shook her head at him.

"Lee's only buffaloed by this news we've thrown at her willy-nilly, and who can blame her?"

She faced Leola.

"Weren't anything made-up about my concerns, Daughter. But we got other things to consider now. Our livelihood for one." She sniffed. "Besides, after what's transpired around here, lately, I'm thinking city folks might be a welcome change from our usual company."

Leola rubbed a bead of moisture from her glass. She'd tried to brace herself for this possibility—Joe and Blanton had discussed opening a market for their roses in Houston, and Mary had said Rice Institute was finally accepting women as students, so she might apply there herself, living in the dorms while Leola boarded at home. Meaning they'd end up at the same college after all. Suddenly, however, such plans seemed farfetched, and Leola wanted to protest, threaten, say she wouldn't go, that Papa shouldn't either—except someone else's tantrum kept her from it.

"Paaaapaaaa!"

Mae again, hurtling from the bedroom, voice pitched not in song this time but outright agony.

"Karla grabbed my treat and it fell and—and rolled on the floor and then—then she stepped on it and it's ruuuuuuuined!"

She held out the flattened candy, its red-and-white surface flecked with grit and dust.

"Don't fret, kitten." Papa scooped her into his lap. "I can get you a new one Monday when I go to town again."

As four months seemed to Leola, two days was for Mae, and when she started blubbering louder, Leola nearly joined in—except Papa caught her eye, tapping his pocket, and she knew he was asking her to sacrifice her own candy to the cause of household peace. Probably he'd not take offense if Leola didn't go along—though of course she did, for no amount of sweetness in her mouth could soothe the dread in her heart.

CHAPTER 14

Every day, Leola sat on the sofa, waiting for Mrs. Gumbs. No, not Nancy Gumbs. Cora Grayly. . . Guidray! Cora Guidray, Leola's dearest friend, the only person who spent real time with her, wouldn't just sit down for five minutes, say a few words, and jump up again like everyone else did. No, Cora would watch an entire episode of Leola's favorite soap—would get upset, too, when a character was unfaithful to his wife or another returned, Lazarus-like, from the dead. Cora never spoke to Leola as if she were a child. Understood she intended to go home, sooner than later.

Today Leola was more impatient than usual for Cora's arrival. She had something to show her friend—a truly astonishing secret, one she'd hidden from the others, who'd only flash her a pitying smile, explaining it couldn't be true. Cora however—Cora would believe.

Leola had been telling her about Papa's visits, the way he'd stand in a corner, moving his mouth. How he'd beckon as if she should follow him. He'd even appeared in the back garden recently and said her name—she'd heard it, clear as a bell.

I think if you're feeling his presence, Cora had remarked, *there must be something to it.*

Now Leola clutched the purse on her lap, counting the bricks around the fireplace. *One, two, three, four . . .* What was next? Eight? Fifty? A thousand hundred? Pshaw! To think she'd had a mind for numbers once.

The doorbell rang and Leola shot off the couch. Her mind might be flim-flam these days, but there was nothing wrong with her body! All that cotton pickin' and horse riding way back must've paid off, for she was spry as ever—though, of course, Rose had to get to the door first, behaving like Leola had forgotten how to turn a knob, on top of everything else!

"Hello there," Cora said, setting down a heavy bag of books. She was doing another degree, in something called *social workings*, and often studied while Leola watched TV or napped.

"You look pretty in that pink dress," she said, "and I see you got your hair done!"

Leola looked down, having forgotten what color her dress was. And when had she gone to the beauty parlor? Still, she smiled in return.

"Thank you, Cora. You look pretty too."

And it was true: her friend *was* lovely, with flawless dark skin and an oval face, thick hair braided tight around her head. She always wore bright pantsuits and dangling earrings, fingernails painted in deep reds or shades of purple. Leola was more of a pale pink kinda gal but wished she had the nerve for such colors.

When they'd first met, Leola had insisted Cora use her given name and Cora had done likewise. *We're friends, after all,* she'd said. *Equals.* Leola had been a tad surprised by this, and also relieved, remembering the cruel etiquette she'd grown up with, even to the way people addressed one another—how Black folk might be beaten for using a white person's first name but a white child could call a Black grandmother *Bessie* or *Mamie* or anything they pleased, and no one batted an eye. As if names didn't matter when everyone knew *how* a person is called and *by whom* speaks volumes about the world.

Thank goodness things had changed—somewhat, at least. Leola

liked to think George Gumbs had something to do with it. She'd gotten a letter from Nancy, long ago, saying her son ran a successful machinery shop in Chicago and was a leader in the community, advocating for racial equality. He'd even been photographed alongside that fearless Black leader, the one everyone called King—*Dr.* King! Despite that—sometimes *because* of that—George had been singled out by bigots, his shop vandalized, his family threatened. *Hate don't always speak with a Southern drawl*, Nancy had written, a sentence Leola remembered clear as a bell to this day.

It hadn't been easy, unlearning the bigotry she'd inhaled with every breath since she was born. Hadn't been easy for her friends and neighbors either, some of whom insisted the way it had always *been* was the way it should always *be*. 'Course, wasn't only Black folk bore the brunt of all that meanness.

Leola had told her children about the Kluxxers who'd thrown shoes at their father because he was considered un-American. She'd described how, during World War II, someone had destroyed an entire greenhouse of their roses, spelling FASCIST on the ground with manure. How the social clubs in town—the Freemasons and Oddfellows, even the Gardening Club—excluded Joe and Leola, saying Catholics weren't welcome.

Not that she needed to explain such things, really. Her kids had experienced plenty of fool antics themselves. When another boy called her brother a *dirty wop* at the bus stop, Rose had given him a pummeling to shame Opal Suggs. Leola had watched from their living room window that day and never said a word about it, possitive the bully would never bother her children again.

Now the grownup Rose had started toward the kitchen, and Cora turned to address Leola.

"You comin', hon?"

Leola lifted her purse, whispering, "I've got a secret to show you."

Cora looked intrigued.

"As soon as I speak to your daughter, we'll go upstairs, okay?"

Following them to the kitchen, Leola sighed. Rose always had to drag Cora away when she arrived, the two of them discussing which pill Leola needed to take, the snack she should eat, how they might take a walk because, as Rose put it to Cora, *you're so much better at making her do these things.*

Leola settled at the kitchen table, watching the birds at the outdoor feeder: two red ones with pointy heads, a blue jay, a wren. No hummingbirds though. If these people hadn't gotten rid of that beautiful trumpet vine Joe had planted maybe they'd return—

"Ready?"

Leola, startled from her reverie, took Cora's arm. She could manage the stairs perfectly well but liked hanging on. Reminded her of when she used to walk with that dear old friend way back, the one who died so young: how they'd clutch at each other, laughing and whispering, never wanting to let go.

On the second floor, Leola checked up and down the hallway before shutting her bedroom door. Then she joined Cora on the bed.

"Can't wait another second to show you this," she said, digging through her purse for the creased bit of newspaper.

Papa had got her in the habit of reading the news long ago. 'Course numbers, like words, were hard to make sense of nowadays, but Leola still enjoyed the pictures. That's how she'd come across this photograph—a man standing at a podium and behind him, a row of other people, listening attentively to whatever he was saying.

"Look," she said, pointing at a person in that row. "It's my father!"

Cora took the page, reading the caption aloud: *Above, Brian Lopez, president of American Wire and Telephone, whose New Innovations division recently moved from Dallas to New Jersey. Pictured behind him are AWT employees helping to lead the transition.*

She fell quiet, studying the photograph.

"Too bad they don't list the names of those employees."

Leola got up, fetching her parents' wedding portrait from the bureau. Returning, she motioned between both photos.

"But isn't that man in back the spitting image of my papa? Look at those eyes, how they turn up at the corners! Those are Papa's eyes, sure as I'm settin' here. And the way he's smiling, a bit crooked . . ."

Cora hesitated.

"I know you *want* it to be your papa, hon." She took Leola's hand. "Think about it; that picture was taken last *week*. It's 1986. Your father would be well into his hundreds if he was alive."

Leola laughed in disbelief.

"That's the silliest thing I ever heard! It's hardly been that long since Papa left. How could he be a hundred years old?"

How old am I, even? she nearly asked, then stopped herself. Best not give the woman reason to doubt her further.

"It was hard, what happened with your daddy." Cora patted Leola's knee. "A terrible thing." Another pause. "But he wouldn't want you to be upset like this and . . ."

Leola's ears buzzed so she couldn't hear Cora's next words. The woman must've been pretending all along that Papa's visitations were real. Must've thought Leola daft like the others did. Hot fury boiled inside her. Fury at Cora and Rose for not believing her. Fury for having a failing mind so no one *would* believe her.

"It's all right." Cora set aside the newspaper, trying to take the portrait from Leola. "Let me put this back, so we can—"

Leola grasped the frame.

"Let go of my family!"

She yanked too hard and the picture slipped from her fingers, shattering against the wall, glass spraying everywhere.

Silence fell as the two women stared at the wreckage. And then Leola's grief rose within her, sweeping away everything except the molten core of her loss.

"Look what you've done, you hoodoo witch!" she screamed. "Trying to steal my best possessions . . ." She pursed her lips. "Was true what folk used to say, that Negroes can't be trusted!"

Cora went still as a statue.

"I know you don't believe that, Leola. I don't think you ever did. Not really. You're a good woman, considering the poison you got spoon-fed from birth. Unlike most white folk in your situation, you did your best to spit that poison out." She pressed her lips together. "Or most of it at least."

Leola's mind felt as fractured as the glass on the floor. When had she been poisoned? And by whom? Faces wheeled through her mind—friends, folks from church, her parents. Good people. Loving people. Or were they?

Is not right . . . The old refrain echoed in her mind, as much a part of her as the influenza cough, Mama's biscuit recipe, the hole in her heart where Papa had been.

She blinked at the woman—Cora—whose rigid expression reminded her of someone else she'd known, someone humiliated by people who'd recite the Golden Rule from one side of their mouths and spew hatred from the other. Leola had considered herself beyond all that, p'rhaps even *above* all that. Yet she knew it was true. Hate's tincture had left a deep stain on her soul.

"Cora . . ." Tears clogged her throat. "I didn't mean . . . I wasn't . . . I . . ."

Cora lifted her chin.

"You forget yourself, sometimes. I think that's what you're trying to say."

She made no move to comfort Leola but smoothed the front of her pantsuit and started for the door.

"I'll get the broom. We better clean up this mess before someone gets hurt even worse."

Smith County, Texas • August 1919

CHAPTER 15

Mama had moved their regular feather harvesting day so Papa could help before he left.

Of all their chores, Leola hated goose-plucking most. Geese were ill-tempered creatures, less predictable even than bull cows and far more likely to wreak havoc on those who trespassed against them. A lumbering bull had to make an effort to get his horns into you while geese could wield their knife-sharp teeth with brutal speed and precision. Tricky enough catching one without injury. Trickier still tying the feet so it could be hung up for plucking. First time Leola attempted the routine, she'd been rewarded with a searing nip to her palm and still had the curved scar as a souvenir.

Things had changed after Papa's accident, when he'd discovered a natural skill for catching geese and could do it better now than folks with two arms. Over the past year, he and Leola had tackled the job as a team, Papa snatching the bird, holding its beak so she could bind the feet, saving her own skin in the process.

Auntie kept the geese on her property, turning them out to pasture each morning and herding them into their pens at night, receiving a share of feathers in return. Besides freshly plumped pillows and mattresses, the only other thing that made the day worthwhile was the feast afterward, for Malvina Hughes was an esteemed chef noted especially for her baking skills.

That morning, as they set out for her great-aunt's place, Leola watched Papa walking the road ahead—Karla balanced on his shoulders, Mae skipping by his side—and knew this would be their last such occasion together. Only by envisioning Auntie's famous raspberry trifle, with its golden meringue and gooey inner sanctum, could she keep her despair at bay.

The Meekers and Rideouts always helped each other with such chores, so Dora and her daughter-in-law, Ceci, were already there when they arrived. Ceci had brought along her chubby son, Guy, who didn't make a peep when he was passed around, marveled over like the first baby ever invented.

And then it was time for the plucking to start. Auntie took Guy and Karla inside to supervise, though Mae was allowed to stay on the front porch to learn how the job was done. 'Course, if things went according to Papa's plan and they became certified city slickers, Mae might never have to use such knowledge—a thought that made Leola glad in a way and also a tad resentful.

Papa turned the goose chase into a comedy, as always, performing dance steps with darting birds, answering their honks with grating noises of his own, crooning lullabies as he held them up. In the end, their group gathered fifteen double-sized sacks of feathers—not enough to make a single new mattress yet sufficient to freshen plenty of pillows.

After setting their bags to dry in the bright September sun, the weary crew washed themselves in Auntie's spring, then spread quilts and set out the banquet: platters of fried chicken, bowls of creamed corn, fresh-churned buttermilk.

As they dug into their food, silence fell, interrupted only by the sound of smacking lips, quick requests to pass a plate, the clank of silverware on china. But once they'd sated their hunger, a determined festivity took over, to the point where Leola could almost pretend Papa wasn't leaving . . . except that whenever someone mentioned an event in the near future—hog-killing, Thanksgiving, Christmas— someone else would quickly change the subject, making the reminder even more obvious. At one point, Ceci remarked she couldn't sleep a wink while her husband was away and a pall fell over the group, lifting only when Papa shaped his hand into a beak and snapped at Mae's elbow, causing her to shriek.

A bit later, Leola noticed Papa frowning into the distance and turned to see Mr. Owen storming across the pasture. By now Mama had seen him coming, too, and exchanged a glance with her husband that meant both expected trouble.

"Did we forget to invite him?" Leola whispered, and Mama shook her head.

"Didn't forget, exactly," she said, which meant he'd been willfully *not asked*. All the more perturbing. Mr. Owen had never helped on such occasions, but some of the geese were descendants of those bred by Big Leola years ago. This, along with the fact that Auntie was his wife's sister, conferred on him a natural claim over a share of the feathers and the feast that followed. Though not, it appeared, today.

Perhaps Mama had excluded Mr. Owen so as not to ruin the family's last moments together. Leola hadn't seen much of her grandfather lately nor heard him mentioned either and, instead of picking up his evening meal as usual, he'd ordered them to leave it on his porch and signal its arrival with a quick rap on the door.

When Leola had asked if Mr. Owen was ailing, her mother had snorted.

That man hain't been sick a day in his life. Too ornery even for germs. She'd paused. *Best keep the wheat from the chaff, Lee, lest you have to do the threshin' all over again.*

Which signified things were worse than ever between Papa and the old man . . . and here her grandfather stood, face shadowed by the tatty straw hat Papa often joked was permanently affixed to his head if by nothing else than dirt and spite.

Everyone had gone quiet. Papa drew Karla onto his lap, watching his father-in-law with a guarded expression. Dora gave Ceci an anxious look and Mae, who'd been petting one of Auntie's cats, ran to hide behind her mother. Even Guy seemed dispirited, blinking at Mr. Owen with liquid eyes before sticking a thumb into his mouth. Only Auntie was unfazed, gnawing on a chicken bone without acknowledging her brother-in-law's presence in the least. No different from any other time, for Auntie had always disliked Mr. Owen and never bothered to hide the fact.

Finally, Mama stood, forcing a gracious smile.

"Howdy-do, Father?" She gestured at the geese in their pasture. "We decided to move the feather-harvesting earlier to accommodate," she hesitated, "some changes in our calendar. Figured you'd be at your Masons meeting today so didn't bother you with the details. 'Course, you're more than welcome to join us."

Leola couldn't believe the bald and very rare lie she'd just heard from her mother. Even *she* knew Mr. Owen's Freemasons meetings were held on Thursdays, never Saturdays.

Mr. Owen seemed unappeased either way, spitting a stream of tobacco into the grass.

"I'm not here to complain of some feather-gatherin' party, but to find out why I am the last person in all of Smith County to learn my *son-in-law*," he curled his lip, "plans to shirk his marital duties, abandoning my daughter and her children to go a-larkin' over the country like some fancy-free bachelor."

Mama's cheeks went pink.

"We'd meant to tell you, Father. And Frank is not abandoning us. We'll join him in due time."

"Ha!" Mr. Owen wiped his mouth, leaving a brown streak on his hand. "Who gave you dispensation, Daughter, to abandon your filial responsibilities? I raised you up and, far's I'm concerned, y'ain't done with obligations owed in kind."

Before she could answer, Papa set Karla off his lap and stalked around the blanket, facing the other man.

"From what I hear, was Orlie mostly raised *herself* up, going out to service at the tenderest age, living in strangers' homes, not only giving you fewer mouths to feed but feeding them herself."

Mr. Owen's eyes glinted like robin's eggs in a grizzled nest.

"You got some nerve, lecturin' me on what mouths I did or did not feed, when you can't hardly feed your own."

"Father!" Mama hissed, but the man didn't flinch.

"Come to think of it, Rideout, you owe me money: for back rent, the mule and chickens and the cow, for the land you—or rather my *daughter*—uses, raisin' what extra food she must due to your lack of provision."

Leola could tell Papa was wrestling his temper as David had wrestled Goliath.

"That's the reason I am going to Houston in the first place, *sir,* to make a better future for my family. And you can expect your rent soon's I get myself a job, not a day beyond." He nodded at their group, huddled around the blanket. "Meanwhile, we'd like to get back to our dinner. Was a hard morning's labor and we earned our repose. More'n I can say for *you.*"

Mr. Owen clenched his fists.

"What I can say for *you,*" he finally replied, "is if you never met my daughter, she could'a had a far better life, one without the toil of feather harvesting and sloppin' pigs, skimmin' blue-john from the milk so there's enough to go around."

"Mama?" Mae's voice trilled. "Why does Mr. Owen got to be so mean? Why is Papa so angry? Can we go home please?"

Mama didn't answer—didn't even blink—so Leola grabbed Mae's hand, then hoisted Karla into her arms.

"Come on, girls. We've that trifle to eat still. Auntie, why'n't you and the others help us serve it up?"

Until then, Mr. Owen had scarcely noticed his eldest grand-daughter and, as he focused his scathing regard upon her, Leola's nerves turned inside-out.

"You can't even raise my grandchildren proper, Rideout," the man said, "allowin' them to associate with the lowest kind'a migrant vermin." He hitched his thumb at her. "Way this one's goin', reckon we can expect a mewling mutt born wrong side of the blanket any day."

Leola could hardly register what he'd said before Papa snatched a bag of feathers and swung it at Mr. Owen, landing such a firm blow that the air shimmered with salt-and-pepper snow. The old man staggered, his fall interrupted only by the split-rail fence along the driveway. As he righted himself, straightening his jacket, Leola thought he might take Papa's advice and finally quit their company. Instead he put his head down exactly as a bull would, charging Papa with surprising speed.

Leola called a warning, but her father was already prepared. Using the half-filled sack like a shield, he shoved Mr. Owen even harder than before. This time the man found no fence to break his fall but landed face up in the grass.

Before he could stir, Papa rushed over, pressing a foot on each of his hands, pinning him to the ground. When the other man yipped in pain, Mama moved as if to help him—until Auntie's faint shake of the head brought her to a standstill.

"You were not invited to this occasion, Columbus Owen," Papa hissed, sweat dripping down on his father-in-law. "In truth, we always have a far better time without you, and will all the more when we've quit this place and left you behind." He narrowed his eyes. "Meanwhile, I best not learn you've insulted my wife nor any of my daughters—nor whomever they choose to associate with—when I am gone or I'll return straightaway to guarantee you never do so again. Understood?"

When Mr. Owen failed to respond, Papa pressed harder with his feet until the old man gave in.

"Understood! Get off'n me 'fore all my fingers is broke."

Papa backed away, watching Mr. Owen with a wary eye.

"This is your share of the yield today." He tossed the sack he'd used as both weapon and armor and which now contained, at most, a few handfuls of feathers. "It's about equal in weight to the feeling you have for us—for anyone in the entire world, far's I can tell."

Before Mr. Owen could charge again, Mama put herself between both men.

"Go," she told her father. "I'm done with your caterwaulin' over things in the past. You've made it plenty clear my so-called *choices* did not suit you." Her gaze sparked defiance. "Yet I would still pick a good man, however poor, over a rich one that thinks everything is his for the takin'. And I'd again choose that same good man over you, my own father, who don't care a jot about me and," she glanced at Leola, "thinks the worst of those I love."

Leola was dumbfounded. Not only had Mama addressed Mr. Owen with open audacity, but her words were eerily similar to Leola's speech at the Old Maids' Convention last week. Then there were the hints of Mama's shadowy past—a lost chance at fortune, that perilous brush with damnation. Leola was certain this must be the cause of Mr. Owen's contempt—p'rhaps was responsible indirectly for why they were leaving in the first place. But this was no time to puzzle over it. All she could do was watch her grandfather grab his skimpy share of feathers, stomping away like a child unjustly rebuked.

Once he was gone, Papa swept Mama in his arms and Leola's spirit revived. It'd been a long spell since she'd witnessed any affection between her parents, and she kept silent, afraid of disturbing this private moment, public as it was. Judging by their own quiet, everyone else felt the same—except for a certain denuded goose honking nearby, chiding them for its own mistreatment. Leola couldn't help herself; she began to laugh and the others joined in, including Mama and Papa, who moved away from each other but not too much.

After the goose waddled off, Auntie picked a stray feather from the potato salad.

"Y'all help me clean this mess and I'll bring out that raspberry trifle as reward." Her mouth rippled. "'Least it's one thing that old ring-tailed tooter can't ruin."

Watching Mama brush bits of down from Papa's hair, seeing the way he gazed at her in return, Leola smiled, thinking it wasn't only the dessert that had prevailed. Thinking if her grandfather couldn't vanquish their little family, p'rhaps a few hundred miles wouldn't either.

CHAPTER 16

How fitting, Leola thought, that this thing she used to smooth Papa's shirt was nicknamed a *sad iron*, for with every pass over the starched cotton, her sorrow deepened. No one had spoken of the affray with Mr. Owen two days ago, but Papa seemed more restless than ever about Houston, wondering constantly if Dell should come earlier to take him to the station, packing and repacking his traveling case every hour.

Leola could hardly blame him for wanting to escape Mr. Owen's spite; still, it hurt to think he was in such a hurry to go. Then she would catch him stroking Mae's hair with a wistful expression, hugging Karla a tad longer than usual, or watching Mama closely, as if trying to memorize the way she half-sang, half-whistled hymns as she worked. Sometimes Leola caught Papa gazing at *her* too—though when their eyes met, he'd smile quickly and go back to his business.

Mama, brow stippled with sweat, held up another of Papa's shirts.

"You think these new buttons are too big?"

Leola set the iron on the burner, wiping at her own face. It was a warm day and the roaring stove didn't help matters.

"Not at all, Mama. They seem perfect in size and right pretty, too, with those streaks of brown and yellow."

Mama gave a halfhearted smile. "Man needs to put his best self forward in a strange place, I reckon."

Her wretched expression made Leola want to embrace her or impart words of comfort, except Papa tromped inside then, holding two bamboo poles.

"Look here, Rosalee! I was cleaning out the shed and came across our old fishing gear. Been since Noah's flood that we spent any time at the creek together." He gave Mama a look. "Could you spare our girl a while, Orlie, allow us a short expedition to our favorite fishing place?"

He didn't add, *for the last time ever,* but Leola could tell by Mama's wistful nod that she understood.

"We're near done anyhow," she said, in spite of the basket of laundry left to press, mostly dresses and underthings that were meaner to unwrinkle than any of Papa's shirts.

Minutes later, Leola and Papa were tromping the wooded path, crickets whirring and cottonwood leaves sighing in the breeze, exhausted by the unending heat. Eventually, they arrived at the rocky outcropping along the creek where they'd fished together since Leola was old enough to hold a pole. As was customary, they stripped off shoes and socks, dangling their feet in the water while Papa baited their hooks with bacon fat.

For a while, the two sat in silence, corks bobbing in the current as swallows wheeled and dipped around them, hunting their waterbug suppers.

"Looks like the fish aren't biting much," Papa said eventually, setting aside his pole. "Reckon they sense night comin' earlier and turned in already?"

Leola snickered. "More like they're aware the lard is rancid and feel insulted by the offer."

Papa laughed, pulling a jar of Mama's lemonade from his satchel along with his pipe and tobacco. As he struck a match against his boot, Leola reeled in her own line, thinking how to word the question she'd wanted to ask for so long.

"Will I ever learn about that business with Mama and the rich doctor, and why Mr. Owen's still so testy about it?"

Papa sucked the flame into the pipe bowl longer than necessary, as he always did when considering a hard question.

"First off," he flicked his wrist, extinguishing the match, "I've heard Columbus Owen was a testy old man from the hour of his birth. And far as your mother's past, there are things only she's privileged to tell you in her own good time." He set down his pipe, uncapping the jar of lemonade. "However, you've gleaned some aspects of the story already, including the fact there was another man—quite wealthy indeed—who once loved your mama. If'n you want to call it *love*.

"Such an association would have benefitted her family, as such associations often do, and when Orlie rejected his *offer*, Mr. Owen felt indisposed." Papa took a drink, handing over the jar. "Didn't help that I came along then and your mama and me fell in love. Guess I was a convenient post for Columbus Owen to whip."

Leola swallowed some lemonade, hoping he'd say more but understanding by his expression she shouldn't pry further.

"I hate how Mr. Owen treats you," she grumbled, "and for nothing bad you did."

Papa exhaled.

"It's a sorry thing, Rosalee, when a parent cannot—will not— accept a grown child's choices, especially where their future help-mate is concerned." His eyes softened. "All to say, Joe would make you a fine husband if you two decide to marry. We had a long talk when he helped me drag the stump behind the barn, other day. It's clear that young man has your best interests at heart which, in my opinion, is the most a father can ask of his future son-in-law."

Leola, a mite embarrassed, still couldn't help smiling.

"I'm glad you like him." She kicked at the water. "Except Mama thinks it more important where his *people* came from, that he's Italian and Catholic and *different*, like nearly everyone else 'round here believes too."

Papa set a hand on her knee.

"Your mama has some stubborn views, child, but loves you more than her own life. She'll come 'round in time, *especially* given the lesson she's learned from her own situation. And as for those other ign'rant folk . . . they are merely bothersome, like the fly buzzin' around our heads, and deserve to be equally ignored. If such people told you oil would quench a fire or that money grew on trees, would you believe them?"

Though Leola understood the gist of what he said, flies could not give her dirty looks nor throw shoes at her sweetheart and, if they got too irksome, could be squashed easily enough with a rolled-up newspaper.

But the sun was dipping toward the horizon, and their time together was slipping away, too—with more urgent questions plaguing her mind.

"Will Mr. Owen throw us off his farm? I heard Mama wonder of it yesterday."

Papa wagged his head.

"That man needs your mother worse than ever. Regardless how impudent he acts, Orlie is a caring person and will administer to his needs, best she can—and he'll not refuse, being helpless to care for himself."

"And what about you?" Leola peered at her father. "Who will administer to *your* needs in Houston? The only person you'll know there is Murl Meeker who's hardly older than me and wouldn't be much help if you got in trouble."

Papa took another swig of lemonade, then fastened the jar.

"I'll be busy—first finding a job, then working, going back to my room at night to guzzle a meal before falling asleep. Trouble will be hard-pressed to find me, and I'll not look for it neither."

Leola must have appeared as unconvinced as she felt, for Papa sat up straighter, instilling a fresh spurt of cheerfulness into his voice.

"Look here. I've something might make you feel better." He dug through his satchel, pulling out the little javelina she'd helped make. "Let me reacquaint you with Flora, who's grown into a fancy lady these past months."

Taking the creature, Leola could see Flora *had* changed mightily since Papa had moved his carving operation, including the whittling arm, to their shed, where he'd painted her pink with pearly spots, giving her bright blue eyes and a tiny rosebud mouth.

"Why you're the wild pig's answer to Dr. Makeover and his machine! She's turned out prettier'n a pie supper."

"Think so?" Papa chuckled, reaching into his bag again. "Hold on. I got something else . . ."

He held out another pig, this one with larger tusks, green eyes, and a painted pipe near its lips.

"Rosalee, meet Flora's father, Francis, a magical beast who can gobble sorrows like real boars devour gardens. He's to serve as your talisman while I am gone, though don't tell your mother I said so. You remember how she is about supernatural so-called *nonsense*."

Leola held Francis to her cheek. "He's a fine good-luck charm, Papa."

She fought tears and he did, too, but he kept his tone light.

"I, on the other hand, will oversee Flora who, being grateful we gave her life, has promised to fulfill each wish made upon her, especially where my daughters are concerned. Every night I'll rub her head, bidding y'all be safe and happy."

Leola couldn't hold back any longer and began to cry. As Papa pulled her close, they watched the sky fill with peachy-pink streaks, the sun staging a goodbye pageant in their honor.

"Here's the thing," Papa whispered. "Flora and Francis must reunite for their magic to stay strong. Likewise, I cannot do without my family, which gives me the power to continue, no matter life's travails."

He kissed the top of her head.

"Sure as I am setting here, we'll be together again, Rosalee. I vow it with all my heart."

Namesek, New Jersey • October 1986

CHAPTER 17

P *apa!*

Leola's own cry jolted her awake. She sat up, trying to remember where she was, noting the afternoon slant of light through the blinds, the housedress she was wearing beneath the afghan. Figured she must've been napping. Must've dreamt Papa this time.

She struggled to recall the dream, already growing dim: Papa was holding out a wooden figure not much bigger than his palm—a tusked animal with the funniest little face. She'd reached and reached but couldn't quite grasp it. And then she'd woken up.

Shutting her eyes, Leola tried to fathom where she'd seen the creature before. And then it came to her: Papa had made it. But how, with only one arm? And where had the carving gone?

She stood, knowing she had to find that pig. Pawed through her bureau, opened her closet, rifled through her dresses. No pig.

A door slammed downstairs, muffled voices turning to shouts.

"Yeah right, Mom!" It was her granddaughter. "Whatever you say!"

Another voice, one with no girlness in it, angrier than hornets in a kicked nest: "Stop being rude, Emma. You'll respect me, understand? *Do you understand?*"

"*Respect* you?" Emma shrieked. "Really? You're such a goddamn hypocrite, lecturing me about everything when you aren't exactly perfect yourself!"

Leola flinched. She couldn't quite remember what a *hypocrite* was but sure as sugar knew that other word!

Sinking onto the bed, she worried about all the recent fighting between her daughter and granddaughter. Leola's grandson, David, was a sweet, affectionate child, cute as a button. Never fought his parents—not so fiercely, at least. Yet much as she loved him, she felt something particular for the girl, who always hugged Leola, asking what she was "up to" (as if she'd be up to anything!). True, Emma could be a harridan at times, wore scant clothing, complained when asked to do the smallest chore, played thrashing music from her room, shaking the walls. Regardless, Leola knew Emma had many a good quality. She'd heard her apologize to her parents after an argument. Heard her giving advice to friends, wise beyond her years.

Leola understood well enough how hard it was, being on the verge of womanhood, how the world expected you to be sedate and pleasing, yet would eat you alive for those very same qualities. Emma sometimes said she wanted to be a lawyer or a banker, wanted babies, too, but wasn't sure how to do it all and why didn't men have to figure it out the same way?

Now Leola heard feet thudding the stairs, Rose's voice calling, "And while you're at it, young lady, clean that room! It's a pigsty in there."

"Pigs are clean actually," Emma shouted back, "but what the hell would you know?"

Bang! Another door slammed. Bang! Leola remembered what she'd been looking for earlier—her good luck charm, Papa's pig. Maybe her daughter would remember where it was.

Downstairs, she found Rose standing at the kitchen sink. When she cleared her throat, Rose spun around.

"Mother! You scared me, sneaking up like that!" She peered at Leola. "Everything all right?"

Leola could've asked the same, of course—she saw her daughter wipe away tears—but didn't want to get distracted and forget again why she'd come down here.

"I'm sorry to bother you. Something of mine's gone missing."

Rose's sad expression changed to annoyance.

"I put your purse upstairs an hour ago, Mom, when you went to rest—on the chair next to your bed like I always do."

"No, no." Leola waved. "Not my purse. I'm looking for . . . the animal. The wooden thing that Papa . . . the one he . . ." She paused, knowing if she got too excited, her thoughts would tangle more. "The pig! I am looking for that little pig of mine."

Rose frowned. "I wasn't talking about a *real* pig before. I was telling Emma what a mess she is sometimes. How her room is *like* a pigsty."

"Do you have it then? The pig in the sty?"

Rose buried her head inside her hands. "Holy Mother of God," she mumbled, and Leola frowned.

"Y'ought not take the Lord's name in vain."

Rose flushed. "Seriously? *You're* giving me grief too?"

Grief. Why would she give this woman—or anyone—grief on purpose, when it was easy enough to stumble upon by accident?

"I want the pig." Her tone was resolute. "Papa's pig."

"I don't know about any pig." Rose winced. "I'm sorry."

"Francis!" Leola was nearly shouting, herself, at this point. "The javelina called Francis!"

Rose's face lit with sudden understanding.

"Ohhhh! The carving! The funny wild boar your father made you."

She took Leola's hand, smiling as if her daughter hadn't cussed her out and her own mother hadn't yelled at her.

"I remember when I was a kid and you showed me that pig. How you said your papa gave it to you before he . . . before he went away. And I *do* know where it is. We never unpacked it after we moved you here. The box is still on your closet shelf, I think. Let's go upstairs. I'll get it down for you."

Relief washed over Leola. "Thank you. You are a good . . . a good . . ."

She gave Rose a helpless look.

"Daughter," Rose replied, gently. "A good daughter. I think that's what you meant to say."

◆

That night, Leola took Francis from her bedside table. She'd been sad at first when Rose had unwrapped him and they'd found part of his leg broken off, the paint on his face nearly gone. Still, it felt good to have her lucky charm again.

And then she remembered Flora, the daughter pig, whom Papa had taken with him. He'd said Flora and Francis needed to reunite for their power to stay strong. Had vowed it would happen, that he'd return and they'd all be together—Flora and Francis, Papa and Leola. But he hadn't come back and fate, luck, God, even *death*, had nothing to do it. Francis had lived without Flora for decades; his so-called powers would have faded completely by now. He was just an old toy after all, a senseless thing, broken as false promises.

Leola shoved Francis into the bottom drawer of the nightstand and didn't look at him again for a very long time.

CHAPTER 18

P apa wrote on a regular basis at first, each letter a story in itself, filled with descriptions of life in Houston: his landlord, Mrs. Grimes, whose name was "downright comical," seeing "she keeps the place so clean, even the hens have to wash before supper"; the Negro jazzing orchestras that played in parks on weekends, how they arranged the same notes a thousand different ways, "so a person can't predict where the tune will end up"; the big ships gliding through the channels of the newly dug port. He mentioned friends he'd made, too, especially Wilburn, a cook for one of the shipping companies, who pined for his family back home in Oklahoma much as Papa yearned for his.

Always his dispatches ended the same way: *Each day is another to cross off my calendar, knowing it is closer to our reunion for I love you, family, better than all the biscuits and gravy in Texas.*

Sometimes, Leola would catch Mama slipping a separate page into her apron, reading it later under the pecan tree, her face flushed and eyes alight. Strange to think of her mother not as the weary, oft-vexed person she was, but one familiar with down-deep affections as Leola was now too.

One day Leola was minding her sisters, who'd gotten on her last nerve. Out of desperation, she took Mama's precious button box from its shelf, instructing the girls to find three matching ones for Mrs.

Durnaydon's gown, which was nearly finished. 'Course, they started fussing right away over who could make prettier patterns with them, forgetting the point completely. Leola was about to take the butter paddle to their bottoms when Mama burst through the door.

"We've had another letter!" She waved a piece of paper. "Seems your papa's finally got a job, clerking for an oil company!"

Leola jumped from the table, snatching the page to read herself.

There are ten other clerks here, all decent men with families to feed, he wrote. *The best part is I will earn $20 a week! Enough for a proper apartment, so we can be reunited earlier than expected.*

Glad as she was of this news, she felt a pain too, realizing that soon she'd be separated from Joe and Ship and all she knew. Not that she could dwell on this truth, as Mae in her excitement knocked over the buttons, scattering them everywhere—between the floorboards, beneath the cookstove, under the front door and onto the porch. It took the better part of an hour to gather them, after which Leola was crosser with her sisters than ever. Mama, on the other hand, was too happy about Papa's job to stay angry, and even baked molasses cookies in celebration of the news.

When they sat down that evening to write their congratulations, Leola helped Karla scratch her name beneath the stick-and-circle figure that was supposed to be Papa, while Mae filled an entire page with a rectangle labelled, *Huston Opry Hous*, the five of them standing in front of it, holding hands.

CHAPTER 19

The following week they heard nothing from Papa.

Mama jested they'd received two letters in a row recently, and it was Papa's mathematical nature to balance an account. But after another week passed with no word, Leola felt that account was overdrawn. She knew Mama was worried, too, for Leola had never seen her tear out and restitch a hem three times in a row, or use too much baking soda for the biscuits, nearly breaking everyone's teeth.

Over the next few days, they were so busy finishing Mrs. Durnaydon's gown, there was no time to visit the post office. Lord knew they needed the earnings from this job, as the money Papa usually sent had dried up along with his letters. Already they'd been surviving on greens, cornbread, and blackstrap syrup, with hog-killing weeks away.

When the dress was finally finished, Leola felt surprised that Mama asked her help in delivering it. Dell had recently loaned them his old mare and cart, making it easier for Mama to visit town while Leola tended the girls. Only when her mother mentioned stopping at the post office did Leola understand it was for the moral support more than anything.

Mama grew unusually quiet after they'd dropped Mae and Karla at Auntie's next morning, and Leola did her best to offer distraction, chattering endlessly about everything under the sun—to which

Mama responded with the occasional, "Ain't that something?" or "Land's sake!" even when such replies didn't fit the conversation at all.

After tying the horse up in front of the Durnaydons', a few blocks from Main Street, they knocked on the door, only to discover the woman was away. Handing the dress to her maid, Mama turned, heading toward their next destination like a homing pigeon to its target.

The post office may well have been the fanciest building in Bronway—the *only* fancy building, in fact—with oak-paneled walls, gold-knobbed letter boxes, and tall windows, streaming light. The place smelled of lemon oil and dusty paper, and the air seemed to vibrate, as if bits of emotion had leaked from the many letters passing through.

Then Leola noticed who was stationed behind the counter and her own heart quivered. She'd forgotten that Dot Furthold's mother sometimes filled in when Postmaster Wells was indisposed, and today was apparently such an occasion.

Leola hadn't seen much of Dot or the other girls since the Old Maids' Convention. The few times they did cross paths, everyone was cordial enough, though Leola always felt relieved to slip away, well aware she'd be whispered about afterward. There were adults, too, who still held her in judgment for her outburst, talking behind their hands when she passed—or worse, looking through her as if she didn't exist at all.

Even Ship, away at boarding school, had caught wind of the gossip.

You will not believe, she reported in a recent letter, *but Mother overheard Mrs. Furthold and Mrs. Slemmons talking about you at the Auxiliary lunch, saying how forward you'd been at the Old Maids' Convention. Saying you were becoming Bolshie, most like from associating with "Macaroni Joe"!*

Given all Ship's underlining, was a wonder the paper hadn't ripped.

Never fear however! Mother inserted herself into the conversation, saying what a shame both their husbands got denied an invitation into the Odd Fellows Society. Said she'd asked Mr. Shipley, being Society president, why a person might be rejected continually from its membership, and he'd answered that any upright, halfway-intelligent man should not have a bit of difficulty getting in. Set those nosy parkers right in their places!

Leola had laughed at this account, yet didn't feel so tickled being face to face with one of the chinwags-in-chief.

"Howdy do, Gladys?" Mama asked as they approached the counter.

"I'm well, Orlie." She gave Leola a cursory nod. "How might I help y'all?"

Mama folded her arms atop the counter.

"We were wondering whether we got something from Houston. Been a while since we could check."

Mrs. Furthold blinked.

"Come to think of it . . . I do b'lieve somethin' arrived here lately." She glanced at Leola. "Thought of askin' that Joe Figgie-what's to take it out to your place. Hadn't gotten 'round to it yet."

Leola couldn't figure which was more irksome, the woman's purposeful mispronunciation of Joe's name or that she'd failed to have this piece of mail delivered, knowing how important it was.

But Mama only flashed a beatific smile.

"I do believe, Gladys, that Mr. *Belfigli*," the name rolled perfectly from her tongue, "is in Jefferson visiting his *Belfigli* kin. So it's good we came along when we did."

The other woman hardly seemed to notice Mama's not-so-subtle correction.

"Too bad you couldn't accompany your husband to Houston," she sighed. "I've heard it's quite the tourist destination these days, what with the canals and fairgrounds and such."

"We'll meet him soon enough." Mama's smile barely wavered. "True love won't be conquered by distance, Gladys. Which is why his letters mean so much."

Sourness flashed across Mrs. Furthold's face.

"All for the best, p'rhaps. I also hear that city is overrun with wetbacks and more on the way. Those folk cannot keep themselves from reproducing which, a'course, is what their Catholic church," she gave Leola another look, "encourages, as it means more coin for their coffers in future."

She picked up a stack of letters, absently flipping through them.

"'Least those greasers work harder than our Negroes 'round here. My cousin Ray got a bunch'a Mexicans helpin' on his lettuce farm. Says they will toil day and night, making do with whatever accommodations are offered—a tarp over a branch, patch'a grass behind the chicken coop. None of this asking for roofs to be fixed or wells to be dug or higher wages than they've a right to demand."

Mama narrowed her eyes.

"I do not know from all that as I have only ever *been* a servant and never used one, good or ill. Now, about our mail from Houston?"

"Ah, yes." The other woman shook herself. "Let me see where I put that thing."

She peeked beneath the counter, then scanned the wall of cubbies behind her until Leola's patience gave out completely.

"Mrs. Furthold, if you could hurry it up, please." She gave her backside a vigorous scratch. "I have an appointment with Doc Hickley this afternoon." Scratch, scratch. "Ever since helpin' Jimmy Suggs, I got such a case of worms. This rash is making me crazier than a betsy bug."

She rested her hand near Mrs. Furthold's, and the woman leapt back.

"Wait right here," she muttered, starting for the office.

Though Mama flashed a scolding look at Leola, she seemed more relieved than anything—especially when Mrs. Furthold returned, waving an envelope.

"Guess I put this on my *do-not-forget shelf* and, haha, plumb forgot!"

As she slid the envelope facedown across the counter, Leola could see it was the cream-colored kind Mama favored instead of the plain white ones Papa used. Mama must've noticed, too, for her face stiffened.

"If'n you'll excuse me, ladies, I've duties to attend," Mrs. Furthold announced, rushing into the office again.

When Mama turned over the envelope, it was exactly as Leola suspected: not a letter *from* Papa but one they'd sent him weeks ago, bearing a red-stamped message on its front, *Addressee Unknown/ Return to Sender* and, scrawled in black ink beside it, *Moved.*

"Moved?" Leola's voice caught. "Papa left Mrs. Grimes's and didn't—"

Her mother slipped the envelope into her bag, speaking in a brisk tone.

"Reckon he ain't had time to send us his new address, what with the new job and all."

Leola wanted to point out that Frank Rideout would never let his family lose track of him, not for a job nor anything else—except Mama knew this already and was halfway to the door, besides.

Hurrying after her, Leola heard a noise and turned to see Mrs. Furthold sprinkling Bon Ami cleanser over the counter, scrubbing as hard as she could.

CHAPTER 20

M ary Shipley flung open her front door wearing the denim driving costume Mama had made.

"I've decided it is time to finally take you out in our Briscoe B," she said, twirling so Leola could get the full effect. "There's nothing better for forgettin' your troubles than a joyride in the open air."

Leola had a hard time imagining that *anything* could help her forget her troubles, given the uncertainty shrouding their household. Mama had barely eaten or smiled since they'd received the red-stamped envelope. Hadn't slept much either, apparently.

Fetching a glass of water from the kitchen a couple nights ago, Leola had found her mother, piecework in lap, staring at Papa's rocker with the ghastliest expression. Even when she'd purposely made a noise, Mama still hadn't noticed her there and afterwards, Leola had a hard time sleeping too.

Still, Mary had been begging endlessly to take Leola for a spin in her family's new touring car and Leola *was* a mite curious. She'd only ridden in an automobile three times and never one as fancy as Ship's.

Minutes later, flying down the road, she realized it was true what Mary had told her. There was something in the forward movement, the wind whipping her hair, even the frisson of terror she felt when Ship took a curve one-handed, nearly turning turtle, that made it hard to dwell on life's problems.

Eventually, Mary pulled the car into a grassy patch by the road.

"Your turn!" she declared and, before Leola could ask what it was her turn *for*, Ship climbed from the driver's seat and ran around the vehicle, yanking open her door.

"Move on over, chum. Henry Scales is arriving at two o'clock. We've no time to waste."

Leola balked.

"I don't have any inkling how to drive! You had a few lessons before taking to the road and I've had exactly none. Besides, this jalopy's newer than tomorrow and twice as fine. What would your father say if I wound it 'round a tree?"

Ship pulled a face.

"Smart girl like you don't need driving lessons. All you do is grab the wheel, press the accelerator handle, and keep your eyes on the road. Besides, you'll have your own car someday; don't want to seem a fool first time you take it out, do you?"

Leola saw some truth in this argument. So she slid behind the steering wheel as Ship took the passenger side, cheering when Leola chugged onto the road.

"There you go, Lee! In no time, you'll be a professional like Alice Ramsey—ever heard of her?"

Leola was so focused on driving, all she could do was shake her head.

"Alice was twenty-two when she traversed the country in her Maxwell Runabout—and that was ten years ago." Ship stretched an arm out the window. "There were no road maps then, so she had to follow telephone poles the entire way. Got stuck in the mud and slept in her car on a few occasions—once drove straight through a pack of vigilantes hunting a murderer! Got shot at too!"

Leola swerved, barely avoiding a passing cart.

"Lordy, Ship! If I attempted a cross-country mission, I'd hardly get 'round the block before getting myself kil't, vigilantes or no."

But it didn't take her long to get the knack of it, and soon Leola was also steering one-handed.

"Slow up, Leola. Go in there!" Ship gestured at a cow path, ahead. "Let's give this thing a run for the money!"

Leola did as she was told, turning onto into an expanse of fields marked off by wire fences, with cattle guards instead of gates.

"That meadow yonder appears overgrazed," Ship said, "no cows to be seen and just enough dirt to give us traction!"

Leola slowed the car. "It's Mr. Turley's ranch. Won't he get mad if he finds us churning up his pastures?"

Mary rolled her eyes. "I doubt Old Man Turley will decide to check this one acre today out of the hundreds he owns."

Sweeping her gaze along the horizon, Leola remembered the Turley homestead was a good three miles away and this patch did seem little used.

She drove across the metal guard, taking a few practice runs until she felt bold enough to rev the engine, maneuvering in ever tighter circles, spinning grass and mud until the windshield was so smeared that she had to lean out to see. Only when both girls were panting with laughter did she finally bring the car to a stop.

"Gad night!" Leola pulled a hankie from her waist, blotting her sweat-dampened face. "This here driving really *is* better than Fourth of July fireworks."

"And to think," Mary snorted, "men get themselves riled, saying ladies ought not be allowed to drive. You wait—womenfolk will be the very ones most liberated by the automobile. No more taking the family nag to town at five miles per hour! Now a lonely farm woman can do her marketing, visit friends, and still get home in time to cook supper."

"Or," Leola added, "be like Alice Ramsey and light out for parts distant if that cooking ain't appreciated."

"Touché, Miss Rideout!"

Ship studied her wristlet, modeled on a popular design from Paris.

"And speaking of husbands . . . if Henry catches me in my current state, he'll be the one lighting out for points distant."

Leola tucked away her hankie, twisting the key in the ignition— but nothing happened.

"Ach!" Ship clapped her forehead. "This may be a cutting-edge car, but that newfangled key gadget fails too often. Good thing they left the crank in front."

She started to climb out until Leola stopped her.

"I'll do it, Ship. You buffed your nails this morning and mine are ragged as it is. I know how much Henry loves those soft, pretty hands of yours."

"You never cranked a car before, Lee. Ain't so easy as it looks."

Leola jumped to the ground.

"Like you said, if I'm to have my own motoring adventures, best learn while I can."

She took her place in front of the crank as Ship called out advice: "Grasp it with all your fingers on one side. That way if the engine kicks back, it won't break your thumb. Then pull it real fast from the top."

Leola was bracing herself for the wind-up when she heard a strange huffing noise and looked up to see a muscle-bound bull glaring from behind the car.

"Hiyo, Lee!" Ship had noticed the threat too. "Get in here this instant!"

Leola knew the car's aluminum shell would hardly protect them if the bull charged, and that they'd never outrun him either. Heart pounding, she cranked the engine, once, twice, three times. Still nothing.

The beast made a terrible lowing sound, scraping a foot through the dirt.

"Hurry!" Ship sobbed. "He's ready to charge!"

Leola gave the handle one last hard thrust. When the car leapt to life, she dove into the driver's seat, pressing the accelerator far as it would go, careening so fast over the cattle grate, it seemed her teeth might fly from her mouth.

Safely outside the enclosure, she stopped, both girls watching, amazed, as the beast bellowed and stomped. When their eyes met, Ship and Leola burst into such loud laughter, the bull finally went quiet, dumbfounded two scrawny creatures might be capable of such noise.

As the animal lumbered away, Ship clapped Leola on the back.

"Dang! You put Alice Ramsey to shame back there."

Leola grinned, turning the car toward the main road, imagining the letter she might write her father. Pictured Papa laughing at their adventure, how proud he'd be of her driving skills. Then she remembered there was no place to send such a letter and her mood darkened. Just as she'd sensed the lurking presence of that bull, Leola knew Papa was in trouble—that her *family* was in trouble. It felt like a truth she might never outrun.

Early October 1919

CHAPTER 21

B lood. Oozing entrails. The nose-prickling scent of singed bristles. Leola had attended hog killings all her life, yet never before felt squeamish about any of it: not when the pig was clubbed over the head, strung up and split open, throat to bung. Not when the blood poured forth, steaming on the ground, nor when the tender ears and dainty feet were severed from its body. In fact, she'd always been fascinated by the humanlike arrangement of blue-tinged organs, nestled within their caverns of bone and muscle.

Today though, when the first carcass was dragged to the kettle, Leola's hands trembled as she ladled scalding water over it. When the hog's innards were ripped from its body, she didn't gape in wonder but turned away, repulsed.

Dragging buckets of bones to a nearby field, memories of the sawmill accident reemerged, reminding her Papa might be hurt again. Tipping femurs and ribs into the hole, she imagined him bruised and broken, left to rot in some alley.

"Look here, Lee-lee!" Mae held up two still-connected neck bones. "It's a *M* as in *Mae!*"

"So it is." Leola could barely choke out a response. "That's . . . that's swell."

Approaching the house, she saw the men hacking at the dead swine. Joe caught her gaze and grinned, but Leola barely lifted her hand in response. And then there was the trail of shiny red dots leading to the back door, like Papa's blood on the kitchen floor the day he lost his arm.

Stifling a scream, Leola fled behind the barn, crouching in a patch of moldering hay. Ashamed as she was of her fear, she felt even more ashamed of shirking her duties, aware of how needed she was—how needed *everyone* was: Dell and his son, Cliff, contributing their muscle power in slaughtering and butchering; Dora and Ceci, helping process raw meat into sausage and head cheese. Though neighbors helped because that's what folks did, they'd also be rewarded with the choicest cuts—spareribs, tenderloins, hearts. Strangers would often come along, too, desperate for work, taking payment in the animal's lesser portions: spleens, feet, tongues. Leola didn't relish the labor but liked the food that came from it—*relied upon* that food to survive the winter and trade for basic necessities. The four pigs they butchered each year, which Mama raised from tiny piglets, were *everything*. And here she sat, useful as a wooden skillet.

"Rose o'Roses!"

Joe peeked around the barn, smile vanishing when he saw her expression.

"What is it?" he asked, squatting beside her.

Drawing a hankie from her pocket, Leola blew her nose hard, not caring how indelicate it appeared.

"The most terrible feeling came over me back there. Seeing the blood made me think of Papa, wonder if he's been hurt even worse than before."

Joe pulled her head to his shoulder, stroking her hair.

"It's too early to fret, Lee. Your mother sent that telegram to Mrs. Grimes only yesterday. I imagine there'll be some reply—some explanation soon—that your father is . . ." He paused. ". . . that he's been overtaken, tryin' to gain a foothold in that city. That he's," pause, "fine."

Leola could hear the waver in his voice. Knew however much he wanted her to believe the words, he didn't quite himself.

"Joe?" A man's voice called out. "You back here?"

Cliff hurtled around the corner, stopping short when he saw them.

"Oh!" His eyes went round. "*Thought* it was y'all."

No doubt he believed they'd snuck off to do some barney mugging.

Cliff, of all people, knew how hard it was to concentrate on a single thing—hog-slaughtering, plowing, even a game of checkers—when your entire being pined for a caress from your love. He'd always been handsome, a favorite with the girls, but only ever had eyes for Ceci Pettigrew, whom he'd met in sixth grade. Even after a year of marriage and the birth of a child, the couple still acted as dumbstruck fools, making goggle eyes at each other during Sunday sermons, laughing at inside jokes no one else could understand.

Yet now he sensed the air of tension and shuffled his feet.

"Didn't mean to be rude."

"It's us who should apologize." Joe stood, wiping hay from his seat. "We been absent too long and the slaughtering just begun. Leola felt poorly; I was makin' sure she was all right."

As Joe helped her stand, Cliff's gaze skimmed from Leola's face to her belly, and she wanted to crawl beneath the barn. He *would* assume she was in the family way, given the rush of his own marriage proceedings, with Mama making last-minute alterations to Ceci's bridal dress, and little Guy arriving not long after they'd said their *I dos*. Leola had never judged them for this indiscretion, especially after Joe came into her life. The two of them had teetered often enough between fervent desire and blissful fulfillment, telling themselves it hardly mattered whether they ate supper before saying grace; they'd planned to marry anyhow. It was Leola who always slammed shut the gate of temptation, gathering her wildest longings like cotton strands in a breeze, packing them away again.

She could not afford to be careless as Cliff had been. The Meekers had owned their Blackland farm for generations and possessed good heads for the business, planting not only cotton in their rich soil, but alfalfa and corn, guaranteeing survival if the bottom fell out of any one market. However much Dell and Dora disapproved, at first, of Cliff's sinful lapse, in the end it was more cause for celebration: a bouncing grandchild, stability for their only son, the extra pair of hands Ceci provided.

Wouldn't be the same party if suchlike happened to Leola. She'd no legacy of productive land nor a paid-off home nor even, for the time being, two capable parents. It was all she and Mama could do to keep the *living* alive. A baby would spell their demise.

Yanking her skirt to emphasize her neat waist, she replied, "I'm fine. Taking a cold is all," and coughed to prove her point.

Cliff gave a relieved nod.

"I b'lieve there's a nice cider posset brewing in the kitchen. Y'ought take some refreshment before gettin' back to work."

Leola tried to smile.

"Something hot could do the trick. Give me strength for the sausage-stuffing."

But as they went their separate ways and she stepped over that trail of blood again, fear rustled beneath Leola's ribs, an embryo of trouble to come.

CHAPTER 22

The latest round of rain had passed, with tepid sunshine filtering through the clouds. As she tossed feed about the chicken yard, Leola's boots squelched in the mud, reminding her of when she was a child and Papa took her for walks after a storm.

Listen to that, Rosalee! he'd say, as their feet slurped in the road. *Sounds like bachelor cowboys at a BBQ, don't it?* Then the two of them would tramp through the muck like drunken soldiers, seeing who could make the funniest noises, not caring that Mama would scold them for mussing their shoes.

She found herself smiling at this recollection—until the weight of reality settled over her again. Another week had passed since the hog-killing and still no word from her father.

Pressing a corn-filled fist to her mouth, she groaned, "Oh, Papa, where are you? *Where?*"

"Orlie Owen! You here?"

At the sound of Mr. Owen's voice booming from the front porch, Leola considered hiding inside the chicken coop. Knew if she did the hens would put up a fuss and get her discovered, and then she'd have some explaining to do. And Mr. Owen was the last person Leola felt like offering explanations.

The old man *had* seemed a tad penitent since Papa went missing, appearing every so often on pretense of fixing a fence or patching a roof, occasionally leaving a gift of sorts on the front porch: a cord of firewood, some moth-eaten quilts Big Leola had made years ago. Too little, too late far as Leola was concerned. The man could bequeath them an entire side of beef and a fifty-dollar bill and she'd not forgive him for driving Papa away.

Hurrying inside, she found her grandfather already in the kitchen, trailing clods of damp earth.

"Afternoon, sir." Leola gestured at the sideboard. "I was planning to bring supper to your place shortly. Fresh ham tonight. Sweet potatoes too."

Mr. Owen shook his head.

"Still got the pork stew left over from yesterday." His gaze darted about as if Mama were the one hiding. "I've news for your mother. Where might she be?"

Leola tried to smile.

"Down at Auntie's getting the girls. That last downpour must've held them up. I'd be more than happy to say you came by."

Mr. Owen plunked down in Papa's rocker like it was his personal throne.

"I'll wait," he said.

As he took a plug of tobacco from his pocket, biting off a chaw, Leola resisted the urge to shoo the man from her father's favorite perch, which no one had sat in since he left. Instead she busied herself sweeping the mud he'd tracked in, trying not to think too hard about what news he carried.

Feeling Mr. Owen's eyes upon her, Leola couldn't help wondering if he'd heard about her "spell" at the hog-killing last week. Wondered if Cliff had whispered ill suspicion to CeCe and she'd shared it around. Imagined the old man catching wind of such gossip, fury turning quickly to self-righteousness. *See what comes of mixing with the wrong kind?* he'd say to Mama. Didn't matter that Leola could fully defend herself. Her mother would be mortified she was the subject of such talk, factual or otherwise.

"Have you heard the influenza is come again to Texas?"

Leola flinched at her grandfather's unexpected question.

"No, sir. Thought the danger long passed. President Wilson said . . ."

"Presidents can be the worst of blame fools." He shifted his tobacco wad from one cheek to the other. "No, they're callin' this round *the boomerang flu,* returned to claim folks it missed before. Some say recent-arrived immigrants are to blame. Hardly seems to bother them but mows down white people like hay through a thresher." He let out a bitter laugh. "Which a'course, is what the newcomers intend, wanting nothin' more than to steal our prosperity for themselves."

Leola didn't answer right away, filling a pot with water though nothing needed boiling at the moment, thinking if last year's pestilence had returned, her virtue would be the least of their worries.

Influenza's first appearance had left their community more or less unscathed, which Pastor Nickles attributed to God's judgment, saying the Lord *recognized righteous folk when he saw them.* After reading the newspaper stories—big-city morgues crammed with bodies, families decimated, towns laid waste—Leola had decided there couldn't be so many unrighteous people in the world and even if they *were* all sinners, surely their orphaned babies were not. She and Mama had been nursing Papa through the worst of his injuries at the time, knowing he'd not survive such a test and relieved when it seemed to be over. Relieved, it seemed, for nothing.

"Is this the news you've brought then?" She set the pot on the stove with shaky hands. "About the sickness?"

"Wish it were," he answered, and Leola knew his tidings were probably worse than she'd imagined—worse than rumors of her supposed indelicacy or even a coming plague.

Right then, Mama burst through the door, Karla drowsing in her arms, Mae close behind. Seeing their grandfather, the younger girl jolted awake, eyes round with terror.

"It Mr. Omen, Mama! Wun 'way!"

Leola nearly laughed at the fitting mispronunciation of their grandfather's name, but Mama only pursed her lips, avoiding the old man's gaze.

"*Shhh*, darlin'," she comforted Karla, "Your grandpappy's just come for a visit. *Shhh*."

Mr. Owen sat ramrod straight, the lump of tobacco unmoving inside his cheek.

"Best get that child settled, Orlena. I came here to tell y'all something and am nearly run dry of patience as it is."

As soon as Mama set Karla on the ground, the girl ran straight to Leola, hugging her legs.

"What is it," Mama asked her father, "that you came to tell us?"

"Not *us*." Mr. Owen nodded at the younger girls. "This news ain't fit for little pitchers."

A brief stillness passed over Mama's face. Then she flew into motion, opening cupboards, chattering to her children in an overbright voice.

"I was savin' some of that fine jam we got at Laird's for a special occasion, but a rainy day is good enough reason to indulge, don't you think? Been so long since y'all had a picnic!" She split two cold biscuits, opened the jar of jam. "Leola, get that old blanket from the cabinet, the one we use outdoors. Set it up real nice in your bedroom."

Leola did as she was told, heart a-gallop.

"Sit and eat, girls," Mama directed when she came into the room, "and after you're done, get into bed. Do not bother us in the kitchen, hear?"

Setting the plates upon the blanket, she managed a weak smile.

"If you behave, we can look through those jewelry catalogs Mrs. Durnaydon gave me. P'rhaps repaper your walls."

She turned to Leola. "Y'ought come, Daughter."

Leola hesitated, uncertain she wanted to be present if her supposed *lapses* were the subject of conversation, but thinking it'd be better to dispel any such tales off the bat. So she followed her mother into the other room.

"Would you like a cup of tea, Father?" Mama inquired. "P'rhaps a molasses cookie?"

The man answered with an aggravated sigh.

"Your girl already asked me as much and I'll answer the same: didn't come for nourishment but to deliver my news and get on home."

Mama clasped her hands against her waist.

"All right then. I'm listening."

Mr. Owen pointed at a chair.

"Y'all might want to sit."

Mama pulled her tiny self as tall as she could.

"I'll stand, if it please you," she said, clearly not caring whether it did.

Leola moved beside her in solidarity and Mr. Owen flicked his eyes between them, sizing up the strength of an army and deciding it held little threat.

"I was in town today," he began, "sendin' a telegram to the Dallas Grange. As it happened, the cable operator had a message for you, arrived not an hour before."

"A m-message?" Mama stammered and Mr. Owen nodded, picking up the chipped saucer Papa used as his pipe stand.

"From that lodging-house lady down in Houston." He spat into the dish. "Concerning your husband."

He fished a yellow paper from his pocket, thrusting it out—though Mama wouldn't take it.

"Lee, will you read the cable to me? I don't think I can."

Leola took the page from Mr. Owen.

Received your cable STOP Frank Rideout not seen since mid-October tho month's rent pd. in full STOP inquiries made per your request STOP report of an affray about that time at saloon Rideout patronized STOP one-armed gringo injured, taken in by Tejano family STOP

Seeing the next sentence, Leola struggled to keep calm: *Word has it, armless man did not survive—*

"Oh my Frank!" Mama shouted. "No!"

Leola caught her mother before she could collapse, leading her to a nearby chair, hating that Mr. Owen had been correct in thinking she'd need it.

"There's more to the message, Mama," she pleaded, rattling the paper, "if you'll listen! It says right here, *no confirmation deceased man is Frank Rideout.* So it might *not* be Papa, the one who got . . . hurt."

Mama didn't respond, pressing her face into her hands.

"You recollect how many men lost their arms in the war?" Leola rushed on. "Plenty, just in our small town! Imagine the number in a place like Houston. Besides, Papa wasn't one to frequent saloons! How could he get caught up in such a . . . ?"

Leola let her words trail away. She'd rarely seen her mother cry and now it was as if all the exhaustion and worry of the past months gushed out, a stream of raw despair.

"You must get ahold of yourself," Leola whispered, "or the girls will hear. We can't lose courage, not 'til we have proof of this thing.

We'll find a way to get to Houston, discover what's happened once and for all." She parroted Joe's words, "It's too early to think the worst."

Mama's tears did dry up after that—but the damage had been done, for Mae stood in the doorway, holding Karla's hand.

"Is somethin' wrong with our papa?"

When Mama wouldn't answer, Leola did instead.

"He might'a been hurt, girls. That's what the message says. We don't know for sure—it could have been, probably *was*—another man."

Never mind her thin assurance. When the girls hurled themselves into Mama's arms, Leola gave in, too, the four of them forming a singular heap of pain. Minutes passed before she noticed Mr. Owen standing by the door, studying them with something like sympathy—except when their eyes met, his face turned back to stone. And then he was gone.

CHAPTER 23

Two days later, Mama and Leola were in town, sending a telegram to the Lone Star Oil Company.

Last night, Joe and the Meekers had visited, helping devise a plan to discover Papa's fate once and for all. Mama had agreed to use some of their meager savings to wire the oil company, while Dell would write to Murl, who'd been working one of the drilling rigs in Arkansas but had recently returned to Houston. If, in two weeks' time, no further facts were uncovered, Dell and Joe would journey to Houston themselves to conduct a search.

Having a strategy seemed to calm Mama better than empty reassurances ever could, and her fresh determination had rubbed off on Leola too. As her mother waited at the telegraph office, she made her way to Laird's, telling herself a company like Lone Star would have the means and connections to inquire around. Office clerks didn't just disappear; someone must have information that would lead to Papa—not dead, despite Mr. Owen's reckoning, but *alive*.

She was so lost in her thoughts, Leola nearly collided with George Gumbs and another Black fellow, well-dressed in a tailored suit and fashionable derby, holding a leather case.

"How'dy do?" George asked, eyes darting in every direction.

"I'm well. And you?"

"Just dandy," George replied, though he seemed fluttery and nervous and not dandy at all.

Neither man stepped off the sidewalk—fine with Leola, who felt a greater disdain for such customs with every passing day. Still, she knew from Mrs. Gumbs that by not moving aside, George was making a statement—knew it for dissent, however small.

Dropping off pennyroyal tincture for Mama's cramps recently, Mrs. Gumbs had mentioned that George was associating more and more with certain "radical" Negroes.

My son believes we got to band together if Black folk are ever to find equality, she'd said. *Vows he'll not go along anymore with the white man's "laws of indignity," as he calls them.* Her eyes had sparked with terror. *I fear for that boy night and day, I do.*

Regarding the two men before her, Leola didn't think they resembled rabble-rousers or firebrands in the least, and left them with a quick, "Good day."

But coming from Laird's a while later, she noticed a crowd next to the blacksmith's shop, surrounding George and the older gentleman. On the ground lay the black leather case the man had been carrying, spilling sheets of paper.

"We weren't planning on bothering y'all," George was saying to Mack Slemmons, "only heading to our meeting down the street. There's no law against bearing pamphlets. It's our right as Americans to gather and also to write whatever we feel—*say* what we feel too."

Leola's chest tightened. Mr. Slemmons was a brawny fellow, perpetually red-faced and known for his short fuse. Judging from his clenched fists, that fuse was down to the quick.

She picked up one of the papers, skimming the masthead: *The Crisis, published by The National Association for the Advancement of Colored People.* Scanned the front page, noting phrases like, *Hew to the line! Democracy is our right! Let the chips fall where they may!*

"Nigras don't get the same rights as us real Americans," Mack was saying, waving his own copy.

"That's precisely it, sir." George's friend stepped forward. "Negroes *are* Americans. Born here, same as you. My ancestors were brought to this country against their will nigh on two hundred years ago, to build the fort in Charleston—the very same one that defended *your* ancestors from the Redcoats."

Another white man snorted.

"Don't care whether your kin lived here one thousand years, boy. You is a Nigra and not allowed to do or say what'cha want." He held up one of the newspapers, ripping it slowly down the middle. "And that is that."

George's friend lifted his chin, face stiff with offense.

"My name's not *Boy*, sir, but Dr. Cyrus Gates."

Mack slapped his thigh, laughing so hard, Leola could see the spaces where several molars were missing. "Well, ain't that something! A colored medicine man of all people, spreading sedition!"

Dr. Gates narrowed his eyes. "I am not a medical doctor but a PhD of Romance languages and a professor at Texas College in Tyler."

"I don't care if you got a ABC or a XYZ, and whether it is in Pig Latin or Zulu. Y'ain't supposed to be stirring things up with this so-called Colored-Advancing Association of your'n." Mack glared at George. "Pastor Nickles warned what y'all been up to. Said it's our *God given right* to break up them secret meetings of yours, which is what we aim to do."

The voice in Leola's ear no longer whispered but shouted, *IS NOT RIGHT.* Daring her to ignore it. Hush it up. Pretend it had nothing to do with her. Yet here she was, caught up in a mob of seething hatred and no pretending about that.

She bent down, collecting as many pamphlets as possible, and held them out to George.

"Here you go," she said, but he only crossed his arms and frowned. It was Dr. Cyrus who took the brochures—yet he didn't look exactly happy for her help.

"You ought not get involved in this, young lady," he muttered, and Leola's cheeks burned. She'd taken a risk to return their property, knowing it might anger the mob even more—might even get herself embroiled in their fury. And instead of seeming grateful, George and his friend appeared insulted!

Before she could reply, Mack Slemmons approached, patting her roughly on the shoulder.

"See?" He addressed the crowd. "For all we try to help our Negroes, this is the thanks we get." He shifted his gaze in her direction. "You're a bleeding heart, girl, selling yourself to the lowest bidder. Time you toughen up, recognize some folk *belong* at the bottom and best leave them be."

Leola yanked away, giving the man a sore look, feeling even sorer that her piteous attempt at bravery had backfired. As the crowd dispersed, whispering and tutting, she tried to comfort herself with the idea that at least her actions had broken the tension, allowing George and Dr. Gates to escape, their crisp white calls-to-action swirling in the breeze.

Late October 1919

CHAPTER 24

L eola held a spoonful of egg custard toward her mother's purplish lips.

"Eat, Mama. Please!"

She'd grown accustomed to the strange, bruised hue of her mother's face, 'specially around the mouth and eyes—what Doc Hickley called *the stain of influenza*. She'd also grown familiar with the hanks of Mama's hair upon her pillow, the rattling sound between each inhalation, the stink of bodily fluids permeating the room. What Leola couldn't get used to was the storm of pain in her mother's eyes, and now they held pleading too.

"The Baptist home . . . in Tyler," Mama murmured, and Leola set the spoon into the bowl.

"I'm aware you want us at the orphanage in Tyler if it even comes to that. We've spoken of it before, remember?"

Her mother started to speak again, but Leola wouldn't let her.

"No need to fret. You're like Mae for not listenin' to others!" She picked up the spoon, again. "You must eat to get strong again."

Leola conversed like it was the two of them in the kitchen on an ordinary Saturday.

"Reckon I added too much nutmeg to this? It doesn't taste a bit like yours."

"The girls . . ." Mama's face sheened with sweat. "Don't . . . don't . . ."

Leola gave up on the custard, kneeling so she could gaze into her mother's eyes, barely flinching when the woman coughed and spittle hit her cheek.

Be careful, Doc had said, when he stopped by last week. *This strain of influenza appears more vicious than the first. City people exposed last year seem better able to fight it off. For us country folk, it's deadly as it is contagious.*

He'd offered Leola a cloth mask like he wore, warned her to wash her hands and the linens with lye soap. But Leola was well past such precautions. Sometimes, after changing Mama's bedpan or blotting her face with a rag, she'd dip her fingers in the water barrel, though it was hard to be mindful with so much else to do. The only thing saving her from this illness, it seemed, was her own fierce belief she would not catch it. Because she *couldn't.*

"No matter what, Mama, I won't separate the girls," she promised, "in case Papa returns. There's no sense in brooding over such things. I can see already your fever's down."

This was a lie, made evident by the cloth on Mama's forehead— cool when Leola first put it there but already warmed by the roaring furnace of her body.

As Leola dampened the rag, Mama raised up, grasping her daughter's hand.

"I want you to know . . ." Her lungs crackled as if filled with glass. "You are my greatest . . . treasure." More hacking and crackling. "I'm sorry for bein' unkind to your Joe. I'd be right proud to have him for a . . . a son."

Leola blinked away tears, easing Mama onto the pillows again.

"You're a treasure, too, and Joe would be—*will be*—proud to have you as his mother. He still pines for his own *maman*, whom he hardly remembers. Thinks you the most capable woman he ever met."

Mama seemed soothed by this and closed her eyes—which was when Leola noticed the basin, nearly empty. Much as she dreaded leaving her mother's side, the cool cloths on her forehead and wrists were Mama's only true relief.

"You rest," she said, reaching for the pitcher. "I'll fetch more water."

As she stood, the walls buckled and she grasped the chair to keep upright. Must be pure fatigue, for she'd barely slept a full night in . . . Leola couldn't recall when she'd first made herself a pallet by her mother's bed, jumping up at every creak of the mattress.

Dora Meeker had brought food over on occasion, except yesterday had left a note saying Dell had passed, and Ceci had taken ill, so she wouldn't be able to check in for a while. Thankfully, old Auntie had been spared so far and was keeping the girls at her place, giving Leola one less thing to worry about.

Now Mama's lips moved in a noiseless murmur—a prayer or part of a hymn or the senseless jargon comes with illness sometimes— and Leola felt the most powerful craving: to be fed and petted, to be *looked after*. It took all her willpower not to curl up beside her mother and sleep. But the basin wasn't filling itself.

"I'll be back, quicker'n a whistle."

In the kitchen, she dipped the pitcher into the barrel, sloshing water across the floor, whispering the whole way, "I'm comin', Mama, I'm comin'."

Except she wasn't fast enough.

Back in the bedroom, Mama lay still, eyes fixed on the ceiling— and no sign of her in them at all.

CHAPTER 25

Mama's funeral came and went but Leola never knew, for she fell ill the next day, bones aching so she wanted to rip them from her body, lungs pulsing hot in her chest, even the roots of her teeth, throbbing and sore. Doc Hickley came by long enough to spoon a foul concoction into her mouth, which she spat up right after he left.

Mr. Owen appeared as well, staring down at her with a disconcerted expression.

"I am lookin' for someone to tend you, girl." He pointed at the bedside table. "Left you water and some biscuits."

Then he vanished too.

And so Leola spent long hours alone, thrashing inside her damp sheets, finding occasional strength to dip water from the basin and bring it to her lips, though more of it dribbled down her nightdress. Sometimes Mama's specter appeared nearby and, while it did not say or do anything, Leola took this as a sign she'd crossed the River Jordan and was at peace.

Papa however did not appear likewise, though her dreams were haunted by him. One such dream repeated often: she'd be standing in the doorway to a strange bedroom, where Papa lay on a bed, attended by a woman in colorful linen clothes. As Leola approached him, Papa would sit up shouting, *I vow it!* and then burst into laughter, after which Leola would awaken, trembling and drenched, relieved it was only a dream.

On one such occasion, her eyes lit on the little javelina Papa had carved, perched on the windowsill. Aware her legs would never support her, she slid to the floor, scooting painfully to the window, reaching for the pig then doing it all in reverse.

Under the covers once more, she recalled Papa's words: *Put all your worries into him and they will disappear.* Leola hesitated. Mama would say it was heathenish to rely on spells and charms, that wooden pigs did not make magic and only God could be her comfort. Yet she *had* prayed these past months: *Lord, bring my father back. Let Mama live. Let me not get sick.* Instead of answering, God had allowed Papa to disappear and Mama to perish. And now he'd let her fall sick, too, her sisters left to fend for themselves.

Leola held the pig tight. *Dear Francis, don't let me die. Bring Papa back to us. Make everything all right. Please!*

The pig remained hard and unyielding in her hands. Leola's innards were still cold, her skin fiery. But in a few minutes, she felt a certain release—not peace so much as resignation. Everything was beyond her reasoning. Beyond her understanding. Wooden pigs, God, Mama, Papa, Ship, Joe . . . they were powerless to save her. People died even if thousands prayed for their health. Others lived who hated God and had no friends. In the end, whether now or at some future date, death would win. That was the order of things, how it had always been. How it would always be. It seemed the simplest, sweetest, most freeing truth she'd ever known.

Soon she fell into a bottomless sleep, not dreaming at all.

CHAPTER 26

The next day, Leola woke to find Nancy Gumbs fixing a warm poultice upon her chest and decided Francis must be magical, after all, for surely she was saved.

"Lord, child, you're a sight to behold! And left alone in your time of need." Mrs. Gumbs held a bitter-scented potion to her lips. "But now I'm here."

Leola took some medicine, then moved her head away.

"My sisters . . . are they . . . ?"

Mrs. Gumbs lay a cool hand on her arm.

"I seen those sprites only yesterday. Pink in their cheeks, not a snotty nose among them." She chuckled. "Keepin' Mrs. Hughes running her ol' legs off."

"Do they know about our mama?"

As she set the potion aside, Nancy's green-brown eyes shimmered.

"'Course, child. However, they did not see the body laid out nor attend the funeral. Mrs. Hughes believed all that might be too much."

Leola's heart ached, imagining the little girls learning their mother was gone, not having their big sister to comfort them—uncertain they would see *her* again either.

"They were worried of you," Mrs. Gumbs said, as if hearing Leola's thoughts. "I told them, what with your spirit, you'd pull through. So you got to keep fightin'. Can't leave those little sprites without you to care for 'em and me, taken for a liar."

Leola drew a raspy breath.

"And Joe? Is Joe . . . ?"

"Fit as a fiddle." Mrs. Gumbs waved. "Stopped by yesterday. Said he would'a come before but got caught in the quarantine over in Jefferson. Made it here soon's he could. Insisted on seeing you but I chased him off. No use *him* falling ill, after all this."

Leola coughed. "Couldn't you fall sick too?"

The other woman leaned in, turning the plaster to its warmer side.

"The good Lord must need my help in healin', child, for it seems he granted me protection from such contagions. Otherwise I would'a been struck down long ago."

Leola licked her sore lips, wanting to ask more—how Ship fared and Dora Meeker and baby Guy—but she was too tired and quickly fell into another boundless sleep.

❧

Days later, Leola opened her eyes and realized they no longer ached. Her lungs were still raw but didn't rattle with every inhalation, and her sheets stayed dry all day. Soon she could sit up, pour her own water, even use the bedpan without help.

When Nancy stopped by again, she insisted Leola try to walk.

"Best get you moving. Those sisters of your'n will be home any minute and you'll need to keep up."

As Mrs. Gumbs helped her stand, Leola's bones nearly crumpled—though after a few steps, her feet moved steadier across the floor. It felt good to sit in Papa's rocking chair with a warm cup of tincture-spiked tea, speaking full sentences without hacking between every word.

"How is the rest of the world, Mrs. Gumbs?" she asked. "Your father? And George? Any word of folks in town?"

"I declare," Nancy laughed, "thought I would never be so grateful to hear you ask questions—like when you was young, always wantin' to know this, that, and everything else!"

She sipped her own tea, made from dried watercress to *uphold her vigor.*

"Far's my kin are concerned, Dad is spry as ever, never took ill." Her face wrenched. "But George . . ."

Leola nearly dropped her cup.

"George got the grippe, too?"

Mrs. Gumbs shook her head.

"Weren't any sickness took him from me and I'm grateful to Heaven for that. No, George gone North, like he been promisin' to do, only earlier than planned and not under the best of circumstance."

"What happened?" Leola asked, and Nancy frowned.

"Seems he made too many enemies 'round here, what with all that talk of change and equality. Meantime, me and Dad got bricks through our own windows and a cross burnt in our field. Wasn't only my father sleeping with his firearm, I'll tell you what."

She let out a long exhalation.

"What saved George from worse misfortune was Mack Slemmons, if you can believe it. Man must've decided he owed me for doctoring his venereal disease—his missus, too, for once a man got the clap, you know the wife's not long behind." She leaned closer. "'Tween you and me, those two got crotch crickets bad on more'n a few occasions. Guess Mr. Slemmons 'membered that a'fore deciding to harm my boy. Warned him to flee while he could."

Leola grimaced, imagining the Bible-thumping Slemmons with dripping, crawling private parts. Grimaced too at the idea of George barely escaping with his life, rescued by one of the very white-robed wolves that would've devoured him otherwise.

"Thing is," Nancy continued, with a shrewd smile. "George already had his arrangements made. That teacher friend of his at Texas College, forget his name . . ."

"Gates," Leola said. "Dr. Cyrus Gates."

The other woman nodded.

"Dr. Gates got friends up Chicago way. Folks who run that outfit George is involved in, the one got him so hepped up 'bout changing everything."

"The National Association for the Advancement of Colored People," Leola recited.

"Mmm-hmm. Dr. Gates said they got plenty of work for someone bold as George. In the end, Mack and his mob only hastened my son's leave-taking by a week or so."

There was a hint of pride in the woman's expression.

"George says he'll be back someday and bring others with him. *Make sure they get listened to,* was how he put it."

Leola pictured the man and his fellow crusaders marching down Main Street chanting, *Hew to the line! Democracy is our right!* Daring anyone to stop them. Impossible as it seemed, still, the idea sent a shiver up her spine.

"I realize you tried to help my son," Mrs. Gumbs was saying, "when he had a run-in with Mack and his gang. George told me all about it, understood how poorly he'd treated you."

She paused.

"It's hard to understand myself. My boy and his ilk, they don't want the white man's—nor lady's—help. *We need do this ourselves,* he says.

Make it our fight. Things been done too long to us and s'posedly for us, but hardly ever by us. High time we put an end to that. 'Course, I tried to remind him you and your family are friends, that you did something most others would not. That there are ways to fix the laws and not be kil't for it. But no. Got his own mind, my son, and hard-pressed to change it."

Leola looked down, remembering that day with the pamphlets, how surprised she'd been by George's disdainful reaction. And now she could see the sense in it. She'd often taken affront when Mama or Papa tried to help her—with a mix-up at school, say, or sweeping the yard on a broiling afternoon. If such offers had come from Ship or Joe, who already saw her as an equal, it would've been different. The fact they came from her parents—well, it felt like admitting she was a child instead of a woman. Black folks had been treated as *lesser than* since time immemorial; who could blame them for not trusting whites any longer to do the right thing?

"I wasn't the one jumped by thugs in the street," she said. "George and Dr. Gates, they weren't doing anything wrong, but Mr. Slemmons and his crew . . ." She sucked her teeth. "Folk like that don't have two good cents in their heads and no business calling themselves Christian neither."

She drained the dregs of her tea, made more tolerable by the sorghum settled at the bottom.

"You must miss George," she added, putting her cup on the table.

Mrs. Gumbs sighed.

"I do, child. 'Least I can rest easier, knowing he's out of harm's way."

Another small silence and then Leola asked, "What about the others? Have you heard anything of our neighbors?"

Mrs. Gumbs kneaded her eyes as if rubbing away all she'd seen of late.

"You know about Senior Meeker, bless his soul. And that little Ceci . . . still weak as a kitten, may never bear a second child. Mrs. Meeker does her best with the baby, who weren't the least bit touched by the sickness, praise be. Cliff, he tries to fill his father's breeches but is so fretful of his wife . . . Nearly knocked me for nine the other day, seein' him thin as a scarecrow and the color of old fireplace ash."

She paused.

"As for Mr. Owen, he didn't take ill—tough as old shoe leather, that one—though seemed at loose ends, havin' no one to look after him. When he came down to our place asking me to tend you, I made him take a sweet potato pie and some bean stew. All my born days, never seen that man smile like he did! Never seen him smile period, come to think of it."

Leola felt buffaloed, but not so much about the smile.

"Mr. Owen asked you to *take care* of me?"

"Sure he did. Seemed right desperate with worry too."

Leola couldn't comprehend her grandfather being worried about *anyone*, much less his errant oldest granddaughter.

"Hard-bit as your grandpappy is," Nancy added, p'rhaps sensing her confusion, "there's good in him as in every person. Columbus showed himself a friend to us when another man tried to cheat Daddy out of his land years ago. Loaned us the money to pay back taxes so there'd be no question it were ours. No reason to do that 'cept *somethin'* right, deep in his character."

Leola could barely digest this revelation before Mrs. Gumbs went on.

"Far's townsfolk go, not much news has traveled the road of late. All's I know 'bout is Opal Suggs and *that* I learned the hard way. Girl came banging down my door one day like a banshee at the gates of Hell. Thought she'd accuse me of witchery or some such nonsense."

She let out a dry laugh. "Yet here she was, hauling a rabbit she'd kill't and skinned, begging for my asafetida remedy, saying both brothers were ill and her Mam's consumption worse."

Mrs. Gumbs wagged her head.

"'Course I couldn't let those children suffer. That Jimmy, for all he was a Suggs, had the face of an angel and a sweet disposition too. Rest his soul."

Leola was on the edge of her seat.

"So, Jimmy . . . he *died*?"

The mournful expression on Mrs. Gumbs's face was her answer.

"Gad night!" Leola pictured Jimmy's dirty little feet, the impish smile belying the hunger in his eyes. "Reckon his mam even noticed he was gone?"

Nancy Gumbs shrugged as if answering would put too fine a point on the matter.

This made Leola more worried of Ship, even as she consoled herself with the fact her friend was hardly a Suggs. If she'd fallen ill, Mary would get the best of care—a personal nurse, proper medicines, nourishing food. When Joe came tomorrow, he'd tell her Ship was good as ever. Might even bring a telegram from Mrs. Grimes or, dare she hope, word from Papa himself.

Leola inhaled, testing her lungs.

"You needn't come by so often, Mrs. Gumbs. You got your own business and your father to attend and I'm getting stronger by the minute."

Mrs. Gumbs frowned.

"Don't like leavin' you high and dry, and no one to help you mind those young'uns."

"It's because of you I'll be fine at all. And as for my sisters—Auntie's only down the road and the girls are good helpers when they put their minds to it."

Leola glanced at the floor, shamefaced.

"You said you refused Mr. Owen's money but it'd vex me not to pay you. I don't have much cash on hand. Mr. McGee still owes me wages and . . ."

"Wouldn't take your pay, no how." Mrs. Gumbs folded her arms. "Your mama was a lifelong friend and my salvation when one of my girls got hurt long ago."

"Girls?" Leola frowned. "I thought Neely was your only daughter."

"Is now. 'Twas Neely's twin, Bethune, who fell into the crick one summer's day."

She gazed at the wall as if watching the memory play out before her.

"I had to put everything into tending that child—by the time we fished her out'n the water, there weren't much else she could do but breathe. And then," she stared into her teacup, "not even that."

Leola was tilting so far forward she nearly fell from the chair.

"Mrs. Gumbs . . . I'd no idea."

"No reason you would. You couldn't even walk when it happened. Would'a been a sight harder on me if your mama hadn't taken Neely in, 'spite of what some folks were saying, how it weren't proper for a white woman to do." She paused. "Two long months, Orlena kept that child and with a babe of her own to mind. Never complained neither—least not to me."

Leola had no recollection of Neely living with them but envisioned her proud, careworn mother making room for another child when it went against her own sentiments and that of most others she knew. Without warning, grief crashed over her, cold and solid as an ocean wave.

"I miss my mama!" she wailed.

"'Course you do, child." Mrs. Gumbs pulled up her chair, taking Leola's hand. "You loved her and she loved you, too, with all her heart. Ain't no loss worse, for our mothers understand us better'n anyone else ever will."

Leola thought this was right. Close as she'd always felt to Papa, she'd shared a special bond with Mama, maybe from all those years it was just the two of them before Mae and Karla arrived. Or because they both belonged to the Society of Womanhood with its various tribulations and rewards. Whatever the case, Leola felt she'd been cut loose from the sturdiest mooring and set afloat, with no guarantee of finding shore.

As she fought a new surge of tears, Nancy Gumbs knelt, embracing her.

"You go on, feel what you feel," she said. "I was a mite when my own mother died. Folk s'posed it unhealthy for a child to mourn, tellin' me all the time to quit carryin' on! That loss haunts me still and most like, that's why." She stroked Leola's hair. "Best get it out now. You'll need to bear your own grief *and* your sisters' when they return."

Leola took Nancy up on the offer, sobbing away the roughest edges of her woe, sure its barbs would grow sharp again in the coming days, yet glad for what consolation she could find.

Later, as Nancy got ready to leave, Leola finally convinced her to take a half-side of bacon, the floral dress Mama had made for herself a year ago but barely got to wear, and nearly all their fresh eggs. In the end, seemed meager reward for one who'd snatched you from Death's door.

CHAPTER 27

Next day, when the girls returned from Auntie's, Leola was glad she'd taken Mrs. Gumbs's advice and shed some of her sorrow ahead of time. Mae and Karla asked endless questions about Mama's death and current whereabouts: Had she felt pain? Would she ever come back? Was she merely sleeping, as some fool friend of Auntie's had suggested, in which case, how would she escape her coffin on Judgment Day? At least Leola felt calm enough to give the girls assurance, however uncertain she felt of it herself.

By the time Joe arrived that evening, bringing a bouquet of dried roses for Leola and a bag of peppermints for her sisters, Mae and Karla seemed so much happier, Leola held back from asking him right away for news of Papa or Ship.

At supper, the girls bolted the pinto bean casserole Auntie had dropped off, chattering endlessly of her new kitten, how Mae had taught her little sister to "read," their plans to make a quilt fort in their bedroom. It wasn't 'til afterwards, as she watched them ride Joe piggyback, that Leola noticed a sag to his shoulders and pouches under his eyes made him seem as if he'd aged years. No doubt he'd borne plenty of burdens lately, worrying not only about Leola but his own family too—all of whom had blessedly survived—and taking up the slack for others laid low.

Finally, supper was over and the girls put to bed. Leola had set aside the last cleaned dish, ready to pose her inquiries, when Joe pulled up Mama's sewing chair.

"Sit down, Rosie Rose," he commanded, his tone so morose, her heart leapt into her mouth.

He knelt as Mrs. Gumbs had, taking Leola's hand.

"You've been through so much, I dread telling you this . . ."

A brutal knowingness ripped through her.

"It's Ship, isn't it?"

When Joe nodded, Leola hunched forward, shielding herself from the same pummeling grief she'd experienced the previous afternoon.

"Mary died four days ago," Joe whispered, holding her close. "Blanton says she spoke of how she loved you, how worried she was of your health. When he told her you'd come through the worst of it, Ship seemed to rest easier." He swallowed. "And not long after, she got called Home."

Leola pressed her mouth against his chest, stifling her cries in case the girls should hear—which brought on such a fit of coughing, Joe had to make a fresh cup of Nancy's tea.

Once her spasms eased, Leola fell silent, remembering the last time she'd seen her friend, three weeks ago.

Mary had driven up to their door, begging Leola to accompany her to Longview, saying she'd *the most awful hankering for sweets.*

What about Laird's? Leola asked. *Seems a waste of fuel, going all the way to Longview for licorice sticks.*

Mary had tossed her head.

Laird's a fuddy-duddy. Spoke to him the other day, after he admonished a Black shopper for touching a bolt of fabric—never mind white customers were doing the very same thing! Told him I'd not frequent his place any longer if he didn't apologize to the lady. 'Course he wouldn't, and so, she'd flicked her eyes at Leola, *Longview, it is!*

Leola had grinned, jumping straight into Mary's car, never suspecting it would be their last adventure together, a thought that brought on such a fit of hacking, Joe had to thump her back this time to make it stop. Little did Leola realize but that cough would stay with her into the future, reminding her of Mary Shipley, best friend she'd ever had.

Early December 1919

CHAPTER 28

Leola's days were soon measured by the wants and needs of her sisters, starting at sunrise: *We need breakfast, Lee! Help us hook our shoes! Let us ride Violet, pleeeease!*

Nighttime didn't offer much relief, as the girls woke often from terrible dreams crying for Mama and Papa—tears that came harder when they realized there was only Leola to give them solace. No matter how they loved their sister, she wasn't their parent and no one would ever pretend as much.

Then came the dawn hours when some small noise—cows lowing or chickens stirring in the coop—awakened Leola and, more than the sweetness of sleep, she'd savor that singular moment of *being unnecessary.* 'Course the idle solitude always filled with the mourning she'd no time for otherwise—for Mama and Ship, the future she'd planned.

And always there was the question of Papa, whether he was alive or dead, if she'd ever get to mourn him outright. As each day passed, their scheme to discover his fate felt less and less possible. With Dell Meeker gone, Dora and Cliff were overwhelmed, salvaging what remained of their family and keeping up their farm too. Dora wasn't even sure whether Murl was still in Houston, for they hadn't heard from him during the last round of quarantine. Leola considered telegraphing Mrs. Grimes again, finding the address for the Houston coroner, but never had the time or wherewithal to do any of it.

Mr. Owen came by often, mucking the stalls and checking on the water barrels, but Leola spoke to him only when necessary, fearing her scorn would show too clearly. Though grateful he'd sent Nancy Gumbs to her aid, Leola still blamed the man for her family's demise, yet also feared his power over their fates, believing each day they remained on the farm meant they might stay forever. Hard as it would be to raise Mae and Karla herself—under her grandfather's pitiless gaze—this seemed better than going to an orphanage and leaving it to strangers.

At least the girls were of an age when they could forget themselves sometimes in play or pretending, and Leola soaked in their laughter like sunshine after weeks of rain.

Mae had taken a fancy lately to a chicken Mama bought years earlier, named Clarice. The bird had been a pretty thing once, with red-and-white feathers, and laid small speckled eggs—at least before she'd grown too old for laying. Now one of her legs was withered, making her stagger like a sot, and her eyes were filmy with cataracts. Not that Mae cared, for she treated Clarice as a child, dressing her in a baby bonnet, pulling her about in a rickety wooden doll cart. Was only a matter of time before the girl began begging for Clarice to sleep indoors, though Leola refused, imagining what Mama would say of such a practice—how the chicken would surely peck holes in the furniture, leaving filthy feathers everywhere.

On an unusually warm day, Leola decided to do laundry outdoors—always easier than hauling water into the kitchen. But before she could light a fire beneath their big black kettle, an ominous crash from the house sent her running, conjuring all manner of tragedies involving her sisters. Blasting herself for leaving them alone.

Inside she found Mae sprawled on the kitchen floor, the lard bucket upended, grease running every which'a way.

"Mae Ellis Rideout!" Leola had to grab a chair to keep from slipping. "What are you about? We borrowed that fat from Dora Meeker and can't pay her back 'til hog-killin' next spring!"

Mae rubbed her scraped knee.

"I din't mean it." She skated, too, as she stood. "Thought I saw a—a ant up there in the cabinet and was climbin' up to—to squash it."

Noting the open peanut butter jar lying nearby, Leola knew this was a fib. Blood boiling, she dragged the child across the room, leaving an oil slick in their wake.

"You don't act as a girl of eight," she seized the broomweed switch by the fireplace, "but like a baby with all her milk teeth. Pull up your dress and take the licking you deserve."

Even as Mae's eyes welled with tears, she obeyed, baring the tender place behind her shins. Meanwhile Karla, hiding in a corner, whimpered, "No, no, Lee! Noooo!" Her protests were in vain, for Leola had landed the lash hard upon its target.

Mae barely flinched, but as a pink welt rose on her skin, Leola gasped.

"Oh, my sweet girl!" She dropped the switch, gathering her sister close. "What the devil have I done?"

"There, there." Mae patted Leola's head, comforting *her*. "Don't fret. It din't hardly hurt at all. I'm a bad girl and you our mama now, who must make us behave even if it pains you *more*."

A strangled sound escaped Leola's throat. Mama and Papa used to say this, the rare times they'd punished their girls, yet she'd never quite believed it—until this instant.

"You aren't a bad girl," she explained, wiping her eyes, "only overdue for your dinner. For that I take blame. I shouldn't have got so mad. Will you forgive me?"

Mae didn't respond, staring into the distance. Forcing Leola's hand.

"I was thinking," she blurted, "after we get this mess cleaned up, let's invite Clarice to keep us company tonight. It's chilly outside. We don't want her pretty feathers to freeze, do we?"

Which was how the chicken had become another member of their little family, with more or less full run—or *waddle*—of the house, sleeping in their bedroom every night . . . until Mr. Owen found out and took matters into his own hands.

One afternoon, as Leola helped him unload coal for their stove, he said, "McGee ain't buying my new foal for a few weeks, so this is all the fuel you'll have meantime. Need to make do with what victuals 'ya got too."

Leola did a mental inventory of their food supplies—a small side of ham, whatever eggs the chickens might lay, p'rhaps ten jars of vegetables, some cornmeal. Seemed they *would* go hungry if they weren't careful—a thought that made her stomach clench like she was starving already.

Then Mae appeared at the door, Clarice limping faithfully behind her, and Leola couldn't help smiling—though Mr. Owen failed to find equal humor in the situation.

"That bird belongs in the henhouse," he muttered, and Leola's pulse quickened.

"It's Clarice, sir. Mae's made her a pet."

Mr. Owen, stroking his beard, glared at the animal.

"Biddy's seen her best days." He started down the steps. "We'll add her to the pot for Sunday supper."

"Leeeee?" Mae wailed. "Don't let him kill my baby!"

"Mr. Owen!" Leola leapt off the porch. "Wait!"

The man turned. "Cain't be burning daylight, girl. Got to get to town."

"Sir." She was panting almost too hard to talk. "That chicken is Mae's dearest chum. There are others we can eat—like the brown one, who's bound to have more meat on her than scrawny old Clarice and . . ."

"The brown hen's still layin'," he interrupted. "She can give us more eggs for eating and earnin' than will far exceed one meal, and you know it. Ain't right to keep an animal in such a condition and y'all goin' hungry. Best make a meal of her before she wanders off to rot in some field."

Leola looked at her sister, sitting on the porch with Clarice in her lap, tears streaming her face.

"Mae's so young, sir, and has lost so much. She loves that chicken." She clutched his sleeve. "Don't let's take that from her."

The old man stepped so close, she caught a whiff of Mrs. Gumbs's camphor salve, which he used for his rheumatism.

"Reckon you should be aware, Granddaughter, that we're in a fix. Without your mama's sewing and your father's—well, what piddlin' earnings *he* ever made when he was whole—I'm barely scraping by on this place. Soon's I can, I'll sell this farm and move to my sister's in Alabama. Meantime, I've made arrangements with the Texas State Children's Home in Waxahachie to take you and your sisters. It's Methodist but the only decent place in Texas with room for the three of y'all." He expectorated into the grass. "You leave right after Christmas."

Leola reeled with shock. Mr. Owen was shipping them, not to the Baptist home as Mama had wanted, but a Methodist one far away—in a matter of weeks!

"I'll come early on Sunday to dispatch of the hen." Mr. Owen began walking again. "Make sure that sister of yours is otherwise engaged."

As Leola watched him go, Clarice let out a harsh squawk like, *Whywhy? Whywhy?* and she wanted to holler to the heavens above the exact same question.

◆

That evening, Leola felt hard-pressed to break the news of the orphanage to her sisters, though it had to be done. Of course Karla understood little, only wanting reassurance that her sisters would stay with her. It was Mae, grappling with Clarice's impending demise, who could not be consoled.

"If Papa were here, he wouldn't let Mr. Owen kill Clarice *or* send us away!" she said, leaving Clarice in her bed to crawl beneath Leola's covers. "He'd fight him and you oughtta too."

Leola gathered the girl closer, noting the sharp edge of ribs along her side.

"I reckon Mr. Owen never had a pet and doesn't understand how you love Clarice. Don't forget: Mama always warned we shouldn't get too attached to our farm animals, put on this earth to serve our human needs, like it says in the Bible."

Mae pulled a face. "The Bible says some folks are meant to be slaves too, Lee, and that ladies are lesser than men. You said that's only some people turning an old story inside out to feel better 'bout treatin' others wrong."

Leola was surprised—and also ashamed—that her sister was smart enough to see through her bumbling excuses.

"You have a feeling for all creatures, that's certain." She smoothed hair from Mae's forehead. "But Clarice cannot come to the orphanage."

"I don't want to go to some stinky orphanage!" Mae's cheeks

flashed bright. "Why can't we stay here with Auntie? I'd be a good girl and make supper every night and not be scar't even of her mean-est geeses!"

Leola sat up, taking the girl's hand.

"Auntie would love for us to stay with her, except she's a spinster with little means, getting older by the day." She exhaled. "Besides, the orphanage isn't a bad place. Auntie's heard it's run by nice folk, and that the schools in Waxahachie are much better than ours too. Most important, we'll be together and . . ."

Mae glared at her. "What if Papa comes back and we're not here?"

Leola had considered this a few times and had a ready response.

"If—when—Papa returns, Auntie'll be around and Mrs. Meeker and others. They'll tell him where we are."

The child flipped over, facing the wall.

"I hope when Mr. Owen tries to catch Clarice tomorrow, she pecks out his eyes. That man ain't nothin' but a ol' jackass!"

Leola flinched. "That's an ugly thing to say! Where did you . . . ?"

She left her question unfinished, remembering that Joe had vis-ited the afternoon of Mr. Owen's announcement, bringing a meat pie from Fiona. Sitting on the front porch together, Leola had battled tears, confiding her grandfather's plans.

Why, that ol' jackass! Joe had hissed—just as a sneeze erupted from behind the wood pile, signifying Mae had been hiding there all along.

Leola got up, pulling a newspaper-wrapped package from beneath her bed.

"I'd planned to give you this at Christmas," she said, handing it to the girl. "But now seems as good a time as any."

Mae tore off the paper, face filling with joy.

"Bettie!"

Leola put a finger to her lips, not wanting Karla to wake, though Mae could barely contain herself.

"And—and she is wearing a new yellow dress like the one Mama made me before she passed."

Leola sighed, glad the doll had served as distraction again and that the blasted hours she'd spent sewing the twin dress had paid off too.

"Bettie's fully yours, Mae. You can give her the kind of coddling I've no time for anymore."

Mae lowered to the bed, clutching her baby.

"I love my present," she said, tone turning defiant again. "But ain't no one gonna make me eat a single bite of Clarice after she's cooked. And when Papa comes home, I'm gonna tell him what a jackass Mr. Owen's been and he'll set 'im straight, throw him on the ground and step on his hands, like he did before. Don't you think?"

Leola tried to smile. "I reckon it's what Mr. Owen deserves, Sister."

Pulling the sheet to Mae's chin, all she could think was, *If Papa ever comes home.*

CHAPTER 29

On Friday afternoon, without asking permission, Leola rode Mr. Owen's nag to Laird's store, trading three of Mama's lace collars for sugar, flour, and what puny apples were left in the bin—hoping to appease Mae's grief with an apple fool, her favorite dessert.

Next she headed toward the Shipley's grafting shed, where she knew she'd find Joe. Along the way her heart ached to see so many landmarks of her friendship with Ship—the withered gladiola fronds, the rope swing they'd played on as children, the verandah where they'd confided their fondest dreams. She didn't need to knock on the door to know the house was empty; Mrs. Shipley had been committed to the asylum over in Longview and Blanton spent every spare minute by her side. Was almost shameful, the relief Leola felt, having an excuse not to visit. After all, what consolation could she offer, having survived when their daughter hadn't?

As she stepped inside the shed, Joe—wrapping gauze around a newly made rosebush—glanced up, and Leola's spirits lifted, thinking him even handsomer in concentration, cheekbones sharpened by the lamp's shadow, eyes bright with purpose. Still, she stayed quiet, for he'd told her grafting was tricky business, especially right after the bud got attached to the rootstock.

Finally, he stepped back to examine his work.

"B'lieve this surgery's a success, Lee! After some bedrest, our patient will be better than ever and making baby roses by the dozen." He peered at her. "And you're a pale and tired-looking rose if ever there was one! You been running yourself ragged, 'spite of Doc's orders?"

His caring tone was all it took for Leola's unspent emotions to burst forth. When he'd visited the other day, she hadn't felt free to fully express her despair—not with the girls so near—but now the floodgates opened. After he led her to a bench along the wall, Leola cried as she hadn't in weeks, wailing of how she missed Mama and Papa and Ship, how tired she was of caring for her sisters yet how she dreaded the orphanage even more.

Wrapping an arm around her shoulders, Joe said, "It seems so daunting. But I do have something good to report, something that could throw cold water over all your grandfather's dag-blame plans."

Leola daubed her eyes with a handkerchief, listening.

"There's a lawyer, Morris Bromberg, in Jefferson. Been a friend of my family's forever. Wrote him recently asking what rights you and your sisters have in this matter. I got his return letter this morning, sayin' the courts will sometimes honor the deathbed wishes of a parent and, as next of kin, you do have some claim to your folks' property. If your grandfather don't abide these rights, Morris said there'd be a long legal battle. Would cost Mr. Owen a pretty penny."

Leola shoved the hankie into her pocket.

"And us, too, no doubt. Pretty pennies we don't have. Besides, we're leaving in less than a week. How would all this happen before then?"

"Morris is the most righteous fellow you've ever met, Lee. Claims he owes my father for all the business he's given him down the years and would consider takin' your case free of charge. Meantime y'all could stay down at your great-aunt's house 'til it's settled."

Leola envisioned traveling the thirteen miles to the courthouse every day, presenting her private grievances in such a public manner. Imagined the spectacle it could bring upon her family when they'd already had so much. Wore her out even to consider.

"It's right kind of you, Joe—and your friend—but Papa might show up still, making all that beside the point." She touched his beard-roughened cheek. "Still I'm a lucky girl to have a champion like you."

Sealing her gratitude with a kiss, she invited him to the Sacrificing of Clarice—which he accepted, saying it'd be a solemn occasion but at least they could be solemn together.

CHAPTER 30

Auntie came over on Saturday afternoon, bringing a basket of apples from her own root cellar to add to the measly ones Leola had bought. They'd decided not only to make the fool for Sunday's dinner but also some traditional apple pies—for no other good reason than they wanted to.

As she was poking around the cabinets, Auntie mused, "Reckon Big Leola's ol' peeler doodad would be helpful 'bout now."

"It's out in Papa's shed, remember?" Leola replied, and Auntie smacked herself on the forehead.

"Land's sake, girl! I'm an oaf to remind you of your papa when you're feeling low to begin with."

Leola knew the woman forgot things often lately and didn't mean ill.

"It's all right." She handed Auntie a paring knife. "Isn't every day that a kitchen tool gets turned into a substitute arm."

'Course Auntie *was* right, in a way. Leola *had* avoided Papa's workshop all these months, unable to bear thinking about him more than she had to, wondering what had become of him, whether he was even alive.

"Wish I could take the whittling machine with me," she murmured, "in case my father ever needs it."

She contemplated the familiar objects surrounding her, some of which had traveled over roiling oceans and rough woodland trails, whose stories she knew by rote. There was the pestle and mortar her Scottish great-grandfather had carved from walnut wood, the tightly coiled basket fashioned by a distant Cherokee cousin, a tiny canvas of bluebonnets painted by Big Leola. Though she'd been taught material possessions meant nothing to the soul, Leola wondered if they might be the only things left, in the end, to show someone had even existed.

"Mr. Owen said we have to sell nearly everything," she said, quietly, "to pay our upkeep at the orphanage. But what about Papa's rocker and Mama's sewing machine and this very bowl, which her sister gave them for a wedding present?"

She wrestled the sorrow from her voice, mindful the girls were in the next room.

"Joe's lawyer friend said we've a right to them, yet there's no time to get a case up and go to court. What if Mr. Owen dispatches of our belongings before anyone can stop him?"

Auntie put down her knife, rushing to embrace Leola.

"If I have to steal into this place 'midst of night, I will salvage what I can. No doubt Joe will find a place to keep everything safe until you can claim them. Don't fret over that, not when you've so much else to think about."

Leola rested her head on Auntie's bony shoulder.

"How I will ever thank you," she whispered, "for bein' such a help to our family all these years?"

"Thank me?" The woman stepped back. "You and your sisters are like my own children. Your parents been nothin' except kind to me since my sister died, despite the bad dealings 'tween Columbus Owen and myself."

Leola laughed. "I hardly think anyone blames you for any ill will toward *that* ol' crank."

"True enough." Auntie took up her knife again, peeling an apple in one continuous stroke. "Even when Columbus Owen was a'courtin' my sister, he were ugly to me—my folks too."

She handed a twisty bit of peel to Leola, then took a bite of her own.

"I had a beau once name of Marcus Smith. Nicest person you'd ever meet. Worked as a stair-and-sash builder, could fix anything." Her eyebrows arched. "Handsome too! Somewhat like your Joe, though 'twas half-Comanche blood gave Marcus his high coloring and striking features."

She stared out the window as if Marcus Smith was striding across the yard that very moment.

"Marcus had a younger brother, Roscoe, afflicted with a wasting disease would not let him use his muscles proper. Didn't matter, for he was the sweetest, smartest person and Marcus loved him beyond belief. Was hard to understand Roscoe's words sometimes yet he had a way about him, noticed things the rest of us didn't." She grinned. "Funny as a jack'o knaves, too, found humor in the direst situations."

Her voice turned gruff.

"One night my mother and I laid out a fine meal. Invited Marcus and Roscoe and, 'course, Columbus Owen. We'd reservations about my sister's beau by then but couldn't leave him out or Sissy would've pitched a fit.

"Moment we sat down that night, Columbus started mockin' Roscoe, mimicking how he moved. Made the boy's affliction seem shameful right in front of him!" Her eyes sparked like the hurt had just happened. "Was so dreadful, I can hardly say."

She picked up the cinnamon jar, staring at its powdery contents as if seeking comfort there.

"Marcus quit town not long afterward. Took his brother with

him. Left a note on my porch sayin' much as he loved me, he couldn't imagine sitting across from Columbus at family meals—which he'd have to if we married. Said he couldn't put Roscoe in harm's way like that."

Auntie set down the jar, tossing her head of snow-white curls.

"Let me tell you, I marched straight to Columbus's place. Told him what Marcus had said." Her mouth rippled. "You know what he answered?"

Of course Leola did not know, but was too riveted by the story to say as much.

"*I did you a favor, Malvina,* said he. *There's tainted blood in that Smith line, passed down from those savage kin'a theirs. You wouldn'a wanted a little id'jut child pollutin' the Hughes lineage, would ya?* Then, I swan, the man laughed!"

Leola exhaled. "That takes the rag off the bush, even for Mr. Owen."

Auntie stared at her shoes.

"Couldn't for the life of me cotton what my sister ever saw in that man. Your grandma was a pretty thing, bright as a new penny. Hardworking too. I always wondered if she settled on him 'cuz she weren't treated right by my own pappy as a child and believed it was what she deserved."

Leola had few memories of her grandmother but didn't recall her ever speaking up to her husband, no matter how obstreperous the man acted.

"I'm so sorry about Marcus," she said. "Ever hear what became of him?"

Auntie, dipping a cup into the flour canister, fell briefly quiet.

"He wrote me once saying he'd settled in Minnie-sota—St. Paul, I b'lieve—helping to build mansions for those rich Swedes. Said the cold weather seemed to help Roscoe's condition, that he attended a school for folks like him. Learn't himself how to paint," she pointed at her mouth, "holdin' a brush in his teeth."

She added the flour to her bowl, mixing until a soft dough formed.

"Later I heard Marcus married a sturdy farm girl. Had himself a wagonload of kids." She rolled out her crust with a few forceful strokes. "Think he passed not long ago."

"Oh, Auntie!" Leola was so upset, she knocked some apple slices onto the floor. "That's a tragedy beyond what anyone should endure."

"No matter, child." Auntie bent to retrieve the scattered fruit, then dipped them in the water barrel. "What's past is past. I've led a good life 'spite of all that—p'rhaps a longer one than if I'd bred children and worked myself to a nub caring for 'em. And soon Columbus Owen will be part of my past too."

"I'm glad for that." Leola threw the salvaged apples into her roasting pan. "Yet I wonder if Mae will ever forgive the man. She's beside herself at the idea of him killing Clarice." Tears clouded her vision. "Makes me mad as all get-out."

Auntie pinched the dough along the pie plate's rim.

"And whatever meat that old biddy possesses," she mused, "will be like chewin' fiddle strings anyhow."

Sliding her pan into the oven, Leola had such a sudden brainstorm, she burnt her hand on the metal door.

"Didn't you say one of your geese is on her last legs?" She slathered butter on the wound, too excited to feel the pain. "What if we hid Clarice before Mr. Owen gets here tomorrow? We could tell him she escaped, so we decided to roast your goose in her stead. I appreciate it's asking a lot, but poor Mae, if only you could see how she . . ."

Auntie set her pie next to Leola's apples, latching the oven with a decided gesture. "No need explaining. That man brought nothin' but heartbreak to this family. I'd be more'n happy to even the score however I can. Besides, that ol' goose is Columbus Owen's equal in temperament. Nearly pecked the feathers off my best pillow-maker, other day! I'd be glad to find a better use for her."

She licked cinnamon sugar from her fingers.

"When we're done here, let's tell Mae. We can bring Clarice down to my place this afternoon, keep her in my potting shed, safe from the cats. Meanwhile, I'll wring the goose's neck and you can carry her back with you to roast in the morning."

Now it was Leola's turn to do the hugging.

"I don't care how pleasing that northern farm girl was, Auntie! I'll bet Marcus never stopped regretting the day he let you go."

Malvina Hughes smiled best she could, for she knew the feeling all too well.

❦

Next day, when Leola described Clarice's daring escape, Mr. Owen seemed ready to protest—until he smelled the sizzle of goose fat wafting from the kitchen and only muttered about *parents who don't raise their children right*. Mae, meanwhile, snuck furtive glances at her grandfather, barely disguising the glee she'd expressed yesterday when Leola and Auntie first confided their plan.

Once it was time for supper, Leola didn't ask Mr. Owen to lead the blessing, as was custom, inviting Auntie to do so instead.

"Dearest Lord in Heaven," she began, "thank you for this food in the service of our bodies, that we might achieve whatever good deeds we can. Thank you, too, for Mae and Karla, so full with your hope and promise, and men like Joe, with fair and kind hearts. Thank you, oh Lord, for my great-niece, Leola, who works hard at holding this family together despite all efforts to tear it apart."

She let the words sink in.

"Lord, we pray no harm has come to the father of these worthy children, that he will find his way back to them post-haste. Meantime keep them safe on their coming journey, see they're treated proper at the orphanage and forgive those who could not or *would not* take care of them here, where they belong."

Leola peeked through her lashes to find Mr. Owen staring at his sister-in-law with consternation, except Auntie didn't seem to notice.

"Heavenly Father," she continued, "send your loving goodness into the spirits of the wicked and cruel lest they burn in the bowels of Hell forever."

The chorus of *Amens* that went up—from five out of six of them—was loud enough to rival Gabriel's horn. Only Mr. Owen failed to answer in kind, spearing a slab of goose from the nearby platter and stuffing it into his mouth.

Chapter 31

It took all Leola's mettle to get through the Christmas holiday, recognizing it'd be her last time with Joe and Auntie for a while. At least there'd be no chance of Mr. Owen spoiling this occasion since Malvina, as host, had full rights to leave him out. Which of course she did.

On Christmas Eve, Leola and Auntie shopped at Laird's, buying plump oranges and hair ribbons for both girls, and a sketch pad and coloring pencils for Karla. Though Mae had already received Bettie as her gift, Leola couldn't resist the tiny comb and brush set she found on a shelf, perfect for grooming the doll's silky hair. She also spied a pair of enamel collar buttons that would suit Joe perfectly—except they cost fifty cents and she only had a nickel left of spending money.

"Go on, child." Auntie pressed the additional coins into Leola's palm. "There's nothin' would bring me more pleasure than imagining that handsome young man, spiffing up for a visit to Waxahachie and these baubles as the finishing touch."

That night they feasted on most of the Rideouts' remaining food stores—ham, stewed tomatoes, and cornbread—before gathering 'round the candlelit pine tree Joe had dragged from the woods earlier. As the girls peeled their oranges, the tangy fragrance, along with the scents of pine needles and beeswax, reminded Leola of Christmases past—a past that already felt cobwebbed and misty, as if she were an aged woman revisiting it from some distant future.

At one point, Leola urged Auntie to open her own gifts, which included some pretty hankies Leola had embroidered herself, as well as a carving by Papa that resembled one of her great-aunt's three cats.

"Land's sakes," the woman murmured. "Your dad's sure got the artist's touch." She showed the figure to Mae and Karla. "What do you think? Ain't she the spitting image of my Lilac?"

Mae took the carving, stroking its head.

"When Papa fetches us at the orphanage, I reckon he'll make Daisy and Marigold, too, with his whittlin' arm."

Leola, wanting to kick herself for choosing such a gift, was glad when Auntie offered distraction, handing her a scrolled paper tied with red ribbon.

"Wish I'd given your mama this when she asked, way back," she said.

It was the famous trifle recipe, which Auntie had copied in a fine hand, illustrating the margins with berry-dotted mayhaw bushes and flapping geese, along with blue-and-red circles to mimic Mama's wedding ring quilt.

"Orlena always teased me," Auntie said, as Leola skimmed the instructions, "claiming I left out certain ingredients on purpose, but everything's in there. All's you gotta do is follow along—though you'll probably want to embellish it, make it your own, over time."

Leola felt her throat constrict.

"I'll only ever make it as it says here." She took Auntie's hand. "And every time think of," her voice broke, "you."

Blinking back tears, both women watched as Joe distributed his own gifts: paper dolls for the girls, a new paring knife for Auntie, and, for Leola, a gold-plated Wilrite fountain pen with matching case.

"This must'a cost you a week's wages or more!" she marveled, and Joe's cheeks flushed.

"It'll prove to those city slickers in Waxahachie that country girls aren't just smart as them, but stylish too," he said.

Treading the edge of emotion again, she offered him her gift.

"Same color as your eyes," Joe marveled, seeing the collar buttons.

They might have kissed then and there—except Mae ran to get the bakery box he'd brought in earlier.

"Open it!" she insisted, and Joe broke the string, revealing a squat Bundt cake snowy with powdered sugar.

"This, ladies, is *panforte*, a traditional holiday treat in Italy. My father carries it in his store every *Natale*."

He cut the first slice, exposing the cake's dark, nut-packed center.

"Panforte means *strong bread*, as it's helped Italians survive countless sieges and perilous journeys over time." He passed a piece to Leola. "Nowadays we eat it to celebrate our own survival and also," he winked at the girls, "'cause it's plain ol' delicious."

Digging in, they all exclaimed over the cake's chewy sweetness, which reminded them of the traditional Texas fruitcake Dora Meeker normally brought them, but hadn't managed to make this year.

For hours afterward, their family lingered around the fire, singing carols, pretending it was a regular Christmas Eve—that Mama and Papa were only down the road visiting neighbors, due to return any minute. That all really was calm and bright.

CHAPTER 32

The next day, with the girls at Auntie's, Leola decided to scrub the house, as if to assure it—and herself—they'd be coming back, despite suspecting otherwise.

Dusting the shelves, she took comfort in the plan she'd made with Auntie and Joe to save some of their possessions. Tomorrow, after Mr. Owen fetched the girls for the train station, Joe would load a portion of their belongings into the company truck. Some he'd deliver to certain friends—Mama's dress patterns to Dora Meeker, Papa's tools to Cliff, their best pots and canning jars to Nancy Gumbs—and the rest he'd store in the Shipley's unused barn.

Leola picked up her parents' wedding portrait from the mantel. There was Papa, handsome in dark suit and vest and Mama, in a cream gown with puffed sleeves, tendrils of hair framing her oval face. For the first time, Leola noted the odd array of jewelry her mother was wearing: a bracelet with dangling locket, a long string of beads, and, pinned over her left breast, a pocket watch, as if she couldn't decide which looked best so wore them all.

Leola thought how young her parents had been; how in that instant, they never could've imagined the disappointments to come nor the too sudden, too soon separation between them.

Not wanting to leave the portrait behind, she brought it into her bedroom to pack. Each sister was allowed only one piece of luggage and Leola's valise already bulged. It was only by refolding a dress, rolling Francis Pig inside a pair of stockings, and shifting around her baptismal Bible that she finally made room, with just enough space for last-minute additions—the shift she currently wore, some under-things drying beside the stove, the new black flats she'd traded with Mr. Laird for their last jars of vegetables.

Returning to the parlor, Leola was picking up her mop when there came a pounding at the door. She flung it open and Joe stumbled inside, bringing the cold air that heralded a blue norther, winter's first real arrival.

"Weren't you coming tonight, for supper?" Leola said, as he hung his hat on a peg.

"Couldn't wait that long." He took a breath. "I've a surprise for you."

Seeing her wary expression, he laughed, kissing her forehead with wind-chafed lips.

"A good surprise, for once."

She beckoned him into the kitchen. "Shall I warm up some coffee then?"

"Don't bother with that." Joe sat, patting the chair beside him. "Let me unburden myself before I explode like a jam-tin grenade."

Leola had hardly lowered down before he blurted: "Blanton's put me in charge of the day-to-day business!" He thrust out his chest. "Miss Rideout, meet the junior vice-president of Shipley-Belfigli Rose Growers!"

She grasped his hand. "That is good news! When did you find out?"

"Couple hours ago. And there's more! Blanton says we'll be moving the entire operation to Tyler, meaning you and I will be nearer each other—at least a little nearer."

Beneath her delight, Leola felt a tug of unease, thinking this opportunity had arisen from the loss of Ship and the ruin of her friend's family. She'd almost prefer Mary Shipley in the world and Joe, still an up-and-comer, dirtying his hands in the fields. But she didn't have that choice. Ship was gone and Joe was crackerjack at what he did, had worked like a dog and deserved recognition.

"Blanton's lucky," she said, "to have you in charge—someone he can trust to keep the company going and make it better in the meantime."

Joe's face turned serious.

"Won't be easy. Blanton wants to plant twenty thousand bushes *per acre* next year, meaning we'll have to build the new greenhouses by March. Which is why—and this is the best part—he's doubled my salary, with further advances if our profits keep improving. And that means . . ."

He dug a clamshell-shaped box from his pocket.

". . . we can be married, sooner than we'd hoped."

Joe lifted the lid, revealing a thin gold band studded with turquoise chips.

"It's lovely," Leola murmured, taking the box but not removing the ring.

"If we get married," he rushed on, "you won't have to stay in the orphanage so long. We can take care of your sisters." His eyebrows did a little dance. "Even have a baby of our own."

"Except my plans for college, Joe." She peered at him. "Auntie heard the high school in Waxahachie is first-rate and sends plenty'a girls to university these days. No college will accept me once I'm married, much less in the family way."

Joe's face was stony.

"I realize that's been your dream, but things have changed. You got your sisters to consider these days, not only yourself."

Leola set the box on the table.

"I'm not thinking only of myself. I'm thinking of their futures too. All our futures! Besides, no matter how improved your salary, it could hardly support three other souls—and a baby!"

Joe glared at her. "What about us? If you go to college after the orphanage, we'll be separated even longer."

"I don't have to go to North Texas. I could apply someplace more convenient, like Holcomb State. It's only ten miles from Tyler. I could visit my sisters and you, regular-like, and . . ."

Seeing his grim expression, her words trailed away.

"This is something I've wanted my whole life, Joe! Mama and Papa wanted it for me too. *Especially* Papa, who always regretted not getting his certificate, qualifying for better teaching positions. He might still have his arm were it not for that! He'd be—*will be*—happy that I won't be held back."

"Your papa should'a considered how *held back* you'd be," Joe sniffed, "before he took off like he did."

Leola let out a disbelieving laugh.

"*Took off*? You make it sound like my father purposely left us. Like he *abandoned* us."

The coldness in Joe's eyes melted.

"It's not that. It's only . . . haven't you thought if your father was dead, you would've heard by now? And if he was alive, why wouldn't he have written?"

Leola felt her cheeks go hot. Such ideas had entered her mind—of course they had—but she'd denied them as a farmer might deny early signs of crop blight, refusing to admit he was through.

"I can only imagine why Papa mightn't have sent word yet. If he was hurt in that saloon fracas, his injuries might'a prevented him from it. Or maybe the epidemic got in the way. Remember how

the telegraph offices struggled to do business with so many oper-
ators taken ill? I heard messages are still piled high, waiting to be
delivered."

Joe clenched his jaw.

"Men take French leave all the time, Leola. Desert their wives and
families, never come back. It's shameful—I'd never do such a thing—
yet there it is. There's the truth you ought to consider."

She stood so fast, her chair tipped over.

"You do not know my father! He loved—*loves*—us and would
never forsake us for another woman. Or for anything!"

This seemed to jolt Joe back to himself and he rushed to scoop
her in his arms—though she stepped out of reach before he could,
refusing his embrace.

"I am the blamest fool this side'a Friday." Joe rubbed his forehead.
"It's only that I feel so helpless. Can't help thinking that if your father
is dead, grieving him outright would be better than pining for him
and always bein' disappointed." He gazed into her eyes. "But you're
right. If there was a father who loved his children more, I've never
met him. Frank wouldn't have left y'all high and dry, not without
good reason."

Realizing he meant what he said, Leola finally leaned against
him.

"How will we stand it, being apart?" she asked, after a minute.
"Reckon I might find some college willing to bend the rules and allow
me to attend, even if I'm married? Then we could get hitched earlier
and all live together and . . ."

Joe touched her cheek.

"Let's see how it goes. We won't be separated for long, either
way. Besides, if you gave up your dreams too easy for me . . . well,
you wouldn't be my Rose o'Roses, would you?" He pushed hair

from her face. "Even if I have to wait 'til you're done with college, I will."

Leola gave him a shrewd smile. "And an occupation under my belt before our first child comes?"

Joe threw his head back, laughing.

"I swan, if all you had to trade at Laird's was a bucketful of air, you'd get top dollar. So since it's useless for me to argue with you and ever win, I'll save the effort for more important things."

As he leaned down to kiss her, Leola held him off again—not out of anger but so she could lead him to the parlor, where they might have some comfort in making their peace. They'd been so careful lately to avoid the judgment of Mr. Owen, whose largesse—however *un*-large it was—Leola and her sisters relied upon. But he'd relinquished that authority by sending them away, and who knew when she and Joe would be alone together again?

So she lay on the divan and pulled him down with her, surrendering to the wild rush of blood in her veins, the bliss of here-and-now, the certainty of *this* and *them,* nothing else in the world.

Ahem!

Joe and Leola sat bolt upright, gasping at the sight of Mr. Owen in the doorway.

"Sir!" Joe stood first, giving Leola a chance to button and tuck herself. "I—I was only just leavin'."

Mr. Owen's mouth twisted. "Reckon so, boy. My granddaughter got better things to do with her time than soil her reputation more'n it's already been."

"It's not true," Leola interjected, "that I have better things to do *or* that I am soiling my reputation. Joe and I were saying our goodbyes as couples do before a separation—a separation not of our making, that's for sure."

Joe shot her a warning look that made her recoil. Was he embarrassed she'd mentioned their mutual love? Angry she'd been impudent to Mr. Owen? Either possibility stung.

And now he retrieved his hat, in a sudden rush to be gone.

"Got to get back to town before the weather changes." Joe flicked his eyes at her. "Goodbye, Lee. I'll write soon."

Write soon? But hadn't they planned for a proper farewell later on? The lump in Leola's throat kept her from reminding him of this and, as he slipped out the door, the chill on her skin sunk all the way to her heart.

"Your behavior is unseemly, Leola." Mr. Owen drew nearer, his expression making her shiver once more. "They'll not abide such goings-on at the Home."

"As I said sir, I've done nothing untoward." She hesitated, forcing the next words from her throat. "I do beg forgiveness if you were offended." She picked up the mop and bucket. "But I have chores to finish a'fore the girls return. We'll want an early bedtime tonight."

She started for the kitchen, Mr. Owen's footsteps echoing behind her.

"Your mother did not like that boy," he said. "Thought he had peculiar manners and smells, and far too much impudence for his kind." He let out an acid laugh. "I reckon George Gumbs had twice as much sense, hightailin' it outta here 'fore he found himself on the wrong end of a shotgun barrel. That cross-back of yours ought to keep his head down too."

Leola speared the mop into the pail, whirling to face him.

"George should've never had to leave. This was his *home*, which he was only trying to make better. Likewise, Joe has no reason to be ashamed, having proven himself in both hard work and character." She lifted her head. "In spite of her prejudices, Mama came to think him a fine man. Gave us her blessing before she passed."

"Your mother weren't much to judge a man's character either way, I reckon."

Leola gritted her teeth, well aware what he was getting at.

"Whatever reason you do not like my father doesn't concern me. I understand the man Papa was—is."

"Oughtta concern you, girl," he grunted. "If your mama had chosen right, you and those little sisters of your'n would not be goin' to a charity-run institution tomorrow but a fine boarding school such as your late friend Mary Shipley attended."

Leola hated the sound of Ship's name on her grandfather's spiteful tongue. She started to tell him again that she had other matters to attend, but he'd already sunk himself into Papa's rocker in that same presuming manner as before.

"There were those considered it disgraceful," he said, staring out the window, "what happened between your mother and that doctor in Kilgore. At least when Orlena returned, tarnished as she was, the man tried to do right, offering her a house with lace curtains and running water, along with monthly income, for doin' nothing 'cept keeping her hair curled and toes up."

Leola flinched at his vulgar expression yet felt too rapt by this revelation of Mama's mysterious past to protest.

"'Course," Mr. Owen continued, "your papa came along then and Orlena got those lavish notions in her head, saying she would not be *a kept woman* but would marry for love."

His tone turned plaintive, like he was recounting past betrayal to a stranger.

"I could'a used the land the doctor offered me if Orlie had gone along. Could'a used my daughter taken care of, one less soul to support. Weren't just the soil on that land that was black, either. Oil were found there, some ten year ago! Sweet deposit producing twenty-two gallons a day." His fists curled on his lap. "And more discovered after that."

Leola shook herself.

"My mother had to live her ideals. She would never have felt right using someone for his money. And my father—weren't his fault he fell in love with Mama and she, him."

"P'rhaps not." Mr. Owen's expression turned dark again. "It *were* his fault though that she had to work her fingers to the bone all those years—even more so after he ran off. If she'd not been so worn down when the influenza returned, p'rhaps my daughter would still be here. Weren't no one to blame for that *but* your father."

Leola felt suddenly tired of standing there, listening to his spleen.

"Was the pestilence kil't my mother, nothing else. Plenty of rich folks who never lifted a finger their whole lives died of it too." She paused. "Besides, if Mama had followed your plan, I wouldn't be here nor my sisters. P'rhaps not even you, for she was the one cared for you all these years—which might not have happened if she'd stayed in Kilgore in her fine kept-woman house." Her mouth rippled. "Kept not only by her lover but her own father too."

Mr. Owen jumped up, wagging a finger.

"Do not sass me girl, or I will tell those orphanage folk not to allow your *Eye-talian* fellow to visit, seeing you two are unable to comport yourselves proper."

Leola fought the urge to hurl herself at him, pound his chest and tear his hair, tell him how much she hated him—for making Mama's life a torment, for driving Papa away, for threatening to separate her from this other man she loved.

Instead she flung the door wide, not caring anymore about the draft.

"It's getting late, Mr. Owen. Auntie will be back with the girls any minute. If you wish us to be ready tomorrow, I'll need to finish my work."

The clock ticked a few seconds before he answered.

"This is *my* home, Granddaughter. I will leave when I see fit."

A laugh came out of Leola—so bitter it surprised her.

"You may own this place, but it's never been your *home*. A home is made of love, which you don't have the first idea about. Most like, you destroyed my family out of jealousy for not havin' anything so precious."

She clamped her mouth shut, but Mr. Owen had already moved in, looming over her.

"I do believe, young lady, you've overstepped your bounds."

As he raised his hand, Leola shielded herself behind the door—until it occurred to her she'd faced more fearsome things recently than the sting of a palm upon her cheek. Not to mention if the old man struck first, no one would hold it against her for fighting back. Which suddenly, she felt full ready to do.

"You should know, Grandfather," she faced him fully, "Joe has a friend in Jefferson. A lawyer who's offered to help us for free."

Mr. Owen dropped his hand.

"Help you? In what way?"

"He says a parent's dying wishes have weight in court. Even if there's no proper will, my sisters and I have rights to our property— and a say-so in our futures too. Would come at some expense for you to fight such a case." She lifted her chin. "I've refused the offer for now, but if'n you come between me and Joe, I may take it up after all."

Mr. Owen hesitated, then stepped over the threshold.

"Yer lettin' the weather inside," he mumbled, without looking at her. "Make certain you and your sisters are ready by sunup tomorrow."

Watching him navigate the back steps, Leola thought his back seemed more bent than she remembered, his gait more uncertain. It dawned on her he'd never make it to his sister's in Alabama, that he'd die on this farm alone, and she didn't feel a moment's grief over it.

❦

That night Leola had just tucked the girls into bed when Joe reappeared, drenched by the storm.

When she let him in, he pulled her to him—so hard, she grunted.

"I couldn't let you go without a proper farewell," he murmured, rain dripping from his hat brim. "I'm sorry for letting ol' Mr. Owen cow me like he did, leaving you to face him alone." He stepped back. "I intended to come back in time for supper. Then the storm hit and I was desperate to get the youngest plants inside before they were ruined."

Leola peered up at him.

"I knew somehow we'd see each other—though I'd started to lose hope." She grinned. "Yet here you are."

Joe eyed the ring, lying exactly where she'd left it hours earlier. After the scene with Mr. Owen, Leola had felt so addled she hadn't wanted to move the box, thinking it might jinx their future. Now Joe traipsed across the room, yanking the ring from its case.

Returning, he slipped it onto her finger.

"I wish you to wear this as a promise not *to* me but *from* me—to always love and help you, come what may." He gazed deep into her eyes. "I don't care how long I have to wait. I only hope when you've done what needs doing, I might still become your husband someday."

Leola's heart felt ready to burst.

"I can't imagine otherwise, Joe. Wish I had a ring to put on *your* finger as my own promise to be faithful."

They kissed then full and deep, ignoring the growing pond beneath them—and the two little girls in the kitchen doorway, gaping in wonder and awe.

CHAPTER 33

Huddled in the back of the cart, Leola felt grateful for the darkness. Grateful she couldn't quite make out their home disappearing around the bend. Glad too that her sisters had fallen asleep beneath the blanket Mr. Owen had thrown over them earlier, as it spared them from witnessing her sorrow.

Soon, however, the sun was high enough to reveal the passing houses of their neighbors, filled with folks she knew: Nancy Gumbs and Old Man Bell; the Meekers, Newmans, and McGees. When Mr. McGee appeared right then, leading a horse from the barn, Leola felt a pang of nostalgia even for the hours spent toiling in his fields. *Goodbye, goodbye, goodbye,* she silently cried, wondering if she would see these folks ever again.

Only when they came to the Dark Road did her spirit lighten. She spun the ring 'round her finger, remembering Joe's promise to visit soon—remembering *all* the promises they'd made to each other. Hoping they could keep them.

The wagon soon came within sight of the tiny cemetery where Mama was buried, grave marked with the rough headstone Auntie had bought with her meager savings:

Orlena Rose Owen Rideout
March 7, 1884–November 5, 1919
The Lord Is My Shepherd

Leola and the girls had visited two days earlier, leaving sprays of bluegrass and dried roses that had probably blown away by now. It hurt to think she'd not be able to tend her mother's resting place. Hurt to leave Mama here alone.

Then she noted the adjacent field where the poorest of the poor interred their dead, usually in unmarked graves. Saw the fresh mound of earth next to a smaller, less recent one, marking the resting places of Jimmy Suggs and his mother.

Leola had run into Earl and Opal last week, coming from a food drive at the fire station. Earl was struggling to keep hold of several packages while Opal balanced her mewling baby sister in one arm and a sack of potatoes in the other.

Without thinking, Leola had offered to help, surprised when Opal handed her the screaming child. As they'd walked back to the Suggses' brokedown cabin near the railroad tracks, she'd sung the baby a lullaby and presently it fell fast asleep.

On the tilted front porch, Opal had set down the potatoes, collecting the infant from Leola's arms.

Mam's dead, she'd muttered. *Consumption got 'er at last.*

Leola had been surprised by the prick of tears in her eyes. She'd barely known Zelma Suggs but understood her life had been a parade of miseries. And here was her youngest child, who'd never remember her at all.

I'm so sorry, she'd replied quietly, the two girls staring at the sleeping infant as if trying to comprehend how any living soul could be so peaceful. Then Earl had come out to get the other packages and Opal followed him inside, shutting the door behind her.

Now, as the graveyard receded from view, Leola realized she and Opal were in similar predicaments: their mothers dead, their fathers, who knew where? She wondered what would become of Opal and

Earl and that baby, if they'd also be sent to an orphanage, one of those seedy places she'd read about in the newspaper where young children didn't go to school but worked all day, subsisting on wormy gruel and hard discipline. Or would their scrappy family be ignored as usual, Opal left to provide whatever pell-mell existence she could, and no one to care either way? At least, Leola grudgingly admitted, Mr. Owen had made some effort to find them a decent situation, one that might offer a better balance between kindness and neglect.

As they arrived at the train station, her sisters began begging for the ham biscuits Leola had packed last night, making her question whether she'd brought enough provisions for their journey. Auntie had given her five dollars, which Leola planned to use for sending additional telegrams to Houston once they were settled. Figured her sisters could share one of the cheap box lunches sold in the third-class compartments and there'd still be money left for a cable or two.

"I need to buy your fare," Mr. Owen was saying, nodding toward the station interior. "Y'all stay put."

A few minutes later, he returned, handing Leola their tickets along with a large paper sack.

"Here's some sandwiches." He fished two smaller bags from his pocket, presenting them to her sisters. "And boiled peanuts for y'all."

Mae and Karla reached out slowly, as if afraid their grandfather might snatch away his offering. He'd never before given them presents.

"That wasn't necessary," Leola said, taking the bigger bag, "but thank you." She nodded toward the heaving train. "Reckon it's time for us to board."

Mr. Owen blinked at the huge black engine. When he looked at her again, his eyes shimmered—though she figured it was from the locomotive's steam and not true emotion.

"Remember," he said, "John Giles will meet your arrival. Knows to be lookin' for a wispy young lady with two sprogs in tow."

"We'll be fine." Leola squeezed Mae's hand. "Bid Mr. Owen farewell, girls."

"G'bye, sir," Mae intoned, though Karla only huddled closer to her big sister.

"Goodbye, Mr. Owen," Leola murmured.

As the three girls walked down the platform, not a one of them looked back.

Namesek, New Jersey • Late October 1986

CHAPTER 34

It was a still, sunless day, the trees mostly gray but for smudges of dusty, leftover color. Gazing out the living room window, Leola had a sudden yearning to see Joe traversing the walkway in his Italian boots—tired after work yet clearly happy to be home.

They'd never grown rich from their rose-growing business. After the airlines began shipping fresh flowers, most folk preferred the showy, dull-scented blossoms from California, so Belfigli Roses had become Belfigli Nurseries, purveyor of everything else. Not that it mattered much when their income had dropped. Leola and Joe had always been watchful of their household accounts—adjusting here, sacrificing there, managing well enough.

Even so, Joe had never denied himself that one indulgence—an annual trip to the Lucchese flagship store in San Antone for a new pair of boots. By the time he'd died, there'd been an entire closet full of sharp-toed footwear, many in immaculate condition, for he'd tended them carefully as his plants. Leola eventually found a buyer for them—a *collector* who paid a pretty penny for *vintage Italian specimens*. Of course she'd kept the ones Joe had worn when they'd courted, which eventually turned so brittle, entire chunks fell off in her hand. Only then had she thrown them away.

Now she reminded herself Joe would never walk this earthly plane again, despite having long made her peace with that fact.

Whatever wrongs had existed between them—and after fifty years of marriage, there'd been plenty—had been more or less absolved before he died. When she finally joined him in the Hereafter, Leola knew it would be a joyful reunion.

But Papa was another matter, his betrayal unresolved. Sometimes she pictured him stuck in that strange limbo the Catholics called purgatory—more a state of being, she believed, than a place, an inside-out version of grace reserved for folks who'd left too many things unsaid in their lifetimes. A state they left their loved ones in, too, it seemed.

Just then a man with three yappy dogs walked by outside, and Leola smiled in spite of her dark thoughts. Their boisterous little parade appeared every day about this time, a spectacle that never failed to cheer her up. Except at the moment, something else grabbed her attention—a blue car passing the house slowly before it pulled over down the block. She'd seen this car before, wondered if it belonged to one of the stringy-haired boys who visited her granddaughter. Suddenly she realized that couldn't be true, as those fellows usually drove rusted heaps, not new and expensive-looking cars like this one.

As Leola watched, the driver's side window rolled down and she gasped. *Could it be?* Hurrying into the dining room for a better view, she noted the shape of the driver's head, the thick tousle of hair over his brow. It was her father, sure as the day was long.

She ran outside, hurrying across the lawn, waving. "Hallloooo, Papa! Yoo-hoo!"

The driver gaped at her a moment before rolling up his window, but as he sped away, Leola kept running.

"Wait! Don't leave!"

She stepped into the street just as another vehicle approached from the opposite direction, swerving around her in the nick of time.

"Dear God, Mother!"

Rose seemed to appear from nowhere, dragging her back to the curb.

"You almost got yourself killed. What were you thinking?"

Leola motioned helplessly. "It was my father in that blue auto! I was trying to . . ."

Rose shook her head.

"Most likely, it was someone who works in town, looking for a peaceful place to eat his lunch." Her face puckered. "It wasn't your father. He died years ago, Mother, around the time I graduated college."

Leola glanced away, not caring what Rose thought. Papa was *here*, not only in dreams and visions but in real life too. She'd even seen him at the grocery store recently, though he'd disappeared before she could say a thing. Impossible as it was to explain, Leola knew he was more than a figment of her imagination. Knew it with every fiber of her being.

"Let's go inside," Rose said, taking Leola's hand. "I made you egg salad and your soap's about to come on."

"No." Leola pulled away. "I'm waiting for Papa to come back."

"Mother, please." Rose exhaled. "Let's go—"

"I said no!" Leola reared back, kicking her daughter hard on the shin.

Rose yowled in pain and Leola's vision darkened with a distant memory—of a child, a gust of anger and raised hand, her own spirit heavy with self-reproach.

"Oh my girl!" She hung her head. "What have I done?"

Rose stared a moment, rubbing her leg. Offered a thin smile.

"I know you're upset, Mom. But you need to let your papa go. What he did—what happened—was terrible. I understand that." Her eyes were like an ocean in storm. "When I was young, you'd tell me bits and pieces of the story and then you'd go back to your usual sunshiny self. It was Daddy who filled me in on the rest, telling me you'd never properly grieved what he'd done." She drew another breath. "It's been such a long time, and it's difficult, seeing you deal with it now when . . ."

She didn't complete her sentence, though Leola guessed what she wanted to say: *when you're so old. About to die. When it is so beside the point.* Which was precisely the point. Leola couldn't ignore any longer her million questions about Papa's disappearance. Her father was here in some form, and she needed to figure out *why.* Not that Rose would understand. She'd never been left behind. Never been betrayed, not like that. Hopefully never would be.

"I'm sorry for causing such a ruckus," Leola said, taking Rose's arm. "Sorrier still for hurting you, my daughter." She hesitated. "You're right. I need to let Papa go."

She didn't speak the other half of her thought: *But not yet. I can't let him go* yet.

Waxahachie, Texas • Late December 1919

CHAPTER 35

B y the time their train pulled into the station, Leola had given up all hope of impressing Brother Giles. The carriage had been cramped and grimy, the trip delayed by two hours. At this point, her sisters were covered in peanut shells, their hair ribbons as unraveled as Leola felt herself.

At least Mr. Owen had provided a good description of his granddaughters for, as they stepped onto the platform, a man in a starched white collar hurried to greet them.

"You must be Leola." He gripped her hand. "I'm Brother Giles. Call me Brother if you prefer."

Leola had always imagined orphanage managers as crabbed and withered, like in fiction stories. Brother, however, was on the young side, tall and erect, with silver spectacles and a thick moustache draping his top lip. Though his serge suit was frayed about the cuffs, the trousers were neatly creased and the shirt beneath his vest, bleachy as snow.

He bent down, gazing at her sisters.

"And you must be Mae and Karla. Pretty as your grandfather said and then some!"

The girls stared back in silence, but Brother Giles didn't seem offended.

"I imagine y'all are tuckered out." He straightened up. "When we get to your new home, you'll have your rest and refreshment, no worries 'bout that."

After finding a cart for their bags, Brother led them to a black car with gold lettering on the door: *Texas State Children's Home, founded 1906.*

"Y'all are among the first to ride in our newly refurbished vehicle, given us by the Mission Society." He tapped the car's hood, proud of the jalopy in spite of its cracked back window and dented fender. "'Course she's an ol' hayburner and gas is dear, so we only use her for special occasions—of which this is one!"

After he'd tied their cases to the bumper, the girls climbed inside, watching as he cranked the engine, muttering words Leola was fairly certain weren't The Lord's Prayer. Finally, the motor turned over and Brother slipped into the front seat, grinning in the rearview mirror.

"Never saw anything—man, beast, nor machine—couldn't be persuaded with an extra ounce'a perseverance!"

As they drove through the bustling town, Brother pointed out various places of interest: the neatly manicured square with its imposing brick courthouse and statue of Johnny Reb; the Freemasons' hall, soda fountain, and movie theater. Occasionally he'd idle in front of an elegant frame house, saying it belonged to an illustrious Mission Board member or local businessman who *believed in their cause.*

A couple miles beyond the city limits, Leola spied a three-story structure sprouting from the prairie, its limestone bricks reflecting the afternoon's glow.

"There it is, girls," Brother exclaimed, "your new domicile!"

The sisters scrunched together, peering out the window.

"We just recently put that addition along the sides and back," the man explained, "to add a bigger dining hall and separate living quarters for the missus and myself."

"Gee whiskers!" Mae murmured. "It's bigger than the post office in Bronway. Big as a castle almost! And golden like a castle too!"

Hardly a castle, Leola thought, and certainly no home. Not that she intended to point this out to her sisters, who'd discover it for themselves soon enough.

"Y'all will be the castle's smartest, strongest princesses," she responded, "and make short work of any horrid Texas dragons that come your way."

Mae frowned as if less than assured by this, but Brother Giles had cut the engine and turned around to address them.

"The other young'uns won't be home from school for a while. Today's the last day of term so I imagine they'll be hepped up more than usual." He let out a rueful laugh. "It'll be quieter at the moment than you'll ever hear again."

Helping her sisters from the car, Leola eyed the lengthy walk-way—a stick-straight path that left no doubt where a person would end up. With each step down it, she felt she was surrendering every-thing she'd known and loved. Felt she was leaving Papa behind for-ever, as well.

When they finally entered the vestibule, a smiling woman awaited.

"I'm Mrs. Jessamyn Giles." She held out a hand. "Brother's wife."

Mrs. Giles was the sort of woman Papa might call *handsome*, her sharp chin and prominent nose offset by a full mouth, shining black hair worn in a single braid down her back. She possessed a more angular physique than Brother, had more lines about the eyes, too, and the beginnings of a small hump between her shoulders.

"Sure glad to see y'all, praise be, though I wouldn't doubt you are sore fatigued . . ."

There was a noise on the staircase and Leola looked up to see a

whirlwind rushing toward them, mostly elbows and knees, streaming wild, white-blond hair, which it was attempting to corral beneath
a bright red kerchief.

"Sorry for my lateness, Brother! I know you wanted me here early,
to greet our new arrivals." The girl-whirlwind came to a halt, panting
as she knotted her scarf. "Mrs. Clymer," she glanced at Leola, "that's
my English teacher at the high school, might be yours, too, when you
start . . ." More panting. "Mrs. Clymer made me stay to finish my essay
and I had to run the whole way here, sweatin' like a stuck pig." She fanned
her armpits. "Did my best to wash up lest I fell you with my stink."

Brother grimaced. "Now, Ruthie. Here are our newest inmates,
already boggled by their journey and you adding to their overwhelm!"

The girl, seemingly unmoved by this scolding, pumped Leola's
arm.

"Ruthie Free's my name. Glad to meet you and apologies for whatever stormin' and overwhelmin' I caused."

Though somewhat thunderstruck, Leola couldn't help smiling.
Maybe it was the way Ruthie stood, legs firmly planted, shoulders
thrown back, like she fully owned whatever space she took up. Or
p'rhaps it was the hint of challenge in her wide gray eyes, as if she'd
peek at what you were selling but probably wouldn't buy. All this,
along with her name, suggested an audacity Leola hoped might rub
off on herself.

"I must take my leave, ladies," Brother said, glancing at his watch.
"Ruthie, you show Leola 'round. Mrs. Giles will escort the little ones
to their own rooms."

As the woman reached for the girls, all three sisters shrank back,
but Mrs. Giles only smiled again.

"It's hard at first to be separated," she said to Mae and Karla.
"However, your room is right beneath Leola's, and you'll see her often.

You've a lovely ward mother, too, named Mrs. Bentham and plenty'a nice children to befriend."

Lowering her voice to a conspiratorial whisper, she added, "Our chef, Mrs. Hooks, baked some of her famous sugar cookies especially for y'all. After you're settled, we'll meet with Leola in the kitchen so you can enjoy your snack together. Would you like that?"

Karla, while still solemn, loosened her grip on Leola's legs and Mae bobbed her head, which was Mrs. Giles's chance to hustle them away.

"We'll see y'all soon," she tossed over her shoulder.

Watching them go, Leola wrestled the impulse to snatch her sisters back and take off in the opposite direction. Only Ruthie's hand on her shoulder kept her from it.

"You been carin' for those mites a while, haven't ya?" she asked, and Leola nodded.

"Since our mother died in November though, in truth, longer than that. Mama's been—or was—awful busy these past years."

Ruthie smiled.

"Y'all are closer than peas in a pod, I can tell. Bein' an only child, I sometimes wonder what that's like. Can't be a picnic minding little ones and now others will take the responsibility. You'll finally find some peace!"

Leola blinked as if she'd just been told the world was round. Having had such constant worry of her sisters, lately, she'd forgotten what it was like not to. But she couldn't ponder over it, as Ruthie motioned her forth.

"Leave your valise by the steps and let me show you what's what."

They toured the ground floor first, with its formal sitting room and small sick ward, Brother's office and, in the back, the Gileses' apartments. Then came the large dining room where the children ate and, next to that, the biggest kitchen Leola had ever seen. As she circled the stove—which would've taken up most of their parlor back home—Ruthie asked, "Are you any kind of chef?"

"Been cooking for my family since I was hardly older than Mae," Leola replied, peering inside the cavernous oven. "Can't say it's my favorite hobby, though I'm told I do make a decent biscuit."

Ruthie licked her lips. "Let's hope you get assigned to breakfast duty then. Lord knows we could use help in that department. My roommate, Verba—the girl you're replacing—was a decent cook and our breakfast leader but, since she's been gone, we been existing on vittles ain't fit for swine. Me, I'd rather get my fingernails yanked out than cook, which is why I work in the barn. Cows and chickens are swell company and don't meddle in my business like others in this place."

Ruthie paused, pointing to a closed door behind the stove.

"Oh—nearly forgot. That leads to the basement, where we have our Bible studies and such. There's a laundry room down there, too, and Brother's developing studio, where he makes his photographs—or as he calls them, his *artworks*." She lowered her voice. "Mostly pictures of sheep in fields and old ladies on porches, which a person can see well enough a'walkin' down the road. Just don't tell him that."

They headed back to the hall, where Ruthie grabbed Leola's suitcase and led her to the second floor, pointing out the large dormitory where her sisters would stay.

"Bigger boys live in the bunkhouse out back, what few we got at the moment. Most of them are presently down in Collins, helping plant the sweet potato crop." They climbed the final flight of stairs. "Whereas we go up here, cozy 'neath the eaves."

At the end of another long hallway, Ruthie pushed open a door, revealing a good-sized room with three beds, two dressers, and a small chifforobe.

"Welcome to your new digs," she announced, setting Leola's valise on one of the two single beds. "You get to sleep alone in Verba's old spot, thank your stars for that!"

She motioned at the double bed.

"Glenda and Euless share that one and are forever gripin' of it. Once Euless punched Glenda in the face while she slept, hard enough to give the girl a right nice shiner." She let out a cackle. "When Verba left, Glenda asked to take her bed, but Brother said she is accustomed to sharing with Euless and can manage a while longer."

Leola snapped open one of her sheets. "What happened to Verba?"

"Got adopted." Ruthie's face twisted. "Or might I say, *hired out*. Couple over in Abilene wanted a sturdy sort. Made no bones about it."

She helped Leola tuck up the sheet.

"Usually such folk choose a boy who can do heavy labor, but this couple liked Verba for her cooking skills *and* the fact she's strong as an ox. Guess they figured they were getting two for the price'a one."

Leola's stomach clenched, imagining what it'd be like to live with strangers who called themselves your *parents* but only wanted you for your skill and stamina. No matter how she'd resented her chores at home, the toil was always balanced by tenderness, plus the recognition Mama and Papa would've given their eyeteeth to keep her from it—if they could've.

"Did Verba have any say in where she got sent?" Leola asked, spreading the woolen blanket over her bed.

"Naw. Verba's got no living kin whatsoever in this world so not much choice in the matter. She did meet the couple beforehand, said they promised her plentiful food and decent pay." Ruthie shook her head. "'Course I got a letter from her last week complainin' the workload's much heavier there than it ever was here. Wishes she'd put up more of a fight."

The bed-making finished, Leola began to unpack, thinking Mama had been in a similar situation as Verba, except farmed out by her own father—as Papa had put it, *like his best mare*—and treated not much better in the end.

"You resemble your mother about the mouth," Ruthie said, startling Leola from her musings, "but mostly you favor your dad."

Leola turned to find the other girl sitting on her bed, studying the wedding portrait.

"How'd they pass, if it ain't too forward to ask?"

Leola refolded a petticoat, trying to hide her pained expression.

"Mama expired from the flu and my father," she tucked the garment into a drawer, "he went off to Houston some months past. Haven't heard from him in a while. My beau is hopin' to travel to Houston and sort it all out. He's busy with work so hard to say when."

Ruthie set the portrait on the wooden crate that would serve as Leola's bedside table.

"Shame about your folks. At least it means you're a half-orphan like me."

Leola left the bureau opened, joining Ruthie on the bed.

"Half-orphan?"

"Mmm—hmm. It's what they call us kids who still have a living parent. My own Pap died when I was a babe but Mam's alive and kickin'—just indisposed at the moment. Our boardinghouse in Dallas burnt down two year ago so she put me here 'til she can set herself right. Meantime can't no one else claim me, like they did Verba."

She raised a pale eyebrow.

"'Course, Brother would say I'm too hard-headed to be an attraction to people anyhow." She glanced at Leola. "And you are too flimsy-lookin', I think. Those sisters of yours though—they're sweet and young. *Moldable,* as they say, the sort people drool over. And Brother's one of them *child-saver* types thinks it better for kids to be in real families, don't matter if they leave brothers or sisters to rot in the orphanage."

Ruthie must've noticed Leola's worried expression, as she quickly added, "All that's beside the point anyhow. Even if he has to beat back the comers with a stick, Brother will abide the law. Half-orphans is half-orphans and nothing else for him to do."

Relief washed over Leola. She'd worried night and day of how she might keep their little family together—had even regretted at times not marrying Joe right away, for that reason. But this meant she wouldn't have to throw herself on the mercy of strangers. Eventually, Papa would claim them and they'd go back to being *no part* orphans at all.

"We got the best lodgings in this place, by far," Ruthie said, walking to the window, "if only for the extra privacy. Our ward mother, Mrs. Larkin, lives down the other end of the hall and," she pointed, "we've the new fire escape to use when the weather's fine. Brother and Mrs. Giles only come up here maybe twice each month for dorm inspection, sit with us at breakfast, dole out discipline and such."

She flounced onto her own bed.

"Mostly they stay busy entertaining our benefactors, attending all kinds of money-raisin' hootenannies and fancy sorries."

Leola had to think on this a moment.

"*Soirees.*" She smiled. "I think you mean they hold *soirees.* It's French for *nighttime parties.*"

Ruthie let out another infectious chuckle. "I reckon you been to France and other parts distant, then, and will tell me all about it?"

Leola was taken aback, wondering if Ruthie actually believed she'd traveled the world, but finally understood it was the girl's way of teasing. As Mr. Owen had pointed out, no child of means would be situated in an orphanage if their parents expired. Everyone knew that.

"Well, howdy!"

A short woman with a frizz of sparse gray hair bustled into the room and Ruthie jumped to her feet.

"Afternoon, Mrs. Larkin. This here's Leola Rideout, who hails from gay Par-ee!"

Another bolt of laughter, replaced by a quizzical expression.

"Actually, I do not know where she really hails from!"

"Just outside Bronway," Leola explained, "in Smith County."

Mrs. Larkin nodded.

"Pretty country, East Texas. I've dear cousins near Mixon. Hain't had a day off to visit them in forever." Her face brightened. "Met your sisters downstairs. Precious things!" She clicked her tongue. "What upheaval they've been through and you, too, losing both parents in such a short—"

"Oh, no!" Leola exclaimed. "My papa . . . he isn't dead. My sisters and I," she flicked her gaze at Ruthie, "we're half-orphans."

"Ah." Mrs. Larkin pressed her lips together. "I see."

A small silence fell during which Leola figured the woman must be thinking ill of her father, figuring him as one of those dissolute men who leave their lambs behind for greener pastures.

"No matter." Mrs. Larkin waved. "You're in good company, all you poor waifs thrown upon the mercy of this world—though if a person's gonna find mercy anywhere, reckon it's here."

She exhaled another of the long sighs that seemed to punctuate her every sentence.

"Now if you'll excuse me." *Siiiigh.* "Got to prepare for my other charges to return from school. Always a bit of a kerfuffle, getting everyone to their chores and studyin' and what-not. Finish unpacking soon's you can, Leola." More sighing as she made her exit. "Your sisters will be down in the kitchen looking for you."

Ruthie waited until Mrs. Larkin's footsteps faded before tugging Leola's sleeve.

"You can unpack later. Mrs. Hooks's sugar cookies won't last once the other kids get back. Whatever mercies this place holds, you gotta grab 'em when you can."

CHAPTER 36

W as no small task, adjusting to the clamor of twenty-three other children, sharing the washroom sink without having her feet bludgeoned, memorizing endless rules meant to keep chaos at bay. No matter how exhausted she felt at the end of each day, Leola's mind was too full of uproar to sleep, so she welcomed Ruthie sneaking to her bed after lights out, sharing stories that went a long way in explaining the girl's bold demeanor.

"It was a gentleman's lodging in name only," Ruthie said one night, referring to her mother's old boarding house, "and bad luck I got my figure early. Those lechers were always grabbin' at me. One man in particular, Garland Higgins, would wait for Mam to leave before getting up to his hijinks, trappin' me on the stairs, reaching for my bubs," she motioned at her sizeable chest, "rubbing against me like he were the washboard and I, the dirty laundry."

Leola swallowed, imagining Mama discovering such a thing, taking a two-by-four to the man's head without a single qualm.

"Did you tell your mother?"

Ruthie shook her head. "Mam was run ragged as it was, keepin' that place afloat. Was me had to put a stop to Garland's trickeries else meet a worse fate than bruised lips."

Her eyes reflected the orange-y gas lamps in the hall.

"So I came up with a plan. Collected a mess of scorpions from the lumberyard, dug a little hole 'neath the outhouse. When it was Garland's usual time to 'tend his necessities, I set those critters loose inside that hole. Bolted myself up hard against the door so he couldn't get out easy."

She covered her mouth, stifling her trademark howl.

"Won't never forget that ol' hound dog begging between the wooden slats: *On my mother's grave, Ruthie, I'll never even* look *at you impurely ever again! Just let me outta this place 'fore I get bit and die!*"

Her imitation of the man's mewling desperation made both girls giggle—so hard that Euless threatened to fetch Mrs. Larkin if they didn't pipe down.

These late night *rondy-views*, as Ruthie called them, weren't only for entertainment, but provided Leola with valuable pointers on how things went: which kids would tattle if you dipped snuff (as if Leola would do such a thing!), the adults who'd look away if you cussed (Mrs. Hooks, though she'd certainly scold you in private), those who'd punish you outright (Brother Giles).

"Woe betides you if that man applies the hand of righteous discipline, as he calls it, to your sinful ways," Ruthie warned, during another nightly meet-up. "Then it's the clothespin or the closet and nothin' righteous 'bout neither."

Leola's chest tightened. "What's the clothespin or the closet?"

Ruthie pulled a foot into her lap, peeling off a bit of toenail.

"Brother's idea of *shaping our moral character.*" She flicked the nail away. "You either have to wear a red clothespin on your nose or get locked in that little closet beneath the stairs, with bread and water for sustenance and a bucket for relievin' yourself."

Leola winced. "And here I thought Brother was a nice man."

"Oh he *thinks* himself nice. Only uses his discipline methods if, as he says, *correction is overdue*—mostly with us older kids. Not the bigger boys however. S'pose he's afraid of them."

Seeing Leola's alarm, Ruthie was quick again to put a better face on things.

"You don't strike me as the disobeyin' type, so no need to worry. And it ain't all tragedy 'round here neither. Next week they're taking us to the Dixie Theater to see *For the Heart's Honor*, a so-called *smashing story of a gamble on love*."

She smirked.

"Sounds like you and your beau, taking a gamble on each other even when folk couldn't abide it! You're some'at like Romeo and Juliet, only without the balcony and the deathly poison."

Leola didn't respond, thinking the fierce disapproval of her grandfather, the *100 percent* signs in store windows, the scowls of neighbors who considered Joe and his ilk worse than dirt, were the worst poisons imaginable.

After Ruthie went to bed, Leola remembered the letter she'd received from Joe recently, full of tender assurances and promises to visit. She found herself unable to quiet the ache in her heart not solely for him, but for everything she missed about home: the mockingbird singing by her window, the soft sheets that smelled of Mama's lavender laundry soap, the idea she could steal outside to gaze at the stars without breaking some rule. She imagined Papa studying those same stars this very moment . . . or buried cold beneath them.

Rubbing away a tear, Leola assured herself she'd adjust to this place—she'd *have* to—but would never feel peace again. Not until her father returned.

CHAPTER 37

Despite all the grownups around the Home, it was the kids kept the place going on a daily basis. Even the youngest children had some regular task—sweeping floors, making beds, gathering laundry—while the older ones were given more substantial duties: washing clothes, making household repairs and, in spring and summer, tending the fields around the orphanage, where they grew food for the table and cotton to sell at market.

Just as Ruthie had predicted, Leola got assigned to kitchen duty, her biscuit recipe soon earning praise from adults and kids alike. She didn't mind the work, as it excused her from other, more onerous chores, and gave her the chance to sneak extra food for Mae and Karla on the sly.

The job also required getting up at the crack of dawn, which Leola had done all her life with little difficulty—except she hadn't had a proper stretch of sleep in weeks. Not long after arriving at the orphanage, Mae had begun creeping to her room during the wee hours, waking Leola to say she'd had a bad dream or that Karla was crying for their mother. Then Leola would have to tiptoe downstairs, soothing both girls, barely making it back to her dorm for some shut-eye. Was a miracle she hadn't been caught wandering the halls yet—a serious offense.

All that changed when Leola woke one morning to find Ruthie leaning over her and realized she was still in her sisters' bed.

"You're late to the kitchen," Ruthie hissed, "and Brother in a fine fettle 'bout it."

Leola untangled herself carefully from the sheets, trying not to wake the girls—without luck.

"Lee?" Mae sat up. "Where you going?"

"Shhhh." Leola glanced uneasily at Karla, mouth slung open in gentle snoring. "Don't rouse your sister. If she makes a fuss, I'll be in bigger trouble than I am already."

As she scurried upstairs to change, Ruthie followed, filling her in on the situation.

"Brother Giles got his tail up higher'n a skunk in a possum trap. I tried to explain about Mae and Karla missing their mama, but he acted deaf as a stone."

By the time Leola arrived in the steamy kitchen, the other girls were hard at work, two pans of gray, lopsided biscuits cooling on the sideboard.

"You're in sore trouble," Glenda whispered. "Brother Giles knows you were out of the ward last night."

"I been told that already," Leola hissed. "Now hush up and help me get these biscuits made."

She'd hardly cut the butter into the flour when Brother Giles appeared.

"Good morning, ladies." His gaze landed on Leola. "Miss Rideout, meet me in my office in five minutes. Glenda, you'll be in charge of breakfast today."

Though the others groaned, Leola's mouth watered as she glimpsed the pan of anemic biscuits, knowing it'd be noontime before she could eat again.

Brother hadn't arrived at his office when she got there so she soothed her nerves by studying his bookshelves, including the biggest collection of Bibles she'd ever seen in one place. Some were the commonplace sort found in church pews while others were more exotic, bound in rich leather embossed with fancy lettering.

"I see you've discovered my library."

Leola, surprised by the sound of Brother's voice, jumped.

"My great-aunt had a Bible like this," she said, pointing to one of the more impressive volumes. "Was in her family more than a hundred years, brought over from—"

As she reached for the book, Brother grabbed her hand and shouted, "No!"

The two of them gaped at each other—until he let go, forcing a smile.

"If your aunt had such a Bible, it was precious indeed. Only two hundred of this edition were ever made. The cover is calfskin and the pages, vellum." He gestured at the shelves. "No one else is permitted to touch my collection. I clean the room myself for that reason." Another strained smile. "P'rhaps one day you and I can look at this particular Bible together." He nodded toward his desk and the small chair beside it. "Presently, we've other, less pleasant matters to attend."

Heart racing, Leola eased herself inside the child-size seat while Brother Giles sat opposite, in a tilting desk chair whose springs begged for oil, screeching with his every move.

"Are you feeling refreshed after those minutes of additional sleep?" Brother asked, and Leola's cheeks blazed.

"Beg pardon, sir. I been on time to the kitchen every day 'til this morning. Guess I'm still not myself since being sick. Must be catching up with me."

Brother leaned back, the squeaky chair echoing his disapproval.

"Many here are recovering from the influenza but do not shirk their duties. Besides, you're aware of the prohibition against leaving your bed, which poses a safety hazard, as I'm sure you appreciate."

"I don't know what to do, sir." Leola gnawed her bottom lip. "I'm worried about my sisters, especially Karla. She has nightmares every night and hasn't said a word since coming here. I feel it my duty to comfort her any way I can."

"Ah, yes." Brother exhaled. "However well-intentioned, a place like this cannot meet the needs of individual children, who deserve a family devoted to their care alone." He traced the edge of his blotter with one finger. "This is off the topic of our discussion but since you've brought it up . . . there's a Mission Society member who is quite taken with Karla. Expressed an interest in adopting her."

Leola sat straight, the chair's armrests digging into her sides.

"I promised my mama we wouldn't be separated! Besides, we're half-orphans. We *can't* be adopted, not until we learn what happened to my father."

Brother folded his hands.

"I'm afraid the law differs where fathers are concerned. Too many abandon their families and never come back."

"My father would never—"

"According to the law," Brother interjected, "if a father hasn't been heard of for six months, his paternal rights are terminated. And if he shows up after that time . . . well, desertion is a felony, punishable by jail."

Leola's chin trembled.

"My father didn't abandon us. He wouldn't! There's some other explanation, I'm sure. And it's only been four months since he went to Houston, so the time limit hasn't expired." She pressed her hands together. "Please sir, if the girls are separated from me—from each other, so soon after our mama died—it would finish them."

Brother pulled a cloth from his vest pocket, polished his glasses, and set them on his face again.

"The state welfare agency will be investigating your father's whereabouts," he said, "contacting the hospitals and morgues down in Houston. Meantime, if the welfare of your sisters concerns you, then you best accustom yourself to the idea of adoption."

Leola swiped at her eyes, embarrassed she'd exposed her sorrow to a stranger—one who'd probably hardened himself long ago to such entreaties.

"I'm sorry to cause you upset, child." Brother's tone lightened. "We must trust the Lord in matters out of our control." He checked his watch. "But I have a meeting shortly and we haven't discussed your transgression and its consequences."

Leola stared into her lap, wondering how much more penance she could take, and Brother seemed to read her mind.

"If I overlook your lapses, the other children will think I'm showing favorites." He drummed the desk. "However, it *is* your first offense so wearing the clothespin should be sufficient corrective, I think."

Leola flinched. Only yesterday, she'd noticed a boy wearing the conspicuous device, which looked even more humiliating than she'd imagined. Still, it was better than being locked in the closet for hours. And so she watched, wordless, as Brother Giles reached into a drawer, pulling out the ordinary wooden object made terrible by its maroon paint.

"You're to wear this until noontime," he explained, handing it to her. "And if you're caught without it, we'll have to resort to the next level of punishment."

Leola, staring at a spot over his head, mumbled, "Yes, sir," and turned toward the door.

"Put the clothespin on here," Brother called, "where I can see you."

There was a strange inflection in his voice, as if he welcomed her indignity. Yet she did as she was told, facing him again and placing the clip where it might not feel so painful, on the fleshly part of her nose.

"No, child." Brother Giles stretched out a finger. "Farther up. Nearer the bridge."

Leola didn't react at first. Even considered defying him. Then she remembered the dark closet, the board member who wanted to take Karla, the fact she had to live beneath Brother's watchful gaze day after day. So she moved the clip where he said it should go and where it did, indeed, hurt worse.

The man leaned back, the chair whining where she could not.

"You're excused, Leola."

As she stumbled into the crowded hallway, the noise of the other children died. Some smirked, but most gave her sympathetic nods, having been in such a position themselves and knowing the worst of the punishment already done.

Mid-January 1920

CHAPTER 38

A s they walked to school first day of the new semester, Ruthie rushed to impart whatever advice she'd forgotten the night before.

"Don't try mixin' with the Town Kids, Lee. They're at the top of the peckin' order and we're at the bottom, no two ways about it."

"Town Kids?" Leola frowned. "They're the rich ones, then?"

"Most are rich but it's also because they have real homes and two parents, whereas we don't."

Leola thought such judgment seemed unkinder even than shunning folks for being poor. While poverty had some hope, however distant, of being improved, losing a parent was a tragedy that could never be righted. She tried to comfort herself with the more hopeful facts Ruthie had shared previously—the afterschool clubs and advanced-level courses this new school offered, the attentive teachers who would *positively swoon* over such a *promising* student.

Myself? Ruthie had sniffed, *Once I'm graduated I don't plan to conjugulate another verb or read another poem by Henry Worthless Long-Winded Fellow ever again.*

Now they'd come within sight of the new brick high school, where kids clustered near the front steps, waiting for the bell.

"There's rain in the forecast," Ruthie pointed at the low-slung clouds, "so we'll have to eat in the basement cafeteria today." Her voice dropped. "Do not under no circumstance sit at the tables, even if there are plenty available. Those are reserved for Town Kids. Most have to wait in line to buy the hot lunch, so it takes 'em a while to settle. If they find one of us in their places, we won't hear the end of it!"

A few more steps and she twirled around again.

"Come to think of it, meet me by the basement stairs at noon. I'll show you where we sit. No chance of gettin' mixed up that way."

As the opening bell rang, a thousand butterflies hatched in Leola's stomach. She wasn't sure which kids to smile at, fearing they'd think her too big for her britches. Imagined the others whispering about the *new Home Kid*, remarking on her secondhand clothes and unfashionable hairstyle, speculating on her father's absence.

Casting her eyes to the floor, she remembered the way George Gumbs and other Black folk lived, turning themselves invisible at will, never sure when the unwritten laws would be enforced—never sure even what the rules *were*. At least, Leola told herself, if she overstepped the social strictures here, the most she'd expect was ridicule or shunning, not getting run out of town or beaten . . . or worse.

Eventually, though, the rhythms of the morning overtook her. The other kids seemed nice enough, pointing the way when she got lost in the maze-like hallways, sharing their books because she hadn't yet bought her own.

At lunchtime however—as Ruthie had warned—the difference between the haves and have-nots became abundantly clear, as Leola and her friends were relegated to the windowsill ledge, nibbling their potted meat sandwiches, ignoring the mouthwatering smells of hot food they couldn't afford. Even the Town Kids who'd been friendly previously acted like they'd never seen her before. Acted like they'd never seen *any* of them before.

But the next day brought one of those glorious shifts in weather that sometimes strike North Texas in winter—the sky so blue, it hurt to look at, and the breeze, lush as springtime. While the Town Kids hurried to purchase their meals, Leola reckoned there was some advantage after all to being a poorly fed orphan, if it meant escaping first into the sweet, warm air.

She aimed for one of the benches surrounding the macadam ball court, hoping to save a space for Ruthie.

As she sat, a voice trilled, "Pardon me."

It was a Town Girl, wearing a fashionable sailor dress and kid-leather shoes, holding a rattan food hamper.

"Me and Willie Belle," the girl gestured at her friend, equally well-dressed, with a decoupage lunch caddie, "this is our bench, if you don't mind."

Leola pursed her lips, minding entirely. It was one thing, getting shunted to the cheap seats within a confined space; another to be so corralled within the wide-open liberty of outdoors. Not to mention there were plenty of other benches available, which Leola was about to point out when Ruthie appeared, red-faced and gasping.

"Hey there, Minnie." She nodded at the other girl. "Willie Belle." She paused to breathe. "Leola's new. I forgot to tell her to meet me at our usual picnic spot over yonder."

Leola followed where Ruthie was pointing, to the chinaberry tree at the farthest edge of the schoolyard. Glancing at her friend, she marveled that this usually bold, unapologetic girl suddenly seemed so cowed. Except then she remembered there were more Town Kids than Home Kids here, that their parents were powerful citizens—some even Mission Society members—whom Brother Giles would not be pleased to upset. And so she let Ruthie drag her away, ducking her head, sure everyone had noticed her blunder.

"I should'a made all of that clear before," Ruthie was saying. "The benches are for Town Kids only. Not that you'd want to waste time in the company of Miss Meanie and her sidekick, Silly Ding Dong."

She plopped down in the shade with the rest of the Home girls.

"Far as I'm concerned, eating on this rock-hard ground is loads better than getting my eardrums scraped by those two sauceboxes." Ruthie mimicked an idiot's voice. *"Why, Silly, did you see that there boy lookin' at us? Bet he'd give his eyeteeth for the chance to lick our boots."* And in a shriller tone, *"Oh, Meanie, he ain't half as handsome as you deserve. By the way, did I mention my daddy's buyin' me one of them there errrr-mine stoles for my birthday, and, if he don't get the right one, I'll cry to the Heavens 'til he does."*

She slipped into regular Ruthie speech with an added edge of scorn.

"Those two got their noses up so high, they'd drown in a rainstorm."

Leola tried to laugh with the others. But unwrapping her skimpy sandwich, she couldn't help peeking at Willie Bell and Minnie, giggling and whispering, probably thinking themselves better than her.

A bit of food caught in her throat.

They *are* better, she figured, for having families to go home to, parents who could afford them hot meals and would never put clothespins on their noses. They'd go further in life, have more opportunities, enjoy better health. She thought of her sisters growing up in the orphanage, grasping at whatever care they could find, destined always for the margins and far corners of everything.

Laughter erupted beneath a tall pecan tree closer to the school, and Leola caught sight of another group of kids, also eating from paper sacks.

"Those are the Cotton Millers," Ruthie explained, "whose parents work at the factories 'cross town. Hardly have a pot to spit in yet are still higher than us in the pecking order, which is why they get the better dinin' locale."

Leola studied the grimy faces and secondhand clothes of the Cotton Millers. She knew day laborers led hard, even dangerous, lives, that they could be dismissed from their jobs with no notice because someone more desperate had shown up. She'd heard stories of workers developing lung diseases from inhaling fibers or getting sliced to pieces in the milling machines. They probably worked long shifts, leaving their children to manage for themselves. Still, those kids were considered better-off than orphans—whole, half, or anything in between.

A breeze rustled the branches overhead and a plume of dust tickled Leola's nose, reminding her of the last time she'd gone fishing with Papa. Sad as she'd felt about their looming separation, she'd also understood—*believed*—it was temporary. She'd had faith in his intentions. *Trusted* his assurances.

She recalled what Brother Giles and Joe had said about men deserting their families—how common it was, even where *least expected*. P'rhaps while dangling their feet in the stream that day, Papa had been hiding his plan. Maybe that was why he'd wanted to set out alone in the first place—to make a clean break.

As the other girls chatted, Leola imagined Papa boarding at Mrs. Grimes's long enough to get his bearings, eventually melting into the crowd with no forwarding address. Watching two Cotton Millers pelt each other with rotting pecans, she realized if the kids who'd lost their parents through tragic accident, illness, or impoverishment sat on the lowest rungs of the social ladder, then those whose parents had *willfully* discarded them must have no place on it at all.

Battling tears, Leola stared into her paper bag, pretending

interest in the peanut butter cookie Mrs. Hooks had added to their lunches. When she looked up again, she could tell Ruthie had noticed her melancholy—as she always seemed to do.

"I've heard the Town Girls talking lately about these posin' parties of theirs," she announced in a jaunty voice, "where they dress in their best fashions and take photos with their Brownies. Seems like larrupin' fun, don't you think?"

Glenda, tearing the crusts off her bread, sniffed.

"Reckon it's easy to pose in fine fashions when you got fine fashions to begin with."

Ruthie gave her a look.

"Don't be so spiteful. Mrs. Giles said she'd take us to Epstein's on Friday to buy new dresses. The Home's gonna throw in half the cost if we contribute earnings from our summer jobs."

Glenda tossed crumbs to a nearby bird.

"You mean the dresses on the sale tables more like. What little we saved won't go far even with the Home pitching in."

"Quit your sour-pussin,'" Ruthie hissed. "All's it takes is a bit of creativity to gussy up a cut-price dress and we got that in spades."

She smiled at Leola.

"You hain't had time to earn much money but you could wear that peachy getup you brought from home. Bet it goes real well with your complexion."

The knot around Leola's heart eased, thinking it might be fun to dress up and take pictures. Grateful, too, she had a friend like Ruthie, who seemed to always sense when she needed cheering up.

"How do we get a camera for taking pictures?" Leola asked. She hadn't personally known anyone who owned such a device—although ever since Mr. Kodak introduced his one-dollar Brownie, everyone seemed to want one.

"We already have the camera."

It was Euless piping up. She was a mousy thing, didn't speak much—somewhat resembled a rodent, too, with dishwater hair, a narrow face, and round eyes that made her seem perpetually baffled.

"The Mission Trustees gave it to us," she added, "few months back."

Glenda crumpled the waxed paper from her sandwich, shoving it into her bag.

"If Brother Giles will let us have it longer than a minute, you mean." She sucked her teeth. "He's been hoggin' it for himself. Other day I heard Mrs. Giles admonishing him for bein' holed up in that darkroom of his at all hours."

She looked at Leola.

"Has he given you the sermon about how we ain't to go into that place under any circumstances?"

"No, but Ruthie mentioned it."

"Don't matter," Euless offered. "I saw he's put a big ol' padlock on the door. Said Mrs. Giles was nearly beside herself, thinking some kiddie might get in there, chugging down chemicals like lemonade and—"

"I was helpin' out with one of the Gileses' supper parties the other night," Ruthie interrupted, "and Catherine Valchar was there." She turned to Leola. "Mrs. Valchar is the newest trustee and the nicest by a long drink'a moonshine. Her husband, Andrew, is a banker, rich as King Midas. It was Catherine's idea to give us the camera in the first place."

She spat out the blade of grass she'd been chewing.

"Anyhow, Brother was all puffed up, showin' off his tedious snapshots—Mrs. Valchar looked ready to fall asleep from it too. Except then she called me over, ask't did any of us ever get to use the camera

ourselves, seein' we were the ones it were intended for? I felt on the
spot, yet considered it my duty to answer honest. Told her we'd used
the contraption once or twice in the beginning and hadn't seen hide
nor hair of it since." Her mouth twisted. "Girls, let me tell you! Mrs.
Valchar may seem sugar-and-spice-and-everything-nice, but she
shot Brother a look to freeze over Hell and give the Devil pneumonia.
Why, John Giles! she says, *I believe you are monopolizin' the gift we
gave for our young people to use.*"

Ruthie lowered her voice.

"I swan, that man's face went red as the cherries on Mrs. Hooks's
black forest cake. Then Mrs. Valchar got what she called *a brilliant
idea,* sayin' us kids should organize a photo exhibit, p'rhaps sell tickets to earn some money." She sighed. "'Course that was weeks ago
and I still hain't seen hide nor hair of our Brownie, have y'all?"

When everyone shook their heads, Ruthie yanked a fresh blade
of chewing grass.

"Mrs. Valchar likes me right well," she mused, "and is a swell
sport besides. I could bring it up with her again and she might ask
Brother about it. He can't get vexed at *her.*"

Before anyone could agree or disagree with this tactic, a red-
headed boy from Leola's chemistry class sauntered toward them.
Leola couldn't remember his name but, with his pomaded hair, cap-
toe Oxfords, and shining smile, had already pegged him for the upper
tier of Town Kid society.

"Well look who it is." Ruthie murmured, around the grass.
"Gordon 'Big Red' LaHaye, visiting us poor urchins in our orphanage
slum."

"Howdy there, ladies!" Gordon called, despite mostly gawping at
Leola—much as she'd caught him doing in class a few times.

"Mr. Kelly found an extra chemistry text in the office." He handed her a thick book. "Says you need it right away, seeing you're such a promising student. There's no charge either."

"Much obliged," Leola responded, feeling somewhat self-conscious about this public act of charity. Gordon, however, seemed too admiring to notice.

"I told the teacher the way you answer questions in class, you could probably write your own science book."

Leola's face warmed as she flipped the pages, pretending not to notice the glances ricocheting between her and Gordon, even though her friends knew well enough she had a beau who was visiting next week.

Another boy appeared then, keeping his distance as if their group might carry some new form of influenza.

"C'mon Gordo," the boy shouted. "Quit killin' the ladies so we can get our teams drawn up!"

Gordon waved, turning back to Leola.

"Guess I better light a shuck." He bowed. "But if I can be of further assistance, just holler. I *am* class president and *do* have some sway 'round this place."

As he trotted off, Ruthie dug an elbow into Leola's side, nodding toward the ball court.

"Lookee yonder, will you? Meanie and Ding Dong appear fit to be tied, seein' Big Red fawning over one of us."

And it was true. The two Town Girls were shooting darts sharp enough to feel even from afar.

"Minnie's craved that boy's attention since she fell off the turnip truck," Glenda laughed, "and he won't give her the time'a day."

"No matter." Leola shrugged. "Judging from those soft-looking hands of his, Gordon's a dewdropper never done a lick of honest labor in his life. I myself prefer *real* men, the kind with color on their cheeks and muscle in their backs, the better to feel 'neath my fingers when we're alone."

As Ruthie gave an approving whistle and the other girls giggled, Leola snuck one more peek at Minnie and Willie Belle, pouting on their sacred bench. Mama used to say vengeance was reserved for God alone, which seemed a mite selfish on His part, like hiding a warm batch of Mrs. Hooks's cookies so no one else could have a bite. Smiling, she twiddled her fingers at the two girls, savoring every morsel of their comeuppance, however paltry it was.

CHAPTER 39

A s soon as church service was over on Sunday, Ruthie hustled Leola toward the back of the sanctuary.

"Mrs. Valchar's the hostess at fellowship hour. It'll be a good time to ask about gettin' our camera back."

They headed across the Commons Room, stopping just shy of the refreshments table.

"That's Catherine Valchar," Ruthie whispered, nodding at a woman chatting with a portly older man. "Ain't she the bee's knees?"

Leola nodded, thinking Mrs. Valchar was a beauty along the lines of Lillian Gish or Mary Pickford—fashionable, too, in a pin-tucked taffeta frock, a brown-and-white cloche hugging her bobbed hair. The way her elegant fingers whisked the air as she spoke reminded Leola of how Ship might've turned out ten years hence, and she felt cheated again of their future together.

But as they waited for Mrs. Valchar to finish her conversation, Leola couldn't help giggling at Ruthie's whispered observations of their company: Mrs. Shaw's abundant crop of chin hairs, Reverend Braithwaite's barking laughter, a little girl picking her nose while ogling a plate of shortbread.

Finally, Catherine—who'd been flashing them discreet SOS messages with her eyes—brought her conversation to a halt.

"It's been lovely speaking with you, Byron," she nodded at Ruthie and Leola. "However, I asked these young ladies to seek me out and have kept them waiting too long. Shall we continue our discussion after the board meeting next week?"

Mr. Stone blinked as if noticing the girls for the first time.

"Yes, of course." He beamed. "No matter we disagree on some issues, Catherine, it's a fine thing you do, taking an interest in our female orphans, modeling what they might become if they stay on the straight and narrow."

After he'd gone, the girls hurried to Mrs. Valchar.

"Sorry to interrupt your conversin'," Ruthie said, but the woman only chuckled.

"I should be thanking *you*." She lowered her voice. "Byron Stone's a nice fellow but does go on. I've no idea what he meant by *straight and narrow* either, for he's always chiding me over my so-called *militant viewpoints*. In fact, he'd just got done arguing against my support of married women owning bank accounts. Believes it will give females more cause to escape unsatisfactory marriages to which I say, *And what is wrong with that?*"

Before either girl could answer, Mrs. Valchar offered her hand to Leola.

"Don't believe we've met. You must be Miss Rideout?" Her eyes sparkled. "I've heard such wonderful things about you. Brother says— and I quote—that you're among his *most intelligent and determined charges*. Said you'd like to attend college?"

Leola nodded, somewhat surprised Brother Giles had spoken so highly of her. Lately he seemed to either watch her too closely or not notice her at all.

"Thinking of becoming a science teacher," she said, and Mrs. Valchar grinned.

"I don't see what would prevent you from it! I'm a college graduate myself. University of Texas, class of 1916. Majored in nutrition sciences. Haven't had a career of it, of course, but figure it will serve me well enough if—*when*—Mr. Valchar and I have children. Poor things will become my personal test subjects, I s'pose, forced to endure marmite sandwiches and veal broth pudding and such."

She shook her head.

"I'm guessing y'all didn't come 'round to hear me prattle on about the dietary needs of my future family."

Ruthie leaned closer.

"It's about that Brownie camera you gave us. I was serving at the Gileses' *soiree*," she glanced at Leola, "and heard you say we should have use of it. I've asked Brother Giles but he still keeps it for himself."

Mrs. Valchar folded her arms.

"Seems we younger members of the board have no authority, after all, when we give our orders!" She paused. "P'rhaps it makes better sense then to buy y'all a brand new camera. Young folk these days do seem to like memorializing their experiences. And what sorts of things are you hoping to capture?"

Ruthie and Leola had discussed ahead of time whether they should be honest with Mrs. Valchar about their plans, worried she'd think taking self-portraits was a frivolous, even vain, undertaking, or that she'd mention it to the Gileses, who could very well quash the idea. In the end though Ruthie insisted Catherine Valchar, of all people, would understand—and by gum, she was right. The minute they explained their idea, the woman clapped like an excited child.

"That seems like perfect fun for modish girls like you." She crinkled her brow. "You could hold the party at my place, if you wish. My living room gets an excellent afternoon light. Fact is, I could use some amusement, what with Mr. Valchar away on business so often."

She lowered her voice. "At this point I've been to enough Temperance Society meetings and sewing circles to last a lifetime."

"We wouldn't want to put you out," Leola murmured, trying to be polite, though Ruthie had no such compunction.

"Thanks be, Mrs. V.!" She hugged Mrs. Valchar so hard, the woman had to clutch her hat to keep it from tumbling off. "The only place we can ever hold a social is in the basement, and then we have to invite the cockroaches and mice too."

Catherine giggled.

"I don't imagine roaches appreciate a thing about fashion, never mind I did see a strange photo in the newspaper recently of mice dressed in frilly attire, posed upon a set of tiny living room furniture!"

"Yoo-hoo, Catherine!" A woman called across the room. "Yoo-hoo!"

Smoothing her Ruthie-crumpled blouse, Mrs. Valchar returned the other woman's wave with half as much enthusiasm.

"Seems my company is requested once more." Her face brightened. "How about we plan your shindig two Sundays hence—the week after Valentine's Day? Mr. Valchar will be in Oklahoma so we can have the place to ourselves. I'll make sure to purchase the new camera by then and broach the subject of your party with the Gileses, pledge to keep things on the up-and-up."

She tapped her bottom lip as if thinking.

"Posing takes stamina so I'll have plenty of refreshment on hand too."

Both girls hugged her this time and, as she started away, Mrs. Valchar winked.

"But no marmite sandwiches, I promise!"

CHAPTER 40

S eeing the envelope on her pillow three days later, Leola felt the same rush of excitement she always did when hearing from Joe—followed by plunging apprehension. Given his upcoming visit, he wouldn't have written so soon unless something momentous had happened.

Ripping open the envelope, she wondered whether Auntie had taken ill or—dare she hope?—if there was news of Papa.

Jan. 25, 1920

Dearest Rose o'Roses,

With regret I write to say I cannot visit as promised next week. Building these greenhouses is onerous, and Blanton still hardly able to keep his mind on what needs doing, meaning I am saddled with most of it. I can't hardly stand not seeing you yet will come the following week, never fear. Meantime keep your spirits up and remember I love you with all my heart.

Leola glimpsed mentions of Mrs. Gumbs and Dora Meeker, something about a Klan march in Jefferson, but couldn't bring herself to read further. Shoving the pages beneath her pillow, she kept from sobbing only because Euless and Glenda were in the room, getting ready for supper.

The next day's busyness, though, made it hard to linger on her disappointment. Besides school, Glee Club rehearsals, and the usual chores, Leola had been promoted from Breakfast Girl to Supper Assistant—an improvement, as she received a small stipend for doing it. She also enjoyed the company of Mrs. Hooks, who didn't change the subject whenever Leola talked about her parents or past life in Bronway, and seemed to sense when she was too downtrodden to speak much at all. On those days, the cook took over their conversation, relating interesting stories about her family back in New Town, the Black section of Waxahachie: the husband who crafted fancy saddles for a living; the daughter who taught at the Colored elementary school; the son, blessed with the gift of oration, who was studying for the ministry.

"Got the spiritual bent from me, I reckon," she said, proudly.

Rebecca Hooks was a lay preacher at the New Town Abyssinian Church, where she was called *Sister Hooks*—an amazement to Leola, who'd never known a woman preacher of *any* color. Sometimes Mrs. Hooks would even ask Leola's opinion on an upcoming sermon, and they often sang hymns together while working.

Still, there was something Leola couldn't understand about her new friend, which was her unusual attitude toward the Gileses. With Mrs. Giles, it manifested mostly in frustration at the woman's domestic skills—or lack thereof.

"Lady's 'bout as useful in the kitchen as hip pockets on a frog," Mrs. Hooks once mumbled after Mrs. Giles had tried—and failed— again to replicate a recipe from one of her magazines, leaving a mess for the cook to salvage.

However, Mrs. Hooks's bearing with Brother Giles—not merely her employer but a *white man*—was a whole other kettle of fish. Once Leola saw her set a plate down so hard in front of Brother, gravy splashed onto his cuff, but she didn't apologize or help clean it up.

Another time, when Brother asked her to make a coconut pie for a Mission Society affair, Mrs. Hooks replied, *I have mince leftover from your last foofaraw and will use that instead,* to which Brother only muttered, *Suit yourself then.*

One day, accompanying Ruthie to collect the Indian tools that littered the countryside, Leola inquired about the situation.

"Reckon Mrs. Hooks believes she can get away with it," Ruthie replied, plucking a stone from the farm field where they walked, "what with so many Black folk beating a path up North and a shortage of cooks 'round here."

She gave the rock a quick once-over before tossing it away.

"And she ain't just any chef neither, but her desserts get raves from all our visiting dignitariats." She peered at Leola. "Did you know she has a business on the side, keeping Mission Society members in rhubarb fancies and currant buns? Buys her own supplies, uses our kitchen in the off-hours. Makes a tidy sum, I warrant."

Leola was surprised Mrs. Hooks hadn't told her this before, but did remember seeing three chocolate cakes and two lemon tarts on the kitchen counter recently that had soon disappeared.

"If she's so skilled, why doesn't Mrs. Hooks take a better position elsewhere? Seems she could find work, easy, with a neat family of five instead of feeding twenty-some-odd bottomless pits."

"Maybe," Ruthie squinted at the ground, "Mrs. Hooks likes that the Gileses let her go home every night 'stead of having to live in. Or maybe she appreciates that they allow her baking enterprise."

Whooping, she bent to retrieve a white arrow point so shiny and perfect, it might have been dropped days, instead of a thousand years, ago.

"This'll make a fine addition to my collection, won't it?" she asked, and Leola nodded.

"You got so many relics in that shoebox beneath your bed," she said with a laugh, "y'ought open your own exhibition hall." She traced her hand in the air, imagining what the sign would read. "Ruthie Sara Free's Hall of Historical Marvels!"

As they started home, their talk returned—again—to the mystifying situation with Mrs. Hooks and Brother Giles.

"Maybe you could ask Mrs. Hooks about it," Ruthie suggested, without much conviction. Both of them knew the woman would never confide such private concerns to a white person—even a low-down orphan, who still had better standing in the world than any Black preacher-chef, however talented.

"By the way, speaking of baking!" Ruthie's eyes sparkled. "Mrs. Valchar came by yesterday to order some pies for our posin' party. Couldn't stop talking about the new camera she bought, how the store owner offered a discount if she'd get our pictures developed there, which she said she would happily do and pay for herself."

She let out an incredulous laugh.

"That woman is better than a fairy godmother. Never seems to put any conditions to her wish-grantin', like in the old stories, where the princess has to live with the ugly beast or trade her voice to wed some prince? It's like Mrs. Valchar is happy *we're* happy and that's enough." She glanced at Leola. "She'd make a good mother, don't you think?"

Leola nodded. "She gets a sadness in her eyes sometimes, talking about children. I wonder if she and Andrew are having trouble in that department."

"Can't be for lack of trying." Ruthie chortled. "Leastways if handsome Andrew was *my* husband, it wouldn't be for lack of trying. Know what I mean?"

And Leola did know. If there was one thing she anticipated about her future with Joe, it was the *trying*.

February 1920

CHAPTER 41

Leola was in math class when the principal's assistant, Polly, bustled into the room.

"Excuse me, Miss Nestor. I believe you have a student, name of Leola Rideout?"

Miss Nestor pointed at the second row, and Polly addressed Leola.

"There's been some difficulty with your sister at the elementary school. You need to get down there at once."

"Is Mae all right?"

"All's I know is there's been trouble. Principal Nylander gave you permission to leave for the day."

Leola didn't say another word but got her jacket and set out for Mae's school, half a mile away. She would've run except there'd been a wintery blast the night before and the slick road made the going slow, giving her time to imagine the worst.

In some ways, it was true what Ruthie had said that first day: Leola's daily burden for her sisters *had* lessened since arriving at the Home. At times, in fact, she wondered if she'd been *too* lax in her worrying duties. Neither girl was thriving—Karla still wouldn't talk and Mae kept to herself, refusing to sing in music classes, rarely playing with other children. Leola knew they were struggling but didn't know where to turn. After that one conversation with Brother Giles, she'd been afraid to approach him, not wanting to raise the matter of adoption again. Most days, it was easier to lose herself in her own distractions than face her helplessness over the future.

Entering the primary school, Leola spied her sister slouched on a hallway bench, hair hanging about her face like a curtain. Looking so alone.

"Mae!" She rushed over, scanning the girl for signs of injury. "You all right?"

Instead of answering with words, Mae began to sob and Leola sat down, pulling her close. "Hush. I'm here. *Shhhh*."

An older woman in a ruffled blouse came out of the office, introducing herself as the principal, Mrs. Erskine.

Leola stood. "What happened? My sister's beside herself."

Mrs. Erskine cast a reproving look at Mae.

"Seems your sister had an *accident* during the spelling contest. Wet herself quite thoroughly, I'm afraid."

Leola's face heated like she'd committed the mishap.

"There must be some reason *why*. My sister's never done that before."

Mrs. Erskine pinched her lips together.

"According to the teacher, Mae was dawdling before lunch and missed her time in the toilet." She gave the girl another barely tolerant look. "She does tend to dilly-dally, I'm told."

Leola felt a rush of emotion—pity, maybe even frustration, toward Mae but mostly anger that grown folk found something amiss in a little kid being, well, *little*.

"My sister's had so many changes. It might take her a while to learn the new routines."

The principal sighed, motioning at the unfamiliar, too-short dress Mae was wearing.

"Lucky we keep extra clothing for such emergencies, though we were hard-pressed to find something she could fit into, since this usually only happens to the *younger* ones." She cleared her throat. "We did our best to dry her underthings. Wait here. I'll get them."

Returning from the office, she handed a damp paper sack to Leola before addressing Mae.

"You must remember to use the toilet when your teacher says. Can you do that?"

Mae gave the tiniest nod and Leola wanted to scoop her up like a baby, but knew it would embarrass her further.

"I do trust Mae will soon find friends here," Mrs. Erskine said, in an almost scolding tone, "and p'rhaps more reasons to smile." She glanced at the clock. "Meanwhile, school's nearly over. I reckon the girl's too distracted to learn much else today. Best take her home—or rather, to *the* Home."

The woman stuck out her hand, but Leola had already started away with Mae and pretended not to notice.

Outside, the girls walked in silence awhile. It was another half-mile to the orphanage and Leola was glad for the stretch of time together.

"How did it really go, Mae," she asked at last, "to make you forget yourself like that?"

The girl kicked at a clump of dirt.

"I was waiting my turn at the washroom after lunch, but everyone kept going ahead of me, sayin' I'd have to get used to waiting, being a *Home Kid* and all."

She ran a sleeve across her nose, talking faster.

"Then mealtime was over and the bell was rung and . . . and I knew if I was late, Teacher wouldn't let me do the contest and I didn't want to miss it. I didn't! I studied hard and knew 'em, too, all those words, and I had to win so they wouldn't think I were just some dumb ol' orphan in a cotton-sack dress." She snuffled. "Then it was my turn and I couldn't hold it no more and," her shoulders trembled, "there it was, a big puddle 'neath me."

She clamped her arms around her sister so hard, Leola could feel the damp of tears through her own blouse. When a car careened around them, blaring its horn, she led Mae to a flat boulder beside the road.

"Sit here," she patted the rock, grown warm from the sun, "and tell me the rest."

After the girl plunked down, Leola lowered beside her.

"Teacher had me clean up my tee-tee with a rag," Mae continued, "and take it to the trash pile out back." She shuddered. "The kids were laughing at me through the window. I seen 'em! Laughin' and pointin' . . ."

Leola ached, envisioning the episode. She made Mae blow her nose again, smoothing tear-drowned strands of hair from her face.

"Your teacher shouldn't have let the others poke fun of you. And she needs to give you more time at the restroom. I'll speak to her tomorrow, see what can be done."

Mae, a little calmer, hiccupped.

"I know these past months have been a trial." Leola touched her sister's cheek. "And you've been brave and good."

She wanted to promise that things wouldn't always be so hard, that there were better days ahead—which felt like a lie, of sorts. Instead she pulled the uneaten cookie from her lunch sack.

"Hungry?" she asked.

The way Mae gulped the cookie was her answer. Probably she felt rushed at lunch, too, and hardly ate. Leola recalled seeing the girl scarf her supper a few times like a racehorse. Remembered ignoring the clammy knowledge that her sister was half-starved and there must be a reason why.

Then Mae wiped her sticky fingers on the borrowed pinafore and Leola winced, realizing she'd have to launder it and Mae's peed-upon garments in secret. If she sent the unfamiliar dress and soiled clothing down the laundry chute, someone might ask questions, and she didn't want Mae getting the clothespin. Not for that. Not for *anything*.

"I only wish Papa would come get us," Mae murmured, "so we didn't have to be Home Kids no more."

Leola sucked her teeth, regretting whatever hope she'd planted in her sister's mind. Recently, she'd come to understand how Joe had felt, thinking it better they grieve outright instead of feeling disappointed every day Papa failed to appear. Those days were adding up, too, the dim trail of clues he'd left growing fainter and fainter. She'd used the last of Auntie's money to send more telegrams to the oil company and Mrs. Grimes, with no response. And yesterday, when she'd asked Brother Giles if the state agency had any news, he'd answered curtly, *They've said they will investigate. I'll inform you the minute they report their findings.*

It might be time, she thought, to steel her sister for the possible outcome.

"Living at the Home has nothing to do with who you are inside, Mae. It's not your fault we're here. The kids who make you feel bad about it—well it could just as well be them someday, in our situation." She paused. "Truth is, I don't know if Papa *will* come back. We must prepare ourselves for that, in case."

She'd braced herself for Mae's despondency, but the girl only shrugged.

"Oh, he ain't dead."

Leola's heart sank, thinking Mae hadn't registered her words.

"I reckon I've made you *think* Papa is alive. But I'm not—"

"Karla sees him all the time." Mae spoke as if describing the sun in the sky. "And he ain't dead."

"*Sees?*" Leola frowned. "I know Karla has dreams of our parents—"

"No, Lee. She don't just see Papa in her *dreams* but also while she's awake."

A chill gripped Leola's spine.

"How do you know?"

"She done told me. Said he comes to visit when she's alone. Once while she was playing dollies 'neath the porch, he was there, watchin' her."

Leola gawped at her sister, a thousand questions crowding her mind.

"Karla's speakin' then? More than a few words?"

Mae nodded. "Only to Papa and me." Her brow furrowed. "'Cept Mrs. Bentham heard her telling me about Papa. She ax't me about it later."

Leola stared. "Oh?"

"Mmm-hmmm. Then those folks came to visit Karla. Last week, think it was. She told me they ax't her 'bout Papa's visits too." A proud expression flashed across her face. "Karla didn't say a thing. Just took the candies they gave her and kept her mouth shut."

Waves of uneasiness swept over Leola. Were *those folks* the couple who wanted to adopt Karla? Sometimes prospective parents did that, Ruthie had said, to *kick the tires before buying.*

"What kind of people were they? What did they look like, I mean?"

Mae studied a passing cloud.

"I dunno. Grown folk, dressed all spiffy, with writing pads and such. Smiling like this . . ." Her lips stretched tightly across her teeth. "Then they took her to Brother's office for *a little talk.*"

Leola tried to quash her anxiety, assuring herself there must be some explanation. Weeks remained before they'd officially become *full orphans*. Interested parties could look all they want. It didn't mean a whit.

Mae picked up a stick, jabbing at a patch of ice.

"I'm tired, Lee. And hungry. Can we go back to the Home now?"

Leola hesitated, wanting to probe further, but knew Mae had had enough for one day. She stood, taking the child's hand, musing more to herself than her sister, "If these visions of Karla's bring her comfort, if it makes her happy to talk to him—"

"*Papa* makes her happy," Mae said, in a resolute tone. "And knowin' he's not dead, that makes *me* happy."

Staring down at her, Leola felt a sudden ferocity. *And if Papa is alive*, she nearly blurted, *and doesn't want to come back to us? What then?* Of course she didn't say this, instead leading Mae toward the road, swinging their arms, happy to change the subject.

"It'll be nice getting to the Home before the other kids. Mrs. Hooks made a big pitcher of buttermilk last night. How 'bout we sneak ourselves a glass?"

The way Mae grinned, Leola understood her sister craved the taste of fresh buttermilk as she did—because it reminded them both of *real* home, a distant place where everyone got the hot lunch and papas weren't pretend.

CHAPTER 42

That night, Mae and Karla's dormitory was a beehive of activity, children running in and out of the washroom while trying to cram in some playtime before bed.

Mae knew Leola would be visiting Karla so didn't protest when the two sisters went off together. Though Karla was clearly pleased by Leola's attention—smiling, giggling, squeezing her hand—she didn't utter a single word as they headed down the hall.

Leola had decided the sleeping porch was their best chance for privacy. Because it was too drafty for sleeping during wintertime, the ward mothers had outfitted it as a playroom, with a few books and toys, and a shabby upholstered chair in one corner.

"Go on, sweet-sweet," Leola urged, settling in the chair, "pick a book for us to read."

Karla chose a story about barnyard animals and climbed into her sister's lap.

The first page of the book showed a brown horse with a bright red barn in the background. *Here is the horse,* Leola read, *the one that says neigh/Here is the horse, eating his hay.* Karla laughed as Leola made whinnying sounds to accompany the verse, but as they turned the next page, sat up so fast, her head bashed against Leola's chin.

"Oof!" Leola rubbed the sore place, surprised Karla didn't seem to feel the rising knot on her own head.

"Papa's piggie!" the girl shouted, tapping the illustration. "Dat his pig, Wee-wee!"

Hearing her sister speak—using so many words, all at once—astonished Leola, though she tried not to make a to-do of it, worried the girl would clam up again if she did.

"That's right, Karla," she replied. "It *is* a pig, like the one we had with the big white spots on its back and the—"

"No, Wee! Not Mama's piggie!" *Tap-tap-tap.* "*Papa's* pig! Flo-ya!"

Leola scanned the page. "I don't see any flowers, sweetheart."

"Da pig, Wee!" Karla was nearly beside herself. "It name—*Flo-ya.*"

Leola's fingertips went icy. Was the girl talking about Flora, the so-called magical charm who was the daughter of Francis, tucked away with Leola's hose and petticoats? Flora, whom Papa had taken to Houston and far as she knew, never shown her sisters?

Karla didn't seem to notice Leola's shock. The dam of silence had crumbled and her words flowed like a springtime freshet.

"Make a wis'!" She rubbed the illustrated pig furiously with one finger. "Wis'! On Flo-ya. Like Papa do!"

Leola felt dizzy, remembering her father's words: *I will rub her head each night, and Flora will fulfill each wish made upon her.*

She spun Karla around, shaking the girl.

"How do you know about Flora? Did Papa tell you, before he went away? Did I tell you, and forget?" Her voice was strangled. "*How do you know?*"

Karla went pale as chalk, sliding from Leola's lap, backing toward the door with terrified eyes, reminding Leola of when she'd switched Mae—the silverfish moment of near-ruined trust between them.

She leapt off the chair, crouching to take Karla in her arms.

"I'm sorry, poppet. You're right. It *is* Flora and she *is* good for wishing upon, like Aladdin's lamp in the storybook." She pressed her nose against the girl's hair. "I didn't mean to frighten you." She sat back, gazing at her sister. "I understand you miss Papa—Mae said he comes to you, *talks* to you, and that you talk to him!" She tried to smile. "Is that true?"

The child gave a solemn nod and Leola pitched her voice calm as she could.

"Where does he appear, Karla? Besides under the porch?"

Her sister gave the faintest shrug. "Ev-wee-where?"

Leola stared again into the huge brown eyes.

"And what," pause, "what does Papa tell you?"

Karla bent forward, answering very quietly, "He say, *I wook for you.*"

Leola blinked, recalling Mae's refusal to accept that their father might be gone forever. How could she expect Karla, so much younger and more fragile, to understand? After all, it was what she wished too.

"Oh, darlin'," she muttered. "I know that's what you want. But if—"

"Ssssss!" Karla's eyes went round, and she pressed a finger to her lips. "Wisten, Wee. He here!"

Leola hesitated, wanting to appease her sister, yet also wanting to shake her again, tell her to stop acting foolish. Wanting to stop the girl's heart from breaking.

And then, all at once, she felt something encircle them, a movement of air—not the breeze around the windowpanes but something more substantial and warm, like a breath or a whisper. *All will be well,* it seemed to say.

Watching Karla close her eyes, seeing the strange smile on her lips, Leola's scalp prickled.

"Karla?"

No response, only the rapturous expression—and the swirling

force around them, the mysterious feeling of peace. Leola wanted to give in to it, too, like her sister seemed to be doing. Instead, she nudged the girl, nearly shouting.

"Karla!"

The child's eyes flew open, her ecstatic expression vanishing—the heavy blanket of warmth lifting too. For a long moment, the two of them were still, Leola trying to sort what she'd just experienced, Karla, limp and blank-faced in her arms.

After a while, Leola picked up the storybook lying nearby. Opened it with shaky hands.

"So," she forced a cheery tone, "if it's Flora in this story then we *should* wish upon her. How about we tell her what you want for your birthday—p'rhaps a trip to town for a malted?"

Karla didn't answer.

"Or," Leola rushed on, "if the weather is fine, a picnic in the park or—"

"Wis' Papa take us back to home."

Leola hesitated, remembering the eerie sensation of moments earlier; eerie, she realized, because it seemed so familiar, like what she'd felt when Papa appeared after her tussle with Opal, or the countless times she'd wrangled with schoolwork and he'd cheered her on. Or the way he'd pledged, before he left, that they would be together again. Leola had no way of making sense of it—to herself, much less Karla. But just because she'd begun to consider the awful possibility he wouldn't return didn't mean they couldn't still *hope*.

"All right." She picked up the girl's hand, pressing it against the page. "Close your eyes and say after me: *Flora pig/Who we love dear/ We wish for Papa/Bring him here!*"

Karla repeated the words and Leola went still, almost longing for the strange presence to embrace them again. Longing at first, then glad when it didn't. Glad she could tell herself it had never happened at all.

"Shall we blow on the pig," she asked, "like a birthday candle, to make the spell extra-magical?"

Karla nodded and they counted to three, blowing hard.

"Will it work 'den?" Karla peeked at her sister. "Will da wish come twew?"

Leola stared at her. *Hope,* she told herself. *It's all we have.*

"I reckon it's a very strong spell," she replied, "and Flora will do her best to bring it true."

This seemed to satisfy the girl. She nestled close to Leola, listening to a verse from *The Turtle Dove:*

O yon doth sit that turtle dove;
Doth sit on yonder high tree.
A'makin' a moan for the loss of his love
As I will do for thee.

The room next door had gone quiet, and Leola knew someone would come looking for them any minute. Before she could rouse Karla, the girl jerked violently, crying out in garbled speech, making Leola think of those strange visions. P'rhaps the recent shocks had knocked something loose inside her sister, something that might never get glued back together. Maybe Papa's "visitations," the self-imposed silence and tearful nightmares, weren't some supernatural force at all—or even hopefulness—but early portents of madness. Leola had read a newspaper story about a special hospital in Boston for young mental patients. *Unfortunate tykes,* the author had written, *whose early trials have crushed their tender souls beyond repair.*

She shivered, throwing off her gloomy notions. Karla was too young to be broken. Too new to be wrecked. As a country child with few playmates or diversions, she'd developed a vivid imagination to keep occupied. That was all these apparitions were—a way of handling loneliness and uncertainty. Karla could still play and eat and smile. When she wanted, she could speak, even better than before! No, Leola told herself, Karla would be fine. They all would. The Rideout girls were strong.

That's what Papa always said.

CHAPTER 43

For Leola and her friends, visiting a department store like Epstein's was somewhat like entering a museum of artifacts, ones far more delicate than Ruthie's relics.

Studying the cases of jewelry and taffeta-wrapped mannequins, the girls kept their hands to themselves, aware Mrs. Giles and Halette Epstein, the owner's daughter, were watching. Smudges left on glass or—even worse—fabric would be met with stern reminders that this was a fine establishment, not a country fair.

"Stars and garters!" Ruthie leaned over a case of pearl necklaces displayed against blue velvet cloth. "Some of these rocks are big as ball bearings!"

The shop girl—dressed like a mannequin herself—glided over to explain the pearls were from the Far East, natural stones that cost two thousand dollars for a single strand. Leola gasped, calculating what such money could afford: her entire college tuition *and* the down-payment on a small house, with enough left over for visiting Houston to find Papa.

Now Mrs. Giles was clapping, ending her flight of fantasy.

"Let's not whistle up the wind, girls, but adjust our sights on more realistic aspirations." She pointed toward the rear of the store. "The sales annex is there. You may shut the door to try on your finds. Just remember whatever you choose should be nice enough to wear at the

Mission Ball in three weeks but sturdy enough to last. And keep in mind your budget!"

As they flew to the sales room, Leola was happy she wouldn't have to press her nose to the proverbial window. Last week Mrs. Giles had informed her and some of the other girls that the Mission Society Auxiliary—mostly on the urging of Mrs. Valchar—would address their *meager wardrobe situation.*

Catherine believes all young ladies should have not only decent, but fashionable, *attire,* Mrs. Giles had explained, *to help make up for other insecurities. So the Mission Society will parcel out monies from their Rainy Day Fund to use when we visit Epstein's next week.*

As she'd handed over the cash, Leola had felt a fair helping of shame along with the gratitude. Imagined the Society ladies clicking their tongues over the plight of the Rideout sisters, commenting about irresponsible parents, judging her father a cad.

She decided to let those thoughts go, for the moment, giving in to the frenzy of the hunt, pawing through the piles of dresses—never mind, as Glenda quickly pointed out, they were last season's fashions, discarded by shoppers who could afford to be picky.

"Quit gripin'," Ruthie huffed. "Even a blind hog finds an acorn every so often."

She held up a mauve dress with a cluster of silk grapes at the waist.

"Look at this number! It's too fitted for me but . . ." Her glance darted over the room. "Maudifrank Swenson, this fairly screams your name! The color matches your eyes right well."

Leola had spotted the dress earlier and thought she might try it herself, but Ruthie was right. Maudifrank could do it far more justice—could do a burlap sack justice, if it came to that.

Leola had been a mite envious of Maudi when they met, for she was a beauty of the first degree, with deep violet eyes, cupid's-bow mouth, and tiny waist. Screaming babies chortled when they beheld her, men tripped over themselves when she passed, teachers put her in the first row, as if to distract unannounced school board visitors from dull lessons. Even Brother Giles seemed taken by the girl, often excusing her from chores because of a "lingering disability" from her own bout of the flu, an irony that didn't escape Leola one bit.

As she'd gotten to know her, though, Leola felt more pitying than envious of her friend. There was a hollowness about Maudi—something removed and distant, as if at times she'd flown away and left her body behind. 'Course she'd suffered more tragedy even than the rest of them. After losing all their money in oil speculation, her father had died of influenza, followed in quick turn by her mother. Then her younger brother and only sibling got run over while playing in the street, with Maudi watching from the window. Leola figured God, in making the girl, had given her an extra helping of attractiveness to compensate for what was to come.

"If you wear this," Ruthie was saying to Maudifrank, "you'll make the best portrait at Mrs. Valchar's next week." She winked. "I don't doubt but Warren Granger would like a photo of you for his back pocket."

Maudi's face fell quicker than one of Mrs. Giles's sad souffles.

"I do not like Warren Granger," she muttered, examining an ugly brown frock that was obviously too big.

"Aw, Maudes." Ruthie shuffled her feet. "Anyone can see the way that boy looks at you, all goggle-eyed. Besides, he ain't half-bad himself in the looks department and has a good job working at the—"

"Don't care where he works. I don't like Warren nor any other boy," Maudifrank answered—so loud, everyone fell silent.

Not that they were surprised by this outburst. They'd all seen Maudi hide when young men came calling for her. *Tell him I'm not here,* she'd plead, as if a police platoon stood waiting in the vestibule and not some Brylcreemed scarecrow with knobby knees.

"I may not attend Mrs. Valchar's social after all," Maudi said, a bit more gently. "Need to catch up on my Latin."

Ruthie hung her head. "I can be more full'o wind than a corn-eating mule." She peeked at Maudi. "But you can't miss a party for *Latin.* Mrs. Valchar has the poshest house and promised us all sorts of delicacies. It'll be a corkin' good time."

Maudifrank stared miserably at her shoes, and Leola was sure she'd either burst into tears or yell at Ruthie again. But she only flashed a remorseful smile.

"'Course I'll go. Sorry I got a burr under my saddle. It's just . . . I hate the way I look in photographs." She poked her cheeks. "The camera makes my face seem fatter, like I got the mumps."

Ruthie sniffed. "If you think *yourself* unbecoming in pictures then the rest of us better save the cost of film while we're ahead."

When Maudifrank chuckled, Leola felt relieved, holding up the moss-green frock she'd found for herself.

"What do y'all think of this? There's a little snag by the collar— one here, too, on the bodice. I have a few embellishments from my mother's sewing basket should cover them."

Ruthie came nearer.

"Why, that's the smart sort of thing Mrs. Valchar would wear." She nudged Leola. "Would make the perfect getup for an outing with Joe the Beau, too, when he comes to visit."

Now it was Leola's turn to blush, though of course she'd already envisioned Joe's helpless expression when he beheld her in the hip-clinging dress, hair swept into a loose chignon . . . the better, he'd say, to pull out the pins and watch it unwind.

CHAPTER 44

"Criminy and cream!" Ruthie muttered, climbing Mrs. Valchar's front steps the day of the posing party. "Catherine's adobe is almost more handsome than her."

Leola wasn't sure if her friend meant to use the Spanish word for *house* instead of *abode,* but was too busy admiring the Valchar residence to care. Though she'd seen bigger, fancier places in Waxahachie, this home's whimsical gingerbread trim, lead glass windows, and wraparound veranda perfectly reflected Catherine Valchar's understated style and charm.

After a few knocks, a housemaid answered the door, explaining that Mrs. Valchar was running late. As she led them inside, the girls *oohed* and *aahed* over the honeyed oak furniture and patterned linoleum floors, all of it like an advertisement from a home decorating magazine. Even more, they agreed, it smacked of being grown and having a life of one's own.

Soon Mrs. Valchar appeared, full of apologies for not welcoming them herself.

"I could not get this pin on to save my life," she said, gesturing at the flowery brooch on her collar. "Took a bit of jiggerin' but here I am."

Smoothing her black hair, which dipped in a perfect curve beneath her chin, she gave the girls appreciative once-overs.

"Y'all are pretty as, well, *pictures*." She motioned toward the dining room. "However, excited as you are for the portrait sessions, I'm not too old to remember being your age and hungry 'bout all the time. Thought you'd want to start with some refreshment."

The girls, already licking their chops, followed her, gasping at the platters of sandwiches and cakes spread about the oval table.

"Gad night a'livin'!" Ruthie squawked. "When I am done with this feast, y'all gonna mistake me for the sow and send me to the slaughterhouse."

Leola glanced at Mrs. Valchar, thinking she might take offense at Ruthie's vulgar expression. Instead the woman smiled like it was the finest compliment she'd ever received.

Back in the living room, everyone was too busy eating to talk, so Mrs. Valchar filled the silence with tales of her college days, including her first date with Andrew.

"We drove his Model T to Travis Lake and were just gettin' to, uh, *know* each other when the car rolled straight into the water and us with it." She let off a gleeful snort. "Seems Andrew had forgotten to apply the brake!"

When the girls exclaimed in alarm, Mrs. Valchar laughed harder.

"Oh we were fine. *Mighty* fine! Trust me, there is no better way for a boy and girl to become acquainted than to find themselves in cold water together." She lowered her voice. "Don't quote me on that or Brother Giles will have me ousted from the Mission Board quicker than you can say *sins of the flesh*."

This got them all laughing—to the point where Ruthie choked on a petit four and had to be firmly pounded on the back until it flew out.

After helping herself to another round of dessert, Leola wandered to a cozy sitting area in the hallway where, despite the mild day, a fire roared in the fireplace. Watching the orange flames curl and leap,

Leola remembered a time before Mae and Karla were born, when her family would gather in the parlor on cool evenings—Mama with her sewing, Papa with his pipe, Leola with dollies or coloring pages. From this distance it felt like watching a film reel about someone else's life.

"What do you think of the trifle?"

At the sound of Mrs. Valchar's voice, Leola thudded back to the present.

"It's delicious." She nodded at her plate. "Almost as good as my great-aunt Malvina's."

Mrs. Valchar, sitting down beside her, looked pleased.

"It's only my first attempt at making it, so that's quite the commendation."

Leola cringed. "I thought it was one of Mrs. Hooks's creations." She slid her eyes at the woman. "Guess I've swallowed both feet whole."

Mrs. Valchar shrugged. "No offense taken. No one else's trifle— even Mrs. Hooks's—could ever measure up to a beloved aunt's. I'll make another stab at it someday and invite you over to see if I've improved."

Setting down her plate, Leola brushed crumbs from her lap.

"Before we left Bronway, Auntie gave me her trifle recipe, including—supposedly—all the secret ingredients she used. I can copy it out and give it to you. She uses butter from her own churn and, in late summer, raspberries or mayhaws. It's so rich yet so light—you can't imagine."

Another surge of homesickness engulfed her and she looked away.

"I expect you miss your family something awful," Mrs. Valchar murmured. "Have you heard from your great-aunt lately or anyone else back home?"

"I do hear from my sweetheart, Joe, often enough." Leola twisted the ring on her finger. "Dora Meeker, our neighbor, wrote to say Auntie's palsy is so bad she can't hardly write or speak. The Meekers sold their farm and will take her with them to Shreveport soon. I'm so grateful—she'd be sent to the poorhouse otherwise." Leola gnawed her bottom lip. "But I wonder if I'll ever see her again."

Mrs. Valchar touched her knee.

"You must've brought her untold joy over the years—and those sisters of yours, too. Such darling things." She smiled. "Every time I see little Karla, with those big brown eyes and that fetching expression, I'm about done in! Andrew looked somewhat like that as a boy. His mother tells me she could hardly keep her friends from pinching his cheeks, to the point where, when *any* woman approached, he'd grab his face and run for the hills!" Her bright gaze met Leola's. "Karla must get her share of cheek-pinchin' too, yet doesn't seem the least bit spoiled by it . . ."

As the woman gushed on, Leola felt weak, realizing all at once it was the Valchars who wanted to adopt Karla. This must explain the donation from the Rainy Day Fund, why Catherine had offered her house for their party, bought the camera, laid out such an elaborate banquet. Maybe it was just an attempt to curry favor so Leola wouldn't fuss when they took Karla away.

"Has Brother Giles told you of Karla's disturbance?" she nearly shouted. "How she's haunted by nightmares and won't speak at all, except to the ghosts of our parents?" She sighed. "Don't expect she'll ever be right again."

Mrs. Valchar's frown was exactly what Leola had hoped for. With so many normal orphans to choose from, surely such an *upstanding couple* would think twice about wanting one *peculiar.*

"I did know Karla has suffered," Catherine said, "although . . ."

"I can only imagine," Leola interjected, "what would happen if, on top of everything else, she had to deal with another sudden change. Would be hard to pick up the pieces after that."

Catherine went motionless, face etched with a visible pain that almost made Leola pity her. *Almost.*

"Both girls are lucky to have a devoted sister like you," the woman replied at last. "I'm sure you're right—Karla needs stability more than anything." Her brow furrowed. "There's a new doctor I've heard about at Shriner's Hospital in Dallas. Studied the Talking Cure in Europe. This doctor—I cannot recall his name, at the moment—adapted those same techniques for treating young orphans during the war. I've some contacts at the hospital. P'rhaps we could arrange for him to treat Karla privately at the Home? The Society could cover the costs."

A lump caught in Leola's throat. Much as she wanted to cling to her initial suspicions of this woman—wanted to think this was another attempt to ingratiate herself or create an obligation to be repaid in the dearest way—the pain in Mrs. Valchar's eyes, along with her expression of concern, would be hard to pretend.

As another girl came over to talk, Leola's thoughts whirred too loudly to pay attention. Catherine would make a good mother, like Ruthie had said. The Valchars could give Karla the love she needed and privileges she'd never experience otherwise. They lived close enough that Leola could visit often, maybe even have a say in how Karla was raised. If Papa did return—even if his parenting rights had been dissolved—there'd be some way to work things out. And if he *didn't* come back, Karla would have the chance at a good life after all. Maybe, Leola mused, she'd been wrong in keeping Mama's promise. Maybe Mama had been wrong in asking her to.

Peering at Mrs. Valchar, she wanted to cry out, <u>You</u> *should be her mother. She needs you. I need you.* Of course she didn't, not least because Ruthie appeared then, announcing the picture-taking was about to begin.

"This is a posin' party, after all, and not just for gossiping and stuffing ourselves to the gills." She rubbed her belly. "Mrs. Valchar has generously offered to let us use her powder room to beautify our visages before we start."

"Beautify our sausages?" Euless murmured to Glenda, who grunted in exasperation.

Some of the girls had brought makeup and accessories—hair pomade and lipstick, even eye kohl and pots of rouge—strictly prohibited at the Home, which Leola couldn't figure how they'd gotten hold of.

"It's all right," Ruthie said, dotting rouge on Leola's cheekbones. "Mrs. Valchar said since it's off orphanage property, the rules don't apply. And haven't you seen how she outlines her own eyes, even for church?"

After they were rightfully primped, Mrs. Valchar gave a tutorial on using the camera, which, being newer than the model Brother Giles had seized, possessed a few unfamiliar features. Then they created a backdrop against one wall, moving chairs around, arranging themselves in small groups or pairs, striking poses from serious to silly and everything in between.

Having taken a picture with Ruthie, then Euless and Glenda, Leola let herself be photographed alone, thinking she'd give the finished product to Joe. He'd recently sent a new photo of himself, asking for one in return, saying he wanted to *gaze upon it every night before retiring.*

Eventually, after most of the girls drifted back to the sunroom, Mrs. Valchar approached Maudifrank Swenson, who hadn't moved from her seat the whole time.

"Come," she held out her hand, "your turn to pose."

The girl didn't answer, sinking into the cushion as if trying to blend with its damask pattern.

"Maudifrank doesn't like herself in photographs." Ruthie emerged from the dining room with another plate of sweets. "Thinks her face looks deformed."

Mrs. Valchar laughed. "Nonsense! A face like yours was *meant to be* captured on film, if not in alabaster."

Maudi didn't respond, though Mrs. Valchar kept insisting.

"It's grand that you're neither vain nor conceited. But didn't you say you had some cousins up in Oklahoma who've not seen you in years? I am certain they'd love to know how you've grown. You may think you look plump in pictures but they, most likely, will not."

Maudi hesitated. Mrs. Valchar was not a pal but an adult with authority and charisma, someone she wanted—and needed—to please.

"All right then." The girl stood, exhaling. "If it'll make y'all happy."

Ruthie pointed at a chair by the window. "Arrange yourself there, Mauds."

She shoved the camera into Leola's hands.

"Your turn to play photographer."

Leola held the instrument at her waist, centering the subject in its viewfinder. Wasn't easy to do, as Maudi shifted continually, yanking at the neckline of her dress, licking her lips, twitching like the tail on a squirrel.

"Be still," Leola directed. "And smile! You do have the prettiest smile."

Finally, the girl settled. Tilting her head to one side, Maudi pouted her lips, the sapphire gaze taking on the wily glint of a woman far beyond her fifteen years. Leola looked up from the viewfinder, hardly recognizing this person before her. Ruthie was the only other person still in the room and, judging by her gruff tone, she'd noticed the change too.

"G'wan and snap the picture, Lee. Maudi's got her pose. Can't be expected to hold it forever."

Looking into the lens again, Leola pressed the shutter button, certain even if she never saw the printed image, she'd never forget Maudifrank's expression that day.

CHAPTER 45

"I've a telephone message for you. From Joe."

Mrs. Giles stood in her dorm room, giving Leola a start. She'd arrived earlier than usual from school—with the other girls still at their afternoon activities, she'd thought the place was empty. More surprising however was what Mrs. Giles had said. The Home only recently installed its own telephone—mostly for emergencies, as placing calls was still dear. If Joe had spent his hard-earned money to reach her this way, it did not bode well.

Leola hurried over, tempted to snatch the paper right from the woman's hand.

"The Hello Girl had it delivered here when no one answered our exchange," Mrs. Giles said. "Thought it urgent enough, I guess."

She held out the message before turning away.

"I'll leave you to read it in private."

Not that there was much to read: *Greenhouses behind schedule. Must cancel visit. Joe.*

This time Leola didn't hold back but threw herself weeping across her blanket, stopping occasionally to reread the note—as if it might have transformed to happier news just because she wished it so. Yet there it was, written in the operator's perfect penmanship, threadbare of encouragement or the slightest excuse: *Must cancel visit.*

Hearing voices down the hall, Leola eventually wiped her eyes and sat up, thinking Joe must not love her anymore, that he was too caught up in his new position and the many enticing possibilities of a big place like Tyler—including beguiling city girls and plenty of coins to shower upon them.

Raindrops streaked the window glass like the dark notions streaking her mind, one fusing with another, Joe's rejection tangling too closely with her father's disappearance. *Men need to be adored,* Mama had always said, *put front and center. Worshipped. That is how they are made.*

Leola had always considered this sentiment bunk, believing both men *and* women appreciated attention from those they loved. Now she stared at the ring on her finger, wondering if she'd failed to worship Joe the *right way,* after all. Hadn't he been insulted when she'd hung onto her dreams of college, refusing to deny her desires? And maybe he was right when he'd said she was thinking only of herself. Look how she'd ignored Mae and Karla recently, avoiding the burden of their grief. And how often she snuck into the school library after classes to study—not only to further her college aspirations but because she wanted her name on the Honors list tacked to the principal's door. Leola *liked* glory and admiration. She *wanted* to succeed in the world.

Ambition is a dangerous quality in a woman, people said. *Detracts from their focus on home. Makes them coarse and hard-hearted.*

Leola noticed a stain on the floor, thinking it resembled a reproving face—Joe's or even Papa's. P'rhaps her father also thought her unbecoming, crass, repellent. Maybe she wasn't good enough as a daughter *or* a fiancée . . . or a woman, in general. It could answer why Papa had never come back for them—because there was this defect in her, this *unsuitability* he couldn't stand.

She reached for the photo of Joe propped on her bedside table. In it, he wore a new suit and fresh haircut, along with the very *un*fresh Italian boots. On his face was the bedazzled smile of a drunken sailor, victorious after a game of dice—an expression she'd seen countless times when he'd say, *I cannot believe my luck in having you, Rose o'Roses.*

Leola scanned the photograph, wondering if maybe it wasn't bedazzlement she saw there, but the look of a person biding his time until something better came along—a real woman, meek and dainty, who'd not question the world or ask a thing for herself. A woman Leola could never be.

She spotted the chemistry book on her bureau and thought of Gordon LaHaye. She'd been surprised when he'd volunteered to be her lab partner, not seeming to care a whit when his friends muttered about *shabby Home Girls.* Was surprised, too, at how patiently he'd explained the fancy equipment, how easily he'd chatted about his two dogs, the fact he might become a dentist like his dad.

Until this instant, Leola had viewed Gordon as a friend and nothing more. As she'd told the other girls, he was hardly her type, would never be caught fiddling with flowers, wearing embroidered boots, or speaking Italian around people who considered it the Devil's tongue. Gordon was bland, predictable as the day is long—except in this, his seeming infatuation for a skinny Home Kid with nothing to call her own. Enough reason, she thought, to like him back, if only to prove that Joe and Papa were wrong, that she *was* worth something after all.

So the following Wednesday, she rubbed some of Ruthie's contraband rouge on her cheekbones, donning the green dress she'd planned to save for Joe. During their lab, she laughed louder than usual at Gordon's jokes, complimenting his performance at yesterday's baseball game, saying how scared she'd been when the batter hit a line drive at his head—how relieved, when he'd caught it. Then, while lighting the Bunsen burners, Leola pretended to stumble, singeing her finger in the flame.

"Ouch!" she yelped, prettily as possible, although not so loud the other kids would be alarmed.

Gordon took her wrist, studying the injury. "Jeeps, Lee! You've done yourself in!"

It hardly hurt—not compared to goose bites or cotton boll stings—yet Leola forced tears, allowing Gordon to fetch the emergency kit, rub salve on the finger, and wrap it in gauze. Afterward she let him walk her home—stopping strategically down the road from the orphanage, making sure he saw her wince.

"You all right?" he asked, and Leola offered a valiant smile, lifting her injured hand.

"Just feeling the sting."

This elicited the response she wanted and Gordon drew nearer, concern etching his face.

"Was my fault you burnt yourself. I feel lower'n a snake's belly too—you'll have a scar in the end, sure's I'm standing here."

Leola peeked at him through her lashes, imagining what a girl like Minnie would say. "I'd never hold it against you, Gordon. And if I do have a scar, it'll be one to remember you by."

This did the trick. The boy's eyes filled with hunger, cheeks blazing the color of his hair.

"I'd like to see you again," he murmured. "Take you to the soda fountain on Saturday evening, if you'd agree."

Leola lifted her face. "Yes," she whispered. "That'd be keen."

After making sure the coast was clear, Gordon kissed her on the lips . . . exactly as she'd predicted—as she'd hoped—he would.

CHAPTER 46

On the night of her date with Gordon, Leola brushed her hair, ignoring Ruthie's peeved expression as she watched from the bed.

"I can't for the life of me cotton why you're giving Gordon LaHaye the time of day," she said, "when you have Joe."

Leola sighed.

"Joe isn't here nor seems any closer to being. Surely no one expects me to pine my life away when he hasn't put half the effort into keeping me from it."

Ruthie puffed out her cheeks.

"You read me his last letter saying how hard he's working, saving money so y'all can set up housekeeping someday. Just 'cause he can't visit at the drop of a hat don't mean—"

Leola set the brush upon the bureau with a loud thump. "I'm late."

She started toward the door then turned back, placing the turquoise ring on top of the dresser, not looking at Ruthie at all.

Most girls waited for callers in the kitchen or vestibule, but when Leola had asked permission for their date, Brother Giles insisted she use the fancy parlor for that purpose. *Gordon's father is a fine friend of mine!* he'd exclaimed. *A friend to so many in this town, in fact, for all the investment he's made in it—not to mention the toothaches he's cured!*

He'd chuckled at his own joke.

I'm glad you're finding such high-caliber entertainment here, Miss Rideout, taking new opportunities from your tribulations.

Perching on the horsehair divan, Leola's scoffed aloud. The only *opportunity* she was taking was to . . . what, again? Prove it didn't matter if Joe no longer loved her and Papa had left her, high and dry? Spending a few hours with some candy-leg she hardly knew and didn't care about would never make up for all that.

Watching his shiny automobile pull up outside, Leola considered hiding beneath a table as Maudi did with her own male callers. But it was too late; she could hear Brother and Gordon carrying on at the front door. Reassuring herself she'd only go on this one date, treat it as friendship and never step out with him again, she ventured into the hallway.

Brother Giles seemed surprised to see her, as if he'd forgotten why the boy was here in the first place. Meanwhile Gordon gave her the same ravenous look he had the other day, if a bit more artfully concealed.

"Evenin', Leola," he said. "You look darb tonight."

"Thank you." She took in his slim-fitting suit and lace-up driving boots, thinking he'd clearly dressed to impress. "You do too."

"I was just commenting on Gordon's new jalopy," Brother interrupted, "sitting there at the curb."

"Isn't mine exactly," Gordon replied.

"Pshaw!" Brother flapped his hand. "What belongs to a father also belongs to his son!"

He gave Gordon a sly look.

"Wouldn't mind having a proper inspection of that apparatus before y'all leave. I've only ever seen a Barley in automotive journals."

"Sure thing," Gordon gestured toward the door. "C'mon."

Leola followed them out to the car, whose glossy pale gray paint gleamed even in the woolly light of dusk. Walking around it, Brother let out a whistle, running his hand along the exterior, patting the red-rimmed tires like they were babies' heads.

"A proper beauty," he murmured. "Resembles those Rolls Royces the Huns made famous in the war."

"Was made to look like one for certain," Gordon replied. "The chassis is aluminum and the interior is brushed nickel. The dashboard and trimmings, polished walnut."

Brother poked his head into the passenger compartment, emerging with a grin.

"It's against my spiritual beliefs to covet worldly goods, but a person can't help being tempted sometimes." He cast a final longing gaze at the car before stepping away. "I'm sure y'all youngsters wish to be off."

Gordon opened the door and Leola climbed in.

"Take good care of her," Brother called as they pulled away, though Leola wasn't certain whether he meant her or the car.

"Sorry this is so open to the elements," Gordon said. "Was designed to give a feel for speed and not so much for comfort. It can get cold in here this time'a year." He motioned behind the seat. "There's a blanket back there you can use."

Peeking sideways at her, he added, "If I weren't driving, I'd keep you warm myself."

Leola flushed—not from passion but because she was glad he couldn't.

"I have my jacket," she replied. "I'll be fine."

As they traveled down the road, Gordon pointed at the tubular devices jutting from either side of the dashboard.

"Once we start really moving, use your speaker there so I can hear you."

Leola laughed, thinking it would be strange to sit within a foot of someone and not make herself heard. But when Gordon picked up speed, the rush of the wind did indeed force them to converse through the metal tubes.

Only as they approached town did Gordon slow the car, sounding his horn whenever someone on the street waved, which was often. He seemed to know everyone at the soda shop, too, introducing Leola to a rookie police sergeant named Bobby Russell on break with his young bride, Inez.

After finding their own seats, they ordered sundaes, and soon Leola found herself laughing at Gordon's masterful imitations of their teachers, the pranks he'd committed on his baseball chums, a recent party he'd attended where a friend got deathly sick on bootleg punch. He turned serious at times, too, relating how he'd nursed one of his dogs after it got bitten by a snake and recently helped his mother deliver used clothing to the Widows' Home in Nash. He also asked Leola about her family, and she responded as she usually did, saying Papa was looking for work in Houston and Mama had succumbed to the flu. Gordon didn't probe further but seemed moved, reaching carefully to take her hand.

For a while, Leola was glad she'd accepted his invitation—even wondered if she'd been wrong about Gordon, that maybe he *was* her type. Did her best not to think about Joe . . . at least, until a small family entered, settling at a table in back.

Leola might not have noticed them at all but Gordon wouldn't stop staring. The man was short and broad-built, with bright eyes and curly black hair like his daughter's. The woman resembled any farm woman except for the neat kerchief covering her light hair and the gold cross around her neck. The boy, with his easy smile and pale tresses, looked more like his mother. As the group conversed, Leola could make out a few English words along with others she didn't understand—not Italian or Spanish but another language.

"Seems we got some of those low-downs from the quarry," Gordon muttered. "Must not know dagos aren't allowed in our restaurants."

Leola stiffened. "They're behaving nice enough," she said, and Gordon regarded her like she had two heads.

"P'rhaps you didn't have many foreigners in East Texas, Lee. Take it from me, there is nothing *nice* about 'em."

He scraped up the last of his ice cream, dropping his spoon into the metal bowl with a loud clang.

"Those quarrymen are trying to unionize and once that happens . . . you can imagine us reg'lar Americans trying to make an honest buck and losing control of the situation."

For a moment, Leola stared at the cherry in her dish, usually her favorite part of a sundae—which now seemed unappetizing. Then she raised her eyes to his.

"We'd plenty of foreign-born folk in Smith County. Czechs, Germans, Mexicans," her voice quavered, "even Italians. Never had more trouble with them than anyone else."

Gordon was already standing and didn't seem to hear.

"Excuse me one minute, Leola."

He motioned Bobby Russell to the side of the room and, after a mumbled conversation, the two strode over to the immigrant family, where Officer Russell—a hand on his billy club—addressed the husband like he was deaf instead of merely unfamiliar with the language.

"This here's a 100 percent business," he shouted, "only serves Americans. Y'all need to move on."

The father glanced uneasily at his wife.

"We done nothing," she said, sitting straighter. "Only wanted to order some supper." She nodded at the frightened-looking kids. "A treat for our children."

Gordon set his hands on his hips. "Feed your young'uns elsewhere. No cross-backs served here."

Is not right. That urgent voice, hissing in Leola's ear again. Since arriving in Waxahachie, she'd seen plenty of 100 percent signs in store windows, knew the Klan had a strong following here. Only days ago, she'd heard classmates congratulating themselves for defacing the new Catholic church with black paint and cruel insults. Mere miles away, a Jewish man had been tarred and feathered, and Mrs. Hooks had told her local police officers were coming to New Town often, harassing Black citizens for fun.

IS NOT RIGHT!

Being in a strange place, her own troubles weighing heavy, Leola had muffled that startling refrain. But then she imagined Joe appearing in this place on a Saturday night, chased off by a soft-palmed boy who wouldn't last an hour tending fields in the hot sun.

She recalled Bill Faye, a classmate back in Bronway, who'd once got a fly stuck in his ear. After unsuccessful attempts to remove it, he'd tried to ignore the insect writhing and buzzing inside him. By the time it did fall out—weeks later—it was dead, and poor Bill, crazier than a loon. Leola wondered if her smothered conscience was like that fly, destined either to die altogether or drive her to madness.

"Sorry if that little interruption upset you, Lee."

Gordon had reappeared, nodding at the puddle of ice cream in her dish.

"Can I order you another?"

Leola shook her head.

"Something's not," she cleared her throat, "agreeing with me. Best I get back to the Home."

"Dang bohunks," Gordon hissed, frowning at the back door. "Nothing good comes from letting strangers where they don't belong."

As they started across the restaurant, Leola couldn't acknowledge the other patrons, who nodded with approval at Gordon. And when Inez Russell thanked him for *defending their rights,* telling Leola how *lucky* she was to have *a knight in shining armor* at her disposal, Leola only stared at the floor.

Inside the moving car, she was glad for the cool breeze against her shame-tinted skin, hardly hearing Gordon as he related another story about his dogs.

"I loved a Catholic," she blurted.

He gestured at her to use the speaking tube.

"What did you say?"

"My beau." Leola leaned forward. "He was—*is*—Italian. And Catholic." She paused. "And I loved him."

Gordon's incredulous expression meant he'd heard her well enough this time.

"A foreigner? Ha! Can't picture you with someone like that!"

Leola narrowed her eyes. "Joe was born here. He's American as you and me."

She was no longer speaking into the tube but yelling, each word clear above the breeze.

"Don't matter anyhow. Joe's a lot more than where he came from. Smart and funny, handsome as the day is long. Invents new rose breeds faster'n Mr. Ford invents cars. Cooks better'n my mama did and can learn any musical instrument."

Gordon slowed the car to a crawl. Good thing, too, as he was staring at *her* more than the road ahead.

"Most of all," Leola kept shouting, though it was no longer necessary, "he knows how to make love better than any so-called *pure* American I've ever met."

They'd pulled in front of the orphanage, where Gordon turned off the ignition, glaring at her.

"Reckon you came to your senses, showed him the back door after all that?"

Leola snorted. "Joe's not my beau anymore and not because I showed him *any* door, front or back. But thanks to you, I've realized I still love him and won't settle for anything less in the future. Certainly not someone thinks himself better than others for no good reason besides the tint of his skin or the language he speaks."

Flashing him a radiant smile, she added, "So guess I *have* come to my senses after all."

As she jumped out, slamming the door, Gordon yelled, "Reckon it's true then, what they say about Home Girls, turnin' up their toes for *anyone*."

Leola didn't reply, didn't even look at him, smiling when the Barley sedan shot into the road, wheels whining louder than a man done wrong.

CHAPTER 47

"Great-Granny's alive!" Ruthie gasped, as they emerged from church the next morning.

Leola's eyes were inflamed from sobbing over her broken heart the previous night and so she didn't see what her friend was squawking about, at first. Then she caught sight of Joe leaning against a nearby juniper tree and ran straight at him, stopping just short of jumping into his arms.

"When—when did you get here? *How* did you get here? I thought you said—weren't you supposed to—"

Joe laughed, interrupting her gibberish.

"My love might be enduring but I am not so much." He reached for her hand. "Hopped the last train outta Tyler yesterday. We were delayed, and I arrived too late to go to the orphanage. So I checked into the hotel, slept best I could and roused myself early, hoping to find you here."

Leola gulped, picturing what might have happened if the train had been on time and he'd run into her with Gordon.

"What about the greenhouses and . . ."

"There's more to this story, Lee." Joe peered about. "Is there a place we can go before I've no choice but to make a spectacle of us?" He edged nearer. "Don't think I can wait much longer to be reminded what I been missing all this time."

Good thing Ruthie showed up then, or that spectacle might've happened.

"Reckon you're the famous Mr. Joe," she said, "of whom I've heard so much." She thrust out a hand. "Ruthie Free, pleased to make your acquaintance."

Joe started to greet her in kind, but Ruthie interrupted him.

"Before we get bogged down in pleasantries, I'm sure y'all will want a private place in which to *reacquaint* yourselves." Her eyes glimmered. "LaSalle Park's your best bet. Not so many of the morality patrol there, handin' out their citations." She pointed. "Two blocks past the firehouse, make a left."

"Shouldn't I tell someone first?" Leola asked. "One of the ward mothers?"

Ruthie wagged her head.

"Most'a the grown folk are attending the Annual Congregational Meeting—they'll hardly notice you're gone. I'll cover for you if they do. Just be back for madrigals rehearsal at four."

As the two girls hugged, Leola remembered how her friend had listened last night as she'd carried on about her ill-fated date with Gordon. How not once had she said, *I told you so.*

"I can see why you've affection for that girl," Joe remarked, as they headed toward the firehouse. "She's lively as termites in a woodpile."

Leola twined her fingers through his.

"Ruthie's been my salvation. But Mrs. Free's close to getting their new boardinghouse in order, so she might be leaving sooner than expected. Ruthie is beyond glad, a'course—her mother can't visit very often, and they miss each other something awful. The new place is ladies-only, too—no small relief after what Ruthie's been through." She paused. "Though I don't imagine what I'll do once she's gone."

"You'll have to visit each other. Dallas is only a stone's throw." Joe gave her a sad smile. "Still, it must be hard, what with losing Ship so recent."

When Leola fell quiet, Joe squeezed her hand.

"It's mostly due to Blanton I'm here in the first place, Lee. When he heard we'd been apart so long, and knowing how hard I been working on those dang greenhouses, he insisted I come. Bought me the train ticket, even drove me to the station." He paused. "Made me promise to say how they miss you 'round their place."

"So Mrs. Shipley's home then?"

"She *is* home, except not much improved. I was in Bronway recently, saw her on their front porch. When I waved, she seemed not to notice, like she was looking for one particular person and wouldn't settle for less."

"For Mary. She's looking for Mary." Leola regarded two small children playing hop-skip nearby. "Always will, I guess."

"Blanton says they'll move soon," Joe said, "to be closer to the new nursery operation—though I imagine it's to escape the memories too."

"Poor Shipleys," Leola whispered, and he squeezed her hand again.

"Blanton was glad to do us some good. Seemed to cheer him up."

They'd arrived at the park and, as they searched for a private spot, Leola's sadness dissipated. After settling on a grassy patch surrounded by a yellow forsythia bush, Joe spread his jacket on the ground and soon they were making up for lost time, pausing on occasion to make sure they weren't being watched—even if, truth be told, the possibility of such a thing did bring an extra thrill to their reunion.

When they finally came up for air, Joe kissed the turquoise ring that—luckily—she'd returned to her finger the night before. Struck guilty by this recollection, Leola sat up, brushing grass from her hair.

"There's something I have to tell you." She could barely meet his gaze. "I went on a date with another man. It was a mistake. I did it because I felt you were throwing me off and I needed to believe *someone* could like me. Thought it didn't matter who . . ." A sob caught in her throat. ". . . but I was wrong."

Joe sat up, too, moving close enough that Leola could see the gold flecks in his brown eyes.

"How could you not believe you'd be liked," he whispered, "a girl so full'a spunk, with such a good nature? No surprise another fellow would want to show you some fun, 'specially when this one's failed in doing so!"

"But Joe—"

He lay a palm gently over her mouth.

"Will you see this person again? Is he what you prefer? Is that what you're trying to tell me?"

She pulled away, smiling. "Not by a thousand miles do I prefer *anyone* to you."

"I'll take those odds if you'll take the same odds I'll never stop loving you." Joe's face shone. "Remember, I'm only a befuddled man who gets caught up in his own consternations at times. If ever you feel insecure again, tell me straight off so I can set things straight, y'hear?"

When she nodded, Joe grinned like in his portrait—not an expression of duplicity, she realized, but the look of a lover who has exactly what he wants.

CHAPTER 48

On Monday morning, after dismissing the others from breakfast, Brother asked Leola to stay and "converse in private." She'd already guessed what the conversation might be about and by the time he'd closed the dining room doors, had her reply in hand.

"It was nice meeting that Mr. Bel—Bel—that Joe fellow yesterday," Brother said, settling in the chair beside her. "I'm glad he was able to eat supper with us, though I *was* a mite confused, having seen you off with Gordon LaHaye the night before."

Leola shrugged. "Gordon and I are good friends. He only wanted to show me the town."

"The way he looked at you, Leola, is not the way a man regards a *friend*."

"I didn't notice," she murmured, unconvincingly.

"Surely you're not innocent as all that." Brother smirked. "I've had reports of you and Joe bustling off in a fever after he first arrived, disappearing for no small interlude."

Leola went still, wondering if someone had seen them in the park or another girl had tattled.

"I need not warn you of the consequences of premarital indiscretion," Brother continued, "and hope I don't need to limit your visits with Joe. I've no idea of his upbringing or values. I imagine they are," he cleared his throat, "quite *different* from our own."

Leola replied through gritted teeth, "Joe's honest and kind, same's any other worthy man."

"Even so," Brother picked up a napkin, dabbing at spilled milk, "I'd hate to offend Mr. LaHaye." More dabbing, and then: "You'd have quite the pleasant life, Leola, if you landed someone like Gordon. Whereas Joe—well, didn't you say he was a *field hand* of sorts?"

"A horticulturist." Leola couldn't keep the indignation from her voice. "He's a master gardener, junior vice president of Shipley Roses, one of the largest flower-growing outfits in the state." She tossed her head. "I reckon he'll start his own business someday and do right nicely by it."

Brother refolded the napkin.

"You may be some years from marrying, Leola," he said, slowly, "yet this is exactly the time to think seriously about your life partner." He set his hand atop her own. "As your rightful guardian, I'm only giving you the same advice your father would if he were here: Y'ought not look a gift horse in the mouth."

Leola nearly laughed aloud. She wanted to tell Brother how Papa had admired and respected Joe—and *her* for choosing him. Wanted to explain that Gordon's too easy shift from kindly to menacing Saturday night was hardly *gift-horse* behavior. Except she didn't say these things because the moment had passed when Brother should've removed his hand, and now he ogled her in a manner that he himself might characterize as *more than friendly.*

Leola pulled away, standing so fast, her vision flashed with green dots.

"I have an . . . an exam this m-morning," she stammered. "Teacher said I have to get there early. For—for review."

Brother didn't flinch, his eyes sweeping her body in a languorous movement that made her feel naked as a jaybird before him.

"Of course you may go." His mouth twisted. "Do mind, however, the signals you send men by your manner of behavior. Once you've let on that you are free and easy, you can hardly blame a fellow for treating you as such. Remember that a girl's reputation is her most precious asset to a future husband, wherever he stands on society's ladder."

Leola, hardly able to stifle her anger, didn't respond, but as she made her way to the door, felt Brother watching her all the way.

CHAPTER 49

As they walked to school an hour later, Leola related what had happened with Brother Giles, and Ruthie stopped dead in her tracks.

"Hell's bells, Lee. Let's hope he don't have designs on you too."

Leola frowned. "Designs? On me *too*?"

Although they were far behind the other kids, Ruthie whispered: "I wanted to bring it up before, but you were so new—didn't want you to be spooked."

"Spooked about what?"

"I think Brother's petting Maudifrank." Ruthie's freckles vanished beneath a bright red blush. "Saw them the other day, coming from the basement together, Maudi looking worse than chewed twine. Wasn't the first time, neither."

Leola remembered Brother's hand, sweaty and insistent, against her own. Remembered his yearning appraisal of her figure. Knew the answer to her next question almost before she asked.

"Are you sure?"

Ruthie nodded.

"Sure as a Delco battery. The way he looks at her—ain't how an old man ought to look at a young girl. I, of all people, can vouch for that. Verba thought the same thing too. Confronted Maudi about it but she got her tail up, saying it was a terrible thing to suggest." Her face puckered. "Then, not long after, Verba was shipped to Abilene."

"And you think it's because Maudi told Brother of her suspicions?"

Ruthie sucked her teeth. "Would seem a mite too coincidental otherwise."

"Why would Maudi *tell on* Verba instead of letting her help?"

"It's a mixed-up situation." Ruthie's brow furrowed. "I know what it is to live with a two-peckered billy goat and feel in his thrall, no matter how wrong it is. 'Course I got more gumption than Mauds, which is why I improved my own situation. Can't imagine *her* being so bold."

As they started walking again, Leola's mind spun. This must be the reason Brother had chosen Maudi in the first place, because she'd been weakened by her tragedies with no strength for fighting back. Probably the first time he'd set his hand upon her, she hadn't pulled away but let it happen—and whatever went beyond. Leola imagined her sisters, singled out by Brother Giles. Mae might have the where-withal to fight him off, but Karla was so much smaller and even more defenseless. It made her stomach ache, to consider.

"Can't we tell someone? Mrs. Valchar, say? Or the police?"

Ruthie stopped short again, letting off a brittle laugh.

"Don't you reckon what would happen if we complained about an upstanding citizen like Brother Giles? Without evidence, we'd get accused of lying. And what would we tell the Valchars? That I saw Brother *making eyes* at Maudi? That he spends too much time helping her with homework?" She made a *pffff*-ing sound. "The Valchars and Gileses are thick as thieves. No one's gonna do a thing if they don't have surefire proof."

She spat into the dirt.

"If we're to help Maudi, we best tell the right people at the right time in the right way, 'else we're all in trouble."

Another few steps, and Ruthie gave Leola a sharp look.

"Good thing the Mission Society gala is coming up. It's our biggest money-raiser and Brother Giles gets outside himself, making sure everything comes off *just right*." She glanced at the kids crowding the school entrance. "He'll be too busy to mess with Maudi, givin' us time to come up with a plan. Meantime we best keep our eyes on the girl, make sure she's never alone with that man."

As the opening bell rang and Ruthie hurried off, Leola thought, *Make sure none of us is alone with that man. Ever again.*

CHAPTER 50

Two weeks later, Ruthie stood before the mirror, studying herself with a glum expression.

"The Lord made me more fearfully than wonderfully, I reckon," she said, yanking at the too-tight bodice of her dress.

Leola rushed over, standing behind her.

"That is not true. With such bright hair and sparkling eyes, you're handsomer than all the lilies of the field."

Ruthie snorted. "I'm a dandelion, Lee, and that is all. What chance have I among so many brighter blossoms?"

Leola knew her friend was thinking about the skinny-legged youth pastor who would lead their Bible study tonight, as he always did when Brother was away. Ruthie considered religion hocus-pocus—a fact she tried to keep secret, living in a Methodist orphanage—but her crush on Pastor E.J. Bottley seemed the next surest thing to redemption. Problem was, just about every other girl at the Home dreamt of a similar Rapture.

"If all E.J. cared about was beauty," Leola sniffed, "he wouldn't be worth a hen's tooth. The man is sweet on *you*. Remember last week, when he said he admired health and vitality in a woman above all else? How he looked straight at you and went red as a tomato? And now you've memorized so many scripture verses . . . well, he'll appreciate how smart you are too."

Ruthie's mouth rippled. "Think so?"

"Don't *think*—I *know*."

Leola gave her friend's arm a playful pinch and Ruthie giggled worse than Minnie Calhoun.

"S'pose I should get goin' then," she said, gathering her Bible and notebook.

"Hold on," Leola said, in a low voice. "I got something to tell you while we're alone."

Though the other girls were long gone, she checked down the hallway before shutting the door.

"Mrs. Hooks arranged for Maudi to work with us in the kitchen. Said the girl's interested in cooking and needs the pay besides. I told her Maudifrank might also help make deliveries to her white customers—Cook's been getting harassed, lately, when she goes alone. Mrs. Hooks thought it a grand idea and got permission from Mrs. Giles. All of which means less time for Maudi to be around," she mouthed the next words, "*you know who.*"

Ruthie exhaled.

"And when Brother gets back from Waco, he'll have to jump right in with the gala." She gnawed her bottom lip. "Still, we got to come up with some plan soon or else do what you said, go to Mrs. Valchar—come what may. I can't hardly stand to think of poor Maudifrank, endurin' more'n she already has."

The gathering bell rang downstairs, signaling class would soon begin, and they shook themselves.

"You comin'?" Ruthie asked, starting for the door.

"Got to find my own Bible first." Leola rifled through her bureau for the umpteenth time. "Forgot it for our last meeting and Brother said if it happens again, I'm in deep dirt."

"Aw, don't worry. I'll make sure E.J. don't report it."

Leola shook her head. "I'd rather not put him in that position. Besides, it's the Bible Mama gave me after I got dipped, with a personal note on the inside cover. Would break my heart to lose it."

Ruthie hesitated. "I ought to stay, help you look—"

"What you *ought* to do," Leola teased, "is get down to the basement, socialize with a certain greenhorn preacher. No doubt he's wondering where you are."

Ruthie grinned like the Cheshire cat.

"Well, don't be long then. I plan to win in Sword Verse tonight. Wouldn't want you to miss history in the making."

After she was gone, Leola peered under her bed, though all she spotted were some dust kittens and one of Ruthie's crinkled scarves. Then, sitting on her heels in prayerful position, it dawned on her: she'd left her Bible on the church pew last Sunday. She glanced at the clock, realizing it was too late to get to town and back, and the sanctuary was probably locked anyhow. All she could do was hope Ruthie was right and E.J. wouldn't mark her lack of preparation.

But passing Brother's office on the way to the basement, Leola remembered his collection of Bibles, and figured she could borrow a plainer one, returning it before anyone was the wiser.

She crept into the room, choosing an everyday volume like the one she'd misplaced, hurrying toward the door again—except before she got there, something slipped from the Bible's pages. She bent to pick it up, saw it was a photograph of Maudifrank, and her spirit went dark.

Brother had taken countless snapshots of his orphans, which he hung in the hallway for prospective parents and benefactors to admire. At first glance, this one—Maudi dressed in a plain white blouse, smiling sweetly—appeared equally innocent. Except Leola knew there was a reason it was hidden here. Knew because, ever since

Ruthie had confided her suspicions, she'd been watching Brother and Maudifrank. Noticed how he'd find any excuse to stand near the girl, brushing a hand against her hip, looping an arm around her shoulder. And when he wasn't outright touching Maudi, his eyes did the caressing—much as they had Leola recently.

But despite her conviction, Leola knew this photograph wasn't the evidence they needed. She imagined Brother confronted with it, claiming it was the kind of souvenir many grown folk kept to commemorate a special child. Then he'd say Leola was the depraved one for thinking otherwise. Wise to her suspicions, he'd send her away as he'd done with Verba, separating her from her sisters with little chance of finding Papa again.

Where there's smoke, there's fire.

Mama's voice echoed in her mind and Leola turned, eyeing the fancy Bible Brother had got so lathered about weeks ago. *My most precious possession,* he'd called it. *No one's allowed to handle it but me.*

If the photograph she'd already found was the smoke, that Bible fairly crackled with flame.

As she pulled the heavy tome from the shelf, Leola could tell this gospel was far more valuable than the one Malvina Hughes owned. While Auntie's was covered in cheap imitation leather with stapled pages and few illustrations, this one was bound in the softest cow hide, filled with colorful maps of the Holy Land.

A gale of laughter floated up from the basement, reminding Leola there wasn't much time. She set the Bible on Brother's desk and licked her finger, shuffling the pages, eventually finding what she'd been hoping—and not hoping—to find.

Buried inside Song of Songs was another photo of Maudi, this time leaning back in a chair, wearing nothing but a frilly slip and garters and, on her face, the same mask as at the posing party: a child's version of womanhood, forced and unnatural.

Leola noted an underlined passage on the page, Chapter 4, verse 5: *Your breasts are like two fawns, like twin fawns of a gazelle that browse among the lilies.* Sourness rose in her throat. She wanted to cry and scream, but needed to keep her head. If the wrong person discovered her here, the fact she'd snuck into Brother's office might cause a bigger stink even than the terrible crime she'd just uncovered.

Hands shaking, Leola shoved the tawdry photo of Maudi deep into her notebook and carefully returned the fancy Bible to its place. Then she slipped the less damning photograph back into the plain gospel she'd planned to borrow and put that away also. Better to get in trouble for being unprepared, she figured, than risk suspicion if someone noticed her carrying the unfamiliar Bible.

Checking the coast was clear, Leola hurried into the hall and down the basement stairs, passing the darkroom Brother had made from an old coal closet. *Poisonous chemicals, my foot,* she thought, imagining John Giles inside, waiting for his latest *artwork* to reveal its sinister outline while life went on above him—children at their lessons or chores, or saying bedtime prayers: *Thy will be done.*

Luckily, when she got to the youth room, everyone was busy forming teams for Sword Verse and didn't notice her slip to the end of one line.

"Ruthie and Marlon," E.J. called, "as team captains, you'll go first."

Silence fell over the room.

"Swords out!" he commanded.

Ruthie and Marlon held up their Bibles, bindings facing toward them so they wouldn't be tempted to cheat.

"Ready?" E.J. warned, and the captains nodded.

"All righty then. Your verse is Proverbs 11:13." He let the tension build before shouting, "Charge!"

Marlon and Ruthie searched furiously through their Bibles, though Ruthie found the verse first: *Whoever goes about slandering reveals secrets, but he who is trustworthy in spirit keeps a thing covered.*

As Ruthie's team applauded, the words thrummed in Leola's mind:

Slandering

Secrets

Trustworthy

Was it slanderous to even *think* Brother guilty of such an offense? He was their superior, after all, a respected adult who must have a reason for what he was doing. P'rhaps there was more to the story, she thought.

She looked over at Maudi, smiling as Bass Williams whispered in her ear. Maybe she'd been wrong and the girl wasn't an innocent victim after all, but had welcomed Brother's advances. *Invited* them even.

Leola recalled poring over a smuggled fashion magazine with Maudi recently. Remembered how captivated the girl had been by the article about flappers and their tradition-bucking ways, how she'd cooed over their formfitting dresses and pearl-embossed hose, the cigarettes dangling from their mouths. *Wouldn't it be swell,* she'd sighed, *to make up the rules as you went, live as you wished, and do as you like?*

Leola had thought the same, of course, plenty of times, though now wondered if Maudifrank was talking about something besides trading their tedious, rule-bound lives for a more interesting existence. Maybe Brother and Maudi had a plan to run off together when she came of age. *You can divorce that ol' wife of yours,* Leola imagined her whispering to Brother, *and then you will be free.*

"Miss Free!" E.J.'s jubilant cry brought Leola back to the present. "I see you been practicing!"

Ruthie beamed at Leola, who did her best to smile back.

Then she snuck another peek at Maudi, noticed how drawn and pale the girl was, how thin she'd gotten, her neck permanently crooked from staring at the ground. Flapper girls took joy in flaunting the rules, but Maudifrank hardly seemed alive at all.

Another verse from Song of Songs came to Leola's mind: *You are a garden locked up, my sister, my bride; you are a spring enclosed, a sealed fountain.* She'd always believed these words, set inside the speaker's longing, were strange, as if his betrothed's modesty—her *virtue*—was the prize and not her love. Leola had been taught her own virginity was *a pearl*, a treasure she'd give away by *choice*. Yet she knew there were menfolk who relished the thrill of unlocking gardens, unsealing fountains, breaking spirits, all for the power it made them feel. Even if it was no contest at all.

Thinking of her sisters dressed in cheap lace and posed like ruined dolls, bile rose in Leola's throat. 'Course they had their sister to stand for them, while Maudi had no one. No one except two half-orphans with nothing—and everything—to lose.

❧

That night, Leola didn't have a chance to tell Ruthie about her discovery, as Glenda and Euless were doing homework beside the door, taking advantage of the hallway light. Not that Ruthie, on cloud nine after helping E.J. put the chairs away, would have been able to concentrate on this revelation.

"He ask't me every sort of question 'bout myself, Lee, like I was the President of the United States and not a plain ol' half-orphan never stepped outside Dallas County." She brought her pillow to Leola's bed, encircling it with her arms. "Not like other fellows, yammerin' endlessly 'bout themselves as if a girl wouldn't possess a tongue or brain of her own."

With the terrible secret rubbing a raw place in her heart, Leola struggled to keep the irritation from her voice.

"It's clear E.J. likes you. Don't understand why you got to be so simple about it."

Ruthie's smile vanished.

"Something's hounding you, Lee." She leaned in. 'You looked like you seen a ghost when you got to Youth Group tonight and hardly tried at Sword Verse."

Leola glanced over at Euless and Glenda.

"It's only my monthlies coming," she lied. "Feeling a bit rough around the edges, I s'pose."

"Well, that's easy enough to remedy!" Ruthie's teeth gleamed in the dark. "You been resistant, but it could be the perfect time to try snuff. Lifts me from my womanly miasmas beyond what Pinkham's pills ever do."

Leola hesitated. She'd already explained to Ruthie her distaste for smokeless tobacco, instilled in her by Big Leola, who'd been a child in Alabama after the Civil War. Even in old age, the woman had grimaced, recounting how silk-enshrouded ladies used to expel chaw juice from carriage windows or sniff the powdered version during church. *Eventually,* she'd explained, *their very tongues and lips would turn white, every tooth gone missing. Minds gone missing too.*

Ruthie always shrugged off such stories, claiming she could quit when she felt like it.

"I found a swell new place to do it, too," she was saying. "A fallen-down house in the woods. Planned to take you there, snuff or no snuff, for it's the kind of picto-risqué spot you like."

Leola hesitated. She'd wanted to take the damning photograph to Mrs. Valchar's house right after school tomorrow. But it made sense showing the thing to Ruthie first, and this solitary setting might be the perfect place for doing so. At most it'd mean a few minutes' delay.

"All right," she agreed. "Tomorrow, after chores?"

Ruthie slapped her knee. "Now you're on the trolley!"

"Shut your piehole," Glenda hissed, pelting them with balled up composition paper. "Can't you see we're working?"

Ruthie ignored her.

"I vouch," she whispered to Leola, "a pinch'a Sweet Scottish Rose is all it takes to be lifted from your earthly strifes."

She stood, twirling the effigy of E.J. Bottley back to her bed.

"Though kisses from flat-footed preacher boys come miiiight-ty close. Mighty close indeed."

CHAPTER 51

Ruthie was in fine spirits as they headed out the next day, hooking her arm through Leola's, laughing when two boys on bicycles collided, ending in a heap on the curb.

Leola, for her part, didn't feel so cheerful. She'd hardly slept the night before, thinking of the photograph tucked beneath her mattress. And today her palms had been so sweaty, she'd found it hard to clutch Joe's fancy pen, causing her to muck up every assignment.

But as Ruthie led her down a wooded path, Leola told herself the ordeal would soon be over, her burden shared, Maudi out of danger.

"Isn't this about the peaceful-est place you ever seen?" Ruthie asked, when they arrived at their destination.

The ruins of the house sat in a shallow ravine bordered by a burbling stream, hidden from surrounding farms. Birds trilled from every tree and the air smelled like new onion grass and water-rusted stones. Compared to the Home's hullabaloo, the place was a real Garden of Eden, and Leola worried that confessing her secret here might ruin it for Ruthie evermore.

As they settled behind a broken-down wall, Ruthie pulled a flowery tin from her bag.

"Here's our magical elixir and the necessary dipping stick." She presented a twig with a frayed end. "I prefer to use sweetgum wood as it lends a nice flavor to the experience. You can see I chewed it extra fine, to make the end brushy. Easier to spread that way."

She dunked the stick into the powder, rubbing it about her teeth and gums.

"Aah!" Her face flushed. "Makes my head spin just enough, though there's advantages to sniffin' it straight up the nose for sure."

She offered the utensil to Leola, who waved it away. The influenza had quieted in these parts, but she still felt squeamish of reckless spit-swapping.

"You're a starchy one," Ruthie laughed. "Yet I came prepared." She held out a fresh twig. "Fashioned you a dipper of your own. You can chew the end yourself, avoiding my lowdown germs."

"That was kind of you, but I didn't come here to sample your aromatics."

Ruthie slouched. "Should'a guessed you'd chicken out."

"Didn't chicken out exactly. I've something to tell you but couldn't last night with so many ears in the room." Leola eased the notebook from her bag, handing over the photograph. "I found this in one of Brother's Bibles."

Ruthie took one look and gasped.

"Great day in the morning! John Giles is depraved as I thought and then some!"

"I'm sure there's more where this came from," Leola explained. "I was gonna ask Maudi about it but after the business with Verba, reckoned not. The girl's hardly thinking right—who knows what she'd do?" She started to her feet. "And now we should deliver our evidence to Mrs. Valchar."

Ruthie grabbed her wrist. "Don't you remember, Lee? The Valchars are in Dallas, not due home 'til the night before the gala."

"Cripes!" Leola lowered slowly to the ground again. "Plumb

forgot." She licked her lips, thinking. "So maybe we could take it to Mrs. Larkin or one of the other ward mothers?"

"You sure can be dense for such a smarty-pants," Ruthie sniffed. "Mrs. Larkin is well aware she'd get blamed for letting," she gestured at the satchel, "*that* happen on her watch. She'd report us straight off to Brother, who'd make sure our claims never see the light of day."

She paused.

"We should wait for Mrs. Valchar, like we planned. It's only another week. Brother's hardly looked at Maudi lately, even when she's leading chorus rehearsals, and we're keepin' an eye out for her. Nothing bad's gonna happen meantime."

Leola's pulse fluttered. "If he finds his picture gone . . . He knows I was interested in that Bible. I'll be the first one questioned. Then what?"

Ruthie hesitated. "Best pray that don't happen, or . . ."

She sliced a finger across her throat and Leola let out a nervous laugh.

"Brother would never be *that* desperate. Would he?"

Ruthie stared. "Don't you know? It's folks with upstanding reputations get most desperate when they have to defend 'em."

Recalling Brother's lecture about her own *precious* reputation, Leola's stomach cramped like it really was her time of the month, and she grabbed the snuff tin, inhaling a sizeable pinch up one nostril before Ruthie could stop her.

"Hang it, Lee! You're new at this! Gotta go easy."

Leola didn't listen, repeating her actions with the other nostril then sitting back, waiting for a sudden burst of lightness to her brain, a momentary sensation of devil-may-care, any release whatsoever.

Instead, all she felt was *fear.*

CHAPTER 52

Tracing the dread path to Brother's office, Leola considered her many recent transgressions: practicing the shimmy with her roommates. Sharing a piece of Mrs. Hooks's coconut cake with Ruthie under the bedcovers. Her newfound habit of cussing.

She'd happily take punishment for any of those things—clothespin *and* closet, carbolic soap on her tongue, a month of latrine-scrubbing— as long as Brother Giles hadn't found his photograph unaccounted for.

Entering the room, it was all she could do not to stare at the fancy Bible on its shelf. Could hardly look at Brother either—until she noticed he was smiling and her fear slackened the tiniest bit.

"Be seated, please."

He motioned at one of the comfortable armchairs opposite his desk, rather than the seat where he usually doled out consequences. His own chair must have gotten its much-deserved oiling, for it didn't creak a bit when he leaned back.

"We're both busy so I will cut right to the chase." He patted the thick file on his blotter. "Folks from the state agency paid Karla a visit few weeks back . . ."

Leola's pulse quickened. "Mae mentioned something about that."

"Yes, well, the agency returned its recommendations this morn-ing. They're concerned, as we all are, about Karla and advise a more stable situation be found shortly."

Leola narrowed her eyes. "What sort of situation?"

"A family, as I discussed with you previously. Two parents who can give her the attention she needs."

"But," Leola's throat tightened, "you said my father still has legal authority over us. That we're half-orphans 'til he's declared dead or officially missing, and it hasn't been six months yet."

Brother raised a hand.

"The agency has written to every morgue and hospital in Houston. I have the responses here if you'd like to read them. No person matching your father's description ever entered their doors nor left in a pine box." He offered a sad smile. "Difficult as it is to consider, seems your father has simply chosen not to return."

Leola bit the inside of her cheek, trying not to cry. Even though she didn't want to believe what Brother was saying, even though she knew Papa hadn't willfully abandoned them, she regretted more than ever her promise to Mama.

Yesterday she'd watched from her room as Karla wandered the play yard alone. Saw her approach Mrs. Bentham, rubbing against her like a hungry cat. Saw Mrs. Bentham frown, pushing Karla toward some older girls.

Mrs. Valchar would never do that, Leola had decided, but would supply Karla with all the cuddling and reassurance she needed. And if—when—Papa returned, the Valchars would honor his rights, Leola knew that for certain by now.

"I understand that my sister needs a real," she swallowed, "family."

Brother's face lit with surprise.

"I'm glad you're taking a more sensible view. I think you'll like this couple, recommended by the agency." He slid a photograph across the desk. "They've two grown sons yet have yearned for a daughter all these years, and . . ."

Leola's mind reeled. "Sons?"

By now she could see it wasn't the Valchars in the photo but a much older couple. The stern-faced woman wore thick glasses; her husband sported a shock of white hair and the befuddled expression of someone on the brink of senility.

"But they're so . . . old," she muttered, and Brother cleared his throat.

"The Nolans *are* older than many adoptive parents, yet the agency says they're sturdy and healthful nonetheless. Mrs. Nolan is some ten years younger than her husband and I'm sure she has plenty of life ahead."

Leola blinked at him.

"I thought it was the Valchars who were interested in Karla."

"Ah." Brother shifted in his chair. "Andrew and Catherine are fond of her. However, they have serious concerns regarding the girl's *difficulties*. I believe they've decided to keep trying for a natural-born child, one with less chance of causing them trouble."

Leola glanced away, regretting she'd persuaded Catherine of her sister's frailties. Regretting too that blood-related children would ever be viewed as superior to the other kind. After all, a begotten child could arrive with any number of deficiencies, passed down through generations or brought on eventually by life's inevitable hardships.

"I don't want Karla serving as nursemaid to elderly folk." She gestured at the photograph. "I can't imagine they'd have patience for a little kid, and one despairing of her family to boot."

Brother's face stiffened.

"It's not always possible to find the perfect situation at the perfect time, Leola. I agree with the agency—the sooner your sister's settled, the better. Besides, the Nolans own a thriving black-eyed-pea operation near Angus." He cocked his head. "Karla will inherit quite a tidy sum when they pass."

"Angus?" Leola choked out. "That's a hundred miles away! I'll never get to visit her there." Her voice was reedy with anguish. "You can't let her go!"

Brother pursed his lips.

"It won't happen for a few weeks, giving y'all plenty of time to get used to the idea. By then everything could look different and the advantages, clearer."

In that bright-flashing moment, it took all Leola's discipline not to threaten Brother with the picture of Maudifrank. But she did her best to stay calm. In two days, the Valchars would have proof of Brother's dark deeds. His authority would be ruined and whatever agreements he'd entered into, meaningless.

Leola stood, feeling a sudden rush of confidence.

"P'rhaps you're right. My mama always said time doesn't just *heal* all but *reveals* all too. Everything will work itself out in the end."

Turning toward the door, allowing herself the quickest glimpse of that Bible, she silently prayed she was right.

CHAPTER 53

Two evenings later, getting ready for the gala, the girls flew in and out of each other's rooms, tying sashes, fixing their hair with the yellow ribbons Mrs. Giles had given them, talking mostly of the glorious banquet to come.

"I can still taste that fricasseed chicken from last year," Ruthie murmured as Leola buttoned the back of her dress.

"Three kinds'a potatoes too!" Euless chimed in. "Couldn't decide whether I liked them better scalloped or in their jackets, so took both!"

Until now, Leola hadn't felt much excitement about tonight's event—not with the constant fear Brother might find his photo missing, her worry over Maudi and Karla, the looming deadline that would mark Papa as officially *gone*. Every time Brother so much as glanced at her she was certain he knew, though Ruthie said it was only the weight of this secret she carried, nagging at her mind.

If I ain't scared, you shouldn't be neither, she'd admonished after they'd snuck off to their snuff-dipping place that afternoon. *Even if Brother did find his photograph disappeared, what could he do in the midst of all this hurly-burly? Besides, he'd be too afraid to make a fuss over it, scared of tipping your hand. And tomorrow it'll all be over.*

Leola sat on her bed, trying to believe this, telling herself their plan was about to come to fruition, she had to have faith. Trying to convince herself that tonight she could forget her recent sorrows—at least for a few hours.

But as she put on her black flats, Leola felt a pain that couldn't be ignored, for the shoes hardly fit any longer. She debated brushing them with water and stretching them out but there wasn't time. Her sisters were so excited about the party—Mae had a singing part in the performances and Karla would present flowers to the guest of honor—and Leola had promised to walk with them to the Mission Hall. If she didn't show up, it'd take the shine off their rare happiness. The flats would have to withstand this one final duty.

"Can you braid my hair, Lee, and twine this through it?"

She looked up to find Maudi holding out her yellow ribbon.

At first, Leola wanted to refuse, saying she didn't have time. But the girl's pinched face kept her from it. Probably Maudi was thinking of the next day, when she'd once again become the object of Brother's vile attention. It was all Leola could do not to reassure her otherwise.

"Sure, Mauds," she replied, taking the ribbon.

Deftly lacing the chestnut strands, Leola recalled the first time she'd tested her braiding skills on Mama the previous summer. *It's a wonder you can't abide sewing, Daughter,* she'd said, examining the end result in the mirror, *for you do have the nimblest fingers.*

Leola's eyes turned so blurry at this memory, she had to start over with Maudi's plait.

"We're leaving in fifteen minutes, girls!"

Mrs. Larkin's voice startled Leola from her sorrow—though her appearance came as an even bigger surprise. Their ward mother, who usually dressed in shades of black and gray, currently wore a floral linen chemise with a matching bow in her freshly permed hair.

"Ain't you the fashion plate, Mrs. Larkin!" Ruthie exclaimed, rushing over for closer inspection.

"Thank you," Mrs. Larkin replied, cheeks flashing bright as the dahlias on her dress. "Couldn't show up at tonight's shindig in my workaday rags, could I?"

"I thought you were staying here," Euless said, "to keep an eye on the place."

Mrs. Larkin shrugged.

"Brother insisted at the last minute that I go. Said it'd be a shame to waste such a grand occasion, as he put it, *keeping company with the ghosts.* So I s'pose we'll dance the night away together, after all."

"Not dance," Ruthie muttered. "We might be modernized Methodists but Brother says there will be too many Baptists there to offend with turkey trots and fish walks."

"Hain't danced in a lifetime no how." Mrs. Larkin sighed. "My husband was Pentecostal, bless his soul. T'was fine to shake with the Holy Spirit in church. Beyond that, I could hardly scratch my knee without him claiming it was Satan's work." Another sigh. "But y'all better head out before Mr. Giles does his own kind'a dance, and it won't be a fish walk neither."

As the other girls rushed away, Leola laughed at Maudi's buffaloed expression.

"It *is* a shock seeing Mrs. Larkin so done up. P'rhaps she's had enough of widowhood and wants to meet a nice older gentleman tonight, a rich Episcopalian who'll let her dance all she wants."

Maudi, staring blankly into the mirror, didn't respond, so Leola gave her a poke.

"You all right?"

The other girl flinched.

"Fine. I'm fine. A tad nervous about the performance is all."

"I wouldn't fret." Leola stepped back, scrutinizing her work. "We sounded near perfect at rehearsal yesterday."

"Let's hope we do tonight too," Maudi murmured, "else Brother won't be pleased."

"You won't have to worry much longer what that man feels."

Maudi frowned. "What do you mean?"

Leola wanted to snatch her words from the air and shove them back inside her throat.

"I, uh, meant with the choir." She reached toward the wrap on her bed, thinking fast. "You said you wouldn't direct us next year, so you won't have to concern yourself with Brother's judgments."

"Never said I was quitting." Two furrows appeared between Maudi's eyes. "Brother wouldn't put anyone else in my place, besides."

Leola, draping the sweater across her arm, forced a smile.

"'Course he wouldn't. And we'd be sunk without you in charge."

When Maudi hesitated, Leola steeled herself for a sudden confession—which didn't come—and as the other girl put her hand on the doorknob, Leola felt the overpowering urge to keep Maudi exactly where she was.

"Wait!" she cried, and her friend spun around, looking more consternated than before.

"What is it?"

Leola had no idea what had set her off and now had to feign another excuse.

"It's only . . . Appeared to be a mark on your dress." She made a show of peeking around Maudi's other side. "Guess it was only a shadow after all."

The two of them locked eyes, then Maudifrank stole away, little more than a shadow herself.

CHAPTER 54

L eola and the other girls sat at the back of the usually spartan
Mission Hall, marveling over its transition.

The windows had been hung with swaths of gold bunting, the
tables set with brass candelabras and vases of colorful greenhouse
bouquets. Leola was surprised to see a ragtime band onstage, for
certain Methodists still frowned on snazzy music—until she remembered there'd be plenty of Episcopalian and Presbyterian supporters
here who'd expect some form of entertainment. What few staunch
Baptists were present would have no choice but to plug their ears or
pray extra hard in church on Sunday. Tapping her feet to the perky
rhythms, Leola felt certain she'd be forgiven too.

The girls watched, transfixed, as guests floated past in fancy
attire probably purchased in Dallas or mail-ordered from St. Louis.
Of course Mrs. Valchar was chicest of all, in a Grecian-style dress
with pleats down the back, holding a gleaming peacock feather that
she waved about, mocking her "high-falutin' airs." Of course, she
fussed over *her girls,* too, like they weren't wearing the same cut-
price dresses she'd seen on numerous occasions already.

"Y'all will have this audience eating from the palms of your
hands," she told them, "especially given what I've heard about the
upcoming concert."

She smiled at Maudifrank.

"Brother can't stop saying how well you've done, leading our madrigals. Says you'll end up at Carnegie Hall one day, if he has to snatch you up to New York City himself."

Leola gawped at Ruthie, thankful when Andrew appeared and took his wife's arm so no one noticed her distress.

"Best get you settled at the table, darling, so I can take my place on stage." He leaned down, whispering loudly, "Catherine would rather spend the evening with you youngsters than the stuffier set but I need her cheering me on up front. Oration's not my strongest suit."

His wife laughed.

"Don't worry, girls. I've made certain Mr. Valchar's speech lasts no more than five minutes, the sooner we can dive into that delectable buffet. I hear there's fricasseed chicken tonight and roast beef too."

After he'd settled Catherine up front, Leola watched Andrew join the row of bigwigs onstage: Brother Giles, Mayor Probst, and another man she swore she knew but couldn't place.

"Dr. LaHaye, Gordon's father," Ruthie whispered, reading her thoughts, and Leola understood why he seemed so familiar. Despite the blotchier freckles and sagging middle, Dr. LaHaye was an uncanny foreshadowing of his son in the future, and a tremor traveled her spine.

Since their ill-fated date, Gordon barely spoke to her during science lab, and when she said hello to him in the halls, he pretended not to notice—except when he was with his friends. Then Gordon would laugh, muttering about *bohunk lovers* and *dago mushers*.

There'd been other slights, too—like when Minnie handed out party invitations to everyone at Glee Club but Leola. *There'll be no mixing at* this *party,* she'd announced, *except between girls and boys,* and even the teacher had smirked.

Not that Leola cared so much. She was on the outside to begin with. What she'd done felt like small potatoes, but she'd do it again, if given the chance.

Andrew had started speaking, so Leola set her mind to listening. As promised, the man kept his speech to the point, inserting enough humor to make things interesting. Alas, the others didn't take his lead, droning on until Leola found her mind wandering. Gazing at the flowery centerpiece, she recollected springtime at home, when bluebonnets turned swaths of grassland into periwinkle seas and Papa would take them to gather bouquets for their mother.

"Ladies and gentlemen, we've saved the best for last!"

Brother's brightened tone finally caught Leola's attention.

"Our next guest needs no introduction! Besides giving you the wherewithal to masticate tonight's victuals," he grinned at Gordon's father and laughter rippled across the room, "tonight's honoree is among our town's greatest boosters."

With a sweep of one arm, he stepped back.

"Please give a warm welcome to Dr. Hiram LaHaye."

The dentist sauntered to the podium, waiting for the applause to die.

"Thank you, esteemed guests," he began. "It's a pleasure to be here, although John Giles is wrong. Given the tender meat we've consumed tonight, I don't anticipate any of y'all needing emergency treatment tomorrow, not while I'm on my first hunting excursion of the season." He jabbed a finger at them. "If you get my meaning."

The place burst into fresh uproar, which Dr. LaHaye quelled with a raised palm.

"On a more consequential note: As you may be aware, I was recently elected Grand Wizard of our local Klan chapter . . ."

Leola, stifling a gasp, seized Ruthie's hand beneath the table.

". . . and our klavern has taken in record-breaking dues of late.

After helping to rebuild the boys' club over in Maypearl last year, we've been casting about for a worthy new charity to support." He paused, allowing an air of expectation to fall over the room. "And that worthy charity, I'm proud to announce, is our own Texas State Children's Home!"

Though most of the crowd applauded, Leola noticed a few guests murmuring among themselves, and Andrew Valchar wriggling in his seat like he'd sat on a pinecone, clearly surprised by this announcement. Meanwhile, Brother Giles picked up a cloth-covered easel and set it near the podium. At the dentist's signal, he whisked away the cloth, revealing a colored sketch of the Home with a small brick building on the side where none currently existed.

"Behold the new vocational department for our deserving orphans!" Dr. LaHaye proclaimed, as a chorus of *oohs* and *aahs* swept through the assembly.

"Here," he pointed to the sketch, "will be a mechanics and woodworking shop for helping our young men become productive members of white society. And here," he slid his finger over, "is the proposed Home Management and Cookery department, where our girls will learn to nurture their hardworking future husbands and the next generation of pure Americans!"

Picking flower petals from the table as an excuse not to clap, Leola noticed Andrew frowning in his wife's direction. Though she couldn't see Catherine's face, she could guess her feelings, as the woman had recently joined the Citizen's League, a group in Dallas that opposed the KKK.

So far, we're three thousand strong, Mrs. Valchar had confided in Leola, though her cheerful expression had quickly faded. *'Course, that won't stop our Klan-backed politicians winning every election it seems.*

"Construction on this project won't begin for another month," the dentist was saying, "but our klavern will deliver the first load of bricks to the Home next week to be unloaded by the orphans themselves, giving them ownership in the endeavor."

"Giving *them* free labor, more like," Ruthie hissed but Leola didn't reply. She'd just spied Mrs. Larkin leading Karla toward the stage and realized it was Dr. LaHaye her sister would reward. As Karla handed over the flowers and the man leaned down to whisper in her ear, Leola held her breath, for the Klan considered mutism as much an *aberration* as being Catholic or having dark skin. Luckily the child's shy smile seemed to charm the dentist well enough—though when he kissed her cheek, Leola couldn't help wincing.

It was hard to put her spirit into singing after that, but she did her best, recalling how nervous Maudi had been about their performance. Of course everything did go fine, the girls receiving even greater applause than Dr. LaHaye had. Never mind when Maudi took a bow, she hardly smiled at all.

After Mae's group had finished their own performance, it was finally time to eat—or rather, watch everyone *else* eat, since the Home Kids had been warned to serve themselves last. If Mrs. Valchar hadn't shown up when she did, Leola thought they might've broken into a riot.

"And why haven't y'all visited the buffet?" she demanded, squinting at their empty plates.

Euless shrugged. "Brother Giles said we should—"

"Brother says lots of things." Mrs. Valchar pulled a face. "However, I am more or less his boss and *I* say y'all have earned your supper." She motioned for them to follow. "So let's get that beef while it's hot!"

At the banquet table, Ruthie practically swooned.

"Not only top-cut meats this year but Waldorf salad and buttered beets too! Weren't I right, sayin' this feast would bring tears to a glass eye?"

Leola's stomach growled in answer and the girls laughed so loud, other guests scowled with disapproval.

After helping themselves to seconds—in some cases, thirds— everyone else drifted off to mingle with the crowd while Leola finished the last of her lime mousseline. Noticing Maudifrank's clutch under a chair, she picked it up, scanning the room for her friend. Found her in a far corner, standing near the old piano and beside her, Brother Giles, holding a plate of uneaten pie. The way he bent over her, the voracious gleam in his eye, was all Leola needed to see.

She took off in their direction, unsure what she was doing, only knowing she had to get to Maudi, fast. Of course Glenda had to buttonhole her, waxing ecstatic over LaHaye's *swell donation*. Then a Mission Board member pulled her aside, inquiring of school.

By the time Leola arrived at her destination, the only sign Brother and Maudifrank had been there at all was that plate of pie, forsaken on the piano.

CHAPTER 55

Leola did a desperate turn around the room, checking the banquet area, the annex, even the steamy kitchen where Mrs. Hooks and her helpers were serving up more desserts. No Maudi. No Brother Giles.

She looked out the window, searching for the orphanage jalopy, which had been parked in the adjacent field earlier: It was gone too. Brother Giles had left and taken Maudifrank with him, Leola knew it. Yet where would they go? Surely, he'd wouldn't park the Model T on some Lover's Lane, not with its blazing sign announcing who was inside, doing Lord knew what.

She recalled Brother's comment to Catherine about Carnegie Hall, imagined it as an unintended hint of his plan to flee with Maudi—not to New York but someplace like Mexico, where the law would stuggle to find them . . . or do much, if it did.

Leola located Mrs. Valchar, surrounded by VIPs—including Dr. LaHaye. Pictured interrupting their conversation, spilling everything she knew. The Grand Wizard had the power to intervene on Brother's behalf. Most likely had friends on the police force, like the officer who'd helped Gordon chase that family from the soda shop. He could make an agony of Maudi's life and Leola's too.

She saw Ruthie on the other side of the room, standing with

E.J. Bottley and some other fellows from the seminary—another chance to cause a scene that could backfire. And then Leola noticed the younger kids being led upstairs where they'd rest until the party ended, and recalled Maudi's strange demeanor when Mrs. Larkin announced she'd attend the gala tonight. In a flash, she realized Brother had probably planned the whole thing, hoping to sneak away while the party was in full swing—giving him plenty of time with Maudi at the Home. The empty, empty Home.

She grabbed her sweater and slipped out the front door, walking fast, at first, but breaking into a run once she'd passed the city limits. Along the way, a car slowed down, the figure inside watching too closely, so Leola leapt into the irrigation ditch, trying not to think what might be hiding in the weeds—snakes, black widows, scorpions, cantankerous after their brief winter naps.

In the end it wasn't sharp-fanged creatures who hindered her journey but the too small flats, cutting into her heels. When the hurt turned to agony, Leola ripped off the shoes and threw them into the field. Soon her silk stockings—bought with precious wages from her kitchen work—snagged and then tore, so she got rid of them too.

Across from the orphanage, bare legs nearly numb with cold, Leola hid behind a tree, gathering herself. At first, the building looked as quiet as they'd left it. But creeping across the lawn and into the back, she noticed the windows of the Gileses' apartment glowing with yellow lamplight. Saw a shadow move behind the curtains then a second, smaller one.

She eased along one wall, crouching beneath the window. Rising slowly, she peeked through a gap in the curtain panels to see Maudi lying stiff as a board on the bed and Brother, in his shirtsleeves, leaning over her.

Leola dropped to the ground, hardly able to breathe, thinking she should've roused Mrs. Valchar—maybe even the police. But it was too late for that and their nearest neighbors were a good mile down the road.

She looked around, thinking what to do. The kitchen door—which may or may not have been locked—was at the other end of the building and the basement windows were too small to crawl through. Of course there *was* the separate entrance to the apartment—though Brother would surely have bolted it, tonight of all nights.

In the darkness, Leola made out a shovel leaning against the coal bin and ran to get it. Inhaling deeply, she aimed the iron handle and all of her 110-pound self at the apartment door—surprised when it flew open so easily.

As she staggered into the room, Maudi screamed and Brother jumped off the bed.

"Miss Rideout!" He fumbled with his trouser placket. "What are you . . ."

She ignored the flash of white at his crotch, rushing over to Maudi, who curled against the headboard like a doodlebug poked with a stick.

"Leola!" The girl wailed. "I am . . . I'm so sorry."

"Sorry?" Leola glanced at Brother Giles, reaching for his glasses on a nearby table. "Isn't you who should be sorry, Mauds." She steadied her voice, pretending a calm she did not feel. "But it's over and we are leaving."

Brother took a step, lips twitching.

"Wouldn't benefit you nor anyone else to judge in haste what you've seen here." He snickered. "The girl was hardly an unwilling accomplice."

Leola clutched the shovel, recalling Maudi's rigid body on the bed. Not exactly *willing*. Then she remembered what Ruthie had said about their friend being in Brother's thrall. Leola couldn't very well pick her up and run; if the two of them were going to escape, Maudi would need to come of her own accord.

"Is it true that you wanted this, Maudifrank?" Leola asked, and the other girl stared into her lap.

"Yes. I mean no," she answered, finally. "Brother said it was natural, if two people care about each other . . . said I was his special girl."

Her face puckered, voice ringing with desolation.

"I wasn't certain who to tell or what to do! Brother said I'd be punished, sent to the poorhouse. That no one would believe me—"

John Giles glanced away. "That's not true," he muttered, weakly.

"You won't be sent to the poorhouse. And you *know* this isn't natural, nor the kind of caring grownups are s'posed to do." Leola rested a shaky hand on the girl's back. "But you should button yourself so we can leave."

After a small hesitation, Maudi did as she was told.

"I need to use the lavatory," she whispered, nodding toward the hall.

Leola hesitated, thought of going with her, but decided it was better to stay and keep an eye on Brother, make sure he didn't try anything. Clutching the shovel with both hands, she faced him.

"Hurry back then, Maudi. I'll wait."

Once the other girl was gone, Brother glared at Leola.

"If you tell anyone what you've witnessed, they'll say you're smearing me because you don't want Karla to be adopted or because you're jealous of Maudifrank, as so many are." He gestured toward the hallway. "And *that* one would hardly back you up. Can't imagine her testifying in court."

"Maudi's stronger than you think," Leola retorted, even though he was probably right. "Besides it's not only me who's had suspicions. There's others too."

Brother pulled out a handkerchief, pressing his brow.

"P'rhaps. But without real evidence y'all could be charged with perjury or defamation, which could prohibit you from applying to college." He glowered at her. "Might even land you in jail."

A wave of anger dissolved Leola's shaky composure.

"I do have evidence," she blurted, "a photograph I found in your precious Bible." She eyed the door, hoping Maudi wouldn't hear. "Anyone I showed it to would understand what you've done is anything but *natural*."

Brother went still. "You can't." Another step closer. "You wouldn't."

"I can." Leola raised the shovel in warning. "And I would."

An endless moment passed as Brother tangled the handkerchief through his fingers.

"Give me that photograph," he pleaded, "and I'll nullify the adoption agreement with the Nolans. You can watch me do it! I'll draw up a new contract, recommending you and your sisters never be separated. I'll say you should remain at the Home while attending college, if you wish, to keep charge of them." He licked his lips. "Just give me the picture."

She lifted her chin. "I won't be bribed."

Another crackling silence and then: "I have some information might interest you, Leola. News of your father."

Leola froze on the spot. Brother Giles was desperate—would probably say anything—yet her heart pattered with hope.

"You've heard about my papa and didn't tell me?"

"A message arrived yesterday morning. I've hardly digested it myself with so much else going on." He seemed proud to take the advantage. "Of course I'm more than happy to share said dispatch with you, soon as this so-called *evidence* is in my possession."

Leola gripped the shovel tighter.

"You'll have to give me the message first. Otherwise how do I know you won't take the photograph and escape?"

Maudifrank had come into the room again, standing behind Leola, although Brother hardly seemed to notice.

"All right," he replied at last. "S'pose I can relate just enough to convince you it's true." He stood up straighter. "Your father had a friend named Wilburn, hailed from Oklahoma. A fellow lodger, chef for some oil company."

Leola fell silent. Mama had planned to write Mrs. Grimes again and inquire of Wilburn—maybe discover his last name—but never did have the chance, and Leola had plumb forgotten about him. Certainly she'd never mentioned the man to Brother Giles.

"What about this Wilburn?" she asked, at last.

"He was visiting kin 'round this county on his way to a new post in Alaska territory. Called at several orphanages—including ours—to see if anyone knew of Frank Rideout's children."

Leola swayed as if blown by an invisible wind.

"Did—did you tell him we were here?"

Brother pressed his lips together.

"He left his message beneath the door. No one saw the man come or go—if he even delivered it himself."

"But *someone* must've read the note before—"

"It was sealed in an envelope, found by Mrs. Larkin and delivered straight to my desk. I didn't even have the chance to tell my wife. After reading it, I put it away for safekeeping to revisit after the gala was over." He sneered. "And now Wilburn is gone, bound for the North. You'd never find him in *those* wilds, I reckon."

Leola tried to imagine what the message might contain. After months of silence, it felt like Papa was outside whispering and all she needed to do was open a window to hear him.

But then she noticed the wreath of welts above Maudi's elbows, as if Brother had seized her with force. Noted the yellow ribbon coiled on the very pillow Mrs. Giles would rest her head upon later on. She'd survived this long unsure of her father's fate, but if Brother hurt Maudi more than he already had—or hurt some other innocent kid, maybe one of her sisters—she could never live with that.

"Doesn't matter." She grasped Maudi's hand. "I'll find out this message myself, somehow. Meanwhile we are leaving." She brandished the shovel again. "You best not try and stop us."

Even saying the words, Leola knew they meant little. Brother was stronger and taller than both of them. The man might even have a gun hidden somewhere and no reluctance to use it. But if she didn't at least pretend confidence, they were surely doomed.

"Open the door, Maudi," she commanded. "You leave first."

The girl slipped outside and Leola faced Brother alone again.

"Don't try anything, Mr. Giles, or you'll regret it."

Inching away, eyeing him the whole time, she'd almost made it to the door when he lurched toward her, hands like claws and teeth bared, howling like a wounded animal.

A brutal strength surged through Leola, ignited by the sudden certainty of death. She landed the shovel's blade as hard as she could against his shoulder, and Brother fell, hitting his head on the table, spectacles skittering across the floor. Only when she noticed his back rising and falling, signifying he was alive, did Leola feel relieved—and terrified.

Rushing to join Maudi on the lawn, she looked back at the apartment, fearing Brother could come to at any moment, trying to figure their next plan of escape. And then she spied the Model T in the driveway. Knew it didn't require a key.

"Get in the car, Maudifrank." She tossed the shovel aside. "We have to go back to town and fetch Mrs. Valchar . . ."

The girl balked. "But if you make a fuss, Lee, everyone will hear about me and Brother! I'll be sore ashamed."

"I won't make a fuss." Leola glanced at the building again. "If we don't get out of here Brother might kill us both. Is that what you'd prefer?"

Maudi only blinked in response so Leola gave up, running to the front of the car, grasping the starter handle with both hands. She'd only cranked an auto once in her life, on a sunny day that felt ages in the past. *Brace yourself!* Ship had warned. *Put all your fingers on one side . . . Turn it down fast as you can.*

This jalopy was more temperamental than Ship's had been but, after a few well-timed tries, the engine sputtered to life. Leola rushed for the driver's seat like she was outrunning another furious bull— until she noticed Maudi in the exact same spot as before.

"Why on earth are you still standing there? We have to leave *now!*"

When the girl didn't budge, Leola stepped away.

"There's nothing more I can do to save you." Her tone was grim. "You'll have to save yourself."

Luckily, by the time she'd climbed inside the car, Maudi had come to her senses, sliding into the front seat—none too soon, as Brother Giles had materialized in the apartment doorway.

"Come back, Leola!" His voice keened through the quiet night air. "Come back, Maudi!"

Leola gripped the steering wheel. There'd been no time to flip the switches on the car's headlights and the road stretched ahead, black as the veins of grief in her heart.

"Maudi, you be my extra pair of eyes," she ordered. "Tell me if I get too close to the ditch so I can concentrate on the way forward. Understand?"

"Yes, Leola," the girl replied, a new note of determination in her voice.

With Maudi acting as navigator—*You got plenty of room over here! Now you're too close!*—Leola pushed the accelerator lever, flying down the road faster than Alice Ramsey fleeing the vigilante mob, not slowing until she spied the Mission Hall, a shining beacon of hope.

CHAPTER 56

I n the parking field, Leola jammed the brake pedal, its sharp edge biting into her bare foot.

"Stay here." She reached down, feeling the trickle of blood on her toe. "I'll get Mrs. Valchar."

Maudi gawped in terror. "But what if Brother shows up? What if he sees me and tries to get me?"

Leola wiped the bloodied finger on her petticoat.

"You can hunker down in back. Brother will never notice you if he even dares come here—which I doubt he will."

Maudi took hold of Leola's sleeve.

"Don't leave," she said, and Leola swallowed, unsure what to do.

And then, like an Almighty vision, Rebecca Hooks appeared on the back porch, readying herself for the long walk to New Town.

Leola tumbled from the car, whispering furiously, "Mrs. Hooks!"

When the woman didn't seem to hear, she pitched her voice to a quiet shout.

"Mrs. Hooks!"

The woman jumped, grasping her chest.

"Lord, you scared the daylights outta me! And what are you doing," she pointed, "going shoeless in this air?" Her gaze bounced between Leola and the car. "Were you driving Brother's flivver, there?"

Before Leola could explain, Maudi stepped from the shadows, tousled and wild-eyed, and Mrs. Hooks clapped a hand to her mouth.

"Oh." A long pause. "Oh child. Do not tell me. That man . . . did he . . . ?"

She rushed down the steps, taking Maudifrank in her arms.

"Lord Jesus," she murmured, as the girl burst into tears. "I am so sorry."

She knows, Leola thought, astounded. *Has* known. Not that there was time to find out for sure.

"Is anyone still in the kitchen?" she asked, and Mrs. Hooks shook her head.

"All the other helpers long gone."

"Can we sneak inside then? I need to fetch Mrs. Valchar without causing a racket."

The chef nodded. "No one'll bother us there."

In the kitchen, Mrs. Hooks sat the girl by the still-warm stove, pulling a chair beside her.

"It's them shenanigans with Brother Giles, ain't it?" she asked, and Maudi sniffled, laying a head against the woman's side.

"I had my suspicions, I did." Mrs. Hooks stroked the girl's hair. "Saw him touch you once in the most disgraceful manner." Her mouth set in a hard line. "Right in front of me too! Guess he figured I were no threat—not 'til I brought it up to him in private. Then he warned if I dared tell anyone, Dr. LaHaye could—*would*—make things hard for me and my family. Which I reckoned was true enough."

She spoke low, addressing Leola.

"That LaHaye was the one accused young Ezra Steele of acting above himself toward a white woman last summer. Got his mob all worked up, nearly lynched that young man—may as well have for the beating Ezra got, and left for dead. Those policemen, they looked the other way too." She took a shaky breath, pulling Maudi closer. "I tried to keep a watch for you, child, best I could. Made sure Mrs. Giles put you in the kitchen with me—for whatever that was worth."

Maudi lifted her head, wiping at her eyes.

"Brother would'a made good on his promise if you'd told anyone. Wouldn'a done a thing neither but torment us into eternity."

Leola, dazed by so many revelations, stirred herself.

"I need to fetch Mrs. Valchar before Brother gets away with his crimes, and I can't do that," she pointed at her bare feet, "like this."

Mrs. Hooks stood, gesturing at her rugged walking boots. "These would get you the wrong kind'a notice. Got my work shoes might be better."

She opened the broom closet, retrieving the black flats she wore in the kitchen, which were not so different from the ones Leola had thrown away.

"I b'lieve we are about the same size," she said, handing them over.

Dabbing her bloody foot with a handkerchief, Leola slipped on the shoes, relieved they did indeed fit.

After thanking Mrs. Hooks, she patted her hair in place and entered the main room, glad the crowd had thinned so she was able to spot Mrs. Valchar at once, conversing with Mr. Stone and his wife.

"Why there you are, Miss Rideout!" Catherine said. "I looked for you earlier and couldn't . . ."

"I have a surprise for you in the kitchen." Taking the woman's elbow, Leola hardly glanced at the Stones. "Pardon us a moment."

"That was rude!" Mrs. Valchar hissed as they walked away. "Whatever you have to show me surely could've waited until . . ."

When Leola veered toward the coat closet, Catherine's tone changed from huffy to alarmed.

"What is going on? Didn't you say . . ."

"I'll explain," Leola replied from one side of her pasted-on smile. "In private."

Leola shut the closet door and cut on the overhead light, pouring forth her story while Mrs. Valchar yanked at her pearl choker, uttering cusses that might put Ruthie to shame.

"Poor Maudi! Lord, how did I not know?"

"Because Brother is a sneaky son of a biscuit. But he's still out there. Someone needs to find him quick, before he gets away."

The other woman smoothed the front of her dress.

"Of course. You stay here with Maudifrank. I'll go gather the men."

Leola caught her arm.

"Maudi's mortified over what happened. Please don't make a to-do, if you can help it. Maybe rustle up Andrew and some others, but not Dr. LaHaye nor any of his Kluxxer friends. They'd find some way to let Brother escape, sure's I'm standing here."

Mrs. Valchar nodded.

"I'll do my best not to raise a fuss and will keep that no-account LaHaye out of it." She peered at Leola. "You did a brave thing, my girl. The *right* thing. When we find John Giles, we shall force him to disclose whatever he heard from this Wilburn fellow, I promise."

After she was gone, Leola closed the door again, cut off the light, and sank to the floor. Never mind Ruthie was probably searching for her, that Karla and Mae must be worried, and Maudi needed her as well. Leola craved the respite, however brief, from making decisions she hardly felt ready to make—decisions that didn't feel like choices at all.

Closing her eyes, she gave herself wholly to her longings: for Mama and Papa, Auntie and Joe and Ship, for a childhood that felt like it had never happened, and the secret wish someone might save *her* too.

CHAPTER 57

While Andrew discreetly gathered a search party, Mrs. Valchar bid the remaining guests goodnight. Then she informed the kids there was *a situation* at the Home, that everything would be fine but they'd need to stay put until morning. Somehow she corralled enough extra blankets for everyone and, with the help of the ward mothers, served leftover dessert to those who'd grown hungry again.

Was no small feat for Leola to get her sisters calmed down. Mae and Karla were ecstatic about the so-called *pajama party*, asking a million questions about the undercurrent of calamity. But once they were settled into their makeshift beds, Leola joined Ruthie on the back porch, both of them wrapped in quilts.

"Knock me down and steal my teeth," Ruthie muttered after Leola gave the full account of her ordeal. "When they catch that piker John Giles, they better cut off his dilly-dally first thing so it can't never do damage again." She flicked her springy hair. "Leastways that's what I would do."

Leola watched a shooting star whisk toward the horizon.

"I'll take him being locked into prison with the key thrown away so long's Maudifrank doesn't have to testify. Hard to admit but Brother was right, saying it would break her."

A small silence passed before Ruthie asked, "Did he ravish her, do you think? Steal her pearl, I mean?"

Leola recalled Brother leaning over Maudi on the bed. His unfastened trousers. The girl, a wooden figure beneath him.

"Not sure. Might not have been the first time they were in such a situation. But it seems beside the point, for Maudi will never be innocent of anything ever again."

As they stared at the diamond-chipped sky, letting this truth sink in, Ruthie touched Leola's knee.

"Catherine will get that mysterious message outta John Giles," she said. "Don't you worry."

Even as she nodded, Leola wasn't so sure. Brother had hurt a child in the worst way right beneath their noses. He didn't seem fashioned from the same flesh as most folk, but some other, more hardened stuff. The man would hold fast to his secret, if only out of spite.

"Lee? Ruthie?"

They turned to see Maudifrank standing in the doorway.

"Y'all coming to bed soon? I can't sleep."

Ruthie jumped up, nearly crushing Maudi in a hug. Nothing more was said but they all shed some tears before going inside, stepping between sleeping bodies until they arrived at the space they'd cleared earlier. Arranging their pallets either side of Maudifrank's, Leola and Ruthie draped their arms around the girl as if it was all the protection a person might ever need.

CHAPTER 58

The men captured Brother Giles in an abandoned barn some miles from the Home, but he broke free and ran into the road. Didn't see the truck careering around the bend—until it was too late.

"Never knew what hit him," was how Mrs. Valchar put it the next morning.

"But the message?" Leola choked out. "From my papa?"

Mrs. Valchar touched her shoulder.

"Andrew and the others are scouring the orphanage as we speak, looking for it. Before he put Mrs. Giles on the train to her sister's this morning, he asked whether she'd heard anything of your father." She gave Leola a regretful look. "At least in this, Brother was truthful. Seems Jessamyn Giles was as ignorant of that as she was of her husband's carryings-on with poor Maudifrank."

The search of Brother's office, darkroom, and apartment did yield more secrets, including additional offensive photographs of Maudi and another girl who'd lived at the orphanage years ago. They found letters, too, from potential adoptive parents, indicating they'd given Brother heaps of money for *select children*—money he must have pocketed himself, knowing the Mission Society would never abide such a practice. There was also KKK literature with notes in Brother's handwriting, and the date of an upcoming rally he clearly planned to attend. But no letter or cable, no sign of any message from a Houston chef named Wilburn—no news of Frank Rideout at all, unless you counted the agency's communiques with the morgues and hospitals in Houston.

The disappointment of this, along with deep-down exhaustion from everything she'd been through, knocked the wind out of Leola—literally—and a week later she took pneumonia. Fortunately, the Valchars were supervising at the Home until the Mission Board could find a new manager, and Leola received the best of care—from doctors but also from Mrs. Valchar, who plied her with veal broth and mustard plasters, reading aloud from *Glinda of Oz*, a story about the good witch who was such a friend to Dorothy Gale.

"Dr. Folds says your lungs were scarred by the influenza," she explained when Leola finally felt well enough to sit up and take a meal. "Says you'll have a tendency to respiratory ailments through-out your life, but that you're physically strong in every other way. With an ounce of prevention, it shouldn't prove onerous at all."

Leola could think of nothing so onerous as Papa's absence, a far sharper pain than she felt in her lungs. Must have shown it, too, for Mrs. Valchar whisked away the bed tray, enclosing Leola's fingers in her own.

"I realize how disappointing it's been not hearing of your father. When you've gained strength, I'd like to accompany you and Joe to Houston, conduct a search. I already spoke to Joe when he came yesterday. He thought it a grand idea. I'd pay for the train tickets and such." She caught Leola's gaze. "What do you think?"

Leola blinked back tears. "It's mighty kind, but I'd hate for you to use your time and money without any . . ."

"Nonsense." The other woman slouched. "It would help placate the guilt I feel for getting duped by John Giles. Not to mention we all could use some respite from this place."

Drying her eyes with the sheet, Leola smiled.

"I appreciate it, Mrs. Valchar, more than you know."

"High time you called me Catherine, young lady. After all, we're not so far apart in age—or so I tell myself." She chuckled. "Besides, I feel more friend to you than superior. Not a bosom pal like Ruthie, p'rhaps, but someone who thoroughly enjoys your company."

Leola grinned in agreement. Mrs. Valchar—*Catherine*—was the sort of smart, interesting pal she'd imagined making at college. If she ever got there.

"Ruthie came to visit this morning," Leola said. "Told me Maudifrank is bearing up, more or less."

Catherine nodded.

"She'll shoulder untold effects from this tragedy no doubt. Let's hope the doctor I mentioned to you can help her sort things a little." Her tone brightened. "P'rhaps when he visits Maudifrank, he'd see Karla too. With your approval of course."

"That'd be swell," Leola replied, thinking unlike Glinda the Good or any other storybook figure, Catherine didn't need a wand to cast her spells. Joe had told her how besotted Mae and Karla were by the woman, who'd even slept in their room when the girls were especially worried about their sister.

But now she noticed Catherine had fallen silent, fiddling with a loose thread on the quilt.

"There *is* something else we'd like you to think upon," she said in a measured tone, and Leola's pulse raced, for she was fairly certain what that *something else* might be.

Yesterday she'd learned the state agency had nullified the Nolans' adoption agreement, though still insisted Karla be placed in a family setting, soon as possible. Knowing this was probably inevitable, Leola had hoped for a certain outcome. Was ready with a reply if it happened.

"We'll not be offended whether you accept our offer or not," Catherine continued, "but," she paused, "we were hoping you and your sisters would let us foster y'all until you can assume their care or find your father—whichever comes first."

Leola blinked, realizing it wasn't only Karla the woman was asking about.

"We'll understand if you don't agree," Catherine rushed on. "Won't hold it against you one bit. There might yet be a Valchar baby to arrive in the traditional way, but we already love you girls as our own so that should make no—"

Leola swooped forward, embracing the woman, smothering whatever else she'd meant to say.

"Yes, yes, yes!" she exclaimed, noticing that Catherine, like Mama, also smelled of lavender and milky tea and the general essence of good, honest things. "A thousand times, yes!"

The two of them burst into such a fit of laughing and crying, Andrew and Mrs. Hooks came running and, when they realized it was a racket of jubilation, joined in the uproar themselves.

Houston, Texas • August 1920

CHAPTER 59

E ven seated in the first-class car, the train ride to Houston felt longer than a trip to the moon. Months had passed since the calamity with Brother Giles. The Valchars had been busy finding a new director for the Home and arranging to foster the Rideout girls, and Leola had endless schoolwork to make up after her illness. At times it'd seemed they'd never make the journey, but now that it was happening, Leola's emotions pitched wilder than an unbroke stallion.

By the time they settled at the Regency Hotel, it was too late to venture far. So, after a sumptuous dinner in the oak-paneled dining room, they wandered to Military Park, watching the ships glide up the canal, as Papa had described in his letters. Leola tried to appreciate the sights, but couldn't help wondering if he'd once sat on this particular patch of grass or strolled a certain walkway, homesick for his family.

The next morning, Catherine, accompanied by an old college chum, set out for Mrs. Grimes's lodging house while Leola and Joe headed to Magnolia Park, where the main population of Tejanos lived. For hours they pressed down the crowded streets, Joe asking questions in Spanish, Leola brandishing her parents' wedding photograph.

Being the rare gringos, most folks treated them with suspicion—

which Leola understood. Mexicans weren't treated quite as badly in this city as Blacks—were allowed to sit at the front of trolley cars and be served in certain white establishments—yet still were viewed as second-class citizens. At the train station yesterday, she'd witnessed two well-dressed businessmen laugh as they purposely knocked down a Mexican newspaper boy and, at breakfast, overheard three Anglo women discussing the "outrageous" fact that "greasers" were allowed to attend Houston's white schools. *At least they're taught in separate rooms,* one of the women huffed. *Those folk are dirty as sin, and why should white children be exposed?*

Entering the bustling market, Leola was too hot and dusty to care much about the wary stares they received or the wooden stalls filled with mouthwatering food and handcrafted merchandise. Not to mention her feet ached in the shoes Catherine had bought her last week, which fit perfectly but hadn't been broken in.

Joe, noticing the drag in her step, pointed out the general store ahead. "Let's get us some Coca-Colas." He jangled coins in his pockets. "Quench our thirsts and rest awhile."

Leola was happy for the break, but as they sat guzzling the icy drinks, felt a sudden, sharp yearning for Mama's lemonade—much more refreshing than cola, in her estimation. This thought, coupled with despair at ever finding Papa, brought tears to her eyes—which she tried in vain to wipe away.

"Oh, Rosie . . ." Joe took hold of her hand. "Don't lose hope. We still have the Second Ward to search and two days left to do it. You're weak from your sickness and need some fuel." He motioned in the direction they'd come. "Don't know about you but the smell from that carnitas stand back there got me hankerin' for lunch."

He stood.

"Stay put. I'll fetch us some vittles. With a bit of nourishment, you'll feel right as rain."

After he was gone, Leola noticed a wooden stall just down the street, festooned with brilliant-colored fabric panels like she'd never seen before. Intrigued, she approached the booth, where a petite woman not much older than she was conversing with some other women. In spite of their rapid-fire Spanish, Leola could tell they were bargaining over some of the smaller textiles.

After money and cloth were exchanged, the group finally took their leave: "*Te veremos pronto*, Martina!"

As Leola drew near, the woman named Martina looked up, her smile replaced by the same uncertain expression Leola had seen so often today.

"*Habla inglés?*" Leola asked, embarrassed by her feeble accent, wishing she spoke fluently like Joe did.

"*Si.* Yes," Martina replied, and Leola gestured at the weavings.

"These are the prettiest things I ever set eyes upon. Did you make them?"

Martina shrugged. "Most."

Leola studied a tapestry decorated with lion-like figures and geometric shapes.

"My mama was a seamstress, made beautiful quilts in every design," she said. "Didn't know how to weave but would have learned, if it meant fashioning something like this."

The woman's black eyes softened. "Your mama," she gestured about, "here?"

"No." Leola steadied her voice. "Mama passed months ago. Influenza."

"Ah." Martina bowed her head. "Many taken in this city too. Is a hard thing losing *tu madre*. My own died when I was . . ."

She held a hand knee high.

"*Condolencias*," Leola said, embarrassed again by her poor diction.

Then she remembered the photograph in her bag and the reason she was here to begin with.

"I have a picture of my mother," she said, offering it to Martina. "That's my papa too. He came to Houston nearly a year ago looking for work, but we haven't heard of him since."

Martina took the portrait.

"He was much younger in the picture, of course," Leola rattled on. "Has more lines on his face these days and," she gestured at his left side, "no arm. Lost it in an accident. Frank Rideout's his name." She peered at Martina. "We heard he might've been hurt in a fight, that a Tejano doctor might have taken care of him. Have you . . ."

"Have not seen," the woman responded, handing back the photograph. "Is a big city, Houston, many Tejano *médicos*." She began rearranging a pile of fabrics, avoiding Leola's gaze. "Many one-armed gringos too."

Leola's hope wilted again. *Have not seen* was a more common refrain around here apparently than the squeal of trolley wheels on metal tracks.

"Well, if you happen to cross paths or hear of my father—please tell him his daughter, Leola, is looking for him. We're staying at the Regency for three more days. After that we'll be living in Waxahachie with Mr. and Mrs. Andrew Valchar. Tell your friends too, in case they run into him."

When the weaver nodded, Leola tucked away the picture—and her longings—yet again. But then her eyes fell on a tapestry hanging behind Martina and her spirits lifted the tiniest bit.

"Those hummingbirds," she pointed at the whimsical pink, green, and purple creatures hovering against a dark background, "remind me of home."

The woman removed the hanging from its peg so Leola could see it close up.

"How much?" she asked and Martina answered, quicker than she expected, "Three dollars."

Leola understood enough Spanish to know the weaver had asked more money for the less-elaborate piece she'd sold to her friends. Maybe, she thought, Martina was offering this bargain because she felt pity over Leola's plight or empathy over their deceased mothers. Whatever the reason, Leola didn't want to hurt her pride by insisting on a higher price.

"I'll take it." She dug around in her bag. "Seems more than fair, for such a marvel."

She handed the money to Martina, who wrapped the cloth in paper.

"Thank you." Leola took the package. "*Gracias.*"

This word rolled more gracefully from her tongue, though Martina, already helping another customer, didn't seem to hear.

Leola, pretending to examine another weaving, found herself lingering, unable to shake the eerie connection she felt to this woman. They came from two different societies, two different *worlds*, and still there was something between them she couldn't put her finger on . . .

Just then, Martina looked over, regarding Leola with a half-curious, half-wary expression, as if asking a question and answering it too—until another patron appeared and their strange intimacy vanished. Leola realized Joe had probably returned to their meeting place, that he'd be worried to find her absent. She told herself a well-connected person like Martina would know about Papa if he were around—meaning that, after lunch, she and Joe could hop a trolley to the Second Ward, pressing on with their search.

Hurrying through the narrow street, she put the weaver out of her mind, hoping Joe hadn't eaten his empanada and hers too.

◆

At dinner that evening, Catherine recounted her discussion with Mrs. Grimes, who'd heard nothing more of Papa but did suggest the name of the saloon, Pearlie Swain's, where he might've gotten hurt. Catherine and her friend had gone there afterward, quizzing old Pearlie.

"He said there *was* a fight 'bout the time your father vanished. The fracas started inside and spilled onto the street, with plenty of passersby hurt—including a one-armed man from East Texas. Mr. Swain never saw the man's face nor heard much else about him." Catherine's eyes turned sorrowful. "Not so different from what we already knew, I'm afraid."

Leola pushed a pea around her plate, thinking of her own foiled search. She and Joe never had made it to the Second Ward, as a raging thunderstorm had broken over the city, returning the streets to their natural swampy state and flooding the trolley tracks.

"Don't lose hope yet," Catherine said, leaning close. "There'll be more leads in the coming days, I'm certain."

Leola slunk against her chair.

"But there's that Klan demonstration planned for tomorrow! People say it'll cause all kinds of upheaval, that we'll have to stay in the hotel all day. What if we—"

She didn't get to finish her question as another guest had sidled up—one of the women Leola overheard yesterday talking about *the Mexican problem.*

"Apologies for interruptin'," the woman said. "I couldn't help eavesdropping upon your conversation. Thought I'd add my two cents." She offered a hand to Leola. "I'm Mrs. Donald Entwhistle from Waco. Met your lovely chaperone this morning."

As Catherine made the introductions, Mrs. Entwhistle flinched at Joe's name like the sound of it hurt her ears.

"Forgive me again," she said, addressing mostly Catherine, "for barging into your affairs. I do have some insight into this upcoming Klan event."

The woman had several chins and Leola couldn't help watching the wobbly layers, moving in rhythm with her words.

". . . it's one of their reg'lar demonstrations against immorality. At midday the entire Houston klavern will march assorted riff-raff— wife beaters, gamblers, tipplers, you name it—down to the canal banks for a whuppin'."

Leola snorted. "It's those Kluxxers ought to be whupped for *immorality.*"

Mrs. Entwhistle narrowed her eyes. "Way this country's goin', young lady, y'ought to appreciate their efforts to keep innocents like you from the influences of," she sneered at Joe, "unsavory sorts."

Joe clasped his knife like he wanted to prune Mrs. Entwhistle's floppy growths from their stalk—not that she seemed to notice.

"Regardless the Klan's best intentions," the woman sniffed, "violence has a way of breaking out over these things. Happened last time I was here, if you can believe it. Was the Coloreds down at the military base causin' trouble, all because the white soldiers gave them some good-natured ribbing. When the Klan tried to bring order, those Black malcontents fought back, too, causing further harm. The city was put on curfew, railways shut down. I was lucky to get one of the last trains out. Had to pay double and even then could only book the third-class compartment."

She curled her lip.

"Took me an entire week to get over *that* misery, but I won't make the same mistake twice—my sister and cousin are down at the station as we speak, paying our *first-class* fare. We'll be gone by sunrise tomorrow and you should do likewise."

Leola, mortified they might have to abandon their search when it'd hardly begun, touched Joe's hand, ignoring another of Mrs. Entwhistle's frosty expressions—which melted when she spotted one of her companions across the room.

"Here's Cousin Nola!" She waved at the other woman. "I best be going. Do take my advice and hightail it out of here while you can."

After she was gone, the three travelers debated the situation, while Leola battled a host of contrary feelings. These past days, she'd felt closer to her father than in months, but the idea of stumbling upon him without warning had also given rise to a darker possibility: that he'd created a new life for himself, one without space for his three daughters. A life she could not imagine—maybe didn't want to. And now this threat of violence, the possibility of Joe being singled out by frenzied Klansmen, of Catherine and Leola getting caught up in the savagery. Her sisters had just begun blossoming under the Valchars' care—Karla speaking again, Mae finally making friends. How could she jeopardize such hard-won progress?

And so, with Mrs. Valchar promising they'd return, Joe rushed off to buy train tickets—though in the end the third-class compartment was their only choice. Not that it mattered to Leola and Joe, for whom such accommodations felt like home.

❧

Next morning, as the train pulled from the station and Houston's skyscrapers receded beyond the vast bayou, Leola felt her connection to Papa stretched to infinity too. Tried conjuring his smile, his voice, how loved she'd felt in his presence. Tried but hardly could.

"I'll be back, Papa," she whispered. "We'll find each other, I promise."

Though she was less certain than ever it was true.

Tyler, Texas • March 1940

CHAPTER 60

Leola gathered the flour and sugar canisters, hurrying to get dessert in the oven. Joe had always loved Auntie's trifle and now they had a son, Peter, who relished it, too. Leola had even left work early today to make one: a surprise treat for a surprise announcement.

Though she'd long memorized the recipe, Leola always propped Auntie's dog-eared instructions nearby as a stand-in—however poor—for the woman who'd been her kitchen companion once.

Cracking eggs against Mama's yellow bowl, she realized she'd have to delay again visiting her great-aunt's grave in Shreveport. Malvina had died soon after moving to Louisiana, but Leola had been ill with pneumonia and couldn't attend the funeral. After that, life had gotten so busy—she'd finished college, become a teacher, married, had a child. She wasn't even certain anymore of the cemetery's name.

Whisking milk into the batter, she hoped at least she'd visit Bronway with her family. The town had lost the old post office— destroyed in a fire—as well as the grand cedars along the Dark Road, bulldozed when the track was widened. She wasn't sure Mr. Owen's old farm was still standing or Malvina's place or the Shipleys' but there were memories there she wanted to share. If she could stand it.

A car door slammed and Leola looked outside, alarmed to see Joe marching up the walk. Her husband's rose-growing business was among the region's most successful, yet he still insisted on working alongside his hired hands, meaning he usually stayed late to catch up on office work. The fact he was home at this hour was not a good sign.

As they met in the hall, Joe pulled Leola close.

"Rose o'Roses." His glum tone reminded her of the night he'd brought news of Ship's death. "I've something to tell you."

Leola made a quick calculation of possible disaster, knew it couldn't concern Peter, whose voice rang out from their neighbor's yard, or Mae, whom she'd phoned minutes earlier. P'rhaps she'd missed a call from the psychiatric institution where Karla currently lived and they'd contacted Joe instead.

She looked up at him. "Did Karla have another episode?"

Her husband shook his head.

"Far's I'm aware, the new medicines are working and she's visiting next weekend, like we planned."

Leola exhaled. Despite the Valchars' steadfast care, Karla had never fully recovered from her early losses. As a young woman, she'd begun to experience periods of deep darkness followed by stretches of wild excess, when she'd spend all her money or marry some hapless cad, only to divorce him months later. *Looking for Papa,* she'd muttered, when Leola had confronted her about one such ill-conceived romance. *Don't you still wish for him, Lee? Still wonder what happened?*

I do my best not to, Leola had replied. *What do you remember of him, Karla? You were so young when he . . . left.*

Not much, her sister answered. *There was one time—think I was playing with dollies. Under our porch?* She'd laughed. *It hardly makes sense; Papa couldn't have fit in such a space. Yet there he was, sayin' how we'd meet again. How we needed to be together "for our magic to work" or something like that.* She'd shrugged. *Guess I'm remembering it wrong.*

Leola still got goosebumps, recalling this incident. She'd never mentioned Karla's strange visions to anyone, and Mae had never brought it up again either. *Let sleeping ghosts lie,* Leola had told herself, fearful of stirring them in her own soul as well.

"If it isn't my sister," she asked Joe, "then what?"

He gestured toward the kitchen. "Let's sit."

Leola didn't offer to take his hat or get him an iced tea, lowering to the table, heart pounding so wildly she thought it might bolt from her chest.

Joe threw his work case and Stetson on the table, then sat in the chair next to her.

"Got a call from Andrew Valchar, couple weeks ago." He raked still-thick hair from his forehead. "Didn't want to tell you right off as there were," pause, "some details I needed to confirm first."

Leola's unease deepened. Joe usually told her of Andrew's calls within days, not weeks, and even then, their conversations were hardly about more than baseball scores and gardening. But now she recalled how distracted her husband had seemed lately—though she'd figured it was some mix-up at work and bound to resolve itself, as such things usually did.

"Details?" she asked, and Joe nodded.

"Something Catherine confessed before she died."

Remembering Catherine's death from cancer last March, Leola blinked back tears. At least that was *one* funeral she hadn't had to miss. Her sisters had gone too—Mae singing "Amazing Grace" and Karla delivering a short elegy for the woman she'd called *Mother* to the end.

"We've long suspected your father was alive." Joe licked his lips. "Now it seems we know for sure."

It took a moment for his words to sink in.

"Papa." She could barely speak. "*Alive.*"

She gawped at him.

"But if Catherine knew, why didn't she say so?"

"She had her reasons, Lee." Joe hesitated. "Didn't want you to be hurt worse than you'd already been."

Leola stiffened. Of all people, Catherine understood her craving for any knowledge of Papa. If she'd willfully withheld such knowledge, it must be wounding indeed.

"Go on," she murmured.

Joe hooked his boot heels over the chair stretcher but Leola lacked the wherewithal to chide him, as she usually might, for scuffing the wood.

"When we were in Houston back in '20," Joe began, "Pearlie Swain gave Catherine the name of some prominent Tejano doctors might've ministered to the man injured in that street fight. She planned to visit them the next day. Didn't say anything for fear of raising your hopes. 'Course we had to leave early so she took up her sleuthing at home, writing letters, making calls. Didn't get much response at first." He hesitated. "But a year later one of the doctors wrote back, saying he had a colleague—a Dr. Curbelo—who'd cared for your father. Said he still lived with the doctor's family and was," Joe glanced into his lap, "*is* doing well."

Leola tried to make sense of his words. "But I don't understand. If he's alive, why didn't he. . . ?"

"Seems your father married Dr. Curbelo's daughter," Joe interjected, "not long after we left Houston."

Leola felt clouted by an invisible force. As with the possibility of her father's survival, she'd weighed this prospect countless times. Convinced herself it couldn't happen, at least not before he'd reunited with his daughters. Not with Mama barely cold in her grave.

Joe cleared his throat.

"What is it?" she asked.

"The woman Frank married. . . she's a renown weaver in that city, named Martina. Used to hawk her wares at," he blinked, "the market in Magnolia Park."

Leola wrung her hands. "The woman I met that day, who sold me the hummingbird tapestry? *That* Martina?"

Joe gave a grim nod.

"But she knew I was looking for Papa!" Leola's voice was a near-wail. "She could've taken me to him! Or told him we were looking for him."

"I reckon it was a shock," Joe replied, "meeting you in such a haphazard way. Maybe she was worried the police would get involved. Her family, being Tejano . . . well, it might've caused them trouble. Might have caused your father trouble too."

Leola's temples throbbed.

"It still doesn't answer why Catherine hid this secret from us."

"By the time it was all unraveled, Lee, two more years had passed. You and your sisters were thriving. Catherine decided it'd be cruel to inform you that Frank had moved on in such a definite way." His face wrenched. "But a few more letters did get exchanged. That's how Catherine discovered Martina and your father already had one child and another on the way."

Disbelief washed over Leola. Papa had not only remarried, but started a new family—like she and her sisters were so easily cast aside. So easily replaced.

Glancing around the kitchen, it felt as if she were viewing her life from an impossible distance. The utensils on the counter were child's toys. The pots and pans, absurd. Big Leola's bluebonnet painting mocked any true beauty she'd ever known.

She turned her gaze to her husband again.

"How many? How many *new* children did my father have? Did Andrew say?"

Joe nodded, rubbing his knees. "You sure you want to know?"

"Tell me," she commanded, and he responded so quietly she had to bend forward to hear.

"Six more. He's had six additional children, the youngest born only last year."

After a few stunned moments, Leola stood up, staggering to the window. Outside, two hummingbirds darted through the trumpet vine, a display she'd always found both miraculous and comical—the unceasing whir of wings, how their curved beaks fit perfectly inside the bright orange flowers, the way they'd be there one minute, gone the next.

But now the scene reminded her of the weaving she'd bought from Martina. She'd never hung it up—never used it at all, even though she'd never understood quite *why*. And last year, she'd donated it to the church bazaar.

Behind her, Joe made a noise, and she knew he was crying too.

"I'm beyond sorry, Rosie." His touch was warm on her shoulder. "I came close to not telling you. P'rhaps I shouldn't have."

Leola turned, rubbing tears from her cheeks.

"You did the right thing." She sloped against him. "At least now we finally understand why Papa didn't wish to be found."

Joe motioned at his work case.

"I have Frank's address in Houston. You could call or write, ask him yourself why . . ."

"I'll share it with Mae," she interrupted, "but not Karla, not until I'm sure it won't set off another of her depressions. If Mae wants to make contact—though I hardly think she will—that's for her to decide." Leola squared her shoulders. "I've made a new life that has nothing to do with my father. Got no need for his excuses."

She took her husband's hand, placing it against her belly.

"Besides, *mi caro*, bitterness isn't good for a growing baby."

Color rose again in Joe's cheeks. "Baby?"

"It's true, darlin'."

Leola tried to summon the elation she'd felt minutes earlier, before her world had changed forever.

"After all these years tryin', we'll have another sweet son in six months' time. Or dare I wish it, a daughter for you to spoil."

Joe's joyful expression changed to anguish again.

"If I'd any idea, Lee, I'd have waited to tell you until afterward or . . . or never at all."

She gave another vigorous shake of her head.

"You had to tell me. Besides, there's no good time for such news. It's better I found out now so I can make some peace with it before she," Leola patted her stomach, "or *he* arrives."

As Joe hugged her, sadness flickered inside Leola like a humming-bird's wings, cutting sharper into her heart, threatening to snag her spirit also. In that moment, she determined not to let it, remembering everything she had, the people she loved and those still to come, allowing this old-new sorrow to float down to the darkest parts of her soul, there and not there—as Papa had been for so long and would be, it seemed, forevermore.

Tyler and Waxahachie, Texas • April 1957

CHAPTER 61

Leola sat in the car, patience wearing thin. Sixteen-year-old Rose was always late, didn't matter how early she set her alarm, and Leola was getting antsy. The ride to Waxahachie took more than two hours, it was already eight thirty, and they'd promised to meet Ruthie at the Home by eleven o'clock.

Sighing, Leola wondered again if she'd made a mistake, permitting Rose to accompany her to the annual orphanage Homecoming Day. *You have to go, Mother, and take me with you,* Rose had protested, when Leola debated the invitation over supper, weeks earlier. *You said Aunt Ruthie will be there and we haven't seen her in forever. Besides, I'll be off to college in two years and who knows when I'll have another chance?*

Leola chuckled, thinking her daughter could argue the tail off a dog. She'd always found it touching, how close her kids felt to Ruthie. They had their own aunts of course, but Mae had been busy over the years raising her brood of five and Karla, fragile as she was, acted more as older cousin than aunt. Meanwhile, Ruthie and her husband, Floyd Wilkerson, ran a thriving horse ranch outside Dallas and never did have children—a fact Ruthie insisted gave her full entitlement to spoil the Belfigli kids rotten. Which she did without apology.

Lately however their visits had come few and far between. Ruthie had been busy nursing Floyd after his back surgery, then her mother until she'd passed. However much Rose missed Ruthie Free, Leola did a hundred times more.

Even so, watching a dun-colored moth climb the windshield, she felt another tug of doubt about her decision to return to the Home. Last time she'd been there was in the thirties, when the vo-tech center was renamed for the Valchars, who'd somehow gotten the place built after refusing the Klan's dubious charity.

Leola had enjoyed the ceremony and visiting old friends but afterward felt a lingering sadness she couldn't quite name. She'd dreamed about Papa, too, several nights in a row. Saw him standing at the end of her bed, beckoning with his one arm. Calling her name. She'd awakened, sobbing, and when Joe asked what the dream was about, she'd lied, saying it had to do with the silly mystery novel she was reading.

Leola hadn't had a dream like that, since. Didn't relish the idea of opening this old wound either. But it was too late to undo her decision, for here came Rose, flying out the front door, spiffed up and looking excited.

As the girl tumbled into the car, Leola had to admit a certain anticipation in showing off her daughter today. Rose had inherited Joe's golden skin and high cheekbones, his intense focus and easygoing manner. From Leola, she'd gotten the blue-green eyes and willowy build, plus a tendency to question everything. Yet Rose was her own person, too, a firebrand who'd recently challenged their pastor's opposition to school integration. Didn't apologize for her views even after she was disqualified as Prom Queen, called terrible names by kids and grownups alike. *Isn't right,* she'd said to her mother. *Isn't right, one bit.*

"We going?"

The girl was glaring at Leola as if she were the one making them tardy.

"Yes, yes," Leola mumbled, backing their unwieldy Pontiac down the driveway.

With Rose chattering nonstop, the journey passed quickly, and soon they reached Waxahachie's town center—which had hardly changed over the years. As they rounded the square, Leola pointed out various places of interest: the Dixie theater and soda shop where Blacks and Mexicans still weren't welcomed, the haughty statue of Johnny Reb on the courthouse lawn.

"Never mind the South fell near a hundred years ago and hasn't exactly risen again," her daughter huffed.

Only in the surrounding countryside did Leola truly feel the passage of time, marking the slew of recent housing developments, the sprawling grocery store and soaring television antennae. The cotton fields surrounding the Home had been replaced by a baseball diamond and parking lot, the old dormitory razed to make way for the cozy cottages where the children currently stayed, with a gleaming Welcome Center in the middle of everything.

"There's Aunt Ruthie!" Rose cried as they parked.

Outside the car, Leola grinned, watching her friend run toward them. Though she'd cut her hair short and gained a little weight, Ruthie still exuded the same bold energy. When they embraced, it did feel like coming home.

Eventually the three women joined other alumni—including Glenda Yokum, née Wanless—for a tour led by some of the Home's teenaged residents. There weren't any orphans staying here anymore—no raging epidemics to devastate entire families, praise be! These children were more like half-orphans, waiting for their parents to get back on their feet or for someone to take a chance on them, as the Valchars had with Leola and her sisters.

After lunch, while her friends regaled Rose with tales of yore,

Leola slipped away to the Memory Garden near the main entrance, reading the plaques on various trees and benches until she found the one she'd been looking for: *In Memory of Maudifrank Swenson, 1905-1949. With Love, Ruthie and Leola.*

Leola swallowed, remembering the night Ruthie had called to inform her of the tragedy that had taken their friend's life. *Police told me the car was fairly wrapped around the tree, not a skid mark to be seen*, she'd said, the phone line crackling with questions neither wanted to ask.

At this point, Leola had arrived at the edge of the Memory Garden, nearly to the road. Turning, she noticed the long concrete path leading to the Welcome Center, marked by a small sign on a metal post: *The walkway before you, installed in 1906 and never altered, led countless children to the front door of the original Texas State Children's Home.*

Inhaling, Leola ventured one step down the path, then another, flooded with memories of that first day, the overwhelming sense she'd had of surrendering everything. Of course she hadn't given up *everything*—still had Joe and her sisters, happy memories, new friends to make and opportunities she'd never anticipated. Yet that strange suspicion that Papa was forever lost . . . *that*, it turned out, had been true.

"Mother?" Rose materialized in front of her. "You all right?"

Leola adjusted her sunglasses, glad the girl wouldn't notice her misty eyes.

"Just admiring the shrubbery." She leaned over, sniffing a peony bush. "Your daddy's favorite flowers—besides roses, of course."

Her daughter hesitated.

"Ruthie and Wanda are looking for you," she finally said, in a quiet voice. "There's a slide show starting in the cafeteria with photos of y'all from some modelin' party . . ."

Leola linked her arm through Rose's, grateful for the distraction.

Later, after tearful farewells and vows to visit Ruthie, the Rideout women started home, but hadn't made it to the highway before Rose blurted, "What were you thinking when I found you in the Memory Garden? You looked positively gobsmacked."

Leola stared ahead.

"Not *gobsmacked*. Just reminiscing. That's what a person does in a such a place."

She felt Rose watching her.

"Were you wondering about your father? If he'd come back, you wouldn't have had to go to the orphanage in the first place, right?"

Rose and Leola had always shared a strange capacity to perceive one another's thoughts, which normally seemed a wondrous testament to their bond. Now it only made Leola feel *invaded*.

"You do wonder about him, don't you?" Rose prodded.

The car in front of them braked without warning and Leola stifled a cuss.

"Mom? Did you hear me?"

"I heard you." Leola cranked her window as if the wind might dispel her daughter's curiosity. "And no, I don't wonder of my father. Not anymore."

"Well I think you should write him a letter. Or call him on the telephone. Daddy says he has the . . ."

Leola drifted into the adjacent lane, nearly colliding with another car.

"Dag blame it, Rose. This ain't the time for such a discussion."

"Then what is the time?" The girl's voice was equally shrill. "Whenever I ask about it, you change the subject. Frank Rideout was *my granddad* after all. It makes me angry, thinking of what he did, leaving you and you sisters, getting remarried—having what? Six, seven more kids? Never going back to . . ."

Leola cut the steering wheel, careening onto the narrow median between the highway and service road—so suddenly, Rose had to brace herself to keep from hitting the dashboard.

"Holy Toledo, Mother! You could'a got us killed!"

Leola turned off the engine.

"I'm sorry." She looked at Rose, speaking as calmly as she could. "You've got to understand, past is past. The things you're asking about I don't wish to relive. I've grieved my father enough."

Rose's cheeks—which rarely showed a blush—glowed pink.

"Have you? Grieved it, I mean?" She cinched her arms across her chest. "Sometimes you're so distant. So *not here*. Daddy says it's you, *dancing with your unburied father*, and the rest of us on the sidelines, waiting our chance."

Leola felt angry that Joe would speak so behind her back, even as she knew he was right. Staring at the Gulf Station and Dairy Queen up ahead, she recalled countless times he'd begged her to confront Papa, believing it might alleviate her anguish. When she'd refused—as she always had—Joe hadn't liked it, but he'd understood. After all, he'd seen her through that loss, knew how it had shaped her and didn't take those dark moments personally. However, the idea her children might've perceived that grief—regardless of how she'd tried to hide it—without the benefit of understanding, tore her up.

She took Rose's hand.

"I had my sisters to worry about after Papa left, then a husband and family, a job and a home. It never seemed right to dwell on such a loss when there was so much else needing my attention. So much else needing my love." She peered into her daughter's eyes, mirrors of her own. "Can you understand that? Or try to?"

Rose let out a sigh. "I *do* try, Mom. It must've been terrible what you went through."

Leola pulled tissues from her purse, offering one to Rose.

"I'm strong, darlin'. Remember, what doesn't kill . . ."

"I know, I know: *What doesn't kill you, makes you stronger.*" Rose rubbed her eyes with the tissue. "But it doesn't seem like strength if it's still hurting you. If you told your father how it made—*makes*—you feel, then maybe you *could* really feel strong. And there could be more to the story besides, things he knows that you don't. Things that might make you feel better."

Leola had considered this over the years. In the end, the possibility he might *not* have the answers she wanted—the idea he might not care *at all*—had seemed too much of a risk.

"I appreciate your concern, Rose, but each of us reckons with our sorrows as we see fit. Besides, if my life had gone differently I might never have had *you,* and that is something I would not trade, for I love you more than all the . . ."

. . . *biscuits and gravy in Texas.* Words her father had said yet hadn't seemed to mean.

". . . more than all the bluebonnets in a springtime meadow," she improvised, and Rose's face crumpled.

"I'm sorry," she flung her arms around Leola, "for bringing up all that bad business." She leaned away. "But if you ever decide to find your father—track him down, talk to him—I want to help, okay?"

Leola nodded, grateful yet again that her daughter had turned out at least as caring as she was stubborn.

"Thank you, Rose. We'll see about that. Meanwhile," she pointed to the gas station up ahead, "we better feed this ol' guzzler while we can." She started the car. "And speaking of feeding—we were gossiping so much at lunch I hardly ate a thing. How 'bout we treat ourselves to some DQ? Nothing better than a burger and shake to set the world right."

"Sure," Rose replied, with a cautious smile, and Leola pulled into the service road, anticipating hamburgers and home. Glad to escape her father's ghost again.

CHAPTER 62

L eola stared at the darkened bedroom ceiling, remembering the conversation she'd overheard between Rose and Cora this morning. Or yesterday morning. Or whenever it'd been.

You're right, Rose had said, in a sad voice. *It is getting harder for me to care for my mother. She almost got killed the other day, running into the road!*

Cora had clicked her tongue. *You've done so much for her, but I don't blame you for considering that nursing home up in Englewood. They'll take good care of Leola and you can visit her a lot . . .*

Leola had been too shocked to hear the rest. Stumbling into the living room, she'd tried to digest the news. They were sending her away again! Back to the Home! Well, she couldn't let that happen, not before she'd found her father, heard what he'd been trying to tell her. It wouldn't make up for what he'd done, but it might mean *something.* And something, she'd realized lately, was better than nothing at all.

So she'd hatched a plan and tonight would carry it out.

From down the hall, she heard her grandson calling, *Can someone get me another glass of water?* Heard her son-in-law trudge the stairs, settling the boy again. Then came the sounds of a television program from the den, snippets of conversation in the kitchen, footsteps in the hallway. A few minutes later, Rose opened Leola's door, as she always did.

"Goodnight, Mother," she said, but Leola didn't answer, pretending to be asleep.

She did drowse a bit after that—until Papa's voice commanded her awake: *Rosalee!*

The glowing clock on her bedside table read 1:32 a.m. Hours had passed!

Leola stood, retrieving her old Sunday coat from the closet. Rose claimed it was *getting shabby* and was too thin for northern winters, though Leola wouldn't let her buy a new one, and not only for the frivolous expense. She liked how familiar this coat was, how it smelled of her old life: the lilies that filled the church at Easter, the strong-brewed coffee at fellowship hour, the suggestion of rich black earth that was everywhere at all times.

It took some effort to fasten the chunky buttons but soon Leola was ready. Grabbing her purse, she stole down the stairs, turning the key in the lock.

"I'm coming, Papa," she whispered, rushing across the lawn.

Though not certain exactly where she was going, Leola didn't need a map. Whenever she got to a corner, she'd listen to Papa's directions: *This way, Rosalee. Over here. Now turn!* Like when he'd helped her whittle.

After a while, however, his instructions were harder to make out. Leola's feet hurt and her heart too. She wanted to give up, fall down, *cry*. Yet she kept going, as she had so many times—when she was too tired to pick another handful of cotton or so full of grief, it seemed she'd never memorize another science term. Or when she was birthing Rose—a breech—and by the time they told her to push, all she'd wanted was to lie back and die. Always in those moments, her willpower had kicked in, propelling her forward—like a nail toward a magnet, doing the only thing it knew how to do.

Eventually she found herself in a park of some kind—curving walkways, open spaces interrupted by stands of trees, branches like demon's arms, trying to snatch her to Hell. A dry leaf skittered across the ground and the cold air made her tremble.

Rosalee, you'll catch your death!

"Papa!"

A scuffling in the grass.

"Papa?" she called again. "That you?"

No answer.

A sob rose in her chest. Where had he gone this time? And what in tarnation was she doing, wandering around in the dark? If only she could rest, clear her head, try to hear him again.

Shifting her purse to the opposite shoulder, Leola took up her journey, rounding the next bend to discover a large building lit by spotlights. After trying a few of the doors, she was relieved to find one unlocked. Turning on the dim ceiling lamp, she could see the room was an office of some kind: rickety desk, scuffed bookshelf, bench with torn cushion. She hesitated, waiting for a hint this was where Papa intended her to be, but the only sound was the wind, rattling the room's lone window, high on the wall.

Exhausted, Leola sunk onto the bench, tucking her purse beneath her head.

"Papa," she said, "if you've something to tell me, it's now or never."

Above her, the window shuddered again. Yet instead of an icy draft, Leola felt something else, a warming breath like a whispered reassurance, a feeling as ageless as it was familiar. *All is well, Rosalee.*

She let the feeling settle. Pulling her coat tight around her, she closed her eyes, waiting for Papa—as she'd waited so long.

CHAPTER 63

"Mrs. Belfigli?" Someone nudged her shoulder. "Leola Belfigli?" *Papa?*

Leola swam from deep-dead sleep, only to discover it wasn't her father but . . . George! George Gumbs, looking debonair in a dark blue uniform. Had she ever seen him wearing it? There were laws saying Black folk could not dress in their regalia at home, didn't matter if they'd killed a legion of Huns. Except that was long ago, she remembered, and this man was not dressed as military but police. Much as he resembled George—especially around the eyes, which were large and concerned yet unafraid—he was a stranger. She didn't recognize the petite woman with him either, dressed in the same outfit.

"Are you Leola Belfigli?" the woman asked, and Leola had to think before answering.

"Yes, I'm Mrs.—Mrs. Belfigli."

The officer grasped her hand.

"I'm Sergeant Garcia and this," she pointed to the man, "is my partner, Sergeant Clark."

George Clark smiled.

"Lucky for you, Garcia noticed the light on in here. Made me check it out. Otherwise, we might've passed you right by."

Leola hugged her purse. "Did Papa send you?"

The officers traded uncertain glances.

"Your daughter called the station last night after she found you missing," the man explained. "She was frantic. *Beside* herself."

"Daughter?" Leola's voice turned plaintive. "But it's *my father* I'm looking for!"

The policeman seemed even more bewildered, though his partner only flashed an encouraging smile.

"I'll bet he's waiting at home, looking forward to seeing you again." She studied Leola. "Think you can walk out of here on your own two feet? Or should we call for a wheelchair?"

Leola had seen friends strapped into wheelchairs and never getting out of them. Dag blame if *she* got rolled away.

"I can walk, thank you," she replied, never mind every muscle ached as they helped her stand.

Outside, Leola squinted in the early morning sun. A few people loitered about, watching as the officers led her to the patrol car, but Leola hardly noticed. She was too busy wondering why Papa had sent her on such a goose chase when he'd been home the whole time. P'rhaps it was her fault for not understanding his directions. No matter. As the policewoman had promised, they'd see each other shortly.

Sargeant Garcia helped Leola into the back and then sat next to her, while George slid into the driver's seat.

"Need to call the station," he said, picking up a gadget on his dashboard, "tell them we have you. Phone's been ringing nonstop since you disappeared, people wanting to help out. Guess those TV bulletins did their job!"

As they started down the road, Leola watched the passing landscape, expecting the close-together houses to give way to familiar farms of tilled black soil, waiting to see her family's sweet little cottage, the limestone yard they'd always kept polished with their brooms. Instead the car stopped in front of a fine two-story house with a grassy green lawn and towering trees.

Officer Clark turned, beaming at Leola. "Home sweet home!"

"But," Leola muttered, "this isn't . . ."

The policeman, climbing out of his seat, didn't hear. "Let me help you," he said, opening her door.

"Don't you understand?" Leola swatted at his outstretched hand. "This isn't where Papa—where *I*—live!"

Sergeant Garcia had gotten out, too, and was standing beside her partner.

"'Course it is." She pointed. "Isn't that your daughter? And those must be your grandchildren and son-in-law, looking very excited you've arrived."

Leola watched as Rose hurried down the driveway, followed by a man, a girl, a young boy—Papa not among them—and the sliver of hope she'd felt melted into despair.

"You said my father would be here! I am not leaving until he comes."

Her daughter approached, looking like a rag thrown out with the wash water.

"Mother! I'm so happy you're safe. Let's go inside, get you fed and rested. I'm sure you're—"

Leola pressed her lips together.

"I will not go back to that—that terrible place! You can't make me!"

The officers glanced at each other.

"You're not being mistreated, are you?" the policewoman asked, bending down. "If so, we should—"

"*Mistreated?*" Leola let out a bitter laugh. "You ever worn a clothespin on your nose, young lady, just for being late to kitchen duty? Or got locked into a closet for sneaking an extra slice of bread?"

Rose gasped. "We don't do those things to you! You're confused with the orphanage."

"That's a lie," Leola hissed, and her daughter seemed about to cry. Instead, she inhaled, motioning the officers aside. Leola tried to hear what they were saying, could make out some of their words—*ambulance, hospital, tranquilizer*—heard Rose reply, *I'd prefer not, hold on, give me a second.*

As she ducked into the back seat, Leola moved far away as she could.

"Leave me be. If I can't see my father, I'd just as soon die!"

Now tears did fill Rose's eyes.

"I'm so sorry you feel that way. So sorry you feel wronged and upset." Her voice cracked. "I try to do right by you. *Try* to make you happy."

"But you're sending me back to the Home," Leola cried, "and if we—if *I*—go there," she drew a shuddery breath, "Papa will never find us."

"We're not sending you back to the Home, Mom. Where did you—"

"You told the woman. My helper." Leola swallowed. "My friend."

"Cora?" A short pause and then: "Ohhh! You must've heard us talking about the *nursing* home, not the orphanage." She shook her head. "I'm sorry I didn't tell you myself about it. We've been exploring the idea is all. Thought you might like it better there—find some friends, not be so bored. When Peter visits next week, we planned to look at some places together. The three of us." She squeezed Leola's fingers. "We'd never make you go against your will."

Leola gazed into her daughter's eyes. Knew she was telling the truth. Remembered she was failing, that her daughter *was* doing her best . . . that it wasn't enough.

"I'm sorry for causing such a to-do. For being such a," she stared into her lap, "burden."

"You're the opposite of a *burden*." Rose embraced Leola. "I feel lucky that you're still with me." Her voice trembled. "Much as I always tell you to let go of your papa, I never want to let *you* go. Ever."

Leola held her daughter, thinking she'd never haunt Rose as Papa haunted her. He was a gaping absence while Leola, despite her many mistakes, had been there for her children, steady and constant. Even when they'd pushed her away—as they'd had to, growing up—she'd kept right on loving them. Made sure they knew it too. Once she was gone, she hoped her memory would be a sweet reminder of their worth instead of a question mark.

"It's all right," she whispered to Rose, patting her hair. "We will see this through."

"Grandma?" Little David poked his head into the car. "Hurry and get outta there! I wanna hug you too!"

Leola and Rose looked at each other and laughed. Then Leola let her grandson help her from the car, into the hullabaloo of her awaiting family.

CHAPTER 64

It was four in the afternoon when Leola woke, rested after a long nap. She'd been too tired to eat after arriving home but now was hungrier than a plow mule.

Sitting up, she remembered her fruitless journey to find Papa, and her heart felt as empty as her stomach. She'd been a fool to think he'd returned. A fool to cause her family so much worry—for nothing. Papa was gone. She needed to forget him, like Rose said.

As if summoned by these very thoughts, her daughter opened the door and peeked into the room.

"May I come in?"

"'Course," Leola replied, sitting up.

Rose offered out a glass of iced tea, setting a plate of cheese and crackers on the bedside table, handing Leola a napkin.

"Emma just left for Burger Shack. Insisted on buying you a cheeseburger and shake to celebrate your return." She sat down too. "Meantime, I thought you'd need a snack."

"Mighty kind of you," Leola murmured, reaching for one of the crackers and gulping it down.

"How're you feeling?" Rose asked, after a while.

"A bit sore." Leola swallowed, patting her mouth. "And I *was* hungry but this," she gestured at the plate, "hit the spot."

She noticed that her daughter looked as she had as a child, keeping a secret she couldn't wait to tell.

"Mother, you're not going to believe this. I barely can myself." Rose paused. "I've had some incredible news about Papa. Something nearly miraculous."

Leola stared, thinking miracles, like luck, were for Bible stories and fairy tales. Still, she waited to be convinced.

"When you ran off," Rose explained, "police bulletins went out over radio and TV. Lots of people heard them . . ." she paused, ". . . including your half-brother, Matthew. He's nearly my age, born when your father was sixty years old. And Matthew lives close by us now—next town over, in fact. Isn't that something?" She shook her head. "He'd been wanting to contact you, kept putting it off. Guess he was worried how you might react." Pause. "But when he heard those bulletins, he knew he couldn't wait. Called me on the phone."

Leola felt smacked by a board.

"I—I don't understand . . ."

Rose turned to look at Leola dead-on.

"Remember that man you saw in the newspaper, the one who looked so much like Papa? Cora told me about that article—honestly, I didn't think much of it at the time. Turns out the story was about the company Matthew works for. He asked to transfer here—to be near you. He says he's the spitting image of your father. It *was* him in that picture!" Rose's eyes were wide. "Not only that, but Matthew did park on our street a few times, working up the courage to ring our bell. You were right all along, Mom. You *were* seeing Papa, in a way."

Given her broken brain, the fact she'd had so little sleep, it should've been too much for Leola to take in yet, somehow, every word made sense. Papa *had* been here—*was* here—in the person of his son, Matthew.

But what about the man who'd beckoned her from corners and closets, who'd seemed equally real? Mama had always reviled superstition, even as she made room for, as she put it, *things we cannot explain but know, deep down, to be true.* Leola realized suddenly that if she hadn't gone on her quest last night, Matthew might never have called Rose. Maybe, she thought, Papa hadn't sent her on a wild goose chase after all.

"I'll be doggone," she murmured. "Papa's son, down the road apiece."

"That's right." Rose paused. "I realize it's a lot to take in, Mom. That's why I didn't tell you when you first came home. I decided it'd be too overwhelming." She took Leola's hand. "But Matthew would like to meet you. He's got some interesting information about Papa. Information you'll want to hear. *Good* things."

Leola pondered this. For years, she'd longed to hear *good things* of her father. *From* her father. At the very least, she was curious about this long-lost brother of hers.

"Of course I'd like to meet him," Leola replied, and Rose grinned.

"I was hoping you'd say that. We were thinking tomorrow if you're up for it . . ."

Leola hesitated again. For so long, she'd buried the fact of Papa's existence, the pain of his betrayal. And tomorrow she'd risk that knife-turn of grief again to meet this man she barely knew, who claimed to have news of her father. A risk, she decided, she owed herself, once and for all.

"That would be fine," she told her daughter. "Tomorrow would be fine."

Before Rose could respond, Emma burst into the room, giving Leola one of her signature bear hugs.

"Your dinner's downstairs, Grandma! Nothing like a hamburger and shake to set the world right again." She peeped at Rose. "That's what Mom always says."

Leola couldn't help smiling, thinking the Belfigli women were somethin' else indeed.

CHAPTER 65

"Hello, Mrs. Belfigli." The man grasped her hand. "I'm Matthew Rideout, your half-brother."

Leola couldn't stop staring. This person was Papa's dead ringer—same gemstone eyes, same rangy build—only he had both arms and was not her father, she reminded herself, but the brother she'd never known.

"Pleasure to meet you," she responded.

The two might've stood gawping at each other all afternoon if Rose hadn't interrupted.

"Let's get comfy in the living room, shall we?" she asked, leading them down the hall, helping Leola to the couch.

"Can I get you something to drink?" Rose asked as Matthew set his leather bag on the floor.

"I'm fine, thank you," he answered.

While Rose settled next to Leola, Matthew watched her intently.

"Seems incredible, Mrs. Belfigli, that we're in the same room together finally."

"Call me Leola." She glanced at her knees. "Papa called me Rosalee."

"I know. He used that name often when he spoke about you."

Leola looked up. "He talked about me?"

"Sure did. I was still in high school, the last kid at home after

Dad—*Papa*, as you called him—retired. We spent a lot of time together. 'Course my siblings and I had heard about you and your sisters, growing up—though our mother, Martina, wasn't too keen on the subject. At least, not 'til Dad got old and she realized he needed to talk about it. About *you*."

"Martina," Leola murmured, a memory flittering at the edge of her mind.

"The woman you told me about," Rose explained, "who sold you that hummingbird weaving in Houston all those years ago."

Matthew glanced between them. "You met my mother?"

Leola didn't answer, picturing a busy market, a sharp-cadenced language she barely understood, a small woman not much older than she. *Martina,* who'd stolen her father away, whom she did not care to speak about when she had far more pressing questions. One in particular.

"Why didn't Papa come get us?"

It took Matthew a moment to answer. "Bad luck and bad timing mostly." He sighed. "Shame and guilt too."

Retrieving his bag, he pulled out a tan folder.

"But you don't have to hear it from me." He waved the folder. "Dad wrote letters to you and your sisters, explaining things. At the last minute he'd always decide against sending them, thinking they'd make you feel worse. Then just before his death, he changed his mind. Asked me to deliver them to you personally, if I could.

"Problem was, by the time I discovered your whereabouts, Mae had already passed. There was a record of Karla in the asylum at Bonnet but they wouldn't supply details. Privacy issues, I reckon. I knew you were in Tyler, even drove up to your place once. Sat there for hours, finally lost my nerve. Then Estella—my oldest sister—learned your husband had died and you'd moved up here.

"I could've kicked myself for not connecting when we lived closer. Considered mailing the letters to you—might have, too, except for what happened next." He shifted in his seat. "My company—based in Dallas—asked for volunteers to open an office here. Of course I had to do it. I'd just gotten divorced, no kids, nothing to tie me down. Seemed the perfect chance to finally get acquainted with you. Set things right."

Matthew jiggled his leg the same way Leola did when she was antsy or nervous.

"Even so, after moving, I began second-guessing myself again. Wondered if you might slam the door in my face, not that I would've blamed you." More leg jiggling. "When you got lost, then found, it seemed like a sign—a warning almost—that I needed to buck up and do as I'd promised."

He handed a yellowed paper to Leola, and she recognized her father's elegant schoolteacher handwriting right away. Of course some of the loops were wobbly and some of the flourishes didn't connect. It was an old man's script, after all. But she was an old woman and could hardly make out his words—any words, for that matter.

"Would you read it to me?" she asked, and Matthew nodded, taking the letter once more.

Dearest Rosalee, he began, *I hope this letter someday finds you, and that you'll read it with an open heart.*

Leola closed her eyes, listening. Matthew sounded so like their father—minus the faint Tennessee twang—that she could imagine the *real* Papa sitting two feet away.

Oh, my daughter! I cannot express how I regret our separation!

Was not only my need for work sent me away but the

never-ending rancor of Columbus Owen that finally pushed me to leave. I could not be the person I wanted in that man's company which your mama understood, finally, agreeing we ought to start anew, and I did so with the highest expectations of seeing my family again.

Except then I got hurt in a street melee and there was the second round of flu. By the time I got back to Bronway, y'all were gone—Orlena and Mr. Owen dead, the Meekers and Shipleys, even Joe, moved away. And I could hardly inquire in town, fearing I'd be arrested for desertion.

I'd heard you'd been sent to a children's home somewhere in Dallas County but there were scads of such places. I'd just gotten a new job, had next to no money. Returned to Houston, broken in spirit.

Not long after, I ran into my old friend Wilburn Parmer. When he told me he'd be passing through Dallas County on his way to Alaska, I asked if he might inquire at some orphanages there, which he promised to do. A few months later, I married Dr. Curbelo's daughter, who'd nursed me to health when I got hurt. Never heard from Wilburn again, reckoned he'd forgotten my request or had no luck in fulfilling it.

Leola shivered, remembering the mysterious message Brother Giles had mentioned. Imagined if she'd gotten it, if only she'd been aware . . .

"Mother?" Rose touched her hand. "You all right?"

Leola's eyes flew open. "I'm fine. Please." She peered at Matthew. "Is there more?"

Her brother nodded, becoming Papa again.

But here's where I'm at most at fault, for I more or less gave up then, telling myself too much time had passed, that further inquiry would hurt more than help. I discovered you all were situated with the Valchars. That you were thriving. Martina and I had one child, then another, and I thought such tidings would open up whatever hurts had healed.

Over the years, my youngest son did more investigating. Discovered you'd gone to college and become a teacher, had two children with Joe, that you were a stalwart in your town, always helping those less fortunate. Not a bit of this surprised me, for you always were a loving soul and had plenty of gumption too. I only regret not seeing you becoming the person you did—and your sisters as well.

Matthew rattled the paper, clearing his throat.

Sweet Rosalee! I cannot get those years back but please know it was happenstance and my own frailties kept us apart, not lack of love nor anything you did. Most of all I hope you will forgive me, as you deserve that peace above all.

Your loving, Papa.

Matthew pulled a tissue from his pocket, dabbing his eyes, and Rose sniffled too. Meantime Leola stared out the window, considering what Papa had asked.

From Day One, she'd been taught the importance of forgiveness. But it was only in adulthood that she'd understood its real value. Lord knew there wasn't a person on Earth didn't commit their share of wrongdoing; if she hadn't been able to forgive—loved ones, acquaintances, enemies, even herself, time and again—her feelings would've turned to concrete and she'd be completely alone. Not that forgiving others came easy. In fact, it could be harder sometimes than being lonely or hungry or scared—harder than loving itself.

Problem was, forgiveness also required some untangling of the *whys* and *wherefores* of others' transgressions, and she'd never had the chance to make sense of Papa's betrayal. Until now.

"Mother?" Rose draped an arm around Leola's shoulder. "You sure you're okay?"

"Only thinking it through, my dear," Leola replied, quietly. "Only thinking it through."

"I've got something else." Matthew rummaged in his bag, offering out a wooden pig with the faintest suggestion of green eyes. Despite the missing ear and chipped snout, Leola recognized it as easily as she did her father's handwriting.

"Papa made this!" she cried, taking the carving. "I forget his—her?—name."

"*Her*," Matthew said. "Dad said he named her *Flora*. I found him once, sitting on his bed, looking at her and crying like a baby." His voice quavered. "That's when he told me about the whittling arm and the good luck pigs, the vow he'd made that he didn't keep. How if there was one thing in his life he wished to do over, it was fulfilling that promise."

Leola ran a finger down Flora's curved back, picturing Papa as she never had before—grieving his daughters. Wanting them back. And so, finally, the tears did come, relief outshining the sadness with perhaps some happiness mixed in.

Rose let a few seconds pass before picking up something on the table beside her.

"I knew Matthew was bringing Flora." She gave Leola the father pig. "So I got Francis from your room earlier."

Leola studied the two battered creatures in her palm. Though she couldn't recall which one gobbled sorrows and which granted wishes, it didn't matter. She'd absorbed life's woes well enough on her own with plenty of room left over for joy. And as for the *wishing . . .* that was nothing more than wanting one thing then finding equal, sometimes *greater,* beauty in what you got. The real magic, it seemed, came from accepting that people, broken as they are, always deserve a second—or third or fourth—chance. That in the end, it isn't our sins that matter but our love.

Smiling at her beautiful daughter and newly discovered brother, Leola pressed both pigs to her heart.

"Together," she whispered, "like they were always meant to be."

ACKNOWLEDGMENTS

I began writing fiction in my late forties, with plenty of ideas but no idea where to start. So I did what writers do, took a deep breath, and flung myself down the well-worn but often challenging path to publishing—lucky to find many worthy guides along the way.

Above all, I'm indebted to my grandmother, Eula Emma ("Judy") Dendy Davidson, whose formidable spirit in the face of daunting obstacles inspired this novel . . . and made my life possible. I'm also thankful to my children, Sara and Jassi, who never once questioned that I was a writer even when I wasn't sure myself. *You can't give up*, they'd tell me after I'd accidentally deleted two weeks' worth of work from my laptop—and so I didn't. Kudos as well to my husband, Edward, whose equal partnership in parenting and life gave me the peace of mind necessary for any creative endeavor.

It's hard to express how important my writing community has been to me, including Mally Baumel Becker, Connie Fowler, Karla Diaz, Eileen Sanchez, Sophia Freire, Deb Green, Linda Broder, fellow SWP authors, and many others. Their insightful critiques, always tempered with compassion, were crucial to shaping this book. Likewise, for my teachers at The Writer's Circle, Michelle Cameron and Vinessa Anthony, whose mentorship and instruction have had a profound impact on my professional development.

Writing is a solitary endeavor, but there were many friends who made it a little less lonely, including Marcia Book Adirim, whose Mary Oliver quotes and coffee breaks kept me sane; my sweet pup, Tuxi, who always seemed to sense when a nice long walk would help me untangle a problematic scene; Cathy Sniado Sapanski, who since eighth grade has insisted I write a novel; and Diane K., for reminding me I didn't have to be *so* hard on myself.

I am also grateful for the support of folks like Sandy Sorkin, Harvey Araton, Joseph Bertoletti, Allison Conyers, Anne Johnson, my brothers, John and William Moyers, my niece, Nancy Moyers, and nephews, Henry and Thomas Moyers, and my sister-in-law, Nell Hurley.

Thanks also to the staff at Bluestone Coffee Company, Sandwich Theory, and Mercado for letting me hang with my laptop when I needed to escape from my home office, and Bob Cumins and A.J. Stavistinuk for photography advice. Shout out as well to the fabulous photographer, Lonnie Juli, for my headshots.

I filled hundreds of pages with research for this book, but want to acknowledge some particularly helpful sources: *Fertile Ground, Narrow Choices* by Rebecca Sharpless; *The Second Coming of the KKK* by Linda Gordon; *Texas Baptist Orphanage: My Heritage of Dreams and Happiness* by Georgia Dorsey Edwards; the Texas State Historical Association; and the staff of the Texas Baptist Home for Children (previously, Texas Baptist Orphanage), who generously shared information about my grandmother's time there. I'm also indebted to the children and grandchildren of her half-siblings—the real Papa's second family—whom I got to know while writing this book. Their insights into his later life not only informed the book's fictional plot but helped me understand this longstanding family mystery a bit better. (To learn more, visit suzannemoyers.com.)

As part of my research, I also turned to the diverse canon of "southern" music traditions, from Baptist hymns to African American blues and folk songs. One work briefly quoted in this book is a version of "HaHa Thisaway" attributed to the blues musician Huddie William Ledbetter, also known as Lead Belly. You can listen to some of his original recordings on YouTube.

My greatest resource, though, was my mother, Judith Davidson Moyers, whose forthright accounts of our family's past—in all its messy glory—not only planted the seed for this tale but helped me understand myself better too. She and my father, Bill, instilled in me a love for literature, history, and ideas that has been a source of comfort and joy throughout my life.

Thank you all.

ABOUT THE AUTHOR

© Lonnie Juli

Suzanne Moyers, a former teacher, has spent much of her career as an editor and writer for educational publishers. An avid volunteer archeologist, mudlarker, and metal detectorist, she's also the proud mom of two amazing young adults, Jassi and Sara. Suzanne resides outside New York City with her husband, Edward, and their spoiled fur baby, Tuxi. *'Til All These Things Be Done,* based on a still-unraveling family mystery, is her first novel.

SELECTED TITLES FROM SHE WRITES PRESS

She Writes Press is an independent publishing company founded to serve women writers everywhere. Visit us at www.shewritespress.com.

Among the Beautiful Beasts: A Novel by Lori McMullen
$16.95, 978-1-64742-106-9
The untold story of the early life of Marjory Stoneman Douglas, a tireless activist for the Florida Everglades in the early 1900s—and a woman ultimately forced to decide whether to commit to a life of subjugation or leap into the wild unknown.

Stitching a Life: An Immigration Story by Mary Helen Fein
$16.95, 978-1-63152-677-0
After sixteen-year-old Helen, a Jewish girl from Russia, comes alone across the Atlantic to the Lower East Side of New York in the year 1900, she devotes herself to bringing the rest of her family to safety and opportunity in the new world—and finds love along the way.

Swearing off Stars by Danielle Wong. $16.95, 978-1-63152-284-0
When Lia Cole travels from New York to Oxford University to study abroad in the 1920s, she quickly falls for another female student—sparking a love story that spans decades and continents.

Talland House by Maggie Humm. $16.95, 978-1-63152-729-6
1919 London: When artist Lily Briscoe meets her old tutor, Louis Grier, by chance at an exhibition, he tells her of their mutual friend Mrs. Ramsay's mysterious death—an encounter that spurs Lily to investigate the death of this woman whom she loved and admired.

Expect Deception by JoAnn Ainsworth. $16.95, 978-1-63152-060-0
When the US government recruits Livvy Delacourt and a team of fellow psychics to find Nazi spies on the East Coast during WWII, she must sharpen her skills quickly—or risk dying.